THE INTERVIEW

DONNA ALAM

ALSO BY DONNA ALAM

Hardly Easy

Hot Scots

One Hot Scot

One Wicked Scot

One Dirty Scot

Single Daddy Scot

Hot Scots Boxed Set

Surprise Scot

And More!

Soldier Boy

Playing His Games

Gentleman Player

Women are fickle, you know. And men are idiots.

~ Marc Levy

1

MIMI

Hello, Whit. It's been a while.

I give my head a tiny shake, frowning at myself in the mirrored walls of the elevator.

Hi, Whit! Remember me?

My frown deepens because that's even worse. I doubt he'll remember me, given I had braces and pigtails the last time I saw him.

Hi, Whit. I heard you literally own your own bank these days, so I thought...

I'd turn up on your doorstep with my begging bowl. *Fine, my résumé.*

My thoughts are interrupted as the elevator comes to a smooth stop. The doors glide open, but I find I can't move as I press my hand to my chest, my poor heart flapping like a landed fish. *This is the chance you wanted*, I remind myself. *Spreading your wings. Doing all the things.* The doors begin to close, and I spring forward like this is the last-chance saloon, turning sideways as I slide between the two.

So it looks like I'm doing this.

No big deal. I haven't seen him in a zillion years, but that's okay.

I slide my phone into my one good purse and hike it higher on my shoulder. No need to check I have the right door because there's only one on this floor. Plus, the guy at the fancy concierge downstairs called up to let Whit know I was on my way. There's no mistake. I'm in the right place.

And what a place it is—the lobby downstairs was decked out like a fancy six-star hotel. The low tasteful hum of music overlaid by the sound of my heels on the onyx marble floors, sofas, and a concierge desk, light fittings that look more like art installations. I guess some important people must live here, given the muscle-bound security detail who insisted on going through my purse with a fine-tooth comb. They even made me take off my cute beret, and I don't think they were expecting to find a marmalade sandwich, even if my new coat makes me look like that cute teddy bear the Queen of England, God rest her soul, had tea with last year. *Paddington, I think he was called.*

I pull off the beret, suddenly conscious of looking like an overgrown toddler. But London is so much colder than I expected. I thought March was supposed to be the start of spring, but it's been gray and gloomy since I arrived. I've seen the sun twice, but I swear it had no heat.

The decorator sure liked mirrors, I think as I stare at my reflection in a passageway that is basically a hall of mirrors, without the maze connotations and crazy shapes, thankfully. Their surfaces are mottled with age or at least made to look that way, the copper and verdigris making a sepia picture of me as I throw my coat over my arm and slide a lock of my summer-blond hair back into place.

At the shiny, onyx front door, I straighten my white shirt

and give my pencil skirt one last tug. When I raise my fist to knock, the first rap of knuckles pushes the door open. No one stands behind it with a *hello,* or *hi, Mimi, I haven't seen you in over a decade.* I pause, hoping for some sign of life before I press my fingers to the wood and push a little more, remembering every *CSI* episode that started this way.

"Hello?" My voice echoes as I take a tentative step inside the darkened apartment.

"Come in," replies a voice deeper than I would've recognized. My stomach tightens in anticipation or recognition, it's hard to tell. Is that truly Whit? He sounds so... grown-up, his tone low and kind of velvety.

Stop being an idiot. He was a grown-up back then. Of course it's him—his mom gave me the address and the snooty concierge downstairs confirmed it, *and* they called up.

I fold my coat, placing it on a console, then make my way deeper into a room where a wall of windows overlooks the shadowy treetops of Hyde Park, the hum of the busy Knightsbridge streets inaudible from below. Recessed lighting falls in distant corners casting shadows against the walls and rendering the stylish space with an intimate glow. I don't have time to process why the lights aren't on because all I can think of is *there he is.* Whit is just a few feet away, seated in a pale-toned armchair. His shiny black oxfords are planted wide, his pants equally dark. My eyes follow the row of buttons up his torso, his shirt folded at his forearms and open at the neck. I can't see his expression—can't tell if he's happy to see me or not because, thanks to the fall of the light, his face is wreathed in shadow.

"Whit?"

"Stop where you are."

My feet halt, my heart rattling in my chest at the softly

spoken words so heavy with command. But that's him, all right. It's Whit. Dark-haired and tan, my brother's best friend always stood out like some exotic animal around my much fairer, blander family. And when he opened his mouth to speak, he sounded like a fairy-tale prince.

"Turn around."

"Excuse me?" My words hit the air a little higher than I'd like.

"Turn around. Let me look at you."

Something delicious yet uncertain flutters through me, but it's just a little déjà vu, right? It's been so long. And it's not like I haven't heard something similar from him before.

Turn around. Let me see you. Look at how tall you've grown since I was last here.

I'm lying to myself because that request was not the same, even if the sound of his voice always filled my stomach with butterflies before I even knew what it meant. So many nights I've lain awake wondering what it would be like to see this side of him. To hear him say my name in a sinfully sultry tone. To feel those eyes watching me. Experience the brush of his fingertips.

"Lovely." The deep and smooth voice behind me reminds me of bourbon. "All the way around now."

My heart pounds uncertainly. What am I doing? What is *he* doing? I'm not fourteen anymore. I know what these feelings are, and I recognize that tone. He's never been anything but courteous, never shown any interest in me beyond a kind of distant, brotherly thing. He knows it's me —the concierge called up with my name. So does that mean he...?

I terminate the thought, unwilling to examine it as whatever part of my brain in charge of impulse control literally short-circuits as he purrs, "Come closer, darling."

My heels tap against the marble floor before my brain registers the motion. "Step into my parlor said the spider to the fly?"

His dark chuckle weaves its spell around me when I should feel embarrassed for my ridiculousness.

"I won't flatter you like the spider," he murmurs, "but I might let you come when I eat you later."

My footsteps almost falter as a throb of sweet percussion strikes up inside. Never in a million years could I have expected anything like this. I couldn't have conjured those words up in my darkest fantasies, despite spending many nights in my head with him. But maybe I lack imagination because this Whit is neither tender nor sweet. I find I'm more than all right with it.

I notice the lowball glass resting against his thick thigh as he lounges back in the chair. My heart dances an erratic beat as he slowly uncoils to deposit the glass on a side table.

I stop in front of him, locking my knees to keep them from trembling, and startle a little as his hand lifts. His white button-down pulls tight over the swell of his bicep as his finger hooks under the strap of my purse, slipping it from my shoulder. Something almost erotic in the motion evokes the sense of being undressed.

"You're trembling." He curls his hands around my waist, but it does nothing to help. In fact, I'm pretty sure amazement has me immobilized.

"I know." I roll my lips together, but the words fall anyway. "I've locked my knees to stop them from rattling like maracas."

His laughter is a shocking puff of air against my midriff. I glance down and realize he's slipped his thumb under the hem of my shirt to expose a patch of skin above the waistband.

"It's just your wings fluttering." His tone is sort of velvety, and I inhale sharply when his thumbs skim lightly across my skin. "Excitement mixed with trepidation."

"You think I'm nervous?"

"You should be. It'll make the night more pleasurable for us both."

The night? What comes after he eats me to orgasm? Not that I've ever had *that* pleasure, but if you're going to take risks, it's not the kiddie pool you dip your toes in.

"Lift your skirt."

"I—what?" What on earth... have I bumped my head? Am I lying out in the street in a coma?

"Show me." His words are a honey-dipped temptation. As though to sweeten the instruction a little more, he leans closer, pressing his lips to the skin above my waistband.

Warmth floods between my legs, and I'm pretty sure I whimper.

"Such a pretty sound." I feel the loss of his heat immediately as he leans away again. "Hurry now. Show Daddy what he wants."

If *show me* made me warm, *Daddy* feels like a burst of wildfire across my skin. Why that flutters my button, I don't know, but I do know Daddy Whit is so freakin' hot.

You're not a deviant, whispers a little voice of dissent.

Shows what you know.

"You look like that might've broken your brain a little bit." His tone is amused. "If you don't like Daddy, we can always go with something else."

"No," I say quickly. "I've just never—"

"A Daddy virgin?"

That is so nasty, yet my insides throb.

"I don't like to be kept waiting."

I get the sudden sense that the balance of the moment is

slipping. I glance down, everything inside me drawing tight at his disapproval. Weird. He's barely moved a muscle, yet I feel the weight of his disappointment like a spikey woolen jacket I want to throw off. Before my brain registers what I'm doing, my fingers are at the button on the back of my skirt.

"Not that way." He makes an indolent motion with his finger that I take to mean I'm supposed to... lift it? My fingers move hesitantly to my thighs. "Yes, sweetheart. That's right."

He settles back as I begin to gather the fabric. His eyes burn through the shadows as I pull it higher and higher until—I can't quite believe—it's gathered at my waist. It feels dirty but somehow on the right side of wrong. And, oh my goodness, he called me sweetheart, and I really, really liked it.

I count the beats that pass between us in the throbbing between my legs before he moves forward, the light catching the blade of his cheekbones as his face comes into the light. He doesn't glance up, seeming to examine my panties before he hooks a thumb into the elastic at my hip. Pleasure pulses through me. I'm pretty sure I'm going to melt before the navy-colored lace slides down my legs. But neither of those things happens as his thumb slides away. Not that my pleasure abates, his expression so serious as he trails a slow finger up between my legs.

His head lifts, his gaze catching mine as though daring me to stop him. I won't of course. All I can think about is how I've never been this close to him and how his eyes are so much more striking than I remember. Flecks of gold shine in the ambient light, amber striations around his dark pupil making his eyes seem tiger-like. A knife-straight nose and broad slashes for cheekbones. His mouth is full, and the divot above his finely carved bow makes me wonder what noise he'd make if I kissed it.

I stifle a sigh, my body jolting, suddenly chasing his touch as his index finger lightly brushes between my legs in one curling *come-hither* motion. It's barely a brush, but God, how it makes me tremble. One brush becomes another, his touch so slow and methodical. So... "Oh God." My eyes flutter closed as a familiar sensation begins to build.

"Open them, little fly," he instructs softly. Something must flicker in my expression as he adds, "I'm following your lead."

"Flies are—"

"Gossamer winged." My body convulses as he increases the pressure, working the fabric of my panties where I'm suddenly wet. "'Will you come into my parlor,' said the Spider to the Fly. ''Tis the *prettiest* little parlor that ever you did spy.'"

"The way into... my parlor is... up a winding stair.'" He smiles as I join in, my words halting and breathless.

"'I have many curious things to show when you are there.'" He delivers the line with such wicked intent.

"Oh, I just bet you have." My feathery laughter halts as he introduces his thumb. As he presses it to my clit, a mewl escapes my mouth.

"'Will you rest upon my bed?' said the Spider to the Fly. 'There are pretty curtains drawn around and the sheets are fine and thin. If you like to rest a while, I'll snugly *tuck you in*.'" His thumb and finger come together to pinch my clit, and I make the strangest noise, my body reacting as though struck by a live line. "I'm not sure we need a bed right now," he asserts softly as his arm slides around me, banding my thighs. "Not when you're doing so well."

"No, don't stop. I've never—" But I have no more words

as he deepens the damp crease of my panties. Blood rushes to my cheeks, and I'm so pleased for the lack of light. My feminist membership card will absolutely be revoked once they discover that Daddy and the patriarchy own my ass.

"Oh, I've no intention of stopping," he whispers. "Yes, that's it. Such pretty fluttering."

"Oh God!"

"Not quite, little fly." His assertion is full of dark amusement. I must pull a face again. "Something more generic?" he purrs, his face half in shadow, half washed in the light. "Shall we stick with sweetheart, or how about baby girl?"

I'd like to assert I don't like either of those options, but that would require at least basic verbal skills. He could call me Genghis Khan, and I wouldn't protest as the mostly unused muscles in my thighs begin to flex and tense. I've never orgasmed standing before—or from a hand over my underwear rather than *in*. I'm beginning to think I might need stronger quads. Better coordination. Something to hold on to.

"That's it," Whit encourages, and oh my God, I know I shouldn't be turned on by his praise, but I am. "You're such a good little slut for me."

That. I'm *not* into that.

No way.

Except for right now as pleasure begins to spiral through me from the tips of my toes to my freakin' hair follicles. My body bows, and I fall forward, my hands grabbing his bicep. Somehow, I also seem to grab the remaining threads of my dignity.

"Oh God, Whit," I whimper, locking my knees against this wave of pleasure. "Me-me. Call me Mimi."

My fingers tighten on his arm as I throw my head back

and do the only thing I can. I let go. I'm a little too preoccupied to notice anything else. So I don't see his shoulders tense, and I don't see the color leach from his face, and I wouldn't have anyway, thanks to the dim lighting. I see nothing, hear nothing, and care for nothing but those bliss-filled moments of my release.

2

WHIT

No. Hell no, and fuck no.

"I told her no." Leaning back in my chair, I watch my younger brothers exchange a dubious glance. "What? What's that look supposed to mean?"

El shrugs, and Brin decides now is an opportune time to examine his fingernails.

"I mean, is she the CEO, or am I?"

"Your name might be above the door, but you're not technically the head of the family. You know how this goes." Brin, one of my younger brother, shrugs.

"Dad might've enjoyed having his strings pulled"—both brothers' faces twist in distaste—"but I don't."

"Yeah, but this is Polly we're talking about," El, the problem middle child, adds, referring to our mother by her name. "I'm not sure she knows the meaning of the word."

El isn't really the middle child, just the middle one out of the three of us. That's not to say he isn't a problem.

"We all know that the word *no* means something else to Polly," Brin says.

"Yeah, like try another way," El agrees.

That's our mother to a T. I'm sure most people don't recognize her machinations because she operates like a steel fist in a velvet glove. But this conversation isn't even about her. It's about what happened in my apartment last week. About how good Mimi Valente's nails felt pressing into the skin of my forearm. How fucking amazing it was to watch her come all over my fingertips. Not that my brothers are aware of what happened because I'm not in the habit of discussing my sex life with them.

Don't stop.

I've never—

I give my head a quick shake to rouse myself from the temptation that seems to play in my mind on a loop. *Never what?* I wonder for the thousandth time before pushing the question away.

I hadn't seen her since she was a kid, so of course I didn't recognize her. And I was horrified when she pulled her bloody résumé from her purse. She was dressed for an interview, not to meet some vague fetish of mine. What happened should be enough to make my balls crawl up my arsehole and never want to come out. Unfortunately, my brain took another path, one that seems to insist on reminding me how perfectly she followed instructions and how beautiful she looked as she unraveled, gripping my arm and pulsing against my fingertips.

It was a busy night. I'd had cum on my fingers twice. Once in the lounge, a gorgeous woman clinging onto me, and once in the shower as I'd replayed the moment in my head.

That she'd turned up unannounced was Polly's doing. That she didn't *quite* get the position she sought is on me. I was expecting someone else. A playmate, if you like. But that's not to say Mimi left feeling discontented. She seemed a little dazed, to be honest. And embarrassed. But unsatisfied? Definitely not. Not the way she wobbled her way back out of my apartment.

I rub a hand down my face. This is all so fucked up. And the idea of her working here? No. Fuck no, and hell no. I'm sure she feels exactly the same. She'd probably hitchhike back to Florida rather than face me.

"Poll is tenacious. Like a terrier."

El's voice pulls me back to the moment. "It doesn't matter how dogged she is because I said no," I repeat with finality. "Amelia Valente might be in London, but she's not working here."

My brothers make a joint high-pitched, *"Oooooh!"* which I choose to ignore as I drop my head to one hand and begin to massage my temples. Of course she's not working here. No way she wants to be anywhere near me. She probably thinks I'm a deviant.

"I don't know what you've got against the idea. It's not like you'd have to see her every day." El flicks out his hand, indicating the size of my office or maybe the space of the floors beyond. "You could just shove her in the basement with the tech team."

"I'm not going to *shove* her anywhere," I mutter as I imagine her expression as I shove her on—full of?—something very hard and very specific.

"You're sure?" The thorn between two sibling roses smirks.

My attention reels back. "Are your ears just ornamental?" Something in his expression pisses me off more than usual this morning. "And please, enlighten us, what's with the smug face?"

"He can't help it." Brin stretches out in his chair, folding his hands behind his head. "Not everyone can be beautiful like us." Brin and I share the same coloring, thanks to the Italian heritage on our dad's side. El is fair, like Polly, and the rest of our siblings are a mismatch of colorings in between. Yes, seven. Frankly, it's a wonder Polly can string a sentence together after raising all of us, let alone find the energy to meddle.

"I'm pretty sure smug and superior are mentioned on your LinkedIn bio," El retorts. "But if you don't want her, I can think of a couple of places I'd quite like to shove her."

"Why would either of you need to shove her anywhere?" Brin persists. "Unless she's got a face like a can of squashed dicks?"

"Valente?" El turns in his chair, flashing our younger brother a meaningful look. One that's lost on him as Brin gives a shrug and a shake of his head. "You are such a twat sometimes. Amelia Valente as in Connor Valente?"

I can almost see the light bulb of realization switch on above Brin's head. "Your college roommate, right? From when you abandoned us for sunnier climes."

"Fuck abandoning us," El says. "I got a bedroom to myself when he left."

Back when we'd been a typical family before I'd started this company and hit the big bucks, I'd been desperate to get out of the overcrowded madhouse that was our family home. When I was offered a scholarship to a college in the US, I couldn't pack quickly enough. It meant I'd have to spend most of the school breaks on my own, but it was a small trade-off for that level of freedom and experience. As it was, I'd missed my family more than I could've anticipated. As luck would have it, I'd been roomed with Connor and he'd pretty much became my pseudo-brother overnight. We partied together, studied together, and he'd insist on taking me back home when college breaks rolled around. I spent plenty of summers at their house in the years following college, too. We were just really good mates. But in a cruel twist of fate, he died while he was on holiday in Thailand. I was supposed to be there with him, rock climbing, but I begged off at the last minute. Work was crazy, and I couldn't get away. The weird thing is, for all the danger in the sport, he hadn't died doing it. He'd passed in his sleep. Cardiac arrest, they'd said.

I should've been there with him.

And I shouldn't have crossed the line with his little sister.

"I still don't get it," Brin says. "Where does Amelia Valente come into this?"

"She doesn't," I grate out.

"It's some commute from Florida." He grins. "Hope she's not planning on taking the bus."

"She's moving here, obviously." No need to mention I know she's already here. "For six months, I think." I turn my gaze to the wall of glass behind me and the million-quid view over the River Thames and the city beyond, wondering if I'd frightened her onto the next flight back to Tampa. It would probably be the best outcome for both of us because the image of her in front of me, trying so hard to stay on her feet, unbalanced and unraveling but taking it all like a good girl, makes me want to fuel the jet and follow her there myself.

Obviously, I won't. For all kinds of reasons.

"She's staying with some dotty old aunt, according to Polly." At his airy declaration, I swing my chair and attention back to El.

"How do you know that?"

"Apparently, she doesn't know a soul here." He doesn't bother to temper his shit-eating grin. "It behooves us to show her the same hospitality the Valentes showed you all those years ago. Polly's words, not mine, by the way. She's going to need friends. Really good ones." Then the bastard winks.

"Sorrel!" His full name explodes from my mouth, my movement from my desk chair not dissimilar. "What the hell are you talking about?"

"Oh, do fuck off," he drawls. Unfurling his long frame in the chair, he kicks one ankle over the other. El hates his name, but to be fair, none of us came off great in the naming stakes. Given that we were all named after some plant or other piece of ridiculousness by pseudo-hippie parents, things might've been worse.

Hemp, get your feet off the coffee table! Can you imagine?

Steepling my fingers to my desk, I loom over it. "When," I demand. "When did you have this conversation with Polly?" I'm not sure how El comes into this. I've already told her this is a business I'm running, not a charity.

"Your knickers are awfully bunched this morning." El gives a sly smile.

"I'll fucking choke you with them if you don't answer me."

"That's more his thing," he says, hooking a thumb in Brin's direction.

"Piss off," he huffs. "I'm not going anywhere near his grundies. For the record, they were *her* knickers," he somehow feels the need to qualify. "My date's, and it wasn't my mouth they were in."

"When," I grate out. "When did you discuss this with *Mother dearest*?" Why the hell did she speak to him? El has nothing to do with the Valentes unless... The fist around my heart eases a little. This is a strength in numbers thing. Get my brothers on my case to see if they can wear me down.

"You're asking when did I learn about the lovely Amelia?"

"I thought she was ugly," Brin mutters, but neither of us pays him any attention.

"When I saw her downstairs in reception this morning."

"Mum was here?" And she didn't appear in my office to continue her campaign?

Mischief flickers across El's face. Somehow, I know what he's going to say before he even opens his mouth.

"Not Mum. Amelia. She was there getting the welcome to VirTu. If I'd known, I would've volunteered for the job because..." He does this weird teeth-kissing thing as he shakes his head slowly.

"So she doesn't look like a can of squashed dicks?"

"I'd like to squash her full of—"

"Shut the hell up, both of you!" I yell.

My skin goes cold, which is odd because my blood feels like it's fast approaching boiling point. Somewhere in the distance, I hear El begin to laugh. A great big belly laugh like a department store Santa Claus. Fake, annoying, and deserving of a punch. But he gets a reprieve—they both do —at the sharp yet familiar rap of knuckles against my office door. I lift my head at the intrusion, and my personal assistant's voice precedes her waddling bulk. The woman is the size of a boat these days. She's got to be a health and safety hazard.

"...and this is the monster's lair."

"Jody, we're in the middle of something."

"Too bad you didn't put it on your calendar," she answers casually, not giving a flying fuck. A manila folder held between her fingertips, she casually flicks her wrist in my direction. "And here would be the monster. And it looks like he's in a *charming* mood today."

The door slides a little farther open to reveal the five-foot-eight-inches of golden gorgeousness I hoped never to see again. And now I'm lying to myself as some kind of primeval recognition zips down my spine. *Out of all the people in this room, I'm the one who knows how beautiful this woman looks when she comes.* The thought curls warmly in my gut, snug and satisfied as my eyes eat up every inch of her.

I watch as her pink-glossed lips quiver uncertainly before a tentative smile breaks free. Jesus Christ, Mimi Valente grew up. Grew up and out in *all* the right places. Not that it matters because I made a promise. A promise I haven't broken yet.

Technically.

"Hello, Whit." Her voice is almost as husky as the last time she'd uttered my name. *Whit! Oh God, Whit!* "How are you?"

Me? Oh, I'm just going to hell...

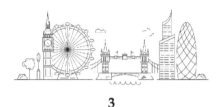

3

MIMI

FOR THE SECOND time in as many weeks in the presence of Leif Whittington, I lock my knees to keep them from giving out. When I'd visualized this moment (and I have at least a dozen times this morning alone), my knees didn't knock. They're not knocking now, either. It's more a case of one look at his hot self, and my whole body begins to pulse and tingle, nerve endings and pleasure points flashing like a dang pinball machine. I guess longtime unrequited lust will do that to a girl. This man was the object of my teenage fantasies and the stuff of my later much more X-rated imaginings, though nothing could top what happened in his apartment. I've never come so hard before and never fully clothed!

It's safe to say that since my dark taste of his reality, my fascination has only increased. *Show Daddy what he wants.* I almost melted hearing those words in *that* voice. In fact, I think my brain might've experienced a little meltdown because it's all I can think of when I look at him.

Jeez Louise, get your mind out of the gutter, Mimi. I barely recognize my own thoughts these days. It's certainly true we're not in Florida anymore, Toto.

Whit's corner office, *natch*, is three times the size of my first apartment. But then, my first (and only ever) apartment was above my parents' garage. Decorated in shades of gray, navy, and black with the occasional streak of white, the color palette might've been inspired by the London skyline frames by the wall of windows. A meeting space dominates one corner, the table a white-gray marble, the eight black chairs around it appearing to have been designed to encourage brevity over comfort. A monochrome rug denotes a more welcoming space with two low leather sofas flanking a matching coffee table. One wall houses library-style cabinetry of midnight blue, and an old-fashioned ladder connects to a brass rail above. The floor and walls are dark and the artwork atmospheric, and in the center of it all is a monolithic stone desk—a piece of art in itself. Behind it stands Whit, and behind him is the city of London. He is a picture of masculinity, sexiness in shirtsleeves, and master of all he surveys.

He can sure master me. In fact, he did. All I need now is for the other inhabitants of the room to disappear and for him to crook a finger at me and whisper *lift your skirt. Show me.*

I suppress a shiver and remind myself he's probably *not* having the same kind of thoughts, judging by his expression. He's shocked to see me, of course he is. And I expect a normal person on a normal timeline would rather pluck out their own eyeballs than see Whit again after such an awkward... decoupling? *De-fingering?*

To put it another way, my post-orgasmic glow disappeared in the length of time it took him to remove his fingers and choke out my name. It's not a moment I choose to dwell on because I also remember his expression as he watched me fall apart. What I saw in his eyes still has the power to take my breath away.

And that's the reason I'm brave enough to stand here. The reason my lady parts are currently as enthusiastic as a tween at a Taylor Swift concert. Externally, of course, I'm more relaxed. I'm a head tilt and a friendly, closed-lipped smile. Kind of *it's* so *nice to see you.*

Can I see more of you?

Pretty please?

I'm here for the experience... here, in freakin' London! Standing in the office of my longtime secret crush with an amended agenda. And oh my gosh, is that London Bridge in the distance?

Jody waddles over to Whit's desk, slapping down the folder she's carrying. My contract, already signed by the HR director. "I forgot you two already know each other."

"H-hardly," Whit stutters, the words coming out like a motorbike with problems starting. *How cute! I made the hot man stutter!*

He seems to give his head a little shake before rounding his desk, so tall, dark, and so freakin' handsome—he's like Superman on attractive steroids. Then he's here, in front of me, his hands on my shoulders, and those tiger eyes intent on mine. My poor little heart goes *"Ah me"* in an echo of Juliet, Romeo's boo. My eyes flutter closed as he leans in to kiss my cheek. I inhale lungsful of his heady scent of cedarwood, spice, and black pepper, but it's the scent of nostalgia that makes me want to melt.

My insides absolutely contract as his warm breath caresses my cheek, and I guess I must make some kind of noise or reaction because then his low voice rumbles, "Behave yourself."

Not even! No way! Not when I'm *this close* to exploding again.

Yep, that's what I said *xxx-plode.*

He moves back a little without moving his hands from my shoulders. "It's been a while," he says as his eyes bore into mine in all their animal intensity, demanding I play along.

"Oh my gosh, a *hot* minute at least." I don't bother to hide my grin because his broad shoulders are already doing that for me. "I bet you're surprised to see me again."

This man, that voice, the experience gives me all the shivers. That night was probably the first time in my life I wasn't worried about my lack of thigh gap. It didn't seem to bother him none, either. While I might not have come to London with Whit in mind, boy do I now want to know what makes *Daddy* tick.

"You could say that," he returns, his expression revealing no hint of his thoughts. He did seem pleased to see me before. Pleased to feel me, too. But then things got awkward, and he said he didn't realize who I was. That he was expecting someone else. *Someone else he confused me for? Someone else he'd never met?* I've spent a lot of time pondering this, and you bet your sweet behind I plan on having that delicious conundrum answered. Just not right now. And not back then, afterward, I mean, because I couldn't get out of the place fast enough. Oh. The. Mortification. But I'm over it now. Mainly because I choose to be.

"But it was nice, right? The last time we saw each other." Well, you saw a little more of me than I saw of you...

"Nice?" If ice had a voice, it would sound like that.

"Well, I thought it was nice."

One of his brow quirks like a question mark. "Refresh my memory. What exactly was nice about it?"

"When you helped me out. You did that, you know, thing?"

"Did I?"

"You know. You helped me with that project?" My cheeks must be aiding global warming right now. "The digital remaster thing?" Help! I'm spouting nonsense!

This time, his lips quirk. Barely. "Digital mastery?" His hands slip down my arms. He folds them across his broad chest.

"Yeah, that was really *nice*." I clasp my fingers in a death grip, desperate to contain my delight. "It was very..." I glance around, unable to bear the weight of his dark taunting gaze, not without giving in to a joy-filled squeal. "Enlightening."

"Was it really?"

I nod, nerves making my mouth hurry on. "How are you, Whit?" My gaze skims over his magnificence. "Are you good?"

Hell yes, you're good.

"I'm well. And yourself, Amelia? Are you well?"

Beats being called little fly, I guess. Maybe? "I am good. Thank you for asking." *For the record, should you require it, I can also be very bad. At least, I think I can be.* "You look good," I tag on. Good as in super-hot. He's obviously older than I remember, but the years look good on him. His hair has a little salt mixed in with the dark pepper. He's larger in the shoulders, but just as lean, his flat stomach denoted by a trim leather belt. He looks like a grown-up. Dark and capable. The kind of man who—

"You look good, too." His eyes flit over me, leaving a buttery warmth in their wake.

Well, I am wearing my favorite shirt. I'm no longer the gangly teen who'd turn beet red at his teasing. I've grown up, but I think we've already established that.

Whit seemed to be a fixture of my childhood home, and I idolized him. I still remember the first time he visited. I couldn't understand why my tummy would flutter when he was near. It was years before I could label the feelings. Each vacation he spent with us, it became more and more clear, but that was before Connor died and the fun was sucked out of my world. Whit had already been living in London for years when Connor passed, but he didn't drop out of our lives like a lot of his friends. *Like loss is somehow catching.* He'd call regularly, just to check in, and send silly postcards from his vacations, and the occasional email. He'd even send *me* emails sometimes. And always a birthday card each year, usually containing a department store gift certificate.

"It helps that my braces came off."

Ouch. Maybe I haven't moved on much from that awkward girl.

Whit stifles a smile as he lifts his hand to his mouth. *Those fingers*, my mind echoes with an internal sigh. This man and his hands have kept me awake many a night, and not just since his *digital mastery*. I don't know if it's his Italian ancestry, but he always seemed to use his hands a lot. It's very sexy. *Even more so now.* His fingers are long, elegant, and tan. I especially like it when he uses them on his jaw and chin, just like now.

"I can believe it." He gives his head a slight shake. "I hardly recognized you."

"Oh, I know," I reply. "I mean, I guessed as much." After last time.

His index finger kind of tugs at his smile, but as someone clears their throat behind him, he turns. I notice El, his brother, sitting in the seat on the opposite side of the desk. Polly, their mom, introduced us this morning when I was getting my ID pass. A second man sits in the adjacent seat, who I guess to be another of the Whittington brood.

"Hi, El." I hazard a little wave, and he scrambles from his seat.

"Hey, Mimi."

"Aren't you going to introduce us?" asks the third occupant of the room.

"No," El says with a laugh. "Not a chance."

"Don't let us stop your important meeting." Jody holds out her hand as though to stop their progress. She waddles back to where I'm standing just inside the door. The woman looks fit to drop. Drop into a chair... drop a baby or three. Any of those. "We still have the marketing and compliance departments to visit."

"Compliance?" Whit frowns, and as Jody passes him by, she gives an exaggerated roll of her eyes.

"Is there an echo in here?"

"Jodes—"

For someone clearly thirteen months pregnant, Jody swings abruptly on her heel.

"What have I told you about calling me that?" she snaps. Whit's brows retract, and he holds up his hands, kind of, *don't shoot!* She shuffles around to half face me, her expression a mixture of tiredness, frustration, and regret. "My ex called me that, and it properly gets my back up."

I make a mental note of the vernacular—to get one's back up means to get annoyed. *Okay.* I nod in solidarity, my hands still clasped at my front like the Goody Two-Shoes I used to be.

"Don't take any shit from him while I'm gone. But don't think you can dish it out, either. He's got a wicked temper. You've got to know how to handle the monster."

The younger-looking brother snickers.

Jody's gaze narrows before cutting his way, her tone withering. "Why don't you have a rest? Take the day off from stupid."

"I just didn't realize you were familiar with the monster," he says with a cheeky grin.

"Are you going to tell him, or do I have to get the handbook again?" Her attention shifts to Whit. My stomach flips because I realize he's still looking at me.

"Get the handbook," Whit says, breaking my gaze. "Hit him with it. It's probably the only use for it where he's concerned."

"That wasn't sexual harassment!" The other brother protests.

"You shouldn't make dick jokes to a woman twenty-eight weeks pregnant unless you don't mind losing it."

"Jody, love, come on!"

"Don't you *love* me. I will throw the book at you —literally."

The pair begin to squabble, and I get the feeling this scene that has played out before. And oh my goodness, I love it!

"Will you two knock it off!" Whit bellows. I jump at the sheer volume, but it does the trick as the room falls quiet. *So this is new. New to me, at least. Maybe I'm a deviant because I kind of dig it.* "I'm not bad tempered," he then adds in a more even tone.

El coughs *"bullshit"* into his fist, and I try to stifle my smile. This is more like a circus than an office. And as of next month, this is my circus, and those are my monkeys. Kind of.

"That's something we'll have to agree to disagree on," Jody says, heading for the door again. I scramble out of her way when she pauses, fixing me with a look. "His not-bad temper can be terrible, but usually not for no reason," she adds. "Whit is a man with a great weight balanced on his shoulders."

His lovely, broad shoulders. "Got it," I agree with a nod.

"But keep him in check. I don't want to have to retrain him when I get back."

"Retrain—Get back? When you get back from where?" I don't know, but I think Whit looks a little panic stricken.

"Oh, you know. A break in the Bahamas." An unamused Jody points finger guns at her swollen stomach. "Where do you think I'm going looking like this?"

"But..."

"I can't keep these two in here forever."

"Oh cool! Twins." It seemed impolite to ask.

Her expression scrunches even as she slides a tender hand over her stomach. "Twin hippos, I'm beginning to think."

"Can someone explain what's going on here?" Whit modulates his tone, holding his hands out in a plea.

"You're complaining, as usual," Jody deadpans. "Unless you're questioning why I'm putting myself to the trouble of showing Mimi around when I should have my feet up."

"I'll show her 'round," the younger brother pipes up, rising from his chair.

"I'm not busy, either," El adds quickly.

"Down, boys." Jody makes a patting motion with her hand.

"Absolutely," Whit replies with a glower. "Put your feet up—take the rest of the afternoon off. But for the love of God, please explain why Miss Valente is getting the grand tour."

"It's part of the orientation," she says as though talking to a halfwit. "How else will she be able to cover for me?"

4

WHIT

I AM SO SCREWED.

What the hell happened to Connor's little sister? She used to be the kind of awkward that was endearing. All spindly legs and nervous hands. Where did that girl go? Who put the saucy siren in her place?

She looks like a modern-day Brigitte Bardot. Is it not enough that I've been torturing myself with images of her riding my fingers that she has to turn up looking like the office pervert's wet dream come to life? Was she poured into that skirt? And that blouse. It was the kind of garment that looked demure at first glance and pure temptation the second, molding to her curves with every movement. I was oddly glad to see years of braces hadn't fixed the gap between her front teeth. It's like the pearl between the oyster of those full lips. Something I think she prefers not to show.

How old is she again?

It's me. I'm the office pervert.

I am so, so screwed.

"What you are is fucked."

I turn from staring at the closed door, wondering if I

need to murder my brother for reading my thoughts before realizing I must've said that out loud. "Jesus Christ," I mutter as I pivot, rubbing my hand across my chin. "Can that woman *not* keep her nose out of my business?"

"Who, Jody?"

"No, Mum," I grate out. "And that was a rhetorical question." Mimi is just a kid. A kid with the body of a goddess and the kind of behavior that reminds me of an eager-to-please puppy. That is some fucked-up combination and far too tempting to have daily in my office. I'll bloody wank myself to an early grave!

"So it looks like you've got yourself a new secretary." El clears his throat as I swing around to glare at him. "If you don't want her..."

"Fuck off."

"Don't let Jody catch you diminishing her title." Brin settles lower in his chair, crossing his long legs at the ankles. "She's not a secretary. She's keeper of big knob over there. He wouldn't know his arse from his elbow if she wasn't about."

"Do you two have no work to do? I mean, do you actually work here? Or do you just swan in each day in a sharp suit and a winning smile because that's all you're good for?"

"Cheers, bruv." Brin slides a loving hand down his lapel. "This one's from your tailor. He did a good job, right?"

I don't answer. Just glower.

"I thought we were meant to be having a meeting? A meeting before the meeting, as it were," El says in an even tone.

"It's a wonder we get any work done because of meetings," Brin mutters.

Ignoring them both, I make my way around the desk,

swipe up my phone, and drop into my leather chair. The call connects as I swing around to face the window and my view over the Thames and London beyond.

"Mum, how are you?" This travesty needs to be undone.

"I'm well, Leif. What about you, darling?"

"Yeah, busy. You know how it goes. Idle hands are the devil's playground." And don't I know it.

"So they say." My mother's laughter sounds down the line.

"Anyway, I was just wondering if you were free for lunch today?"

Steel fist in a velvet glove, my arse. The woman is as subtle as a brick through a plate glass fucking window.

I stand as my mother glides into the courtyard restaurant and watch as she waves away the maître d's outpourings of assistance as though the pair are old friends. As she weaves between the tables in a cloud of gardenia perfume, flowing skirts, and tinkling bracelets, it's hard to ignore the attention she attracts, particularly from the opposite sex. She might be in her sixtieth year, but she's still a very striking woman.

"Sweetheart." I try not to wince as she carelessly drops the Birkin purse I'd bought for her last birthday to the floor.

Note to self: ten grand's worth of handbag gets the same treatment as a grocery sack.

Hands freed, she presses them to my cheeks and a smacking kiss to my forehead. There's little point in complaining. This has been her standard greeting for me forever.

"Thank you, Stefano." The server pulls out her chair, and she takes her seat before sending him a radiant smile over her shoulder. Smoothing her shiny coffee-colored hair, she doesn't notice the man turn pink with pleasure. She never does. It's just her way. She makes everyone feel seen. Appreciated. This earthy loving is written into her DNA and part of the reason she always gets what she wants.

Not this time.

"Just the usual for me," she says, waving away the offer of a menu.

"Salmon again?" I give a tiny shake of my head. "You'll turn pink and get gills."

"If it's not broken." She smiles back. "Oh, leave those," she says as he begins to clear away a third setting. "It's a table for three today."

Oh, do fuck off, I want to yell. Instead, I wave the server on. "No, just two today. I should know. I booked the table."

"Yes," she says, ignoring my heavy tone, "but I rang and changed the booking."

Change the booking to a private members club... she's not a member of. This is the magic of my mother.

"Who?" I put my menu down because... "It better not be who I think it is."

"Calm down." Reaching out, she pats my hand. "You'll have an aneurysm."

"That's not funny." Especially not if our third is who I think it is. "Don't make those jokes in front of her."

"Do you think I'm so careless?"

"No, of course not. But what the hell, Mum? I don't even know how you've gotten involved with the Valentes. It's not like they live down the street."

"They took you under their wing, Leif. Of course I made it my business to get to know them. After Connor died, I wanted to offer my condolences, and we were quite close back then. Well, telephone close. I'm sure things were very changed. It's been very hard on Mimi."

"I know that." I press my elbow to the table and drag my hand down my face. "I mean, I can imagine it."

"Can you, really? Imagine losing Sorrel or Brin or Orion." Orion, who prefers to go by his middle name of Daniel. Not that Mum pays any attention to that. And poor old Sorrel... "Or one of the girls."

Sometimes I do imagine losing my siblings, but not in the way she means. Maybe more like losing a toddler in a grocery store for ten minutes and being blissfully unaware of it. I love my family. I'd die for any one of them. I'm also dying for a little peace *from* them.

"I don't know why you're making such a song and dance about this." Avoiding my eyes, Polly lightly rearranges the silverware.

I am neither singing nor dancing about Mimi Valente working for me, and it has nothing to do with her coming so beautifully for me. My reluctance began way before that moment—the moment Polly suggested it, actually. But that's not to say I can explain the reason behind it. I kept in contact with the family when Connor passed, too. I've even sent Mimi a gift card every year on her birthday, or at least Jody has done on my behalf. I just hadn't realized she was as old as she is. I thought for some reason she was still a kid. Is it not enough that I have practically half of my family on the payroll?

"I know you're a little grumpy about Mimi working for you," my mother begins again, "but if you were really set against it, you should've sat in on the interviews or mentioned specifically to Jody who you didn't want."

I doubt Jody interviewed her quite so thoroughly as I did. *Fuck it all to hell. Come on, brain—get with the program.* "I might well have done if I'd realized you were up to no good," I grumble.

Maybe I should offer her a second interview. But a second interview would only mean she'd come twice.

"It wasn't like that," Poll says with a tinkling laugh. "You're so suspicious!"

No, Mother dearest. What I am is so fucked.

"Jody knows her job inside out. She was the right person to choose her temporary replacement."

"Exactly." She nods. "It might not be temporary, either."

"Don't put a hex on this for me."

"Jody might not come back. Have you considered that? New babies, such bundles of joy. She might find it hard to leave them."

"And she might be desperate to get away from them."

Mum laughs again. "There speaks a man with no idea of what makes the world keep turning."

"That would be sex, obviously."

"Yes, in a way. That's how your father and I ended up with seven children."

I groan like I'm in pain. Because I am. It's called childhood trauma. "Remember the line we spoke about?" I mutter. "You just samba'd your way over it."

"However did I raise such a prude!"

"We're not having this conversation. Ever again. Remember?"

"Fine. So Jody gets to choose."

"Yes."

"And choose she did."

"Jody wouldn't have given the job to a kid out of college." Not without outside interference.

"You're being ridiculous." She turns in her seat, attracting the attention of the server. Two blinks later, he's hovering at her elbow. "Could you bring us some water? Sparkling, not still."

He nods and scurries off as she turns her attention to me again.

"You made your feelings clear. You said *no,* and I heard you perfectly." I open my mouth to dispute this when she raises a finger. I close it with a snap. And a scowl. "I also heard Jody complaining about the caliber of candidates. I simply passed over Mimi's résumé without offering an opinion."

"Jody has fifteen years of experience. Nearly ten as an executive PA. She wouldn't give the job to just anyone."

"Darling, you keep making my point for me."

"But she's just a kid!"

"She's a young woman of twenty-four"—the exact number gives me a start while also somehow making me feel ancient—"who is more than capable of fulfilling the role. Quite honestly, I don't understand where this reluctance is coming from. I'd think it would be the least you'd want to do."

The least I want to do with Amelia Valente is put her on her knees and her head in my lap. The worst I could do would be to dwell on what happened in my apartment. The best I could do for her would be to send her far away and not just because of what happened, or how seeing her makes me feel like I haven't done right by Connor. It makes me feel like I've failed. Knowing she's sitting on the opposite side of my office door day in and day out, dressed in that skintight pencil skirt might just make me really fail.

Fail to keep my hands off her.

Fail to do what's right by her.

After all, I promised Connor.

"Oh my goodness!" My internal flagellation is cut short

as the chair to my right is subjected to a brief battle of ownership as whirlwind Mimi arrives at the same time as the water-bearing server. "Oh okay." Her lips tip with amusement as she allows him to do his job, lowering demurely onto the seat. "Oh my goodness," she repeats, this time at a volume that makes me think of secrets. "The ladies' room is out of this world! It's pink," she adds, her nose scrunching adorably. "The sinks are pink marble and scalloped like flowers—they look like something you might wear, not wash your hands in!"

"They were carved from onyx," my mother says.

At the same time, I repeat, "Wear a basin?"

"They're just pretty," she replies without an ounce of embarrassment.

Her smile is infectious, and that gap between her front teeth feels like it could be the beginning of a fetish. I find myself biting back a grin. Then I clock Mum's twinkling eyes as they dart between us. *Don't even think about it, Polly.* I send her a narrow-eyed glance. She better not think of making a pet project out of this.

Especially if it's *Project Grandkids.*

"I didn't realize you would be joining us." I could bite my tongue the minute the words are out, but I needn't have worried about upsetting her as she throws back her head and laughs.

"I was just thinking how you haven't changed. But I guess I was wrong because that smooth tongue seems to have become a little worn." Her expression twinkles mischievously, and I don't miss how her gaze dips to my lips. I almost want to tell her my tongue is just as smooth as my fingertips, but that would be wrong. It doesn't matter if she's thinking about my tongue because I can't think about *her* thinking about *my* tongue under any circumstances.

"I misspoke." I move the linen napkin a little to the left. "I meant to say I was surprised to find you in the country." Then because it's going to be one of those days, I order a stiff drink. My companions decide to stick to water.

"Weird." Mimi glances at my mother as though in confirmation. "Polly said she'd told you I was here."

"Yes, I did," she agrees happily. "I said Mimi was looking for a position, remember?"

The positions I'd like to give Mimi are wide and varied.

Fuck, I don't appreciate being tag teamed. Not in this manner, anyway. It's so heartening to hear they've been bonding.

"Today wasn't even my first trip into the office," Mimi adds. "You were in Brussels when I came for the interview." She stumbles a little over her words. Nervousness or remembering?

"Was it a thorough interview?" Come on, what's with the tone? No wonder she's looking at you like a bunny in headlights. But then she smiles like she thinks she knows where I'm going with this—like she's hit her stride or something.

"Honestly, I've had better interviews."

"Oh?" I lean back in my chair, spreading my legs to accommodate what's coming next.

"I once had an interview with a typing test."

"And you preferred that?"

She tilts her head as though considering the question. "Maybe there was something about the levels of manual dexterity."

"Typing tests? How old-school." Poll scoffs. "You know, years ago, I had an interview for an office job where the boss tried to squeeze my bum *and* see up my skirt."

Thanks to a sudden, spluttering cough, I cup my hand to my mouth.

"Are you all right, darling?" Poll's tone turns concerned.

"Fine." With my free hand, I make a motion that Mimi should go on. Just ignore me, I'll just die quietly over here. Then I won't need to worry about what comes out of Mimi's mouth next.

"You were telling us about your interview." So much for a mother's concern as her attention turns back.

"Oh, yes. Whit was in Paris, I think, when I spent the day with Jody. She showed me the ropes."

Read: We haven't been keeping this from you. It's just one big cosmic coincidence.

Utter bullshit.

Also ropes really aren't my style. They're a little too prescribed for my tastes.

"I'll admit, Jody is a little scary."

I perk up. "Maybe that means you're not suited for the role."

"Really?" Mimi tilts her head to the side in a questioning manner. "What makes you say that?"

"If you can't handle Jody," I reply kindly.

"Oh, I think you'll find I can handle a lot of things."

Like my balls? my brain unhelpfully inquires.

"No offense, Mimi"—and only for the sake of my mother's involvement—"but Jody's been in the role a long time. I'm not sure you're ready to step into her shoes."

"Thank God! The poor woman has been reduced to wearing Crocs." She glances my mother's way with another adorable nose scrunch.

"Swollen feet are the least of her worries," Mum replies.

I hold up my hand. "Cutting that conversation off before

it starts." No pregnancy war stories today, thank you very much. "I just don't think it's going to work."

Hands out, Mimi gives an expansive shrug. "Too bad. I guess no one told you I already signed the contract."

"You know, I think I've changed my mind." Polly interjects. "I will have something to drink." It doesn't smooth over the fact that I've been well and truly played. "We're celebrating," she tells Stefano, "not hardened day drinkers."

"Was Jody in on this?" I ask, pitching my voice low. Polly, I can understand, but what's Jody's game? She knows I'll do whatever I can to get her back into the office as soon as possible. I've even offered to open a creche in the building!

"You mean, was Jody in on hiring the right person for the job?" Mimi blinks innocently. It must be for my mother's benefit because I've already seen the other side of her. The sultry side, languid lips, and come-fuck-me eyes. "I heard I was, like, the eighth person to be interviewed and fourth to spend the day in the office with her."

"She's very thorough," Polly says with an enthusiastic nod.

"Or she's angling for a colossal raise when she gets back," I mutter unhappily.

"This isn't my first rodeo, Whit. I've been out of college a couple of years now." I snort dismissively though she ignores me. "I majored in business in college and was an executive assistant to the CEO of Blankman and Reid."

"Oh, Blankman and Reid?" I almost throw up my hands in fake amazement.

"I didn't know you were into amateur dramatics." She does that thing again where she tilts her head to the side like a curious terrier. "I bet you just *love* being cast as the villain."

"I'm sorry. I must've just forgotten who those titans of industry are."

"I know you haven't heard of them. Why would you? They're a midsized architectural company based in Tampa."

"There are companies, and then there are powerhouses," I say, leaning closer.

She folds her arms on the table and mirrors my movements. "There is also being patronizing, and then there is just being an asshole. Guess which one you're being right now?"

"Both," Polly answers. "He gets that from his father. Don't worry, sweetheart. His bark is worse than his bite. Oh look, here's the champagne I ordered!"

"I can handle both." She smiles a little provocatively before bestowing Stefano, the server, with a dazzling smile. The kind that inexplicably makes me want to punch him in the face.

"Do you even know what we do?" My mouth works on autopilot as I try not to stare at those pink-painted lips, try not to imagine working my hand into her hair to hold her in place while I taste and tease them. While I bite. Because, oh yes, I would bite. Delicately at first, then less so, pressing my teeth into her neck, her breasts, and her—

"What kind of idiots have applied for this job?" she demands, snapping me out of my dirty musings. "Who goes for a new job without doing their research? Of course I know what your company does. In fact, I've been watching the company since start-up. I was super impressed when you decided not to go down the IPO route. Raising capital couldn't have been easy."

I'm not sure if I'm disturbed or taken aback. Of course she knows I wasn't some rich boy with money to burn or else I wouldn't have been staying with her family all those

years ago. My start in this venture was pure bootstrapping.
There was luck involved, of course, when Miranda, my
cousin, suddenly married into money. It opened up a new
world to me. I got to know the Becketts, a husband-and-wife
angel investor team who, I'm pretty sure, consider corporate
meetings as foreplay. They spar endlessly, then I think they
go home to fuck because that energy has to go somewhere.
Anyway, with their investment and acumen, I was able to
raise the necessary capital.

"It wasn't easy." Polly brings the rim of her glass to her
lips. "But Leif has always had incredible drive. He always
gets what he wants."

"Not always," I grind out, refusing to look at my most
recent failure.

"Well, it shows. VirTu is the banking of the future,"
Mimi says enthusiastically. "I can see how you've been able
to attract so much business with the way you operate. The e-
money license was genius. Modern banking isn't about
depositing your money in brick-and-mortar institutions
where it almost costs you to store it." She's been watching
me when it should've been the other way around. I try not
to be flattered even though she's talking about my company.
"Your money should work for you, no matter how little you
have in your checking account. I love how with VirTu you
can access cryptocurrency, stock trading, and other
crossover services."

"I can see you've done your homework." It's hard not to
be impressed, not to be enchanted by her eagerness.

"But you're still not convinced." She sighs, and I try not
to notice how her chest rises and falls with the action. Try
and fail. I'm a pervert. Too old for her. And then there's the
promise I made to her dead brother.

Oh, so *that's* the antidote to my stiffening cock. Good to know.

"Honestly, Mimi, I'm impressed. But you're young. Jody has had years in the role and—"

"And is about to have twins." My mother interjects. "Tell Leif how you were promoted in Tampa."

"Well, I started as an assistant, basically admin for a bunch of accountants, but the exec PA for the FEO and CFO had a hiking accident, and I was asked to step in. I did, and by the time her leg was healed, they'd created a new position for me. She got the CEO, and I got the other guy," she says happily, surely unaware of how sexual that sounded. Or maybe she is. She was certainly up for teasing me in the office.

"I can manage a schedule like it's nobody's business," she adds, "and while I don't have any contacts in the travel industry, you can bet your butt I'll have some soon. I'm fully conversant in Microsoft, and I have excellent verbal and written communications skills."

I bring my drink to my lips as I consider she does vocalize her climax beautifully.

"Verbal you can attest to, dear."

My head does a double take. How would Polly know...

Ah.

"I'm resourceful and innovative and an independent thinker. I'm proactive, and I work well under pressure," she continues, leaning closer, her gaze solemn and her tone passionate. "I'm a hard worker, creative and detail-orientated. I can work on my own initiative, but I take instructions well, too."

Dead brother, dead brother, I begin to silently chant as my cock perks up, beginning to pay attention.

"Given time, I think you'll come to appreciate having me around."

And that's what I'm worried about.

"I'm very thorough. I never leave a job half done."

Fuck, I'm half done. The dead brother trick didn't last long.

"I promise you, Leif, I won't let you down."

"Of course she won't," Polly says, lifting her glass. "And I think that's something we can all drink to."

Fuck.

5

MIMI

WHIT OFFERS me a ride home after Polly's planned lunch ambush, and I try not to get too excited. I know what the topic of conversation will be.

Spoiler alert: not the fun stuff.

"It's three houses down from here," I say, pointing at Aunt Doreen's house. "You really didn't need to drive me all the way out here, you know. I have my Oyster travel card. I really enjoy taking the Tube."

"You enjoy the novelty," he states. "It won't last long."

I give a little giggle. "You are like a dog with a bone."

"What's that supposed to mean?"

"Don't tell me you weren't about to suggest I live too far out to travel into the city every day."

"As if I'd even presume," he mutters flatly.

"You totally would if you thought it would work to keep me from the office."

"Edgeware might as well be Middle-earth," he huffs as his fancy sports car glides to a stop on the tree-lined residential street. Uniform red-brick terraced houses flank both sides, neatly painted front doors and garden gates showing the inhabitant's individuality.

"Why are you staying with your aunt, anyway?" Whit's hand slides from the leather steering wheel, and as he turns in his seat to face me, the heady scent of his cologne blends with that of the expensive leather interior.

"It was a compromise." I slide my hair behind my ear and duck my gaze. Now is probably not the right time to wrap my hands in his jacket to jerk him closer so I can sink my nose into his collar. "My parents," I say with a tight shrug. "They didn't want me to leave."

"They were against you moving to London?"

"They're against me going anywhere," I say, shifting against the warm leather seat.

"You're twenty-four." His brows pinch a little, but I don't expect him to understand.

"I'm aware." And ready to make up for lost time. The new Mimi has limited time and a limited budget and a mantra to live by: life is short, so get you some. Life. Sex. Eat the cake. Whatever. "After losing Connor, they became fearful, I guess." They see danger everywhere. I'm only sad I let it get this far.

"I'm sure that's understandable."

"So is wanting to live my own life." My reply is more than a touch defensive.

"And your aunt is... nice?"

"She's kind of crazy," I say with a chuckle, glancing toward her house. Aunt Doreen isn't really my aunt. She's more of a distant relation. My grandmother's second cousin or something. When I made my intentions clear to my parents, when I told them I was coming to London before—

Deep breath. In for three, out for four.

When I told them I was coming to London, they were

dead set against it. Tears were cried and guilt was doused, but given I'd recently undergone a literal *come to Jesus* moment, I'd dug in my heels and put my needs and wants in front of theirs for the first time since Connor died. My stubborn streak had come as a shock to them, though there wasn't a whole lot they could do about it. But because I'm also a loving and mostly dutiful daughter, I agreed to stay with family to give them some peace. My parents weren't always like this, but they have more reason than most to want to wrap me in cotton.

"The good kind of crazy, I hope," he says, ducking his head to stare out the passenger side window. "Is that a pink front door?"

"Yep. That's the kind of crazy Aunt Doreen is."

"Is she a fan of Barbie, this aunt of yours?"

"That's more Pepto-Bismol pink than Barbie."

"Did she get the paint cheap?" He frowns at the door as though it offends him.

"It's bright and cheerful," I say in her defense. "And we can't all live in a fancy penthouse or hire a decorator. Or live in palaces of monotone."

Those striking eyes flit my way, and I know what he's thinking. I've been to his apartment. *And I found a little bit of paradise there.*

He clears his throat. "Palaces of monotone?"

"Yes." I nod like I mean it. Like the color palette offends me when I haven't even thought about it.

"I suppose it is a bit..."

"Boring," I mutter, supplying the word he wasn't looking for.

"Are you enjoying living in London?" he says in a subject change.

So we're going to beat around *all* the bushes. Now that

we're alone, we're going to ignore what happened that night. Fine, I can play along. "So far, I like it a lot."

"You don't mind the weather? Surely, you must miss all that Florida sun."

"The sun shines here, too." I glance out the window to where the sun is just setting in a watery orange haze. The spring days have been pleasant, but the sun has been little more than a yellow ball in the sky, lacking heat and intensity.

"What about friends? Have you made friends?"

"This is beginning to sound like a phone call from home," I reply with a huffing chuckle. "I'm not fifteen, you know."

"It's hard sometimes not to slip into old roles, I suppose."

"You're not my brother." Not even close. "I don't need anyone to take care of me." Not in the way he's talking about. "What about you, Whit? London looks good on you."

He doesn't answer, though his brows pinch.

"Do you date very much?" I ask, not playing along.

"I didn't ask you about your dating life," he answers carefully.

"I assumed that's what you meant when you asked about friends."

"It was not."

"Aren't you curious?" I twist in my seat, mirroring his position. Okay, exaggerating it. It wouldn't be too much of a stretch for my lips to brush his.

"Mimi," he says, filling my name with a warning.

"I am. I am so, so curious. Especially in light of recent *developments.* You see, I have this insatiable"—his eyes flare —"curiosity."

His eyes hold mine before dropping very deliberately to my lips. He leans forward, just a touch, and my breath halts, half in and half out of my mouth. I almost anticipate him moving closer, my body tilting of its own accord. I want it so bad I can almost taste it... when his head dips and his gaze slides to the house again.

"It's going to be a buzzkill taking a date back there," his low voice rumbles.

Dammit, Whit! He totally played me. I swallow and brush aside the moment, not ready to throw in the towel. "That was an excellent sidestep. I'm pretty sure that makes you the buzzkill in this scenario."

"I think it's better if we keep it that way," he says as his eyes cut to mine. "In fact, if you want to work for me, I insist on it."

"I'm not working for you right now."

"Behave."

"I am behaving!" I protest with a giggle. "Come on, Whit. Put yourself in my shoes. Wouldn't you have questions? Wouldn't you be curious?" He doesn't answer, and his expression gives nothing away. "Fine, you play the monster. I know better than that."

"No, you only think you do."

At his dark tone, something hot and sweet flares between my legs, though I silently congratulate myself when I carry on as though unaffected. "Do you think this whole hot and enigmatic thing will kill my curiosity?"

With a pained groan, he tips his head back. The long line of his throat makes everything below my navel tighten. It doesn't matter that he's probably pleading for divine intervention through the car's fancy panoramic sunroof because that's not where my mind has tripped. Tripped, skipped, and jumped its way to some dirty musing. In this scenario, I'll be straddling him, his head thrown back and his hands balled into tight fists. I'll press my lips to his throat to feel the ripple of his taut swallow and the vibration of his moan as I do strange, wild things to him.

Note to self: discover what strange, wild things I could offer.

Addendum: maybe explore porn for inspiration.

It wouldn't be the first time.

His chin drops with the gust of a sigh, those dark eyes refusing to meet mine. Meanwhile, I rub the backs of my fingers over my mouth in a surreptitious drool check. How the heck is it possible that I'm turned on by his Adam's apple?

"Go on, spit it out," he says, resigned. "Let's get it over with."

"Really?" *No drool, thankfully.* "I should just rip off the Band-Aid?"

"If you must."

"Is that your thing?" I ask a little too enthusiastically.

"Yes, because I'm the kind of deviant who enjoys having the hairs on his legs pulled out by the follicle." He scowls. "No, Mimi, that is *not* my thing."

"I'm not a child. I know that's not your thing." But now I'm wondering if that might be someone's thing. "You know that's not what I was asking. I was talking about what happened in your apartment." More specifically, my orgasm. "Is that, I mean, I know you said you didn't recognize me, but that only leaves me with more questions."

"I don't pay for sex if that's what you're asking."

Could I pay you for sex? I'm tempted to ask.

He'd totally be out of my budget.

"I wouldn't judge. It's the oldest profession in the world for a reason." I adjust my purse on my lap and glance out the windshield. One of the neighbors and his four-legged friend trots out of his front gate, his attention doubling back on Whit's fancy wheels. I smile because the Labrador retriever isn't so impressed, yanking his human by the leash. I take a deep breath. "Do you... do you often hook up with strangers?" It takes supreme effort to turn back to face him.

He doesn't answer, at least not right away. He just presses his elbow to the leather seat back as he kind of examines me. "Does that titillate you?" The sultriness to his tone catches me off guard, but he's already played me once.

"There is something kind of hot about it." I blow out a nervous breath. "You were so... and I felt. And honestly, I can't stop thinking about it."

"Fuck!" Whit snaps back as though my answer offends him.

"You asked! If you weren't prepared for the answer, maybe you shouldn't have."

"I wasn't prepared for *that* answer, Mimi. You can't go around admitting to things like that. You barely know me."

"I know you well enough."

"I might be a massive fucking pervert!"

I shrug as my mind whispers, *a girl can only hope...*

Whit blows out a frustrated breath. Leaning closer, he suddenly takes my chin between his thumb and forefinger. "Do you always say what comes into that head of yours?"

"If you don't like the answers, think before you ask the question. Also, don't give *me* the answers if you want to keep me thinking about it." Who am I kidding? Answers or not, I'll still be thinking about it.

"She wasn't an anonymous hookup. Not completely." I feel the loss of his touch as he draws away. "So don't get any ideas."

I give my head a slight shake, my eyebrows riding high on my forehead. "What kind of ideas?"

"The kind you've already begun imagining. Anonymous hookups are dangerous, especially for women."

"There's a double standard if I ever heard one."

"I don't make the rules," he retorts.

"I hear there are places for anonymous hookups." I might be sheltered, but I've had access to the internet. I also read the occasional *Cosmo* article online. "I'm sure there would be in a city like London."

"Are you looking to get hurt?" he almost splutters.

"Death by Band-Aid isn't really my thing. If you want the truth, I don't know my thing."

"What do you mean?" By his expression, he immediately regrets asking.

"I'm not a virgin, Whit." *Yep, he definitely regrets it, judging by that face he just made.* "I'm just inexperienced, but I'm open to exploring. To seeing wherever this takes me."

"Where what takes you?" He sounds almost panicked.

"Life." I affect a short shrug. I'm grabbing mine with both hands. "I'm not saying I didn't enjoy what happened between us. But I get it. Things need to remain professional between us. But that doesn't mean I can't explore what London has to offer, right?"

"You are dangerous, Mimi Valente. Imagine if it hadn't been me in—what if I'd been a stranger? What if I'd wanted to hurt you?"

"But you aren't a stranger," I reply softly. "I knew it was you, even if you didn't recognize me." His eyes darken as they roam over me. The effect feels like hot, caressing fingertips. But then his gaze shutters, and he takes a deep breath.

"I'm sorry," he says with sincerity. "I'm sorry for not realizing it was you. I'm also sorry for what happened."

"I'm not."

"That's *not* helpful."

"Well, sometimes the truth is inconvenient." I should know. It's why I'm here in London, after all. "I won't take it back. I'd never felt so turned on, and I don't know what to do with that information."

"I suggest you put it to the back of your mind," he recommends coolly. "If you want to work at VirTu, it can't happen again."

Oh, Whit. Is that really what you think? "Fine," I say instead, hugging my purse a little closer. "But that still leaves me with the question of who you were expecting. Did she turn up later? Did you do it all again? And what was with the whole..." I can't bring myself to say it, even if thinking it draws my nipples to tight points under my shirt. *Daddy*. I want to say it—I really do. Just thinking that word makes an electric current work its way down my body. "Do you really like being called that?"

"Really, Mimi," he chides, "these questions are invasive."

"Don't you get it? I'm trying to make sense of what it meant. It was the hottest thing that's ever happened to me, and I have all these..." *Feelings*. "Thoughts."

His gaze slices my way with a flash of surprise, then what looks like pain.

"If you can't answer me, then who will?"

"The internet." His voice sounds strangled. "We can't have this conversation. It's inappropriate on so many fucking levels."

"Oh, we passed inappropriate a few miles back," I argue. "A few days back. Inappropriate was when I lifted my skirt because you told me to. Inappropriate was when you slid your hand between—"

"Jesus Christ, will you stop!" He shoves a rough hand through his hair.

"Sure." I give a tight shrug. "When you explain it to me."

"Explain?" he asks with a dash of alarm.

"Who was she? The other girl."

"I'd met her before at a party." I feel my eyebrows dispute this, because how? Unless she was my double. "She was wearing a mask," he adds, perceiving my doubt. "A mask and very little else."

"Oh, it was *that* kind of thing." I nod sagely as though I have firsthand knowledge of such gatherings rather than intel gathered from hot billionaire romance books.

"She was blond and of a similar build to you." I can literally feel his eyes strain not to look at me again. I guess that makes me Whit's type. "When the porter called up, I obviously wasn't listening well enough. I just assumed it was her, that she'd taken me up on my invitation."

"Your invitation to..."

"To fuck." The way his teeth graze his lip, the harsh sounding fricative makes my insides a puddle of goo.

What if we'd gone further? What if I hadn't said my name? *Then he would've screwed some random woman,* my mind whispers. *He wouldn't have been screwing you.*

"So did she turn up after? After me?"

"No," he answers simply.

I don't think he realizes my relief. But then, I didn't expect to feel it, either. "But she likes that kind of stuff?"

His soft laughter makes my arms feel all goose bumpy. "What kind of *stuff* would that be?" he all but purrs, like he can't help himself.

"Calling you Daddy." There, I said it—I said it as I resist the urge to wet my parched lips. "Showing you her underwear because you told her to." My words sound shaky as I glance down at my lap. "Being touched like that. Being talked to like that." *Being owned,* I add mentally. Thinking about it makes my insides pulse and my outsides hot and shivery. When I glance up again, it's with a jolt of pleasure that I realize he's eating my words up.

"Yes, I think it's fair to say she enjoys that kind of thing."

"Why do you think that is?"

"Because she gets off on it." His voice is a low rumble, his gaze owning mine. "She enjoys the dynamic."

"What do you mean?"

"That she enjoys being directed. She gets off on the praise."

"Oh." Story... so it checks out. "You think?"

"I do. She probably revels in the power play because she's a little sexually submissive."

My answer is a puff of air. I'm submissive? Because the *she* we're discussing is obviously me. I blink and look up. "Submissive," I whisper to myself before my attention switches to Whit. "So that would make you, what?"

"That would make me..." He crooks a finger, and I lean in closer before he closes the space between us. I shiver as his soft hair brushes my cheek, his lips just a breath from my ear. "None of your business," he whispers.

I spring back, my cheeks not the only part of me burning. He watches as I lift my hand to the spot beneath my ear as though I could further experience that caress. He observes me without bothering to hide his satisfaction.

"You play dirty."

"If you're going to play..." He frowns, leaving the end of his sentence dangling in the air.

"How does a person find someone to play with?" I ask with wide-eyed innocence. I'm not even kidding. I'm not a virgin, but I might as well be as far as this conversation goes. I'm not kidding. All my knowledge of this stuff comes from books and *Cosmo*. "You know, should someone be interested."

His jaw flexes. The shadow of bristles suits him, somehow highlighting the broad strokes of his bone structure. I'm disappointed when he offers me nothing else but a narrow-eyed dark-gold stare.

"I mean it. If a girl thinks she might like that sort of thing, how does she find someone who also—"

"Mimi." He makes my name sound like a reprimand. "Cut it out."

"What? I'm only asking! You can't get angry with me for that."

"What you're asking is impossible."

"What you're picking up *isn't* what I'm putting down," I retort, folding my arms. "This is the same as me turning up at your house unexpected, and you serving me cake I've never had before. Cake that, it turns out, I like. I'm only asking what the recipe is. What store I can visit. Because honestly, Whit, I kind of want a bigger portion. I want to taste it properly."

"Get out of the car," he grates out, all commanding. "Whatever your start date is, wipe it from your calendar. I'll help you find something else."

I laugh. If he wants to get rid of me, he's going to have to change the way he speaks to me. That whole dominating *do as I say* just seems to ring my bell. "I don't want something else. I don't want to work anywhere else."

"This isn't going to work."

"How? I have no idea what you're talking about?"

"You're not that innocent."

"I'm talking to you as a friend, not as my boss. I'm not trying to seduce you. I wouldn't even know what that looked like." True story. This is just my own brand of wearing him down.

"Friends don't do to you what I did," he replies with a glower.

"That depends on what kind of friendship you have. This woman you were expecting. Wasn't she that kind of friend? What do they call them? Friends with benefits?"

"I'm rarely friends with the people I fuck. And I never fuck people I work with."

"Well." I flick my shoulder. "We haven't fucked, so cool beans." *Urgh. Cool beans? Do I have to regress to fourteen? What next? I'll ask him if he wants to listen to my iPod?* "Look, Whit, I will be working for VirTu. I respect Jody too much. I won't make problems for her. And like I said, I've already signed my contract."

"I'll get someone from an agency to fill in." His words fall rapidly. "I'll write you a check to keep you afloat until you find something else."

"That sounds suspiciously like you're trying to buy me off."

"That's not what this is, and you know it."

"You're making such a big deal out of nothing," I say with a chuckle that I hope doesn't sound too forced. The next six months of my life is the *only* time I'll get to live for myself and do what I want. And what I want to do is him. I just have to get him on the same page. "I won't do it, Whit. Jody has enough to deal with without worrying about you and what kind of mess an agency will leave her to clear up."

"Mimi, come on. I can't take that night back."

"I wouldn't give it to you," I reply softly. It was the hottest experience of my life, so to hear him deny me would break me a little. But I also don't believe him. I was there. I saw the way he watched me. Sensed his desire through his fingertips. "Would you really take it back? If you could?"

"You shouldn't ask me that."

And there is my answer. The truth in his troubled expression, and I'm sorry for it. Sorry he feels troubled, at least, as he frowns and rubs a knuckle over his left eyebrow, refusing now to look at me.

"I don't want to turn the clock back." Relief rushes through me at the admission I thought I'd never hear. "This is exactly why you shouldn't be anywhere near me. Because every time you step into my office, I won't see you professionally. I'll be remembering how wet and warm you felt. How your body bent for me. And every time your mouth moves, I'll hear the sounds falling from your lips and think of how exquisite you are when you come."

A blush runs across my skin, my eyelashes fluttering as I take this all in. That right there sounds like a beautiful sort of work-life balance.

6

***

WHIT

I was right about one thing. Every time I see Mimi Valente, no matter what expression she's wearing and no matter what she has to say, I see her mouth softly open and her eyes glaze. Hear her soft, tortured breath in my ear. Feel her fingernails digging into my forearm.

Wouldn't you be curious? she'd said in the car.

The answer is fuck yes. I can't stop thinking about all that I could show her. I can't stop imagining it, and I just... *can't.*

"Have you got a tic?"

I blink, glance up, then scowl as I notice Mimi standing on the threshold to my office. And here comes the start of another hard-on.

Our conversation two weeks ago was nothing short of a revelation. I've never met anyone like her. That she says what she's thinking is refreshing. She's so open and unaffected, and that makes her more than a little dangerous. The things she'd had to say seemed like a lot of information to take in. A lot to digest. But as I'd driven away from her aunt's house, I'd done my best to push it all away. I told myself that I wasn't too worried. I had another few weeks of running interference before the day she'd end up working for me. Enough time to wear her down, to encourage her to find something else. I'd pay a finder's fee to an agency, whatever it took. And if it came down to it, I'd decided I could always take El's suggestion and place her with another department. Out of sight, out of mind. As opposed to not only being within sight but also within reach for eight hours a day while dressed like she's auditioning for the part of a sexy secretary on *Mad Men*.

"You're doing it again."

So much for plans. So much for making sure she wouldn't be my PA because just the day after our lunchtime showdown, Jody had been instructed at a routine doctor's appointment that she needed immediate and complete bed rest. I don't know who was more annoyed: me or Jody. But I do know who was most excited when she'd bounded into the office the following morning like an eager-to-please puppy. Almost two weeks in and constantly having to remind myself that the ways I'd like her to please me are not on offer is wearing.

"What?" I mutter, not bothering to hide my exasperation this time. "Doing what?" My pen clatters as I drop it on the desk, the chair creaking as I thrust myself back in it. She probably thinks I'm an arsehole because every time I look her way, it's with a scowl. But, as the saying goes, it's not her, it's me.

"It looked like you were having a silent conversation with yourself. There are all kinds of thoughts flitting across your face."

"That's because this *is* my thinking face." My thinking I must've pissed someone off in a previous life to have to put up with this.

"Really? It looks more like a *needs more fiber in his diet* kind of face. There are supplements you can take, you know."

"I'm not constipated. Or geriatric," I add when it occurs to me what she might be suggesting.

"I know." Her shoulder lifts and falls casually but our staring match continues. "No one would look at us together and wonder *is he her daddy or is he her dad*?"

"What?" I give my head a shake, not sure if I heard that right.

"I'm just saying, you're in good shape for a man of your age."

"I'm thirty-six. That hardly makes me Methuselah."

"That's exactly the point I'm trying to make."

This woman drives me to distraction. Short of firing her for an inauspicious start that wasn't her fault, what can I do? That's not to say I hadn't considered it as a course of action best for us both. But the prospect of the shitstorm that would follow—Jody's potential stress, Polly's emotional blackmail, my brothers' interference—I'd decided having her here might be the lesser of those two evils.

"Whit?"

I realize I'm still staring, so I roll my eyes with the finesse of Primrose, my youngest sister. I can't have her, but it doesn't stop me from wanting. "Shut the door and come in, for God's sake. I'm not going to bite you."

She turns and reaches for the door handle and murmurs something that sounds like, "I wouldn't mind." Whether that was wishful thinking on her part or mine, I'm not sure. "We need to go over your schedule."

"Fine."

She crosses the space between us, coming to a stop at one of the Le Corbusier chairs placed on the opposite side of my desk, close enough for me to see the tiny pearls she wears in her ears but far enough away not to be tormented by her scent. *Frangipani, sunshine, and holidays.* It sounds ridiculous, but since her car confessional, I've tried very hard not to be within sniffing distance. The scent of her makes me want to press my nose into her skin.

"You have an interview scheduled with the FT on the fifteenth," she says, leaning her thigh against the leather arm. *Lucky arm.*

"What about it?" I make a vague gesture to the chair, but she shakes her head.

"I'm good."

"I wasn't asking. Sit."

"Fine," she huffs out. But, of course, it would've been too much to ask for her to walk *around* the chair. Instead, she slides over the arm, the expensive leather easing her slide with a flash of leg and a soft giggle. "Sorry," she says, smoothing her skirt as she demurely crosses her legs.

Curious. So curious. Is she wearing her blue lace underwear? Her blouse is pale and diaphanous, high at her neck and tight at the wrists. Her skirt is knee length and navy, yet coats like a second skin. Stockings, I'm guessing, and heels, but nothing too obvious. Her foot begins to bounce, my gaze sliding from her electric-blue heels to her knee. Those fucking legs. What I wouldn't give to have them wrapped around my head.

Uncross your legs, darling.

That's it. Press your knees nice and wide.

Slide your skirt a little higher.

Let me watch you grow wet with my words.

"Whit?" My eyes snap to hers to find them dancing with merriment.

It's not like she needs to guess what I'm thinking because

I told her—in very explicit terms—in the car. It was an error in judgment, but I didn't think for one minute she'd end up working here. Telling her I'd always be imagining her riding my fingers was supposed to be ammunition, something to worry her, not titillate.

Not that she ever says a word about it. Not that she needs to—I can tell when she's thinking about it, when she's replaying my words or replaying that night from her own perspective. Her cheeks take on this rosy hue, and she has this way of looking at me with those clear gray eyes. It's almost as though she can see right into my dirty soul.

Fuck it, I need to get laid.

"What's with those?" I make a negligent gesture in her direction. Clearly, I can't help myself.

"What?" She sits up a little, her gaze sliding to her blouse, then the floor.

"Those. The shoes." The bright-blue fuck-me heels. "You didn't have those on earlier." She wore black flats, not that I usually notice these things.

"Oh yeah." She holds out her leg, turning her foot this way and that admiringly. I've stopped looking. But only because she's flashing a little thigh. "I'm wearing them in."

I'd like to wear her—

No. No, I would not.

"They're pretty, though, right?"

"They're hardly workplace appropriate."

"They're shoes. Enclosed toes. Seem plenty appropriate to me," she argues.

"Yes, if you want to break your neck." Or wrap them around mine. "Listen," I add gruffly, "if there's a problem with my schedule, I expect you to bring it to fix it, not just my attention."

Her smile dampens as she lowers her leg, then reaches

for her iPad. "You have a meeting with Alexander Beckett scheduled the same day. There's a chance they might overlap. I thought I should ask which you'd like to reschedule."

"Postpone the FT interview. Beckett is more important." He's the reason I was able to raise the finance for this venture. "Is it just Beckett or Olivia as well?"

"Jody made a note," she murmurs as her attention dips. My attention remains on her face. *By sheer force of will.* "Both." She glances up, seeing right through me again anyway.

"Better order lunch. She likes the sashimi from—"

"Okaish."

"That's the one," I return brusquely. I feel like a complete shit. I bring up her shoes, then turn on her like a dog with a sore tail.

"You've got emails from another couple of publications requesting interviews... got it!" she tags on, tapping the screen because I'm already shaking my head. "There's also a note to remind you that Lavender's birthday is at the end of the month."

"Shit." I rub my hand across the bristles already sprouting on my jaw. "I completely forgot."

"What can I help you with? Lavender is your sister, right?"

"Yeah, she'll be turning twenty."

"Then I can definitely help. I was twenty not too long ago."

I try not to scowl. When she puts it like that, I feel like an old pervert. But Mimi is nothing like petulant, combative Lavender. I mean, I'm thirty-six, not sixty-six, but that still puts a dozen years between us. A dozen years and the fact that I'm her boss. It sounds like a recipe for disaster. For both of us.

"Is there something wrong?"

Me. I'm wrong. Wrong for wanting to bend her over my desk in nothing but a garter belt and stockings. Wrong and such a cliché. I give my head a quick shake and come up with some bullshit answer. "I was just thinking that Jody wasn't up for shopping for personal gifts. Corporate was the limit. She said it was too much responsibility."

"I don't mind." Mimi's shoulders jump along with her words. "Who doesn't love shopping?"

"Well, me."

"I bet I could convert you."

"No, Mimi. You really couldn't."

"I bet I could," she retorts happily. "My enthusiasm knows no bounds!"

"Yes, I've noticed that about you." *Wouldn't you be curious?* The phantom of her soft words curls around my ears again. Yes. Yes, I am. Curious. Hungry. And ignoring my impulses. Clearing my throat, I reach down and adjust my cock, thankful for the cover of my desk. "Would you book somewhere for dinner that night?"

"On the twenty-eighth? For how many?" She angles her iPad.

"Well, there are seven of us," I say with another frown.

"I cannot imagine growing up with so many siblings. It must've been amazing."

"Yes, amazing, if you like to spend your childhood banging on bathroom doors," I murmur. "Seven plus Archer," I say, carrying on. "That's Heather, my sister's husband. Then Polly and also whichever fuckwit boyfriend Lavender has on the go. Miranda, our cousin, her husband,

Harry, and their two boys. And you could ask Brin and El if they'll be bringing a plus-one before you book."

"Is El dating?" she asks.

"No, not as far as I know. Not seriously, anyway. Why do you ask?" I add, casually.

"He asked me out next weekend." She makes a diffident gesture with the pen. I frown as I notice her foot begins to bounce again. "That's not a problem, is it?"

"Why would it be?" I answer a little too quickly.

"I'm just being a good little employee."

"Well, ask, all the same." I'm surprised I'm able to form a full and coherent sentence when all I can think of is El seeing her—really seeing her. Feasting his eyes on her long legs. Maybe even getting her out of her underwear.

"Do you suffer from headaches?" At her question, my gaze sharply lifts. "All that jaw clenching can't be good for you."

El is taking her out, and she's treating me like I'm in my dotage. "No. I don't suffer from headaches." I just have six siblings who are headache-inducing. And a thing for my PA that makes my cock ache.

I definitely need to get laid.

"Where's he taking you?" I ask casually, I hope.

"To dinner, some Thai-Italian fusion place."

"Sounds like a stomachache in the making," I mutter. It's little wonder she treats me like I'm an old git when I behave like one.

"Then we're going to a club."

Maybe I should have a word with him, remind him of Mimi's position in this business. Of how close she is to Mum. Yes, that's it. A quiet word with Polly should piss on his fireworks.

"Getting back to your sister's birthday, we're looking at

thirteen people, possibly fifteen. Sixteen if you're taking a plus-one." She gives a small, polite smile.

I briefly consider lying. Then remember I'm not a teenager who plays games. "Thirteen. Potentially fifteen."

"No date for you?"

"I feel like we've already talked about this." Her cheeks pink, and I get a very visceral kick out of knowing she's recalling our car conversation about a nameless, faceless woman. Why she likes the things she likes. Why she's sexually submissive.

"We spoke, but it wasn't what I'd call an edifying conversation."

My smile slides into a tease. "You don't think so?"

"Not where you're concerned. You don't date, but you have...assignations. I think that was about the strength of it."

"How prim, Mimi. You can use your big-girl words, you know."

"Curse, you mean?" I nod. "I don't like to," she adds. "It's not my thing."

But I'm not yet ready to give up. "My dad used to say that vulgarity is like good whisky. That it should only be shared with the right people and on the right occasion."

"Is that what you believe, too?"

"No. I did once try to give up swearing, but I found I *cunt*."

Her expression darkens, unimpressed.

I set off laughing. "So prim and proper," I tease.

"I just don't swear," she proclaims as my chuckling draws off.

"You will." At least I'd like to make her. Make her eyes roll back in her head as she spews a filthy stream of consciousness.

"You think you can make me?" she answers with a little

too much daring. She barely moves, but her answer is all cocked hip and attitude.

"Working with me will drive you to it." It's the nearest I'll allow myself to get to the truth of it. "And being at Lavender's birthday dinner pretty much guarantees it."

"I'm invited?"

She looks surprised. And happy. I hadn't meant to invite her, and while Polly would've done so anyway, I find I want her there. I bet she'll turn up wearing a pretty dress, the kind that makes her look like a gift. A gift I'd love to unwrap but will end up just staring at longingly instead. But I'm not about to say any of this.

"Of course you're invited. I'll need your help as a referee."

"You'll have games?" Now she looks slightly confused.

The game I want to play is let's unravel Mimi. It's a bit like pass the parcel but with only one player. Me. I get to unwrap each of her layers as I unravel her mind with my filth.

"Games? Only if you consider frightening whichever boy Lavender is currently dangling from her black-painted fingernails."

"That's not nice." Her lips purse in disapproval.

"No, but someone has to do it. She has terrible taste in men."

"And the role automatically falls to you?"

"Sadly, yes. At least since Dad died."

"So you play the dad—" Her eyes fly wide as she bites off the end of the word, her cheeks going from pink to beet red.

"Like a dad, yes." My lips quirk as I consider this. "Which is not," I add, dropping my tone, "at all like playing a daddy."

She swallows, her lashes fluttering as her breath leaves

her chest in a *whoosh.* "That's what I meant about your explanation not covering all the bases."

"That's a curious turn of phrase," I purr, unable to help myself, it seems.

"I was kind of surprised how much fun skipping straight to third base was."

I curl my hands around the arms of my chair, anchoring me to it when all I want to do is round my desk, pick her up, and slide *home.*

This is becoming a bit of a recurring theme. But then her phrasing penetrates my lust-filled brain.

"You've never..." *Shit.* "Don't answer that," I add quickly, but she's already shaking her head, those gray eyes wide and solemn.

"They usually start north of my waistband, not that I have a *ton* of experience."

Why do I like the sound of that? I've always preferred experience over a novice. *Haven't I?* "Right, well, this conversation has crossed over into inappropriate, so let's—"

"I thought there must be a guy manual or something." She gives an adorably pensive twist to her lips.

"A manual?" I'm really not sure what's going to fall out of her mouth next.

"I don't know. Like sexual lore or something." She scratches her temple with her index finger, still in contemplation. "Maybe something on the internet?" And now she's looking at me as though I have all the answers, which is flattering but also slightly daft. "It's just, the handful of guys I have been with have all, you know." With her palm, she makes a circle over her breasts. "Sung from a very similar hymn sheet?"

"Did they make you sing?" Fucking hell. Maybe there's

something in the water. Something more dangerous than listeria.

"What do you mean?"

I'm definitely going to hell. "Did they make you come?"

She bites her lip but doesn't answer, which is probably for the best.

"If I answer your question, you have to answer mine."

"That's not how I work."

"It's not like I'm gonna jump you. I just want to know what you like."

"Why? What good could come of it?"

"I guess I'm trying to make sense of what made me enjoy it so much." Her gaze dips to her lap where she picks at a piece of invisible fluff. "Why I didn't stop you. Was it you? Was it the role you were playing? It was shocking, but I felt kind of compelled. No, that's not the right word," she adds as her gaze lifts, her expression not quite beseeching. "Why did it make me feel so good?"

I almost groan. Why does she have to be so fucking perfect?

"I can't answer that for you." More importantly, I don't want to because then I'll have to admit there are other men like me. Other men with whom she might find what she's looking for. Other men she might share the experience with.

"Well, that's okay." I almost fall off my chair. Mimi Valente giving up—listening? "Because that's not what I want to ask."

"No?" So much hesitancy in that word. Rightly so, as it turns out.

"No. What I'm asking is why you like it."

"I like it when people do as they're told." It's the truth. But I could also be trying to put a stop to this dangerous interrogation.

"People?"

"In a general sense." Who doesn't like to be in charge and have those around them pay attention? It would make my life a lot easier if they did. "More specifically, I enjoy it when women do as I say." Again with the truth.

"In the bedroom," she whispers.

"Sexually," I amend.

"You like them to be a little submissive? Like me?"

"Stop." I bring my head to my hand, ostensibly to rub my temples. The reality is, I need to hide the truth from her. The truth of what her questions mean. "This is ridiculous," I add with an unhappy frown.

"I'm just saying." She gives a tiny shoulder shimmy that I suppose is meant to convey her innocence.

But yes, Mimi. I like them when they're like you, even full of questions and pushing boundaries. I like to call them my good girl when they're compliant and punish them in a way that meets both of our satisfaction when they're not. "This conversation is edging territory I'd rather not discuss." And I'd rather not suffer my hard-on edging the underside of my desk. "You should go back to work."

I expect another question, an *oh, but I haven't asked you about*—

I'm surprised when she stands.

"Yes," she demurs, "I should get back, just like the boss says."

I have nothing to offer, nothing sensible, anyway. Except... she didn't answer my original question. She pauses when she reaches the door, and I think for a moment that she might've read my mind as she lifts her gaze. My gray-eyed guileless temptress. Or should that be agitator? "Does Lavender have a favorite restaurant?"

"Somewhere that serves lentils, probably." Has Mimi

really led such a sheltered life, or is she playing a part? And there's that question again... have previous lovers made her come? "I'm not really sure," I add, pushing the thought away as I draw my laptop closer.

"No problem. I can ask El." I suppose that answers that conundrum. Temptress or agitator, good girl or bad? Try frustrating to the end.

"Just don't book a steak restaurant," I reply, refusing to bite.

"And a budget for her gift?"

"Spend whatever you think."

"No budget? You should probably come with me."

I can't restrain the twist of my lips. Mimi Valente is not bad. She's an out-and-out brat. "I don't think that's a good idea."

"Fine. Have it your way, Daddy Warbucks." She tips her gaze again. It doesn't hide her smirk. "One last question." *Thank fuck.* "What kind of things does Lavender like?"

"Edibles," I say with a sigh.

"O-kay." She marks something on the iPad when she looks my way again. "I wonder if El likes people to do as they're told, too."

I send her a withering glance. "My brother is nothing like me."

"I expect you're right. He seems way more laid-back. Maybe I'll just ask him to hook me up with a dealer."

"It was a joke," I say repressively.

"Yeah." She sighs. "I'm beginning to wonder if you think that's what I am."

And with that, she flounces out of my office.

7

MIMI

"Aunt Doreen!" The brass letterbox rattles as I push the door.

"In here, dear," she calls from the kitchen.

I make my way through the slightly musty hallway into the bright kitchen where Aunt Doreen, dressed in a terry cloth robe and head full of pink spongey hair curlers, is pushing her fat tabby cat from the kitchen table. "Bloody moggy." She scoots it away from an earthenware teapot, patting her silver-blond hair. "Oh pretty!" she coos as her gaze snags on the flowers in my hand.

"I'm glad you like them because they're for you." Her eyes sparkle as I present her with the modest bunch.

"For me?" she repeats with genuine pleasure as she brings them to her nose and inhales. "Oh, how lovely! I don't remember the last time someone bought me flowers. Thank you, Mimi, love."

"None of your harem buy you flowers?" I press my hand to my chest with mock affront before sliding off my jacket and draping it over the wooden chairback. "Sounds like you didn't train them right."

"My date tonight would probably just pilfer a bunch from the local cemetery."

"He sounds like a charmer," I say as I pull out the chair.

"He really isn't." She gives a little laugh. "I picked him up during my bad-boy phase."

At seventy-nine, Aunt Doreen, who isn't really my aunt, lives life at full tilt. From mornings spent volunteering at the local food bank and soup kitchen, to coffee dates with her friends, then onto a diary that's just bursting with *actual* dates.

"So Wednesday night is Alan?" I hazard.

"No, love. Alan is Thursday." She turns and opens a cabinet door before banging it shut again. "Wednesday is my reformed bad-boy Frank. Well, *boy* might be stretching it, but he is younger than me."

"You cougar!"

"He keeps me on my toes," she trills.

"Does that mean he tries to get fresh with you?"

"One can only hope, dear. One can only hope!"

Aunt Doreen has a different man every night of the week (except Sunday night when she puts her feet up) because, in her own words, she's "grabbing what's left of life by the short and curlies." Which I think means she's grabbing life by the balls. She's certainly ball*sy* and doesn't give a "flying fig" what anyone thinks. Personally, I think she's got the right idea. I also think my family might not have been so calm about me staying here if they knew what kind of crazy she was.

We might not be related but she's my kind of woman, and I've decided I'm taking a page out of her book. Not that I intend to date a different man every night. I might have considered it prior to what I've come to refer to in my head as "the interview." But now I'm only interested in Whit.

"Frank is a good little mover," Aunt Doreen says, snapping me out of my thoughts. "And tonight is salsa night." She does a little shimmy that belies a recent hip replacement. "I'll be as stiff as a board tomorrow. If I'm lucky, Frank will reach that point a little sooner, eh?" Turning her head over her shoulder, she sends me a bawdy wink.

"What time were you thinking?"

"Of coming back for a nightcap? Oh, I shouldn't think I'll be home before eleven o'clock tonight."

I make a mental note to be in bed and fast asleep *way* before then as, from under the sink, she pulls out a vase much too big for this modest bunch. She begins to fill it with water from the faucet. "These are beautiful. You really shouldn't have."

"They're just a little thing to say thanks for putting up with me."

"None of your nonsense," she scoffs. "You're not a bother. You brighten the place up."

I eye the orange-painted walls, pink fridge, electric kettle and toaster. Who knew my energy was so... vivid. "How long has Frank been part of your rotation?"

Aunt Doreen pauses, a yellow tulip in hand. "Maybe two months?"

"A new boy." Pressing my elbow to the table, I brace my chin on my palm. "Did you meet him at your salsa class?"

"No. At the little supermarket on the corner. My friend Betty was popping 'round for lunch, and I needed salad stuff. Would you believe he accosted me in the veg aisle? I was holding a cucumber, and he said, 'ah, a lonely lady's favorite companion.'"

I almost choke on my tongue. "And you let him take you out after that introduction?"

"At first, I thought about hitting him with it. Only, I hadn't paid, and it seemed a bit unfair. After all, Ravi, the owner, didn't deserve a bruised cucumber. And I'm not sure his wife would've liked it."

Cue choke number two. "Aunt Doreen!"

"What? It's true. I would've kicked Frank in the wotsits if I was a few years younger, only this new hip gives me some jip when I lift my leg too high. Anyway, I gave him the once-over and decided he wasn't bad looking. He still has most of his own hair and not many men do at that age. Anyway, there he was, standing in the veg aisle, like the cock of the walk, a box of teabags under his arm when I realized he'd come out in his house slippers. So I said to him, 'nice slippers,' you know, all unimpressed, thinking I'd take the wind out of his sails. But do you know what the cheeky devil said? 'How would you like to find them under your bed in the morning?'"

"Oh, my gosh!" I say with a laugh, partly at her storytelling and partly at her wiggling eyebrows.

"But I do like the bold ones. That's why I decided I would like to see what they looked like. Those slippers. Under my bed. Or at least, to see if he was all mouth and no trousers. Maybe you'd call that all hat and no cattle."

"All talk and no action? And he wasn't?" Or else he wouldn't be a fixture on her rotation.

"Well, there *is* a lot going on in the trouser department, if you know what I mean."

I roll my lips inward to prevent something careless from falling out. Something like, *ew, no, Aunt Doreen, I do not need to hear about elderly man penis performance!*

Thankfully, she's not looking at me as she concentrates on her flower arrangement. But coy isn't in her wheelhouse.

"The wonders of modern medicine," she murmurs with a secretive kind of smile.

I don't think she's talking about her hip replacement.

"Don't these gentleman callers of yours mind that they have competition?"

"If they do, they know to keep it to themselves, or they can sling their hook elsewhere. I was married once before. I'm not doing that again. This keeps them on their toes and it doesn't land me dirty socks and underpants to wash."

"Well, it's clearly working for you." Because a more vibrant senior citizen I've yet to meet. Maybe I should be sad that Aunt Doreen has a more active social life than I do, but I'm not. I love that she's squeezing out every drop of this crazy journey. Not that my life has been crazy so far, but I have high hopes. *Very high hopes.*

"Variety, dear Mimi, is the spice of life. Maybe you can find that out for yourself when you make a couple of new friends. That's all it'll take before your social life becomes a whirl. A gorgeous girl like you will have the boys trotting after her like tom cats."

"We'll see." I'm not planning on settling for a boy. I have my sights set on a man. A whole lot of man with eyes like a tiger and a bite I want to experience.

We fall quiet for a moment, lost in our own thoughts. Doreen continues to arrange her modest bouquet as my mind returns to musing about Whit. I'm beginning to wonder *how* he fits women into his schedule—never mind *who.*

The days Whit is in the office, he arrives before I do and leaves after I'm gone. According to his expense reports, he orders a lot of dinners to his desk. His calendar is jam-packed with meetings, in-house and remote, and one afternoon a week is blocked out for some NGO he's on the board of. When he's not in the building, he's jetting between the European operations in Paris, Brussels, and Zurich. And then there are the requests for interviews from financial publications and the more tabloid ones. I've gone months ahead and back in his calendar driven by my curiosity and can see the vacations he occasionally takes are still of an extreme nature. Snowboarding in Verbier winter past. Free climbing in Greece coming up in the fall.

Given the pace of his life, I'm beginning to wonder when I'll get to seduce him.

"This was my mother's vase," Doreen murmurs absently, bringing me out of my dissatisfied musings.

"*Varse*," I mouth the word silently, exaggerating the movement by dropping my chin when she looks up and catches me.

"I hope you're not pulling faces like that at work."

"Only when his door is closed." Which isn't very often, as it seems Whit likes me to be within bellowing distance.

"Your boss still being a pain?" she asks, not without sympathy.

"Eh." I shrug. "Nothing I can't handle." I've had terrible bosses before, and he is not a terrible boss. He's a little cranky, but who knows whether it's because he's stuck with me or because he thinks he needs to resist me? All I know is, one minute, I feel like he's looking at me like he said he would, like he's replaying *my interview*, and the next, he's stomping around the place looking madder than a wet hen. I can't stop thinking about the daddy version of him. Daddy Whit makes me feel all... *ooh-hoo-hoo*. Hot and kind of shivery and I know there's no one on this earth I'd be more comfortable exploring this side of me.

"Are you cold? Do you need a cardi?"

I jolt back to myself and give a quick shake of my head.

"I have some of that cannabis oil if you want to slip some into his tea."

"No!" Gosh, Aunt Doreen is a trip.

"It might mellow him out," she reasons.

"He's really not that bad." And I'm not sure I want him mellow. Whit has been the object of my fantasies since before I knew what a fantasy was. Twelve-year-old me just knew he was the best man on earth. I'd assumed that when I grew up, we'd get married. After all, he treated me much better than my brother did. Of course, Connor was just trying to get me out of the house so they could have their wicked way with their harem of women.

But that's fine. Women have always been drawn to Whit like hummingbirds to a fire bush. I remember when Connor and Whit would take me to the mall for ice cream, usually at Whit's insistence. The looks he'd draw from women of all ages—some of them old enough to be his mom! The year I turned fourteen, I suddenly became very popular at school when Whit visited, but it was the girls his own age who annoyed me most. He was my fairy-tale prince, but I had to share him. He had *such* a way and an innate magnetism. And the girls who hung around the pool in the summer, the ones that led him into the pool house by the hand? Well, I'd decided back then that they were just placeholders until I got boobs. At that age, boobs seemed to be the pinnacle of adulthood. The other thing I learned about boobs was that, like watched pots, they take their time.

As for how he treats me now, it's worth noting that people only treat you with as much (or as little) respect as you'll allow. While Whit's moods might be mercurial, he hasn't once disrespected me, not even during my clumsy attempts at seduction. That's just not him.

"You can always look for something else. No point

staying in a job that makes you miserable. Life is too short." Her hands suddenly still on the vase. "I'm sorry, love," she says, her mouth turning down. "You don't need me to tell you that, do you? Not after all you've been through."

I send her a bright smile and shake off her concerns. I won't feel sorry for myself. "What are you taking the oil for, if you don't mind me asking?"

"My dodgy hip. Just when it's acting up."

"Well, I don't think he needs it." I'm sure his hips work just fine. In fact, I'm counting on it. I find myself smiling as I trace my finger over an old scar on the tabletop. Whit's temper is fleeting, and I keep expecting him to burst out of his shirt like the Incredible Hulk. *A girl can hope.* "I kind of like him the way he is." It's a new side to him, and I kind of like it on him. I think a lot of the time I might goad him to it because while I've had crankier bosses, I've never had one I wanted to bend me over his desk in punishment.

"Oh-*oh.*"

My smile shrinks as I glance up.

"You like him. Your boss. You *like* like him." It's not an observation. More like an accusation.

"No. I told you, he was Connor's friend. We have a history." It's not as torrid as I'd like it, but I live in hope. "But if I did like him..." Urgh, this is crazy. I cannot confide in my elderly relation. This wouldn't be happening if I'd stood up to my parents. I should be living in semi-squalor with girls my own age! But then again, Doreen does have *years* of experience...

"But if you did like him like that?" Doreen hesitantly repeats.

"What would I do about it?" Not in a fatalistic, woe-is-me way. More like give me a hint, naughty Doreen. Show me your temptress ways!

"Well, if you did," she says, looking at me over the top of her pink-framed spectacles, "I'd suggest you write down all the things you want to happen between you and him. What you'd like to do to him and what you'd like him to do to you."

"Yes?" Better buy a new notepad because it sounds like I'm making a list. A long list!

"Jot it all down. Get all the dirty details down on the paper."

"And then?" How do we action this plan?

"Then you take the paper outside with a box of matches and set it on fire—"

"Like a pagan ritual?" I sit straight in my chair. I like it, even if my Baptist parents would have a fit.

"—and never think about him that way again."

"Oh." I slump back in my seat. That's not what I was expecting. "What happened to being bold?"

"I'm an old lady, love. No one is going to be talking about me around the water cooler. And if they did, I wouldn't hear them on account of my deafness."

"You're not going deaf."

"What?"

"I said—never mind." I fell for it again. I don't bother hiding my smile. "Does that go for your neighbors, too? You don't mind if they gossip?"

"They're all upwardly mobile types around here. DINKs," she says as though the word tastes bad. "Double income, no kids," she adds when I look confused. "No one to fight over in a divorce if you discount the dog. They already look at me as though I'm cheapening the street when I've been here since I was three years old. Quite frankly, Mimi love, they can kiss my Irish arse if they do mind."

As well as not being deaf, Doreen isn't Irish.

"You know, that's kind of how I feel. I'm done living my life by other people's rules." I'd gone to the college my parents wanted me to, an all-girls Christian college just an hour from home. They said it would be for the best, but the best for who? Not me. It was the best they could do short of wrapping me in cotton and never letting me out of the house again. I'd done it because they were all so changed after Connor died, and I would've done anything to ease their pain. I'd toed the line, and I'd taken all the precautions, given Connor's cardiac arrest. He was so fit and healthy—such a gym junkie—that we couldn't believe it.

In the aftermath, I stayed close to home. I rarely drank, ate healthy meals, and promised I'd avoid strenuous activities. *Including sex.* I attended doctor appointments when I was supposed to—monitoring cardiology appointments, too. His death made me want to squeeze as much life in as I could. I wanted to travel and explore, but instead, I chose their needs over mine. In the end, it made no difference. It makes me so sad when I think of all the time I've wasted, time I will never get again.

So I'm here, in London, with a list of experiences where I've wanted to live for years. Even staying with Doreen is a compromise to help my parents sleep at night. Someone to check on me and make sure I'm tucked safe in bed, not—

I cut off the internal noise, closing the door on a mind of crowded thoughts and recriminations.

"Screw what anyone else thinks," I announce. "None of us are here forever, so we should make the most of it while we are."

"You're right. Of course you're right. I just wouldn't want to see you hurt."

"Whit isn't like that. He's one of the good guys."

"I hope so," she adds with a sad-looking smile. "Anyway, it's not like you'll be here long."

"Ouch, Aunt Doreen. You never know when your number is up, but that was brutal!" This conversation might've turned a little dark, but perky is more my style.

"I meant here in London, you silly mare! It's not as though you're looking to make a life here, is it?"

Are we talking horses, or am I a night*mare*? And what constitutes a life? Twenty-five years? Thirty-six? Fifty? All I know is I'm going to squeeze as much enjoyment into the time right in front of me because who knows what's just over the next hill.

"Is Frank taking you to dinner?" I ask, segueing a change of topic.

"No, I bought a nice quiche from the bakery. I thought you and I could have that with a bit of salad."

"Great." But not as great as ordering in sushi. I guess my people-pleasing days aren't exactly over because that's how my day ends, eating cold quiche and salad with my elderly relation, who, despite being more than three times my age, is definitely getting more bedroom action.

8

WHIT

I HEAD BACK to the office after taking Mimi home when Mum texts.

> Brin is coming for dinner this evening.

I stare at my phone, abandoning a dozen responses ranging from assumptions about his motives to him turning up with a bag of laundry.

Eventually, I settle on:

> Have fun!

> Should I set you a place at the table?

> Sorry. I'm busy this evening.

> Doing anything nice?

> I'll be in the office quite late, and then I have a date.

With Mimi?

Bloody hell. That was quick. She must be using the talk-to-text function.

Mimi is my PA. She is not dating material.

Rubbish! Mimi is a doll. I can absolutely see you together.

I hope she hasn't got binoculars.

Better get yourself to the opticians because that is NOT happening.

Who's the date with, then?

Angelo from the Italian place on the corner.

Leaning back in my chair, I smile as I watch the little blue bubbles flutter across the screen of my phone. That'll give her something to think about. How to answer that strategically.

You're thirty-six. I think I would know by now if you were gay.

Maybe I've been keeping it a secret.

I'm sure you have lots of secrets, but one of them isn't a hankering for a little man love.

Angelo isn't little.

Angelo has hairy fingers and sweats excessively. Even if you were gay, I can't in a million years see hirsute middle-aged men as being your type.

Maybe I'm into bears.

Darling, there's more chance of you getting Yogi to roger you.

I burst out laughing, but she isn't done.

Now, Mimi is another story. I see the way you look at her.

Bye, Mum.

Why does no one in this family want to give me grandchildren? I'll have arthritic fingers before I get the chance to hold them.

Your grandchildren have four legs and shaggy coats.

Just like Angelo.

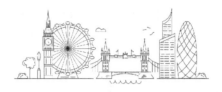

9

***

MIMI

THE LIGHTS overhead flicker as they move faster and faster like some reverse runway. A girl in blue bends over me.

"She's tachycardic, looks like VT, we need to defibrillate..."

It's too late, I think to myself. I'm not on a plane. Did I even get on one? Did I make it to London? Did I get what I was looking for?

It wasn't supposed to happen this way.

I put off living, and now it's too late.

They said my choices were foolish, that I was making a mistake. But I told them—I shouted it from the top of my lungs—there were other ways to die. Fear is the death of choice, and a mental death has to be just as agonizing.

I want to laugh at the irony, at my foolishness, but a mask covers my mouth. I want to laugh and laugh and laugh, but I don't have it physically in me.

I wanted to live my life on my terms. I refused their fear when I should've listened because now it's too late.

The lights blur bright against a pale-yellow ceiling. Machines beep as my mother wails that I *just wouldn't listen*.

I feel fear. I feel anxiety. No, those don't feel right. Enough. This thing I'm experiencing is something else. Something stronger.

Doom.

The word comes to me with a cloaking of black.

My life is over before I get a chance to really live it.

Something brushes against my fingers, and I physically recoil at the sensation. It all happens so quickly, this sense of a happening from someplace else. Some other time and space. I inhale a life-filled gasp, my body jerking upright as though yanked by a force greater than my own.

Meoowwww.

I press my hand over my heart as I begin to laugh. I can feel it pounding under my skin—*it's still there, it's working, I'm okay*—as I glance down. Aunt Doreen's ginger cat stares back at me through the gloom.

"Oh, it's you." I press one hand to his thick fur without moving the other from my still-racing heart.

Just a dream.

Just regret.

It's not real.

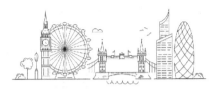

10

WHIT

"You all right?"

Brin's voice pulls my attention from my laptop, his long frame visible through the open door. He's not dressed for the office, or maybe he is. He doesn't work corporate and can often be found wearing jeans. More interesting than his outfit are the takeaway coffee cups in his hand. *Two of them, not three.*

"Am I... all right? Is that what you're asking?" Amelia's voice sounds hesitant. Meanwhile, I'm irrationally annoyed that I can't see her, bar the brief flash of her hand, her shoulder, and the flick of her ponytail. How is it I'd never realized Jody's desk is placed so inconveniently? Maybe because I never spent half the day trying to perve at Jody.

"Yeah," Brin says with a delighted laugh. "It's a greeting. Same as hello, how're you doing? That sort of thing. I bet you're ending phone calls wrong as well."

"How are you supposed to end them? I say *bye* like everyone else."

"Everyone else who doesn't live here, Mimi, love. The standard ending of a conversation in the UK goes a bit like this." The idiot clears his throat. "Alright, that's great, thanks very much, cheers, thanks again, *bye!*"

"You're weird," she says with a cute laugh. She's not wrong, either. About him being weird. He's also weirdly annoying.

"Says the one defiling British telephone etiquette. I'm surprised there haven't been complaints."

"Maybe there has been." She lowers her voice. "It might be what's put the monster in a bad mood."

Brin's head lifts as he slides a smug smile through the open door. "Is Whit being a twat?" he asks, looking right at me.

Me? I just stare back.

"You say that differently."

Mimi's comment brings Brin's attention sliding back. "Because you lot say it wrong."

"And you're just a tease."

My stomach turns to a lump of fucking concrete. Is she flirting with him?

"Am I?" Brin asks with a chuckle I think I might ram down the back of his throat. With my fist.

"Well, yeah. Unless one of those *isn't* for me."

I try to concentrate on my laptop screen again, but no deal. My attention slides back to Brin and I watch as he glances down to the takeaway cups he seems surprised to find in his hands.

"Sorry." He passes one over with a shy grin. "This one is for you."

It's the Amelia effect. She dazzles everyone. At the investor meeting last week, we had the usual array of sharp brains, straight-talking titans of industry, and the mega-wealthy, yet a number of them sat like starstruck schoolboys, gazing up at her as though she'd offered them the moon and not the standard coffee and pastries. It's just her way. She has this knack for treating everyone like they're the sole focus of her attention. She knows everyone's fucking name, and according to security, she's been feeding half her lunch to the homeless bloke who's often camped outside the building. Helena from HR called and asked me what I wanted to do about it. As a company, we do our bit for charity and even sponsor a local homeless shelter, but no financial institution wants a symbol of poverty sitting on their doorstep.

That said, I told Helena to leave it. What kind of a bastard tells someone to knock off being charitable?

"You, Brin Whittington, are a prince among men." Delight seeps into Mimi's tone. It's just her way. She even had Olivia Beckett eating out of her hand, which annoyed me no end because Olivia has a way of making me feel like I'm still wet behind the ears.

"Mmm. That is *so* good."

That is *so* unfair. Why didn't I think to bring her coffee? Then I'd be the one watching her expression. She looks so lovely when she's enjoying herself, all languid eyed and blissed out. Not for the first time today, I find myself adjusting my swelling dick.

"Are you okay?" Mimi's voice turns concerned, and my brother clears his throat.

"Sorry. I must've spaced out for a minute."

I bet you did, you filthy fucker. I force my attention back to the screen, but the numbers might as well be hieroglyphics.

"Thank you for this. I really needed it."

"No problem." Brin's reply sounds a little strangled. The fucking Amelia effect. Blessedly, she walks with her head in the clouds, or else she might see what she does to men. "The place around the corner has the best coffee. Small batch freshly roasted. Have you been yet?"

"I can't say I've come across it."

My fingers splay out on the keys while, in my mind's eye, Mimi earnestly shakes her head. I hope Brin gets fucking priapism.

"Where is it, did you say?"

And there it is. His way in. Bad enough that El thinks he's taking her to dinner next week. *Think* being the operative word. I'll just get Polly to throw a spanner in those potentially dirty works if I know El.

"Why don't I take you for lunch there Monday?" the little shit offers. "They do the best canelés," he adds, not giving her the opportunity to brush him off gently.

"Cannolis?"

"No." He gives a soft laugh. "Canelés," he says, pretending he's a native Parisienne. Brin doesn't speak a word of French, so unless he's about to sing her *Joyeux Anniversaire*—happy birthday in French—I think he's about done. "They're, like, these delicious little cakes." He flicks out his hand as though holding one. Like she's eating out of it.

"Oh, I love cake."

"Yeah?" The fucker sounds turned on. *She said cake, not cock.* "These have this crispy, rum-glazed crust and soft, fluffy custard inside."

"Stop," she half moans, which I do not like. I don't have a problem with the sound; it's more the fact she's moaning in front of that arsewipe. I feel antsy. Like my skin is a size too small. Irrational is what it is—Mimi is my PA. The little sister of my dead mate. I knew her when she wore braces, for fuck's sake. There's no call to give in to these feelings because I'm not a horny teenager.

She just makes me feel like one.

I can't seem to help myself. I mean, I haven't *helped myself*. Not in the office, at least. I might've come close to it once or twice, especially when I get a whiff of her perfume. At home, though...

I'm surprised I haven't wanked myself raw to the image of her—

"They're native to Bordeaux." I snap back to myself at the sound of Brin's voice. He's still banging on about cakes. And the way he says Bordeaux? He's a beret and a string of onions away from being a caricature like the ones you can find being drawn on the banks of the Seine. "It's the only place that makes them in London."

"I highly doubt that," I mutter, returning my attention to my laptop. For 1.4 seconds.

"Oh my goodness." Mimi gives a snorting hoot.

"Mimi!" my brother exclaims playfully. "How many decibels do you reckon that was?"

"Stop! I'm not responsible for the noises my stomach makes when I'm hungry and you're talking about food."

"Don't tell me you're one of those girls who eats lettuce leaves for lunch."

"Does it look like it?"

"You look like—no, forget it." He shakes his head.

"Forget what? You didn't say anything." A pause. "But now you have to."

"I'm not falling for that."

"Falling for what?"

Brin places his coffee on her desk, pressing his palms on either side of it. "You're just fishing for compliments," he all but purrs.

My jaw tenses as I link my fingers and crack them noisily.

"I am not!"

"You're sure it's not because you already know you're gorgeous?"

"Don't get fresh, mister." I'm pretty sure that was the sound of a plastic ruler being rapped across his knuckles. As far as brush-offs go, it'll do as Brin straightens. But if I know my brother, he's not giving in. "I just forgot lunch."

"Who forgets to eat?"

"People who are busy. And... people who leave their lunchbox on the Tube on the way in."

Or maybe people who see fit to feed two homeless people today.

"I'll tell you what." Here it comes. *Let me take you to the best coffee shop in London.* Brin's version of *come up and see my etchings.* I love my little brother, so I hate myself—just a little —when I spoil his fun...

"Amelia," I deliberately call across the space.

Brin's darkly amused gaze swings my way, then back to Mimi again as he fakes the kind of shiver that might indicate someone just walked across his grave. *It can be arranged, Brin.* "That brought back a horrible memory." He hooks a thumb over his shoulder. "Like being summoned by your dad for a dressing down."

I don't resist the evil smile that creeps across my face. *If only you knew, Brin. You'd be one jealous fucker.* I clear my throat and pull my head out of the gutter.

"I didn't realize your working contract was part-time, Brin." My tone drips with derision, even if the only person I should be disgusted with is myself. I'm not.

My brother pulls a face that is one hundred percent *fuck you.*

"If you'll excuse me," Amelia says, her body coming into my line of vision. She touches his arm lightly, and a moment later, she appears at the doorway, unaffected by my sullen expression. "Yes, Mr. Whittington?"

Well, the purr is new.

"Come in and close the door."

She turns as she does so, giving me a stellar view of her round arse, and the bonus sight of my brother's unhappy expression. It's even less happy as I flip him the finger the moment before he disappears behind the wood.

Amelia—no idea why I full named her—clasps her hands behind her back as she takes a couple of steps closer. The afternoon sun falls over her curves, yet all I can see is her smile. A smile full of secrets. Full of knowing. The smile of a lover who seems to intuit just what you're thinking. Does she know what she does to me? That she's playing with fire? *Hell, this is Mimi*, I remind myself. She hasn't a calculating bone in her body.

Meanwhile, my bone...er

"What have I told you about calling me Mr. Whittington?" My voice is a low, unhappy rumble.

"That it makes you want to look over your shoulder to see if your father is there."

"Exactly." I frown a little more just in case she's not getting the picture.

"Well, no one ever calls me Amelia, either. But I get the sense we have similar reasons for using something different."

"Meaning what?"

"That I have a hard time putting this Leif Whittington together with the one who hung out at my parents' pool. And I guess you find it hard to think of me as anything but Connor's little sister when you call me Mimi."

I wish that were true because what I see when I look at her isn't the gangly kid with braces who I barely remember.

But it's a good reminder of how I should be thinking. Of which head I should be thinking *with*. In an effort to return things to how they should be, I've tried to banish what happened in my apartment, but it's no use. I've also tried being the hard-arsed boss, with the same kind of effect. Maybe I need to try harder to be a brother to her. Bring her into the family fold. Make her one of the flock.

As if I haven't got enough looking after them.

"I'm the same person as I was back then." I rub my hand over my jaw and watch as her gaze follows the motion before rising to mine.

"Not even! Before, you would've never barked and huffed, and never explained what I'd done wrong."

"I don't huff," I retort. Huffily. "And you haven't done anything wrong." Because none of this is your fault.

"Back in the day, I could've made you coffee with mud, and you wouldn't have complained. Now you won't even *let* me make your coffee!"

"I have arms and legs. Hands, too."

"Did Jody make you coffee?"

"What has that got to do with anything?"

"I know she did. You act like I have cooties. You haven't had one word of feedback for me, and I know I'm doing a helluva job covering for Jody. You even sent someone else to deal with your dry cleaning yesterday." Despite the lack of accusation in her tone, she cocks her hip as she folds her arms across her chest, making a perfect cradle for her—

Stop.

"My dry cleaning?" I repeat as the words belatedly penetrate my thick skull. "I thought I was doing you a favor. The delivery was late, that's all."

"Yeah, but those little tasks? That's what I'm here for."

I doubt my idea of "little tasks" aligns with hers.

Lean over my desk.

Lift your skirt.

Loosen the buttons of your blouse.

Now, open your mouth like a good girl.

"I know what you're here for," I grate out. *Jody's swollen ankles. Crocs and maternity smocks.* The dead brother trick no longer works.

"I'd like to feel a little less ornamental."

I open my mouth and snap it closed again before I suggest she stop wearing skirts that look like she's been poured into them. The issue isn't what she wears. It's in the cesspit that is my brain. How can I try to be a brother to her when I want to fuck her from here to Land's End?

"You just told Brin you worked through your lunch," I say, remembering the conversation. "That says to me that you have enough to do."

"I do." She inclines her head. "Things that Jody left for me. Things she'd diarized. But you've got to do your bit, too. Whoever heard of a CEO chasing his own damn laundry? You, boss man," she says, pointing my way. "Me," she adds with a tap to her chest, "here to do your bidding."

"My bidding?" My answer falls from my mouth far quicker than it should, the thoughts accompanying it pure fucking filth.

"Yes, Mr. Whittington. I'm happy to assist however you see fit."

Her words are like a lick of warmth against the lining of my stomach. Fuck me. Was that a come-on?

Stop being a cock, the little angel on my shoulder says. It's got a dirty fucking mouth, that angel.

"So Mr. Boss man," she says stepping closer, "what can I do for you?

"I'm the same person as I was," I grumble. "Just a bit older." A lot wealthier.

"A little crankier." She comes to a stop a couple of feet from the other side of my desk. "What did you want me for?"

I force my eyes to remain on hers as a dozen wants prickle on my tongue. *Get on your knees, open your mouth, and stick out your tongue.* "Last month's P & L account."

"What about it?"

"I haven't gotten it yet."

"It should be in your inbox," she replies breezily. Too breezily, maybe. Was she hoping for a different kind of request?

"Well, it's not."

"Well… I sent it yesterday."

"I also need a hard copy."

"There's nothing about that in the book." She looks mildly confused.

"What book?" I find myself frowning.

"Jody's instructions. The first Monday of a new month, the report comes to me. I'm to reformat it and forward it on to you. Which I did."

"I need you to print it out."

She makes as though to stand on the tips of her toes.

"What are you doing?"

"Seeing if your fingers had all fallen off. Your laptop has a print button, right?

"Don't be a smart arse."

"Then stop staring at it."

"What did you say?"

"I said you started it."

I give my head a shake. I must be fucking losing my marbles. "The report?" I repeat.

She glances behind me to where my personal printer sits on the cabinetry.

"It's not working," I say with a glower.

"What's wrong with it?"

"What's wrong with it is that it's not working." I know I'm being a prick, but now that I've called her in here and the door is closed, I need her to leave before I do something very fucking inappropriate.

"Can't you fix it?" she asks.

"If I could, we wouldn't be having this conversation."

"But you're the man who brought modern banking to the hands of the masses." I feel even more ridiculous as she holds out her hand as though waiting for an explanation to drop into it. "Via their phones."

"I didn't create interface." My voice betrays my frustration. Frustration that makes her glower as she presses that hand to her hip. "I'm a banker, not a coder or a software engineer. And even if I could do all those things, it doesn't mean I'd be able to fix a bloody laser printer."

"A laser printer doesn't work by 'laser beams.'" She has the audacity—the fucking temerity—to make air quotes around those two words. "Fine." Before I can properly protest, she makes her way from the other side of the desk, her hip brushing my shoulder as she leans to examine my laptop. "Let me check the settings." She begins to busily tap the keys, and I don't even protest.

Why does she smell so amazing? Would she notice if I sat back in my chair right now? Would she be able to feel my eyes roaming over her delectable arse? I'd never considered myself an arse man, but hers is the kind I could stare at for days. *And I probably have.* But it's not just her arse that makes me feel like a pervert. I watch her plump lips as she speaks just waiting for a flash of that tiny gap between her front teeth. I've probably spent hours wondering what it would be like to kiss her, and my imaginings don't stop there. I curl my fingers into my palm when the notion to slide my hand over her rear flits into my head. Over the firm roundness, I'd run my hand down the back of her thigh before slipping it under her skirt and traveling back the other way. Her stockings are holdups, I'm sure. I haven't seen the outline of a garter belt, though I look again, just to be sure.

I'm such a fucking pervert. I glance at my balled fists, wondering how stupid I'd look if I just sat on them. It would serve me right if she turned her head and caught me staring. It's with gut-twisting comprehension that I realize she already has.

"See anything you like?"

"What?" I resist the urge to shake my head.

"I said, what are you like. You know, Brit speak." She *tsks* and rolls her eyes, affecting what I think is supposed to be an English accent. "What are you like, you total plonker?"

"I don't know..." What this moment is about.

"I thought it was meant to be rhetorical." She turns back again.

"Does that mean you've found the file?"

"No." She stands straight suddenly. "I just thought I'd make myself feel better. I know I sent it. It's weird that it's not there."

And now? Now I'm staring at her tits. It's hard not to because they're *there*—right in front of me. Maybe I should stand, then my eyes wouldn't be at tit level. But then she might notice this massive hard-on.

"Like I said..." I clear my throat, the words rusty. "I've been using email longer than you've had adult teeth."

"I doubt that."

"You saw for yourself." I gesture to my laptop. "The email wasn't there."

"That's not what I meant," she says softly. "You're trying to remind me how much older you are. I was just disputing that fact."

I don't have an answer because the top button of her blouse has slipped free to reveal the smooth valley of her cleavage and the scalloped edge of her bra. A hot prickle runs the length of my spine. Since when has a little lace been so titillating?

"Why are you here?" I find myself asking.

"Because you called for me."

"No, Mimi. Why are you here in London?" Is it to torment me? Because it's pure torment having her here and that's without the inadvertent flash of her cleavage, her inappropriate questions, the sight of her stellar arse, and the way I'm tempted to touch it constantly.

She doesn't answer for a beat but turns her attention back to my laptop. And I go back to contemplating her arse.

"Found it!" I startle at the announcement. "It was in your spam. Do you want me to print it out for you?" She glances toward the cabinet that houses my laser printer.

"That one's not working, remember? Just... have it on my desk first thing Monday. Now, I want you to answer my question." Reaching out, I take her hand in a brotherly fashion. "Tell me why London? Why now?"

"Because I needed a change." When it becomes obvious that isn't going to cut it, she inhales and starts again. "Look, when Connor died, my parents' lives fell apart. They became so fearful, Whit. They saw danger around every corner for me. I understood why and wanted to help them, so I chose to live the kind of life they wanted. I went to college nearby in the kind of setting they wanted."

"Meaning what?"

"I went to an all-girls Christian college," she says, sliding her hand to her hip. "It wasn't at all like you see in the movies."

"Are we talking mainstream or..." *Not a very brotherly inquiry.*

"There were no parties and no pillow fights," she says with a knowing smirk.

"You sound disappointed."

"And you sound like you're enjoying this a little too much. Do you want this answer or not?"

I make a gesture with my hand. Please, go on.

"I moved back home after college. I moved into the apartment. An apartment *above* my parents' garage. You can guess how that was. But I did it for them. And then, well then I realized I only have one life, and I have to live it for me."

"So being here is about distancing yourself from their influence?"

"It's about experiencing life, Whit. I've always wanted to come to London. I guess I have you to thank for helping me discover that London isn't just a city of skyscrapers. It's like a patchwork of places, each quite unique. Art galleries and cozy pubs, lush green parks and filled-to-the-brim museums. It's castles and palaces and tiny, crooked streets and walls daubed with artwork. It's music and food from all over the world!"

Her face lights up as she speaks. I bet if I pressed my hands to her cheeks, I'd feel the heat of her sunshine.

"That's all on you." She seems amused and discomforted to have revealed so much, judging by the way she reaches up to slide away her hair. "You and your accent. My fairy prince."

"I'm no fairy tale. I more like a horror story."

"To work for, sure."

I narrow my gaze, not sure if she's teasing me. "I guess you're a little better now that you've realized I can do the job, and I'm not going anywhere. But yeah," she says, hurrying on. "I loved your accent, dreamed about coming to London, and life is about living life and not giving in to fear." She holds out her hand in culmination. Sort of, *so here I am.*

I feel like a complete shit. Of course her parents were devastated after losing Connor, but I never imagined they'd smother Mimi in the process. "I'm sorry I wasn't a better friend," I murmur, drawn to take her hand again.

"It's not your fault."

I nod as I turn it over in mine, my gaze not lifting from her dainty fingers. "I should've done more." Like a flash of sin, I see her hands tightening on my forearm, her eyes lust hazed, her breath on my face. I drop her hand on instinct.

Mimi straightens, possibly disappointed, but then she winks. "Well, keep your eyes peeled for that report, Mr. Whittington."

"Just Whit," I mutter, twisting my laptop back to where it was.

"Mimi and Whit. Whit and Mimi," she says as she sashays her fabulous arse over to the closed door. I slide open my desk drawer, pull out a rubber band, and slip it over my wrist. "Oh, I forgot to tell you." She swings around. "El said that Lavender likes this new vegan restaurant in Shoreditch."

"Not vegan and not Shoreditch," I mutter, dropping that hand to my lap and furtively palming my tortured dick. *Down boy.*

"No?"

"It might be her birthday, but not all of us enjoy eating jackfruit masquerading as barbecue."

"What was that? That thing you just did?"

I look up at the sound of her confusion, then back again when I realize how ridiculous this is. "When I complained?"

"No. If your lips are moving, you're complaining. I meant the thing you put on your wrist."

"They don't have rubber bands in Florida?" She pulls a dissatisfied face at my answer. "Maybe I'm starting a new fashion."

"You're ridiculous."

"If I needed a rubber band, where else would I keep it but on my wrist?"

"In your pocket. Or maybe the drawer you've just taken it out of."

"Why, when clearly wrists were made for such things?"

"If you say so." She gives a miniature shrug and pivots away.

Meanwhile, I wince at the sharp *ping* of the elastic on my wrist because her wrists are not made to be pinned to my bed. *Thwap!* I do it once more because I'm looking at her arse again. This time, the bright-blue rubber snaps.

Was it a sign?

Probably.

A sign that I'm going to need a lot more rubber bands.

11

MIMI

"Coward," I mutter, slapping the sheaf of papers down next to the binding machine. "He gave you the perfect opportunity to lay your cards on the table, but instead, you're in here trying to impress him with your admin skills." Jerking open the drawer, I pull out a binding coil and a couple of random colored front and back pages. "Could've had him eating out of your hand... maybe even some other place," I add, lining the body of the report between the two. "But why settle for hot sex with your hot boss when you can get a hearty pat on the back for not only finding the damn report in his email but printing him a hard copy and binding it, too."

It's fair to say I'm disgusted with myself. It's also fair to say I spent the rest of the afternoon trying to make sense of our exchange. I'm trying not to make my interest in him too obvious (because desperate is never attractive) while Whit pretends not to notice it. I know he's not that oblivious—I'd studied his interactions with the opposite sex on many occasions. Granted, those were different times, but the man still has it. *In spades.*

To make matters worse, my coffee was cold when I got back to my desk. I was counting on it to tide my appetite over until I left the office for the day because it's true, I had left my lunch on the Tube, which meant I felt compelled to give Joe, the homeless veteran who camps near the building, my last five dollars. I mean, pounds. This was problematic, to say the least, because I hadn't realized I'd left my bank card at home. It wasn't a great start to the day, and I haven't eaten since a slice of toast at breakfast. As Doreen would say, I was so hungry that my bum was eating my knickers.

Whit had left for a meeting off-site not long after our exchange, which I thought might leave me plenty of time to overthink. About ten minutes after he'd gone, a courier turned up with a pretty box wrapped in a blue ribbon instead of the usual paperwork. It had my name on it so, of course, I opened it. Inside was a gourmet packed lunch that outshone the ham and cheese roll I'd left on the Circle Line line. My very fancy-looking late lunch included an edamame salad, two tiny salmon and avocado bagels, a packet of gourmet nuts, a berry fruit salad, a strawberry smoothie, and a delicious lemon tart. All for me!

But did Brin order it or Whit? I know who my money is on.

For all its loveliness, I pick at my lunch while barely tasting it. My mind is awash with conflicting thoughts. Did he call me into his office to stop me from talking to Brin? I see the way he looks at me, and I feel the electric-like attraction bouncing between us whenever we're close. He runs so hot and cold, yet even when he's being a grump, I still find him so hot.

I've got nothing. No ideas and no place to go. Which is how I find myself in the copy room after six thirty, in no great hurry to go home, completing my not-so-grand admin-overachieving plan.

"No!" My specially designed cover sheet snags on the coil, tearing at the corner. "Dammit!" *What kind of idiot company buys a wire coil when plastic coils work much better?* Sliding the cover sheet from the top of the pile, I scrunch it into a ball before launching it at the box designated for paper waste. Still muttering my disgust at binding machines, paper, men, and the universe in general, I whip out my phone and send the cover sheet to the colossus of a printer again. I slap my phone down, anticipating the machine's whir as it digitally rouses itself.

It takes a moment or two for the machine's lack of whir to penetrate my black mood. But when it becomes clear nothing is happening, I indiscriminately stab the buttons with my finger. The thing beeps in protest, then gives me a little attitude on the display panel.

No paper.

"Asshats," I complain, tugging at the paper tray as though the thing is lying to me.

But it isn't.

I stomp my way over to the supply closet and flip open a couple of lids because why wouldn't people put the lids back on empty boxes? It makes so much sense! Urgh. I toss the empty boxes behind me, find a non-empty one, and pull out a couple of reams. Flattening the paper to my chest, I swing around in the cramped space when something hinders my forward motion in the doorway. The second law of motion states force equals mass, multiplied by acceleration. That this mass is accelerating at a rate powered by frustration means I ignore the resisting tug at the door. At least, until I hear the ripping sound. I try to turn, but my stupid skirt is caught on something.

My stupid skirt is caught on a stupid nail, and my stupid self is about to make matters much worse.

"No!" The fabric rips from my hip to the middle of my back. Worse, as I twist, I force the tear in another direction, making a huge flap over one cheek of my ass. A literal ass cheek envelope—a window to my butt! I think I might've caught myself on a nail too, but I'm too angry to pay any attention to that.

"This day is *the* worst," I grate out as I try to work the fabric free. Of all the days for this to happen, it would be one when I haven't paired my outfit with a longer jacket. Bare-assing it home on the London Underground is not the kind of experience I want to endure. Not that it matters because, at this rate, I won't have a ripped skirt to wear because it won't budge from the *fudging* nail!

But then, success! Success that sends me stumbling, a nearby desk the only thing preventing my fall.

My skirt is ruined, my ass might be bleeding, and my temper is more than a little frayed. I'll need a dozen safety pins or maybe some duct tape. If anyone asks, I'll just tell them it's a new look. *Straight off the Milan catwalks.*

I return to the store closet, much more carefully this time, and begin pulling open more boxes. Pens. Ballpoint. Sharpies. Highlighters. Folders. Toner and ink. There's not even a packet of rubber bands in here. I find myself pausing in my rummaging. Why did Whit slip a rubber band over his wrist? Is it some kind of anxiety prevention? He doesn't strike me as the anxious sort. *Aversion therapy?* Maybe it was just what he said it was; just somewhere to keep it. I forcibly push away my pondering. I have bigger problems, like getting home tonight without exposing my ass to half of London.

A search through the rest of the copy room offers

nothing in the way of a solution. I end up slumped over the small desk, raking through the drawers, but there's nothing there, either. Nothing beyond a couple of grungy old hair ties, at least, which might do in a pinch. Maybe? Somehow? Lord, I don't know! I guess I should be relieved most people have gone for the day because maybe I can make it back to my desk and...

I have a stapler! I could staple this sucker together, then wrap my jacket around my waist! This is as far as I get with that plan as, in the periphery of my vision, the door begins to swing open.

"Don't come in here!" I yell. Yeah, that'll work because panic *never* sounds suspicious.

To my deep mortification, Whit's head appears around the edge of the door. "Amelia?" Before I can whip around or protest, his eyes dip to where my ass is flying its underwear freak flag in the guise of a pair of tiny bright-red silky panties, the kind that bare more of my ass than they cover. "What are you doing in—"

"Oh, you know. Just hanging out." I laugh a little. It sounds really weird. "Literally hanging out."

His eyes dip to my ass, and it's all I can do not to groan, and not in the sexy way I want him to be responsible for.

"Is there anything I can help you with, Mr. Whittington?" a perky female voice asks suddenly from the door.

Whit tilts his head like he's about to ask if I'd like whoever that is to help. I give my head a sharp, adamant shake. *Hell no!* This does not require a larger audience. I'm not a circus!

"Ah, April, is it?" he says pleasantly as his head disappears again.

"Yes, that's right," she answers, sounding as pleased as

punch, as Doreen would say. "I work with the back-end team. Downstairs."

Urgh. I roll my eyes so hard, I'm surprised not to hear them rattle in my head. I don't know, but I think I might be *pleased* to *punch* her because her words weren't dripping with invitation—they were swimming in it. Girl, get your own boss man. This one is taken!

"Good for you," Whit replies, and I actually snort. "Well, see you tomorrow. I just have to grab some... supplies." He slips between the door without opening it wider than necessary.

"Hello, supplies," he kind of taunts.

"Funny," I answer, as my stomach turns over. He can grab me anytime. "Has she gone?"

"Think so." He rests back against the door before his eyes coast down the length of my body. I realize I haven't moved an inch—I'm still bent over the desk, my palms pressed to the melamine surface. Like I'm waiting for something, like I'm waiting for him.

"What have you done?" he drawls, his dark gaze belying the note of amusement in his tone. He pushes away from the door, and my heart does this wild, stuttering thing. Something has changed. Something has changed in him, I'm sure of it.

I swallow, forcing my heart back into my chest cavity as I grab this opportunity. Hold on to it. Run with it.

"What do you mean?"

Whit arches a brow and makes a lazy gesture to my ass.

"You mean my skirt? You know what they say." I arch my back, knowing full well he sees me do it. "Dress for the job you want, not the job you have."

"Oh?" The corner of his mouth tips provocatively, and he

slides his hands into his pockets. "I can't think what job you want dressed like that."

"Can't you?"

"What is it you want to do?"

His low spoken words feel like a taunt, and my heart seems to be in my throat as I answer, "You."

He freezes—not one muscle of his seems to move. Panic floods my system, my mind flicking over a dozen ways to take it back. I need a joke to steer this back on course, some kind of time machine to make it go away. *He's my boss. My pseudo-big brother. I'm nothing but his PA. A friend of the family.*

But then he pushes languidly from the door and begins to move toward me, those tiger's eyes of his unrepentantly staring at my ass. He comes to a stop, not beside me but behind me. I force myself to turn my head over my shoulder. God, those eyes. So full of heat and dirty promises.

"Amelia." I've always loved the sound of his voice, low and smooth, but he's never said my name like that. All growly with the lick of reprimand. But let's be truthful. The man could read the Tube timetable and get me off.

"Yes, Mr. Whittington?" I purr. In for a dime, in for a dollar, right?

My breath catches as he reaches out, fingering the envelope of fabric. "It's quite a view." My fairy-tale prince is more a dark knight. "I just don't know what it is I'm supposed to do with you."

"Don't you?" I drop my head, my answer almost a whisper. My mouth goes dry as I sense him moving, and a second later, his palms are suddenly pressed next to mine. The heat of him feels immense, though our bodies aren't touching. *At least, not yet.*

"Maybe you could enlighten me." My heart begins to hammer as he shapes the words against my neck. "Because for the first time in a very long time, I don't know what the fuck I'm doing."

His words, his lips, set off a wave of internal reactions I fight hard to resist. My insides pulse and flutter, and my heart yearns for him to mold those soft lips into a kiss.

"My suggestion," I begin once I've gotten a hold of myself, "would be for you to stop wearing this." I slide my finger under the rubber band around his wrist. Wasn't the last one blue? This one is red. *Red for warning. Red for stop.* I inhale a shaky breath as I continue. "I really don't want you to have an aversion to me."

"How about a partiality?" His body drops briefly, and the hard length of his cock pressed against me makes my insides pulse emptily. I almost groan, rolling my lips together to prevent the sound. "How about a near-constant hard-on?"

"Yes." I roll my bottom lip inward, my whole being suddenly parched and aching for this.

"Is this what you want, Amelia?" His hand closes on my hip, holding me tightly. "Do you want me to fuck you? Here, in the copy room? Is that what you're here in London for?"

My gaze drops to where his hand is splayed next to mine. He has such long, elegant fingers. Square nails. A strong wrist dusted by fine, sun-kissed hair. I'm in London for so many reasons, for so many things. But most of all, I'm here for the experience.

"Which of those questions do you want me to answer?"

Behind me, he swallows audibly. I can almost sense his internal struggle, but I need him to want this the same way I do. To want me with the same intensity.

"I can get fucked anywhere, Whit." I tentatively slide my pinky finger over his thumb. "Maybe you should be asking why I'm here with you."

"Why you're here with me," he repeats, "wearing such interesting underwear." He caresses the back of my bare hip.

"They're just panties."

"They're very *brief*." The word is a low growl in my ear.

"You bought me these panties. I wear them for you." Sensing his hesitation, I hurry on. "Every year on my birthday, you send me a gift certificate. Every year since I turned eighteen, I've bought panties with it." It's the truth, or at least, part of the truth, but I can't believe I'm sharing it.

His hand slides from the curve of my hip and down over my thigh. Regret balls in my throat before my brain connects the dots because he's turning me...

"Whit?"

... and dropping to his knee.

"I think you should show me how generous I've been." Tipping his chin, he angles his gaze my way, those tiger striations more like flames. "Go on," he instructs. *Orders. Commands. Makes my insides turn to throbbing, heated goo.* "Show me what my money has been buying."

Something sweet and sticky winds through my insides as I slide my hands over my hips, gathering my tight skirt higher in tiny increments.

"Holdups," he murmurs as my stocking tops come into view.

"The garter belt seemed a little obvious for the office."

His head lifts sharply. "You bought one?"

"*You* bought it," I whisper, loving the intensity in his expression. "Along with a matching bra."

"Which you don't have on right now." His eyes are amber, his words honey dipped. "You think I wouldn't notice."

"I wasn't sure you were interested."

"I don't get on my knees for just anyone, Amelia." His

finger and thumb tug at the hem of my skirt. "Less talk and more action," he softly instructs.

His eyes watch my face as I pull the fabric the rest of the way, the thoughts of what he might do swimming through my head. I tremble. I want. I ache as I stand in the copy room with my skirt around my waist.

Whit gives a satisfied hum as his touch skates up my thighs. "You're shaking."

"I'm not afraid." I bite my lip against telling him this moment has been years in the making. I've spent half of my life wanting him in one form or another.

"You're very lovely," he whispers as his big hands curve around my hips. Curve and squeeze. "And I'm probably going to hell for just looking."

"I hope you're not just going to look."

Once more, he tips his gaze my way. "Are you sure that's what you want? Here, in the copy room, where anyone might walk in?"

Very few people are left in the office this evening, but there's always a chance. But I'm just... "I'm worried I'll never get this chance again."

Relief washes over my skin as he leans forward and presses his lips to my bared stomach. The touch of them against me does something beautiful and frightening to my insides. Frightening because I'm terrified this is as far as he'll go.

"Definitely going to hell," his low voice rumbles as his lips make a pass over the elastic waistband of my underwear. Biting, he snaps the garment against my skin.

"In that case, you should definitely make it worth it."

His shoulders shake with some semblance of a laugh, and he tips his head. "Were you always like this? Did I just not see it?"

"You never saw me. I was just a kid. But I'm not a kid now."

"No." He sounds almost resigned. "No, you are not."

"As for what I want, I don't really know. Not in these circumstances, at least." That seems to give him pause for thought as he pulls back almost completely, his gaze suspicious. "I'm not—" Why is this so hard? "I *have* done this before." The tension seems to drop out of him. "Just not a whole lot. Or maybe with anyone who'd had a whole lot of practice."

"I see."

My heart dips to my heels as he begins to stand. I want to protest—shout *no, that's not how this is supposed to end!* But I can't because if I do, the words will sound all warbly and watery, and I might just have a breakdown.

"Lovely Amelia," he says, beginning to pull my skirt back into place. "As tempting as you are and as much as I want you. God, do I want you." He shakes his head, refusing to look at me. "I don't see how we can."

My stomach dips, desperation curling my hands into fists at the sides of his shirt.

"You can't do this, Whit. You can't get on your knees and not—"

Voices sound in the corridor, and the sound of wheels before the door begins to swing open. Whit grabs my arm, pulling me toward the supply closet.

"Watch out for the—"

He shakes his head, pulling the door closed behind us.

"Aren't you the boss?" I whisper. My heart pounds as my eyes adjust to the lack of light.

"I think that means I'm supposed to set an example," he mutters. "Not to mention your arse is on show." I don't think I imagine the displeasure in his words.

"You weren't complaining—" My words halt as he presses his finger softly to my lips. Voices carry, accents I don't understand. Rustling, banging, a *pfft* of a spray, and the door handle rattles. My hands ball in the sides of Whit's shirt as I pull him closer, anxious we're about to be exposed.

"It's just the cleaning crew," he whispers, pressing his lips to my ear. I gasp as his teeth suddenly scrape the soft lobe, the noise shock but also part wonderment. How can the slightest brush create a wave of effects through my body? "And that wasn't a complaint. I'm trying very hard to resist you because I feel like your arse should be seen by no one but me."

Tingles. All the possessive tingles everywhere.

From the room beyond, the photocopier fires up.

"Illicit use of the copy machine?" I whisper.

"Hmm."

"It's just human nature. We can't help but be drawn to break the rules."

In the darkness, his expression is impossible to read. His soft, velvety laughter not so much. "Subtlety isn't really your thing, is it?" But then his words are no more as, in a fit of daring, I reach for his zipper. "Amelia." He makes my name a delicious reprimand.

"I can't help it, Whit." I press my hand over his rock-hard length. "You make me want to be a bad girl."

"In here?" His hand loops a circle around my wrist.

"I know you're not shy."

"I'm not sure how you'd know that." He drops his head to my shoulder as he slides my hand away with a quiet groan.

"Because you've always been beautiful. You've always been comfortable in your own skin," I whisper. When I move my hand back a second time, he doesn't stop me.

"Sweetheart, you don't have to pay me compliments." His soft breath feels like a kiss blown across my cheek, the rasp in his voice inspires me to wrap my fingers around his hard fabric-covered length.

"My God, you're so hard." The recognition is a throb of desire between my legs.

"That's not to say I don't like to hear you compliment me," he says, his tone hushed and hot, yet his fingers wrap around my wrists to pull them to my sides. His grasp tightens, and for a moment, I think it's meant as a warning for me. But as he bends his head, I wonder if the caution was meant for himself. His lips brush mine before he presses a kiss to the corner. "I want you so badly," he whispers, sweeping back and sucking on my bottom lip. "You make my life impossible."

I make the kind of noise that's full of encouragement, my body straining to get closer, to feel the brush of his.

"Shush, darling." His lips make another pass. And then it's happening. Oh God. It's really happening. Whit is kissing me—really kissing me. It's not just a dream. And what's more, I'm kissing him back. Albeit with little say in the matter as he holds my wrists in his, his mouth fully in control as he coaxes and teases. The moment seems somehow more intimate than his fingers skimming my panties. More intentional, at least.

"Amelia, Jesus Christ. I've been desperate to kiss you since the day you turned up in my office. I should've known then. I should've sent you away then."

"I wouldn't have let you." I'm surprised I can manage words because I'm pretty sure my feet have lifted from the ground as part of my ascension to heaven as light and heat and ecstasy wash through me. "Let me touch you," I whisper tremulously. The tenor of the moment seems to change instantly. His hands loosen from my wrists and slide around to my ass as he pulls me flush against him. His mouth is on my jaw, my neck as I press up onto my toes, rubbing my soft to his hard. "Please, I want to feel you." I slide my hands around him, spreading my fingers wide on the taut cheeks of his behind as though to maximize the contact, to make sense of this moment of fantasy.

"I want to fuck you," he rasps in my ear. I make that noise of approval because I want that, too. I imagine it as he flexes against me, hot and thick. See his strong shoulders working over me in my mind's eye. "But not here."

"I wouldn't mind." In the dark, our chests heave, our harsh breath mingling when he huffs a quiet laugh.

"You're such a pretty little thorn in my side." His broad palm skims my waist and my ribs before the pad of his thumb skates across my nipple. It aches and stiffens under his touch. "I've no idea what to do with you."

"That must be a first for you." My body jerks beneath the rasp of his nail, and he swallows my moan before pulling back as though my words have just sunk in. "Because I remember more than you think and saw more than you probably realize. Like how the pool house was a favorite haunt of yours."

"Amelia, were you a dirty little voyeur?" His reply is more approval than reprimand. Heck, it sounds more like supreme satisfaction. "Did you enjoy watching me kiss other girls?"

In the dark space, I push up onto my tiptoes and bring my mouth to his ear. "And more."

"Fuck," he groans, "that shouldn't be hot." More kisses, harsher, deeper than the last. He tastes of fresh coffee and cool mint, and he feels like every temptation a cunning devil might offer. But this is not the devil. This is Whit. And I now know those summertime girls will remember those hours of his attention forever by the strength of his kisses alone.

"We shouldn't be doing this." He presses his teeth to my shoulder as though to restrain himself. But I'm not done. I won't let this moment slip away.

"At school, the kids would talk about porn, but I didn't need any of that. I'd just close my eyes and think of you as I slipped my hand between my legs."

He gives a quiet groan, the kind that makes me wish I could bottle the sound. Maybe I should whip out my phone and ask him to repeat himself. *Aural for later?* Thankfully, he can't read that piece of ridiculousness from my mind.

"Are you trying to make me embarrass myself?"

"Whit." His name sounds like a chastisement, though my insides pulse at the strange compliment. "I know you better than that."

"Do you, now?"

"And these days, I have more to work with. My porn reel is more *real*. Whenever I want, I can slip my hand into my underwear and think of how easily you made me come during our interview."

"That fucking interview." His fingers tighten on my thigh. Lifting it, he widens me, cool air hitting damp fabric. "Fuck, I wish I could see. I can feel how wet you are." It's not an accusation, more an expression of praise as his thumb passes over the fabric, making my insides ache. A brush, a touch, a scrape of his nail over my most sensitive place as he begins to play with me, play with my responses. I whimper and twist, so ready for this. I know one firm touch is all I need.

"*Please.*" I cant my hips to increase the contact. I wonder if he can feel my pulse through fabric and flesh, if he can sense my needy pull. He slips his fingers under the elastic, my body jolting as I moan. I think I almost came from that slightest contact.

The outer door slams shut, but he doesn't stop. "I need my mouth on you," he rasps, his fingers swiping through my wetness.

I gasp a desperate, *"yes!"*

His body begins to lower. Then halts as a phone begins to ring.

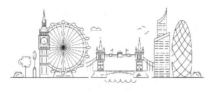

12

WHIT

"You're in a rotten mood." Lavender halts in the action of licking yogurt from the back of her spoon to complain.

"I'm trying to work," I mutter, unable to completely ignore her as I continue physically abusing the keys on my laptop. I'm working from my dining table ,and while I wish I could say I usually keep my work life from bleeding into my personal life, it would be a lie. The lie being I *have* a personal life. Work is all-consuming, and I often work from this space on the weekends and evenings. More so since a certain off-limits blond bombshell became a permanent fixture in the office.

A permanent fixture = a semi-permanent hard-on. A semi-permanent semi?

In other words, I can't seem to concentrate when she's around. My brain seems to revert to its teenage state, becoming a morass of pornographic thoughts and perpetual fucking longing. It's not even like I can send her away because she does her job brilliantly. Other than that one report I was a complete dick to her about, I don't have to ask her for anything. She pre-empts my work needs; everything is as it should be. She hasn't slipped up once.

She's impressed the fuck out of me for someone so young. Impressed me with the quality of her work, her diligence, and her work ethic. Then last night, she impressed me in an entirely different way.

I'm worried I'll never get this chance again.

Her honesty cut right through me, slicing me to my very core. Mimi, I'm sure, is pure, sexual alchemy. She's honesty and naivety mixed with blatant desire. I've fucked some women in my time, women who've owned their own desire, who know what they want and go for it. But they had nothing on this woman. *Nothing for me.*

Yet she can be nothing to me.

"Why are you working from there and not your *super posh* home office?" Lavender doesn't make actual air quotes, but I hear her sneery intention anyway.

"A change of scenery," I answer without biting. Working here feels like a concession of sorts, not that I bother explaining it to her. I can't spend all my waking hours in one office or another. I know I'm probably just fooling myself, but work is all I seem to do these days. I mean, I haven't even made it to a certain club I'm a member of. A club where I find like-minded women. Women who are down for a session of no-strings fucking.

"Could you just, like, *not* ignore me? I said I was sorry." The spoon clatters against the granite as Lavender drops it. Her shoulders suddenly hunch over the kitchen island as she rubs the heels of her palms against her eyes.

"Apologies don't count when you don't mean them." I continue taking my frustration out on my email. "You're just hungover and feeling sorry for yourself." Not at all regretting your ridiculous life choices or any kind of stress or inconvenience you might've caused.

"I am sorry," she retorts, not quite shouting. "Sorry I dragged you away from your *very important job*."

"My very important job pays for your university fees along with your accommodation," I grate out as my volume increases, "the car that was impounded last week, not to mention your fucking love rival's window!"

"She's not my love rival. She's just some skank I caught blowing my boyfriend."

"Such wonderful choices you're making, Lav."

"Fuck you, Whit. Just because you're a cyborg who lives his life above the need for human contact."

I shake my head. I get all the fucking human contact I can take from this family. It's little wonder I'm not interested in relationships given the shit I put up with from my siblings.

"Life is supposed to be messy. We're emotional beings— you should try it sometime."

"I'd rather you try not to drown your emotions in a bottle of Belvedere. Maybe next time, try an adult conversation before you decide to commit criminal damage."

"Talk?" She verbally holds the suggestion between her thumb and index finger. "I'm not talking to him after what he did to me."

"Did you catch him, or was this intel from your so-called friends?" She glowers my way. "I thought so. You just got drunk instead, then lashed out. Again."

Why do people have relationships? Why do they get involved? I can barely deal with what I have on my plate already.

"Why do you have to be such a—"

"Watch it, Lavender. I suggest you choose your next words very carefully."

"Or what?"

"I'll cut you off," I answer simply. "You can do what everyone else does, what I did, and work to pay yourself through university." Though I did a proper degree, not the ridiculousness she's studying. *The Psychology of Fashion.* What's she going to do with that? Help a Vivienne Westwood dress deal with its existential crisis when it goes out of style?

Lavender turns her back to me, muttering about the injustices of her world and being treated like a leech. I don't bother to answer, mainly because I have nothing pleasant to say. If I did answer, I'd tell her she leaches my bloody energy. The money means nothing. It's not like I haven't made enough not to share. Though sometimes I do wonder if we'd be better off living a normal life, paying off mortgages and car loans, being in thousands of pounds of university debts. It might've helped steer Lavender away from this self-destructive streak because she might be too busy growing up to act so ridiculously.

I roll my shoulders, trying to stretch out the kinks from spending much of the evening on a plastic bench in the Chelsea nick. *Chelsea police station.* Lavender's accommodations were probably more comfortable than mine, not that it would've mattered as she'd spent the evening before her criminal damage spree cozying up with a bucket of top-shelf White Russians. Stupid enough that she got so drunk and behaved so recklessly, but then she'd also hung around to scream obscenities when the police turned up. She's lucky the girl with the broken window accepted my offer of compensation. Whatever job Lavender ends up with, I can't see her employers looking well on a criminal conviction.

The police had plonked her in a cell to sober up. Because they couldn't tell me when she'd be released, and because Polly would freak if the coppers had called her, I waited until they kicked her out. And this is the thanks I get in return.

"Thank you," she mutters examining her black-painted fingernails as her bottom lip wobbles. "I know you think I don't mean it, but I do."

I'm saved from answering (thank fuck, because I have no idea what to say) when my phone buzzes with a text. Like a teenager with a crush, my stomach flips. Then like an adult male who had lots of time to dwell on his inappropriate behavior last night, I push the excitement away.

> I hope everything went okay with Lavender.
> Mimi x

This is the second time she's texted me, but it will be the first time I've answered. *Because I'm a dick.*

> She got a caution. They didn't press charges, and we're home now. Sorry I didn't return your text last night. It was hectic.

No sign off. No kiss. No admissions of *you're all I can think of.*

As well as a dick, I'm a fucking coward.

I feel like such a shit.

I should at least apologize for the way I left her. For not

being there to take her home myself. I might also apologize for my cockblocking sister's terrible timing.

Or maybe I should look at Lavender's timing as perfect.

God knows I'd tried to resist her, but in that illicit dark space, I'd caved. I was moments away from dropping to my knees to bury my face in her sweet-smelling heat. My mouth watered as I'd anticipated the slide of my tongue through her soaked slit. I had fully intended on eating her out until her throat became hoarse and her legs weak. Until pleasure coated her thighs, my chin, and cheeks. I would've fucked her then, blind to consequences, blind to everything.

Is it relief I'm feeling or is it regret?

By the time I'd finished the call, Mimi had pulled herself together as best as she could. *Kiss-swollen lips, wet knickers, and a torn skirt.* I was the one leaving, yet she was the one consoling me.

"It's fine. I'm okay. I get it. Go! Family comes first."

I'd asked her to wait in the copy room, then ducked into my office, grabbed my jacket, and made a call. She'd looked shaken as I burst back through the door.

"*It's just me,*" I'd said, shaking out my jacket for her to slip on.

She'd laughed as she'd slid her arms into the sleeves, and I'd murmured something about her growing into it. As she'd turned, I'd pulled on the lapels, bringing her her body against mine.

"*I look silly, right?*" She'd looked up at me, her gray eyes suddenly shy.

"*You'd look gorgeous in a burlap sack,*" I'd replied before pressing a kiss to her head. "*Take the executive elevator down to the basement. George, the driver, is waiting to take you home.*"

I wanted to squeeze her so tight one last time. In the

moments we'd been apart, regular programming had resumed. I think she felt it, too. She'd protested, said there was no need to make a fuss. But there was no way I was letting her take the Tube home. I'd slid my hands into my pockets against the notion of squeezing her tight one last time, then she'd left me in that tiny room.

Fucking her would've been the pinnacle of my year. But it would've been wrong.

"Are you listening to me?" Lavender's petulance pierces my unhappy musings.

"Not really," I admit, putting down my phone and continuing with my email.

"You're such an arsehole sometimes."

"Yep. I'm the arsehole who bails you out of scrape after scrape. I'm the arsehole who also keeps vegan fucking yogurts in my fridge." The arsehole who dropped everything, including the hottest yet most perplexing woman he's ever encountered to bail his troublesome little sister out of shit again. Despite what they might think, I do like having my siblings around. I just wish they'd have a bit of consideration sometimes.

"They're nice, the yogurts," she qualifies. "Thank you for buying them."

"You're welcome."

Honestly, I still don't know whether to consider Lavender's phone call a blessing or a curse. As much as I want to fuck Mimi, something tells me it would've been one night of pleasure followed by many more of grief because more and more lately, I keep remembering the last time I was with Connor.

I'd been in the States on business but had made time to catch up with him. On a whim, we'd headed to Utah to climb in Moab. If there's anything that'll get you thinking about the smallness of your existence, it's spending a couple of days in a red rock canyon, hanging from a piece of sandstone sculpted by millennia of rain and wind. You want to contemplate your mortality? Be sure to rappel down a couple of vertical cliff faces while you're there. Want to kick back after finding joy in surviving? Head from Utah to Vegas, which is exactly what we did.

Our weekend of debauchery began with a steak followed by a few drinks, which had then turned to getting laid, the peacocks that we were. Needless to say, neither of us had gone to our hotel rooms alone. But at breakfast the following morning, Connor had seemed unusually pensive.

"*If anything happens to me, look after Mimi, would you?*" he asked out of the blue.

I'd barely looked up as I'd worked my way through my omelet. "*Why not. What's one more sister added to the pile,*" I'd replied.

"*At least your sisters have each other. If anything happens to me, Mimi will be all alone.*"

"*Are your parents also kicking the bucket in this scenario? Did you all die in the same car wreck? Maybe a grand piano or a supersized anvil fell on your heads.*"

"*Fuck, man. I know it sounds weird, but I just feel like, a girl like her needs someone to look out for her. Someone to make sure she doesn't end up with some dick.*" He's swung a finger between us. Like us, he'd meant.

"*Speak for yourself,*" I'd muttered, reaching for my coffee. But then I realized he wasn't laughing along with me. "*What's brought this on?*"

"*I don't know.*" He wiped his mouth with the napkin, then tossed it down. "*It's just, that girl last night was kind of* sweet." He hunched forward in his chair. *"I can't think of Mimi—"*

"Then don't," I'd retorted, horrified. I had three times the number of sisters he did. I couldn't afford to think of them as women with potential sex lives and all that entailed. I'd suffered a hard enough time when Heather met Archer. I was happy for them when he proposed, but it didn't stop the urge to punch him in the face whenever he touched her.

"I mean it," he'd insisted. *"My parents have no fucking clue what the world is like, and Mimi is so—"*

"Young," I'd offered. I hadn't seen her for a while at this point. In my head, she was still the kid with white-blond pigtails and legs like pale toothpicks. *"There's loads of time before you start tying yourself up in knots."*

"She's such an innocent. She's kind and too sweet for her own damn good." His words choked off, his expression flickering with something akin to pain.

I'd bit my tongue against saying that's what we all like to think.

Jesus Christ, what would he say if he saw me last night? He'd doubtless want to rip off my head.

"Fine." I'd put my coffee cup down and folded my arms across my chest. *"I'll do it."* It was not like he was dying anytime soon, right? He was just hungover and regretting his choice of pussy.

"I mean it. No one like me, right?"

"Scout's honor," I'd said, giving him an ironic salute.

"Or you."

"Fucking charming!" I'd laughed.

"Aren't you gonna ask me to look after your sisters?" He'd stretched in his chair. He'd seemed satisfied or at least lighter in his mood.

"That feral lot?" I'd asked with a huff. *"I like you too much to saddle you with them."*

It wasn't a declaration signed in blood, and he didn't specifically mention me by name. Just someone *like* me. And who is most in the world like me? Me, obviously. But I reckon he'd include El and Brin in the same category.

I drag my mind from the past as my phone buzzes again.

I guess I'll see you on Monday.

I don't respond because fuck bro code, a decent man wouldn't screw his best friend's kid sister no matter what.

After Lavender takes a cab home, I go for a run through Hyde Park to clear my head. The early evening rolls around, and I contemplate ordering Thai in when Brin and Primrose, the baby of our family, appear in the kitchen.

"Oh, Thai food. Yummy!" Prim claps her hand like a cute performing seal.

"I'm having Thai," I say, taking the menu back. "In peace, if I'm lucky."

"Meanie." She pouts and puts down her bubble tea, which probably means she's been wandering around China Town with her mates all day. "I'm starving."

"You're always starving," Brin says, pulling open the fridge.

"I'm a growing girl," she protests.

"Yeah, growing dafter." When the fridge door closes, Brin is holding a beer.

"Make yourself at home," I mutter.

"Do you want one?"

"Do I want one of my own beers? Chance would be a fine thing." Despite the building having a shopping service, which operates a bit like the minibar in a hotel with a member of staff checking stock levels daily somehow, I rarely get more than a couple of beers down my throat each week. "To what do I owe this pleasure, anyway?"

"I was shopping and too tired to go home," Prim says.

"Same," Brin says, pulling out a bottle opener. "But I'm tired because I haven't been home since last night."

"Ew," Prim exclaims, scrunching her nose. "You dirty fuck boy! I bet you're wearing the same clothes."

"Yeah, but to be fair, they're pretty clean. I was out of them most of the time."

"Double ew! I can't believe you got in the elevator with me. I've been breathing in your sex particles!"

"Not sure it works like that."

She swings around and ducks under the kitchen sink. When she stands again, she's holding a bottle of some kind of organic Febreze alternative. "That's what they said before Louis Pasteur discovered germ theory." She begins to spray Brin with the bottle. "Be gone, vile sex particles! Out, damn spot, out!"

"I never let a lady sleep in the damp spot," he says with a laugh, dodging around the kitchen island.

"You're such a dirty ho bag!"

"A dirty ho bag the ladies love." He makes a dash for her, snatching the spray bottle out of her hand. "This suit cost me five grand!" A tussle ensues. Squealing. Tickling. Profanity.

I sigh. There goes my evening.

"Am I ordering Thai for three, or what?" I yell over the din.

"Oh yes, please. I want dumplings," Prim says, abandoning the sanitation of her brother. "And some of those yummy noodles you got last time."

"Not for me." Brin pours half the contents of his beer down his throat. "I'm going out."

"Burning the candle at both ends." Prim *tsks*. "You'll never make as much money as our illustrious leader."

"Who'd want to," he says. "Look at him. At thirty-six, he's going gray and eating takeout with his little sister on a Saturday night."

"Someone has to be with him," Primrose says, not exactly rising to my defense.

"No one has to be with me," I protest. "I'm not ancient!"

"Besides, I'm his favorite sibling," Prim continues as though I haven't spoken.

"Suck-up." Brin snickers.

"It's all part of my life plan. I'm going to look after him in his dotage, and then when he dies, he'll leave *all* his money to me."

"Charming." Neither of them looks my way. "Go ahead," I say, folding my arms across my chest. "Discuss me as though I'm not here."

"There, there, Leif." Primrose pats my arm. "Try not to get *too* wound up. The stress you're under is already immense." She grins.

"The stress I'm under is suddenly increasing."

"It's all part of the plan," she says, laughing. "We'll knock a few more years off your life yet."

"I'll cancel your food."

"No, you won't," she says with the kind of smile you see nurses wear in care in retirement homes. "Look, we all know you're at home on Saturday night because you're just far too busy mastering the universe to be interested in love."

"I have a date," Brin pipes up. "That's nothing to do with love."

Primrose spins around. "Don't make me get the spray bottle again."

"You might need to take it home with you. Mum's doing a roast for lunch tomorrow, and I'm not the only one out tonight. El's bound to turn up reeking of sex particles." He wiggles his finger in the air as though sex particles were an actual thing.

"Urgh, why are my brothers so gross?"

"Looks like I'll be leaving my money to the cat and dog's home."

"Not you, Leif, obviously. You're my favorite." Prim flounces away, snatching up the TV remote as she throws herself into the middle of one of the sofas. "I'm going to catch up on *Love Island*. Is that all right?"

"Go ahead. They're your brain cells to lose."

"I'd rather eat my own feet," Brin says, lifting his beer bottle to his mouth as the panel concealing the TV begins to slide automatically apart. The monied classes don't like to admit to owning idiot boxes, it seems, despite there being one in almost every room of this house. Even in the bathrooms.

"Where's El off to tonight?" I pull out a stool at the kitchen island.

"You mean you don't know?" He puts the bottle down, wiping his mouth with the back of his hand.

"Would I be asking if I did, arsewipe?"

"He's taking Mimi out tonight, the bastard."

"What?" Something pinches between my shoulder blades, forcing me to sit straight.

"You know why, don't you?" Picking up his beer, he tips the base my way. "It's because he heard I was taking her out to lunch on Monday."

"You were what?"

"I brought her coffee and offered to take her to lunch. Speaking of which, you know," he adds, shifting his weight to his left leg, "it's not right, making her work through her lunch hour. A girl's got to eat."

"I didn't—" Fuck it. What's the point in arguing when there are more important matters at hand. "I thought they weren't going out until next week." That's what Mimi said, hadn't she? Something hard and cold settles in my belly, and I begin to wish I hadn't been such an avoiding prick and called her after yesterday. She probably thinks the worst of me, feeling her up like that, then ditching her. Not taking her home. This family sometimes...

I realize Brin is still talking.

"I told him, you're just jealous because she smiles at me."

"She smiles at everyone," I mutter. Sunshine is second nature to her, but what neither of my brothers know is that she burns in my arms a hundred times hotter than the sun.

"Yeah, but she smiles more at me," he persists.

And that's all she's offering them, but she tells *me* she's curious. That she enjoyed my direction. That she wants to know more. She playfully suggests she takes me shopping then accuses me of being everything from a grump to a voyeur. She vies for my attention and I'm entirely too aware of it.

I see so much more of her than they do, and I'm not just talking about her arse hanging out of her skirt.

But that doesn't mean anything. It can't mean anything. I have to let this go. El is nearer her age, and he's fun. If you have a thing for gormless idiots, I suppose. Hell, Brin's even closer to her age. Either one of them would be better for her.

"Anyway, he only brought the date forward because he wanted to get in before me."

"*In?*" I sort of growl, the connotation making my blood boil.

"Yeah, you know. In with a chance." He makes a rough gesture with his fist, the kind that pisses me right off.

"If either of you lay a finger on her..." I mutter, rapidly changing my stance. Fuck that. Neither of them is worthy of her attention, let alone her kisses. *Or more.*

"Come on, bro. You can't blame us. Mimi is fucking gorgeous—she's banging!"

"Urgh! Can you actually hear yourself?" Primrose's disgust carries across the room. "That's an actual human person you're talking about!"

"Yeah, a gorgeous human. Anyway, what are you griping about? Banging is a compliment!"

"You're a sexist pig!" Prim launches a pillow at him before turning back to the TV.

"Calm down, Frieda!" Brin says with a stuttering laugh. "I'm a feminist, too."

"Yeah, right. I have an even funnier joke. A male feminist walks into a bar. Because the bar was *just that low*." Folding her arms, she swings around with an audible huff.

"What's up with her?"

"She has a point. Not only is Mimi an actual human person," I murmur, "but she's also my PA."

"That sounds like a *you* problem, brother dearest. And a reason for you not to dip *your* wick." Brin pokes me lightly in the shoulder. "I'm barely ever in the office."

That's a discussion for some other time. "She's also my best friend's little sister."

"Again with the *you* problem. I never knew the bloke, so what do I care? He's dead now, anyway."

"I'm not sure what that has to do with anything."

"Well, what's he gonna do about it? Haunt me?"

"Have some fucking respect." I rake my hand through my hair because what I want to do is slap him across the back of the head.

Unaware of my simmering temper, Brin drains his beer then sniffs, running the back of his hand under his nose. "Anyway, her brother would be rattling his chains at the bottom of El's bed, not mine because he's the one who'll probably get into her knickers tonight."

The fuck he will.

13

MIMI

"You've barely touched your champagne."

"I'm not really much of a drinker," I say for the third time tonight, the first time being at the restaurant when El tried to top up my glass. Now we're in the club of the moment after a delicious (and very expensive-looking) dinner. The kind of expensive with a menu that doesn't include prices.

"But it's vintage," El persists.

"I'd rather have a soda," I murmur as his attention turns to his own glass.

I'm pretty sure El is just trying to be hospitable, not get me drunk. He's been a gentleman the whole night. He's opened doors for me, walked closest to the curb, and insisted on picking up the check, which I appreciated but didn't like a whole lot. *Even if going Dutch meant selling a kidney on the organ market.* But I only agreed to come out with him tonight as friends, and El had pretty much stuck to that script. So far, at least.

We're seated upstairs in what I'm told is the VIP area. It's pretty swish; bloodred velvet banquet seating with tables dotted around made from golden spheres cut in half and upended. Huge, tubular chandeliers making the servers' glittery minidresses shine like mirrored disco balls.

A girl in little more than a bikini, gold chains, and spiked-heel thigh-high boots struts past the table, El's eyes, and almost his tongue, following in her wake.

I can't help but laugh—I'm not offended—but tug self-consciously at the hem of my dress anyway. Black and short (thigh length, not ass grazing), it's the most daring thing I own. Despite being long-sleeved, it cuts across my collarbones, and where the skirt and top meet, the fabric is slashed. You can't really see skin unless I move. But I thought I'd looked the part—my hair tied back in what I like to call my sexy assassin ponytail, heels, and earrings that look like drops of silver rain. I thought I looked stylish *and* sophisticated. But I'd forgotten I live in London, not Tampa.

This dress is like a spot of Amish in a sea of *Baywatch*.

But who parties in a little more than a bikini?

I'm gonna need to do some window shopping to get a sense of the style vibes of London.

"The music's banging, right?" El's head moves in time to the beat of the ambient dance track as his gaze travels over the heads of those on the dance floor below. The executive DJ in a silver dinner jacket and jeans is doing his thing, his minions moving to the magic he weaves. Magic. Noise. I don't really care for it. I can count on my fingers the number of times I've been in a club, given the experience was one my parents frowned upon.

Too dangerous. Too risky. Those places aren't exactly calming spaces, Mimi.

I don't at all feel excitable. I also don't think I've missed much.

Huh. Maybe it's not the dancers El is looking at, but the podium girls. Podium girls dress in mirrored bikinis, athletically swinging around poles.

I feel the weight of El's gaze and glance his way and realize I didn't answer. "Yeah, it's amazing." It's giving me a banging headache, anyway.

The music reaches a crescendo as a cloud of glittery, golden confetti flutters down from the ceiling. I'd hate to be part of the cleaning crew tomorrow. Of course, that thought slides like keys on a chain to how I'd ended up in the supply closet with Whit last night.

It was... everything.

And it was nothing.

And it's the reason I'm here with El right now. Not for revenge or a *make-the-man-jealous* attempt. I guess I'm just craving company over my thoughts right now.

"Who tucks you in at night?"

"Sorry?" El's voice pulls me from my musing.

"It's the music." He lifts a finger. "The lyrics, at least. You were miles away."

"Yeah." I smile my apology. "My mind drifted off for a minute."

"So who tucks you in at night?"

"At the minute, my elderly Aunt Doreen."

"What?" The word is more chuckle than anything else.

"I just mean that's who I'm living with." The words fall quickly as discomfort stings my cheeks. She doesn't tuck me in, of course, but that's not to say I don't know that she pops her head into my room at least once during the night. I also know who put her up to it. My parents would have me wired up to a monitor 24/7 if they thought I would go for it. Like it would even stop—

Stop.

Those are not *now thoughts*. Those are *later thoughts*.

"Working for Leif must be a tough gig," El says in a not-so-gentle segue.

"No, not really." I tip my head to the side and give it a tiny shake. "Why do you say that?"

"He's my brother. I love him, but he's not exactly what you'd call relaxed."

"I guess in his position you can't afford to be." But I think it's more than the job. I can't help but notice how often his family calls him. Not just Lavender last night. Working within hearing distance of him, I'm privy to most of his phone calls. He gets a lot of work calls, but he also gets a lot from his family. Questions to answer. Favors to grant. Help to dish out. It's mainly from the youngest of the three, but that's not to say El and Brin don't cause him concern either, though it mostly relates to work.

He's always there for them. Like last night, when his phone rang during the hottest moment of my life. Am I feeling salty about it? Yep. In a purely selfish way. The hottest moment of my life, remember? But then later, it reminded me how much I miss Connor, too.

So I got over myself. I respect that Whit has taken on that role, that he takes his responsibilities seriously. He's the head of his family. The person they all lean on when they need a crutch.

As his phone had begun to buzz, we'd disentangled, and he'd slipped it from his back pocket. The illuminated screen just seemed to etch resignation into his face. He'd answered the call, stepping from the supply closet and leaving me inside to compose myself. Maybe he realized I needed the shelves behind me a little longer because they were the only thing holding me up, the residual energy of my almost-orgasm had sapped the strength right out of my legs. My chest heaved like I'd been running, and my thoughts were nothing but tattered remains. Initially, when I heard the echo of a woman's voice from his phone, I'd wanted to cry. I felt about three inches tall. Another woman minutes after kissing me, after saying he couldn't wait to taste me. The woman sounded hysterical, and for the briefest of moments, I wondered if it had something to do with me. *And the closet.* But then Whit had said Lavender's name, and I realized I'd gotten it all wrong.

"*What are you still doing in here?*" He'd appeared in the doorway, phone still in hand.

"*I didn't want to pry.*"

"*Come on out.*" He'd held out his hand, his tone resigned. "*I'm sorry,*" he murmured, pulling me against him. "*Lavender is drunk and...*" He sighed and dropped his forehead to my crown. "*I have to go and sort it out.*"

And that had been that.

No talk of what just happened. No promises of later. But at least he didn't apologize. And he'd made sure I wouldn't be molested on my way home.

"Yeah, I suppose." El lifts his champagne flute to his lips. "It's a tough gig but someone's got to do it."

"Being the eldest brother?"

"Nah, being Mr. Rich and Successful. Men want to be him." He sighs. "Women want to be with him."

"I'm sure you're no slouch." My gaze flicks over him. El is one good-looking man. Fair-haired and tan, he's probably fun to be around. *When you're in the right mood.* His suit is well-tailored, and his personality seems pretty uncomplicated.

I bet he wouldn't leave me in a supply closet, I think to myself. It's not a very complimentary assessment. For him, at least. Maybe I'm not wired right for casual relationships because a man who steps up to fill his father's shoes in his siblings' lives, a man who puts his loved ones first, is the stuff of dreams. *If not fantasies.* He's spent the eight years fathering his siblings, which I guess must be a little like herding cats, thanks to their sheer number. No wonder he likes people to do as they're told.

I'd like to volunteer as tribute, Daddy!

Not wired right for casual? If only that was the issue rather than not being wired right at all.

"Well, you are sitting here with me and not him." I come back to the conversation, turned off by El's edge of smugness.

"As friends," I remind him. "I just moved here. I'm not interested in a relationship."

"Not all relationships have to be serious, Mimi." Hooking his ankle to his knee, he spreads his arms along the back of the low sofa. I guess that's what you'd call a nonverbal invitation. And the look he sends me speaks volumes. But then he jerks forward in his seat, his foot dropping to the floor. "What the fuck?" he mutters quietly. "Speak of the devil, and the fucker will appear."

"What?" I turn my head over my shoulder, following the direction of his gaze. He can't mean—

I inhale a tiny, sharp breath. Is that Whit coming out of the crowd? His dark hair gleams under a flash of light as security steps aside to let him pass. My stomach swoops because, oh my God, it is Whit. A form-fitting dark suit and shirt, his jaw covered in equally dark stubble. As he makes his way toward us, everything inside me begins to flutter. He is so, so infinitely gorgeous, like he just stepped from the set of a fancy cologne commercial. Debonair top notes, base notes of something forbidden and sinfully sexy. Hot. So hot. And the way he's looking at me? Sets those flutters to pulse.

But my excitement is short-lived as I realize this commercial is a couples shoot, and the redhead on his arm is so beautiful.

"What are you doing here?" El frowns as the couple winds their way around the table, the gorgeous redhead's arms stretching out, pre-hug. Or maybe not as one of her hands curls around his shoulders, the other a poked finger between his brows.

"I could almost sit on that," she says with a laugh.

Ohh. Do the brothers, like, share? That was kind of familiar and maybe a little—

"Not the size of your arse." El swipes her hand away as he steps back. "You'd smother me.

The redhead's eyes tighten at the corners. "Tempting," she retorts. "You were obviously wrong, Whit. *Of course* he's pleased to see us." She glances back at him, and I find myself doing the same. With a start, I realize he's looking at me. No, he's not looking at me. He's drinking me in, and the whole thing feels like a prelude suddenly.

"I don't know, Heather." His lids drop, shuttering the effect as he straightens his cuffs. Dark French cuffs with silver cuff links, the hint of a leather-strapped watch peeking from beneath it. "That looks like a frown to me."

The redhead's sleek and straight hair moves like a shampoo commercial as she shakes her head. "Nope, that's just his Neanderthal brow, the primitive being he is."

"Piss off, Heath."

"Nice to see you too, dearest Sorrel."

El's frown deepens. He really doesn't like his name. "What are you two doing here?"

"I wanted to go dancing, and Archer didn't. Whit offered to come in his place."

"You don't dance," he retorts flatly.

"That's never stopped me from busting a few moves before." She makes an adorably uncoordinated krumping move with her arms.

"And you hate clubs." He points an accusing finger Whit's way.

"I'm just being a good brother," Whit answers mildly.

"One out of four aren't great odds," the redhead says before turning her attention to me. "Hello!" She holds her hand out over the table. "You must be Mimi."

"Er, yeah." As my hand meets hers, she gives it a no-nonsense shake.

"I'm Heather. Another of the Whittington brood." She slices a look El's way. "Budge up." El just stands there. Heather tuts. "El, *move*." Without waiting, she pushes between him and the table, sliding in next to me. "I've been dying to meet the woman who's stepped into Jody's capable clogs."

"Crocs." The word is propelled from my mouth as Whit lowers himself into the chair opposite me. His eyes fall over me, making me feel as though my innermost thoughts are exposed. Dirty thoughts. Flashes of last night mixed with those from my imagination.

"Hello, Mimi," his low voice rumbles. "Fancy seeing you here."

"Ditto." It's all I can manage. I've never been happier to be in a club as I am right now. Obviously, because Whit's here, but also because of the low lighting, he can't tell I've gone beet red. And my cheeks aren't the only part of my body that's heated. And I'm not sure my parents' assumptions were wrong because my heart feels like it might burst from my rib cage at any moment.

"Really?"

I turn my attention to Heather's distasteful expression,

then remember what we were talking about. *Crocs.* "Jody said it was because of pregnancy cankles. She left a pair of them under her desk."

"I hope you sprinkled them in salt and burned them." She glances down at her own shoes. They're red and sparkly with spiked heels. "It's enough to put you off ever experiencing the blessed state," she adds, twisting one foot this way, then that admiringly.

Kids? Not touching that. "Your shoes are so pretty."

"Thank you. They are lovely, aren't they?" Heather smiles down at her feet. "My husband bought them for me. I call them my Dorothy Gale slippers." She clicks her heels together. "Because there really is no place like home." I don't miss the look she and Whit exchange. "I'm not here to dance, really." Mischief dances in her gaze as Heather glances my way. "I'm here to make sure El is treating you properly."

"Properly?" I sound pretty amused.

"To make sure he's not trying to get into your knickers."

"What?" I press a hand to my mouth to suppress a giggle.

"Panties?" She scrunches her nose and gives her head a quick shake. "I prefer knickers. I think the word sounds a bit more regal, don't you think?"

"I've never really..."

"Anyway, I'm here to keep an eye on him." She dips her head El's way. "Polly sanctioned. If this were a regency romance, El would be the family rake."

"A what?" El demands.

"The cad—the bounder."

"Oi!" El protests indignantly. "I'm not. At least, I'm no worse than Brin."

"That doesn't exactly recommend either of you."

"What about the dark horse over there?" El asks unhappily, nodding to the eldest of the Whittington brood.

"What about him?" she asks sweetly.

"I should've known you wouldn't have any beef with old golden balls."

"Old and golden." Whit glances Heather's way. "Should I be worried about his fixation with my nutsack?"

Heather barks out a laugh, and El drags his unhappy gaze her way again. "It didn't stop you from marrying Archer."

"Archer's reputation was overstated," she answers tartly. "He's a reformed character. A happily married man."

"I can't see how, considering he married you."

Heather slides me a look that speaks volumes. Kind of, *see what I've saved you from?*

"I was being perfectly well-behaved," El protests. "I've treated Mimi like a sister all night."

Well...

"That's quite a broad scope of works," Heather murmurs, sliding her hand over a wrinkle in her own little black dress. "In my experience, that could mean anything from a noogie to emotional blackmail." She turns my way. "He hasn't tried to fart on your head, has he?"

"Heather," El moans, aggrieved.

Meanwhile, I snort-laugh as I shake my head. Too late, I press my hand to my mouth as though to cover the horrible sound.

"Oh good. A normal one," Heather announces happily.

"That noise was anything but normal," I assert, still laughing.

"If you'd had to endure the standard of dates my brothers have introduced me to, you wouldn't argue. I like this one." She turns to Whit, tipping her head my way.

"I have been on my best behavior," El mutters belligerently.

"And I maintain your best behavior still leaves a lot to be desired."

"Am I supposed to sit here and take this?" El's attention swings to his brother who, I notice, is drumming a tattoo with his fingers on the arm of the chair. He stops, flattening his hand against the velvet. "When have you ever asked my permission for anything?"

Permission for what? To ask me out?

The brothers trade a look that speaks of a language only siblings can understand. Despite the hilarious conversation, it seems Whit is not happy.

"Well, I think I'll have a drink," Heather says, moving from the chair like a chic jack-in-the-box.

"You don't drink."

At his utterance, her gaze sweeps to El. "I don't drink *much*, but I think I deserve a glass of wine tonight. Well, come on, walk your sister to the bar," she demands, staring down at him.

"This is the VIP area," he mutters.

"Is it?" She glances around. "I thought it was a bit posh. Just goes to show how long it's been since I was last in a club," she admits. "It was certainly before Whit hit the big bucks."

At the sound of his name, he glances behind him as though his sister might be talking about someone else. He really doesn't like accolades, I've noticed.

You're so hard. My words curl around my ear.

Sweetheart, you don't have to pay me compliments. That's not to say I don't like to hear them.

I guess he's okay with some praise.

"What are you smiling about?"

"Hmm?" My head lifts.

"That's not a grin," Heather says, correcting El. "That looked more like a secretive smile." She turns to Whit again, his expression impassive. "What do you think?"

"I think you were going for a drink," he answers.

"So I was. Lead on, Sorrel," she demands.

"Sit down," he complains. "Because of Whit's big business brain, VIPs are offered table service."

"I'm not ordering drinks from girls dressed in chains and leather underwear." Heather's expression is the embodiment of distaste. "What is this? A bacchanal feast."

"For fuck's sake," El mutters, gesturing to the girl who'd passed by the table earlier, the one in the gold chain bikini. "Just sit your arse down, and I'll order the drinks."

"What can I get you lovely people?" the server asks, stretching her neck to sweep a high platinum ponytail over her shoulder. *Even higher than mine.* And boy, she moved quick on those spiked-heeled boots.

"My goodness," Heather announces. "Aren't you just gorgeous!"

The server gives her a genuine smile. "That's very sweet of you to say so, hon. Oh my God, is that the new Gucci?" She points at the clutch Heather has pressed between her arm and ribs. Heather gives a closed-lip smile and shakes her head as she holds it out for inspection. I note El inspecting the girl's long, toned legs. Whit, meanwhile, seems content to watch me.

"It's a dupe from Camden market," Heather admits with a laugh. As bikini girl hands it back, Heather asks, "I hope you don't mind me asking, but is that your uniform?"

The woman's shoulders move with her amusement. "Management doesn't make me wear this, if that's what you're asking." Her eyes dart from El to Whit.

"Ignore my brothers, they're not a part of this conversation. Besides, El here knows snitches get stitches, don't you?"

"Does that mean you're gonna chuck a brick at me again?" His hand lifts absently to a scar in his hairline.

"I was eight. He told me redheads have no soul."

"All I wanted to do was order a round of drinks," El mutters.

"Yes, let's do that." Heather steps around the table, patting her brother's knee as she passes, curling her hand in a nonverbal *up you go*. "We're going to help this gorgeous creature carry our drinks."

"That's not usually how it works," the woman says with a smile.

"Don't worry. El will still tip, and tip well. Especially if you don't mind him walking behind us while he stares at your backside."

"The tips are why I dress this way." She slides El a look, then flicks her ponytail over her shoulder. "If he stares, I don't mind."

"Up you jump," Heather says over her shoulder. "And don't forget your wallet."

The trio traipse off in the direction of the bar, leaving Whit sitting across the table, staring at me. Like *really* staring at me.

"Kind of a surprise to see you here, Whit," I say when it becomes obvious I'm not winning this staring match any time soon.

"I imagine so," he offers blandly.

"What exactly are you doing here, if you don't mind me asking?"

He makes an impatient noise as he leans forward in his seat. Elbows resting on his spread knees, he links his fingers in the space between. "I was going to ask you the same question." My heart does a little two-step at his tone. There's something indefinably reprimanding in it. Despite my internal reaction, outwardly, my shoulders twitch in a tiny shrug. Not that he notices because he's staring at those elegant hands. Elegant hands that seem to hold a lot of tension. "You're not really interested in him."

At his sharp tone, I glance up to find his gaze on mine, corkscrew sharp. Excuse me, but direct, much? It also happens to be true. El is fun, and he's made his intentions obvious. Well, as obvious as he can without saying something like, *hey, wanna screw*? The answer to his question would be yes. But not you. Not that I'll admit that to Whit. It's not like *he* invited me out this evening. It's not like he checked to see what my weekend plans were. Suddenly, I feel annoyed about that. About the way we left things.

"Why not?" I eventually offer. "El is cute. He's uncomplicated."

"Which is just another way of saying he's stupid."

"Far from it," I say, pressing my back against my seat. "I think he's pretty astute." I keep my eyes on Whit's face as I slowly cross my legs. "At least he's not one of those men who play at willful ignorance."

"Oh?" His shoulders stiffen minutely in a way that might convey a *no*, a *maybe*, or a *what do I care*. But I know he cares, or why else would he be here? Why else would his sister be here, running interference?

"I don't have a whole lot of experience." Lowering my lashes, I slide my silver bangle around my wrist. "But I know when a man wants me."

"It's just a shame you don't want him." A flare of exhilaration lights in my stomach at the way he's looking at me. "It's me you want," he asserts curtly. "You just haven't *quite* been able to bring yourself to say so."

"Wow. I'm learning all kinds of things about myself tonight." Though my words are delivered with a scathing kind of laugh, the dark intention in his gaze makes me feel all jittery. Before the closet, we'd danced around this. I've hinted and asked questions, but he's right. I haven't had the nerve to state my intention. Sure, I offered myself up willingly in the supply closet yesterday, but that's not the whole of what I want. "What about you, Whit? I'm not the only one not *quite* able to voice what I want." My words mirror his, but with a little more mockery.

I came to London to be bold, to be audacious. And Whit is the only man I've ever truly wanted even if he isn't who I thought he was, that ideal version of him I'd held for years in my head. The real Whit is harder. More worldly.

He huffs an unhappy laugh. "If you knew the strength of my *want,* you'd be on the first flight back to Florida."

"You wish."

"You think you've got it all sussed out, don't you?"

"I don't even know what that word means, but you could tell me, tell me about this want," I say, channeling a demanding femme fatale. "Spell it out for me, Whit."

"It's complicated."

"Didn't seem complicated from the supply closet."

"Do you want me to apologize?" I give my head a tiny shake. "Good, because I'm not sorry for what happened. I know I should be, that I shouldn't have—"

"You didn't. We almost did."

"Like I said, it's complicated."

"I'm here for less than six months, then I'm gone. Back to Florida." Or else. "What could be less complicated than that?"

His fingers twitch, then loosen. Reaching out, he traces a long index finger along a vein on the gilt table between us. The action seems sensual, almost erotic. Or maybe that's just how he makes me feel. It's certainly mesmerizing because when I try to move my gaze, I find I can't.

His hand drops, and he offers nothing else. Embarrassment washes over me as my heart sinks.

"You could just say if you don't want me." I avert my gaze as tears suddenly prick at my lids. I won't cry over this.

"You know that's not it," he admits unhappily.

"Then I don't know what else to say, and I'm tired of dancing around this. Either explain it to me or..." I almost say something like *I'll sleep with your brother,* but it seems my femme fatale has already left the building.

"I made Connor a promise," he says quietly without meeting my gaze. "I swore I'd look after you if anything ever happened to him, and I hadn't even done that. I didn't even know how old you were until lunch with Polly that day. In my head, you were still a kid."

"Well, you did live pretty far away."

"That's not a good enough excuse."

"You did what you could." My denials fall quickly. "If you knew what his other friends—"

His gaze slices up. "I doubt your brother tasked his friends with the same thing. I didn't do enough. Then you turned up in my apartment, and I did too much."

"Don't take that back. Don't you dare take that back," I retort as a fist tightens around my heart. "That was the most real moment of my life." The most sensual.

"It doesn't make it right, Mimi," he says wearily.

"I'm just going to point out the obvious," I say, my voice hardening, "but you do realize Connor isn't here."

"Surely, that's all the more reason to remember what he

asked of me." Yet from under his lashes, he stares at me with such intensity. Such longing.

"To look after me? I'm a grown woman. I don't need looking after." Lord knows I've had enough mollycoddling in my lifetime. "And if Connor was here, do you think he would have a say in my life? My decisions?"

"Neither of us can know that, but you'd have your brother to guide you if nothing else."

"I don't need help in knowing my own mind. And you know what? I think if Connor was here, he'd want me to be happy."

"Connor would want you anywhere but with me, Mimi. He wanted you to be with a good man."

"And you're not?" I demand, folding my arms across my chest. "Turning up here with your sister, caring enough about me to stage an intervention makes you the villain?" Jerking out my hand, I flick my fingers angrily in the air. "Well, does it?"

"El isn't the kind of man you should be with, either."

I jerk forward like a striking snake. "I get to decide who I'll screw." His eyes widen, turn molten, and harden at my coarse language, but I carry on, pointing a finger across the table at him. "Me. Not you, and not my dead brother. Enough with your bull. You tell yourself you're here for Connor, but you're not. Tell the truth, Whit. This is more a case of, if you can't have me, El sure as hell can't."

"And we come back to the point that it isn't El you want."

"So?" I flick my shoulder. "El asked me out. It was either that or another night in with the cat," I admit spikily.

"You're sure it has nothing to do with yesterday."

"I don't take your meaning."

"Payback, maybe." He glances down at his hands as though he could find the answer there.

"You left because your sister needed you."

"It didn't make you angry?" He seems to study my face for the truth, but what kind of person would that make me? "Angry that I didn't at least call."

"To say what? To suggest we pick up where we left off?" Because I totally would've been down for that. Maybe not so much right now. Who am I kidding? I would've crawled on my knees to Knightsbridge if he'd asked me to. I just want him, even when he's making it hard for me.

"It's not that I didn't want to. That I *don't* want to," he qualifies.

Wow. An admission. But not one that makes me feel giddy when he looks as serious as he does right now.

"I'm not here to make you jealous, and that's the truth. Now you tell me the truth. Why you're here."

"That's easy." His gaze slices up, his eyes more tiger-like than ever. "Whether you meant to cause it or not, I am jealous."

I begin to chuckle. "You mean that works in real life? I've just got to go out with—"

"My brother, who, you can't fail to notice, wants to fuck you."

My attention slides to the intrepid trio. I guess Whit's plan has gone as he intended because it looks like El has decided the hot server is a better prospect. "He doesn't seem too hung up on me."

"Because he's an idiot." He rolls his shoulder, the fabric of his jacket tightening against the bulk of his bicep. But he's still not looking at me, which just lights a fire under my butt. I had no intentions of going home with El, but I will not have my future dictated to me, not when I might have so little of it left.

Six months. Or what's left of it.

"Is idiocy the curse of all Whittington males, or just you two?" I say as I stand. "Let me spell it out for you." I yank my dress over my thighs, refusing to look at him. "You don't want me going home with your brother. Fine. But I'm not in London for long and I intend on getting the full experience." My head lifts and I level him with a look that says *last-chance saloon*. "So you better understand, if not him and if not you, I will be going home with someone tonight."

14

WHIT

"Well, that seemed to go well."

I give Heather no more than a cursory glance as she places her glass down before taking the seat Mimi recently vacated. "You think?"

"Sarcasm, Leif. I know you live your life on a different cosmic plain to the rest of us up there on billionaire row, but you remember sarcasm, don't you?" When I don't answer, she adds, "I would hate to think you'd dragged me out to watch you sit and wallow after Mimi served you a slice of angry scowl and pointed finger."

"I'm not wallowing." I'm watching, staring at Mimi on the floor below. Her arms rest on the railing running around the dance floor, her body bent forward to reveal a slash in the fabric of her dress. She's not flashing a lot of skin, yet my gut twists with the desire to slide my fingers there. To press my hands to the sinuous curve of her hips, to feel the softness of skin not ordinarily revealed. Actually, I don't know what the fuck I'm doing.

"Looks like wallowing to me."

"I'm observing."

"Well, *observe* how I've occupied our manwhore of a brother, leaving the path wide open for someone else. Someone else like *you*." She gives a careless flutter of her fingers.

"That's not why I brought you here."

"Isn't it? Come on, Leif. I know I'm not here because you were worried about our brother defiling your PA, sacred soul that she is, disrupting your office Zen. You asked me to come along because you have feelings for Mimi."

"I didn't say that, either. I thought you went for drinks?"

She reaches for her glass. "Your drink will be along when El has stopped flirting with the server. And you didn't need to say. I do have eyes in my head. They work perfectly fine, you know."

"I might be worse than El. Worse for her, at least."

"If you are, you hide it well. For a start, you don't kiss and broadcast it. You're not delusional, either. You don't bang on about how you're God's gift to women."

"El's okay. He's just young."

"He's not *that* young," she replies with a snort. "And he's older than me."

"Yes, but you and me were born with old heads on our shoulders."

"I think the word you're looking for is sensible. Well, I'm sensible. You're a bit more reckless, but I think that comes with the penis-owning thing."

"I'm not reckless." Just ask Mimi, I almost say. If I was, I wouldn't be sitting here, watching the sharks circle as she hovers at the edge of the dance floor downstairs. Neither of us would be here. We'd be in my bed, and I'd have my head glued between her legs.

"No, you're right. You're not reckless. You take calculated

risks, I think. You work the numbers. You like to know what's at the end of a play."

Something in Heather's assumption tugs at my attention, her words morphing into Mimi's.

It was the most sensual moment of my life.

I want the full experience.

I'm only here for six months.

The last isn't a thread that tugs but yanks forcibly. I promised my best friend I'd make sure she wouldn't end up with a man like me. And she won't. Not if she's only here for six months. I can protect her, can't I? Ensure she's not trawling bars and nightclubs, picking up the wrong kind of man. I could make it so she has the best experience with none of the upset.

"Can I go home now?" Heather asks, draining her glass. "It looks like you've just come to a decision. I assume that means my work here is done." She puts down her glass and pulls her phone from her purse.

No. Well, yes, I suppose. Jesus Christ, what am I thinking? Connor must be spinning in his grave because fucking Mimi for six months is not an act of service. It's one of pure selfishness. But short of wrangling her into a chastity belt, she's going to do what she wants.

And what, or who, she wants to do is—

I cut off the thought the same way Connor would cut off my dick.

"Whit?"

"Yeah. Yes, of course you can leave. Thanks for coming." Not that I've achieved what I set out to do. If anything, I've made things worse. "Is it okay if George takes you home?" George is the company chauffeur, not my personal one. Mainly because I prefer to drive myself around. He's parked outside, getting paid triple time for napping. "If El is otherwise engaged," I add, making a futile gesture with my hand.

"You didn't drag me here just to use me as an excuse to leave with your tail between your legs," Heather murmurs, examining her phone screen.

"You don't understand. I just don't want to leave her here alone."

"Oh, but I do understand." Heather pushes to her feet abruptly and, rounding the table, gives my shoulder a brief squeeze. "I feel like bashing your heads together. You live your life at full tilt, and according to Mum, Mimi has had a pretty hard time since her brother died. You'd probably be really good for each other."

"That's nice of you to say, Heath, but—"

"You're a big boy, Whit. You've always done what you think is right, even when it's to the detriment of yourself. But this is where I leave you because my lovely husband whose guts I once hated, incidentally, is waiting in the car outside. If someone had set Archer alight back then, I wouldn't have parted with my pee to douse him. That's how little I liked him. And now he's the center of my universe. Life is funny like that, Whit. You can plan, hypothesize, and minimize the risks until the cows come home. But at the end of the day, life has a plan all of its own."

"That's not what this is," I reply with a weary shake of my head. Her hand tightens briefly before I feel the loss of it as she pulls away.

"I'll have to bash some sense into you another time because the love of my life is parked on double yellows."

Despite her protests, I escort Heather out of the VIP area and down to the lower floor. At the exit, she gives me a hug, which is both uncharacteristic and a bit worrying.

Am I such a sad sack?

Turning back to the dance floor, I make my way through the throng of people whose lives appear much less complicated as they laugh and drink, and deliver drunken pickup lines over the ear-splittingly loud music.

I must be getting old, I think as I dodge a dropped glass, then a drunken, unsolicited kiss, but when I find myself at the last place I'd spotted Mimi, she's nowhere to be seen. I glance up at the floor above, but there's no one at our table. So where the fuck has she gone?

"Nice handbag," some joker yells, making me look down at the sparkly square my fingers tighten on. Mimi left her purse on the table when she'd stormed off. She can't very well have gone far without it.

I swing around, my gut twisted in a tight knot. She's about as far from flighty as Heather is, and it's not like she has a drink to spike. *Or money to buy one.* She's probably just dancing, I tell myself, as I cast a glance over the writhing bodies on the vast dance floor. It's like a scene from hell, the knot in my stomach joined by another between my shoulder blades.

"Want to buy me a drink, gorgeous?"

"Not particularly," I mutter, untangling myself from some nameless woman's arms and ignoring her pout. I swing away. This place is a fucking meat market.

If not you and not El...

Her words drift through my head. No. I don't for one minute think Mimi is—

Someone in front of me moves one way, the person in front of them another, and I see her through the crowd. See the back of her head, at least, the light catching her blond ponytail. There's a man in front of her. He towers over her, all smiles and slick hair.

No. Whatever that is, it's not happening. No and fuck no, I decide, beginning to push my way through the crowd, ignoring the complaints of those between me and her. My chest expands, my heart seeming to salsa somewhere inside it. It doesn't matter if she's trying to make me jealous because we've gone way past that.

The closer I get, the more the arsehole looks like the poster boy for steroid abuse. A pounding starts at my left temple as he puts a hand the size of a shovel on her shoulder. I'm not small, but fuck me, he is huge. A strobe light passes over the pair, making it hard to tell if he moved his hand or if Mimi moved her shoulder, not that it matters because I'll snap his hand off if he touches her again. I don't care if he's built like a brick shit house—his dick could be dipped in chocolate, and it's still not happening. She's not leaving with anyone but me tonight, even if that means I have to chuck her over my shoulder and drag her kicking and screaming from the place.

Connor, my friend, better me than him, surely, I think, the moment before, thanks to a dip in the music, I hear:

"... not interested!" Her irritation is clear. "Don't touch me!" she demands as her shoulder jerks out of his reach again. In three steps, I'm by her side, and I realize the prick is holding her wrist. "Get off." Her voice shrill with distress.

Something inside me snaps. I don't see red. I see black as a veil descends over me.

"Sweetheart." I press a kiss to her temple as I give her shoulder a light, reassuring squeeze. She slants me a narrowed glance, which could be Mimi speak for *took you long enough.* In the time it takes for this exchange, I've slid her sparkly clutch into my jacket pocket and wrapped my fingers around her arm, just above his.

"The lady isn't interested." I turn to the prick, whose biceps are so big, he probably has difficulty taking a piss.

"Fuck off," comes his less-than-eloquent reply. If anything, his fingers tighten. Mimi tries to yank her arm away, but I still her, curling my fingers over hers.

"Have it your way," I mutter. Tightening my grip on Mimi, I hook my leg behind his, unbalancing his footing just enough to make him stumble. Which isn't really the point of the exercise. I just need him to turn a little so I can...

Thwack

I punch him in the kidney. I get him a good one too, judging by the strangled groan he makes as he drops to all fours.

"Come on." I twist my hand from Mimi's wrist to her fingers, tugging her along as I move briskly away.

"What was that?" she yells near my ear.

"A bit of MMA," I answer over my shoulder, mainly to see if the dick is back on his feet. It won't do to hang around.

"Em em what?"

"Mixed martial arts. Let's not hang about, eh?" He might be pissing blood, or he might just be really pissed.

"Oh. Yeah, right."

"Don't look behind you," I say, wrapping my arm around her back as I pull her into my side. "And don't look guilty."

"What? Are we going to get in trouble?"

"Nightclub owners aren't keen on their patrons fighting, no matter which side of the velvet rope they've paid to be on. More importantly," I add, pulling her closer, "VirTu could do without the publicity."

We get almost as far as the door when a hand on my

shoulder yanks me from Mimi. Without saying a word, the slightly green-looking arsehole catches me with a right hook. I twist from the majority of the impact, though I'm conscious of Mimi's shrill scream. My instinct is to protect her as I barrel into him, getting my hands around his waist to slam my knee between his legs. There's no such thing as dirty fighting; ask any one of my brothers. There's only winning and making sure you've still got a pretty nose at the end of it. But we don't get that far as security piles onto us, landing a few indiscriminate punches before pulling us apart. Mimi yells about how she was attacked, pointing a finger at the now raging bull of a man as he's restrained by the bouncers. He doesn't do himself any favors as he spews a mouthful of obscenities.

"This place is a fucking joke," I begin, ranting over the top of him. "What the hell are you doing to protect your clientele? I'll have my legal team on this come Monday morning."

"I thought you didn't want any attention," Mimi mutters, pulling on my arms.

"Smoke and mirrors, sweetheart." Pulling her close, I press my lips to her ear. "Play along."

"That man attacked me," she says, bursting into an impressive bout of fake hysterics. "I want to go home!" It isn't long before we're escorted to the door rather than ejected, which I assume will be what happens to the arsehole. But hopefully not right now.

"Let me look at your lip."

I instinctively twist away as she reaches out. "I've had worse," I say, taking her hand instead. "What were you doing with him, anyway?" Her brows flicker briefly with confusion. "The meathead," I elaborate.

"Excuse me?" Not so confused now, darling.

"Was he part of your full experience?" I don't mean for the words to come out cold and derisive. Or fuck it, maybe I do. First El and now that twat. "Maybe you were planning to take him back to your aunt's house for a cozy fuck."

"Screw you!"

"Oh, but you'd like that, wouldn't you?" I growl, stepping closer.

"Yeah, well, at least one of us can be truthful," she parries.

"You deserve better. Don't you get that? Better than him," I say, throwing out an arm. "Better than me! Don't let anyone make you feel like second best, Amelia. Don't you fucking dare!"

"You haven't..."

"Haven't I?" One hand on my hip, I rake the other through my hair. What the fuck am I doing out here, yelling in the street, my head fit to explode? "I haven't treated you like I should have," I mutter, making a *v* of my hand over my chin.

"What on earth are you talking about?"

"The fucking supply cupboard!" I yell.

"You want me to be angry because you left?"

"You should be angry. You should be telling me to go fuck myself."

She pulls a face and mutters, "I'm getting close. Your sister needed you, Whit. It's not like you left me to make my way home with my ass hanging out. What do you want me to say? Do you want me to soothe your feelings, your little peccadillos? Tell you that you're a good man? A good brother? There, I said it. Do you feel better now?"

"No," I say, taking a predatory step closer. "My peccadillos aren't small." A flash of mockery sounds in my head. *Better to convince her.* "I don't feel very good about any of this." She startles a little, inhaling a gasp as she steps back. "Maybe you should ask my sisters what kind of brother I am."

"I know what they'd say. You're a good one. Dependable and... and considerate." I take another step. Mimi takes another back.

"Yes, a good brother. Like the time Primrose fell off her bike and bumped her head."

"I'm beginning to wonder if she wasn't the only one."

"Her knee was grazed, too. I picked her up and kissed it better. Is there anywhere you hurt, Amelia? Anywhere you'd like me to kiss you?"

She gives her head a tiny shake as though doubting her own ears.

"But you're thinking about it." I huff an unhappy chuckle. "God knows you're not the only one. I would drown myself in you, Amelia. Gorge on you until only your sighs remain."

"Are you trying to frighten me or turn me on?"

"That's just the thing. I'm not sure anymore. I've tried being brotherly. I've tried being a pain. I've even tried being considerate, tried to do the right thing, but you thwart me at every turn." I know these sound like complaints, but they're actually more like compliments. She knows it, too, as her lips tip upward.

"I don't think I've ever thwarted anyone in my life."

I reach out, wrapping my fingers around her elbow. "I can only think you haven't been paying enough attention. Saved by the Bentley," I add as the company's SUV pulls quietly up to the curb. I suppose George must've spotted us from where he was parked.

"Maybe I don't want to be saved," she says softly.

"And maybe I don't want to fuck you in a cold back lane," I lie.

I ignore her shock as the car pulls up, and the driver's door closes with a heavy *thunk* as he slips out.

"Hello, George." Mimi's expression reflects surprise as he opens the rear passenger door. "You're working late tonight."

"Overtime." I glance over my shoulder just in time to see him shoot her the kind of wink that would earn a younger man a punch to the ribs.

"Gotta make hay when the sun—moon—shines." Adjusting my hold on her arm, I turn her toward the rear of the car.

"Gov'nor," George says with a decisive nod as Mimi slides inside. "Looks like someone got you a good one," he says, tapping his jaw.

"You should see the other guy." Mimi ducks in the seat, her flushed expression appearing at the other door. "The man was *huge,* and Whit—"

"Narrowly avoided extensive dental work."

"You look like you came out on the right side of it," he says, moving around the car with the kind of quick march that reveals his military history. He doesn't bother opening my door. It took months for me to persuade him my arms aren't ornaments.

"My hero," Mimi whispers as I climb in next to her.

"It might easily have worked out very differently."

"Yeah, but it didn't."

"He definitely had 'roid rage," I murmur, gingerly

touching my jaw. I feel very far from a hero or a good man right now.

"Road rage?" she asks, confused.

"'Roids," I clarify, sliding her a look. "He looked the type to be a steroid abuser. If you were looking to take someone home, better to look for a man who doesn't walk around like he has a rolled carpet shoved under each arm."

"Oh my God, he did look like that, right?" She gives a ridiculously adorable giggle, deliberately refusing to take the bait. I decide to be a little blunter.

"He wouldn't have been able to reach his dick, never mind fuck you with it."

And then sledgehammer blunt.

And because it's just that kind of moment, George climbs into the driver's seat in time to hear my less-than-eloquent summing up of the situation. His wide eyes meet my unhappy ones in the rearview mirror, though he glances quickly away. A second later, the Bentley starts with a throaty purr.

Fuck this—why am I feeling uncomfortable? George is a hardened East Londoner, so I bet he hears worse language on a daily basis. Shit, I bet his five-year-old grandson has said worse at the breakfast table. *Maybe not about steroid abuse.*

While George might not be embarrassed, when I turn to Mimi, her jaw seems to have unhinged. Which is weird, because that's exactly how she makes me feel. Fucking deranged with lust and the need to shake some sense into her. I don't know whether I'm on my arse or my elbow with her. I don't know whether I want to fuck her or spank her.

Probably all of the above.

Agog, that's the word to describe her reaction. Good. The

woman needs shocking, and I'd be lying if I said I didn't feel satisfied that I'd managed it. *For once.* It's like the return of my equilibrium, the sense of how things should be as I lean over the center console and press my forefinger under her chin.

"Close your mouth." I lean closer still. My next words are a sultry purr at her ear. "Unless you want me to put something in it."

She swallows, and her gaze turns inward, stunned or imagining just that. Again, both work for me. I shift in my seat in an attempt to discreetly adjust my now tight pants when George's voice plucks at my attention.

"Where to?" His tone might be casual, but it looks like someone has shaved off his eyebrows and painted them just below his hairline. I never realized before, but it seems George has the hearing of an elephant.

I open my mouth to reply, still conflicted and unsure if I'm going to take her home or to my—

"We're going to Knightsbridge," Mimi answers clearly and without hesitation.

15

***

WHIT

THE CAR IS silent but for the swish of tires against the road, and we've barely spoken since Mimi's direction. Why did El have to choose a club so far away from my place? I'm pretty sure I'll combust before we get there.

"Whit?" I no sooner turn my head than words tumble from her mouth like water over rocks. "I've never had sex in a car before."

I almost groan. Combust? I'm pretty sure I'm about to *bust* a nut. I'm not in the habit of denying myself but having Mimi so close to me, day in and day out, has been torture. I wake in the morning to the phantom feel of her riding my fingertips, then spend my days trying not to stare at her arse while mentally undressing her. It's been torture—a pure, ball-aching torture I've tried hard to ignore. I know I said I wouldn't, and I know it's wrong, and if I was Connor, I'd be rattling more than chains at the bottom of my bed, but fuck it all to hell, how can I not want her when she's just so fucking adorable?

Full of truth and enthusiasm.

I've never known anyone like her. Never wanted anyone

like I want her. If I'm not careful, I'll end up reciting the periodic table in my head. That or embarrassing myself.

"George?" His eyes flick to the mirror at his name. "Have we got any booze in this thing?" I spend a fair chunk of time being ferried back and forth from the airport by him, but I'm always working. I've never thought to ask before.

"Mini fridge in the center console, Guv." He leans forward and flicks on the radio. The sound system fills the front of the car, not the back. Tactful, right?

Opening the console, I cast my eyes over the contents. "Would you like—"

"Oh, like a plane," she says, peering at the miniature bottles. "Do you have a soda?"

I half lift a couple of the tiny soda cans, but she shakes her head with a murmured, "No, thanks."

Grabbing a glass, I select a bottle of Laphroaig and twist off the lid before dumping it in. "I wasn't about to ask if you'd like a drink." I glance up from under my lashes in such a way she can't miss my meaning.

Her eyes wide, her head swinging to the driver and back again. "Rude!" But then. "You mean... now?"

Her head slices sharply George's way, and I chuckle. I can't tell if she's thinking about it, titillated, or scandalized.

Maybe all of the above.

"There really isn't enough room." My pelvis tilts as I stretch back, an action she doesn't fail to notice.

"We could make it work." Her voice drops, her eyes along with it. My body prickles pleasurably as she takes me in. "The seats recline, don't they?"

"And you, what? Climb over this." I pat the polished teak console, though my attention is on her tight dress. "Should I ask George to pull over? I'm sure you wouldn't want him to watch." I find myself sucking in a sharp immediate breath as she leans over me, curving her dainty hand over my thigh. A quicksilver pleasure shoots through me, my balls drawing tight and the hairs on the back of my neck standing high.

"So thick." The muscles flex beneath her fingers like a warning.

"I'm learning all kinds of things about you tonight."

"Meaning?" Her attention lifts, her breath sweet on my face.

"That you're either a tease or an exhibitionist."

"I said I'd never had sex in a car. Does that sound like I want to be watched?"

"So you're a tease."

"So, so thick." Her gaze dips to my crotch, the dig of her nails harder now. "Think of it more as a prelude. Since yesterday, I haven't been able to stop thinking about that other *thick* part of you." The word is all curling tongue and filthy intent.

"*Amelia.*"

"You love making a warning out of my name, don't you?"

"I love it as much as you love making me do it."

"I wouldn't have to if you didn't make it so hard for me."

Under her hand, I flex my thigh muscle again. "You have no idea how hard."

Her eyes darken as she leans closer, her eyes dipping to my mouth. "Poor Whit." She slides her thumb across the tiny cut. "Does it hurt?"

"Sweetheart, the part of my anatomy that's hurting is a little farther south than my mouth."

She stifles a smile. "Should I kiss it better?" She pouts, playing the part to perfection. My balls throb, and if it's possible, my cock becomes even harder. She only needs to move her hand a few inches and...

And George would probably get a very good show.

My heart ticks up as Mimi suddenly reaches out, her breasts brushing my arm as she lifts the crystal tumbler from my hand. I feel the loss of her heat immediately as she sits back in her seat.

"Is it good?" She doesn't give me time to answer before tipping the contents down her throat. She comes up spluttering, the alcohol burn obviously not quite what she expected. "*W-why!*"

I chuckle as she gives a violent, whole-body shiver. "You don't like whisky?"

"I've never had it before." She shivers again, but not quite so severely. And the face she pulls? It's a picture of violent distaste.

"It's meant to be savored."

"It tastes like soil and burns like fire." She begins to cough, and I jerk forward, aborting the movement when her hand flutters to her chest and she gives a tiny huff of a laugh. "Why would anyone drink that? Not for the taste, that's for sure."

"Again, it's not meant to be thrown down your neck."

"Mmm, but it's spicy now," she murmurs, rubbing at a spot in the middle of her breastbone. "Warm and tingly," she adds, rubbing her lips together provocatively.

This time, I don't bite. But that doesn't mean I don't have plans to do so later.

16

MIMI

THE CAR PULLS AWAY from the curb, the beat of my heart making a symphony with the sound of the tires. We're here. Finally almost here.

"How far do you want to take this?" Whit's fingers loop my wrist. Light from the streetlamp falls across him in ripples as he closes the space between us, his steps as fluid as a cat. "How far, Amelia?"

"Mimi," I whisper. I don't sound very bold.

"I can call you Mimi," he says, reaching out to run his thumb and fingers down a lock of my hair. "Or I can call you Amelia. But I can only fuck one of the two."

"And Mimi doesn't do it for you?"

"Mimi belongs in the past." His knuckle brushes my teeth. "The woman in front of me, she isn't a kid anymore."

Why does that sound so right?

"You've done this before." The question is in his expression, not his words.

I laugh softly. "I'm twenty-four, Whit. I haven't saved myself for you." A pause. "I would have if you'd been around." I bite my lip from adding, *I imagined it was you.*

His breath leaves his chest in a rush, and he looks stunned. Maybe that was too much. But as the doors to Whit's building automatically swish open, he sort of jolts back to himself, his fingers moving from my wrist to my back.

"Shall we?"

I smile up at his serious expression and shrug. "Why the heck not?"

This time, there's no security request to check my ID or the contents of my purse as, with a clipped nod from Whit, we pass by the evening's security detail. My heels echo as we cross the sleekly stylish lobby, Whit's hand a hot presence at my back. Before we even reach the elevator, the doors begin to glide almost silently open.

"That's a clever trick." I glance up at him, the sudden longing in his eyes catching me off guard. My God, this is really happening. "The doors," I clarify unnecessarily as I resist the instinct to cross my legs as a sudden hollow throb strikes up in my panties.

"Apparently," Whit's low voice rumbles as he adds a little pressure to my back to get me moving, "the rich should never do something as mundane as wait." He guides me into an elevator car of bronze mirrored walls and lattice screening. The doors no sooner close than he's pulling my back flush to his front. His hands rise to my hips, sliding to where the fabric separates. The contact sets off a wave of sensation I can't control. "They also don't share space."

"So this is your elevator?" My ridiculous question sounds high and my heart flutters wildly as he bends, brushing his lips against my neck. The sound he makes is more a satisfied hum than an answer. Not that I really need one as I sink into his chest, lengthening my neck for the path of his tongue. The sight of us in the mirror opposite paints quite a picture. My mouth softly opened, my eyes wanton, wanting, and full of encouragement as Whit's hands circle my waist. His dark head bent, his lashes are like a sweep of dark angel wings.

"Poor Mimi," he gently taunts. "Never had sex in a car."

"Oh!" I suck in a sharp breath as his teeth find my earlobe. "You have?" I begin to move my head to look at him, only to find his finger at my chin, maneuvering me back.

"A misspent youth," he murmurs as his hand drifts to my breast. He cups the full weight, and I inhale sharply as his thumb brushes my stiffening nipple. "That and a house full of siblings made for ingenuity. Lie back against me, sweetheart."

"Why?" My mouth questions as my body does it anyway. There isn't one thing about him that doesn't thrill me, the chemicals swirling through my body so seductive.

"Because I want you to." I almost moan as he tweaks my stiff nipple through my dress. "Because you want to please me." He doesn't wait for my confirmation, but I guess he doesn't need to. "You know where I've never had sex? In an elevator car."

My insides start to pulse, yet the chuckle that fills the tiny space is far too loud.

"That's funny, is it?" he asks.

"I was thinking about cameras." I don't move my head because that would involve moving my neck, but my gaze does flick around the small space.

"Do you have a thing for watching?" Heat courses through my veins as both hands slide over my rib cage and down over my thighs. "Being seen? You do seem very studious."

At his taunting tone, my eyes catch his in the mirror. The tiger and his prey.

"I'm not…"

"What?" he purrs, toying with the hem of my dress. "Watching my hand?" He roughly pulls at the hem of my dress, his hand sliding between my legs. His fingers curl inward, gripping my thigh, and my knees almost buckle on the spot. "Willing me to use my fingers on you again?"

I begin to tremble as his hand slides higher and my body bows, chasing his touch. But then I remember where we are and how the doors might open at any time. My body protests reflexively when his hands tighten, and he whispers a quiet, "Hush."

Of course. This is Whit's floor. He isn't expecting anyone to come.

Well… in that way, maybe. Because the way he begins to slide my dress higher makes me think he might be expecting *someone* to come.

"What will I find if I pull your skirt higher, Amelia?"

I startle at the sight of myself. My cheeks flushed red, my feet planted wider than I recall, and the skirt part of my dress looking more and more like a belt.

"Answer me. Did you go out with my brother wearing panties that *my* money paid for?"

"You make that sound like a bad thing." Oh my God, I'm blaming Whit's sexual voodoo for my response because I have no idea where the words are coming from. "Better than going out bare assed."

"That would be something I'd certainly punish you for."

My brain buckles, the synapses misfiring, my thoughts making not one bit of sense. That… that's not sexy. So why are my internal organs slut dropping at the thought of it?

"You look shocked." I roll in my lips to stifle a whimper at the hot drag of his fingers up my thigh. "Are you imagining just that? Have I broken your brain a little, sweetheart?"

"Punishment isn't my thing."

"Such a sweet little liar. Unless you don't really know?"

I gasp as his hand ghosts my pussy, my body throbbing in anticipation of the contact that doesn't come.

"Who are you in the dark, darling?"

"I... what do you mean?"

"Who are you just for you? When there's no one around, and you don't have to be the sunshine."

"H-how would you punish someone?" My voice is tremulous because he's not supposed to notice. Who I am inside is not his business, and those thoughts are to be held at arm's length.

"Punish *you*, Amelia. How would I punish you?" This time, oh yes, his fingers are a fluttering brush between my legs. "There are so many ways, so many parts you and I could play. Tell me about these." He cups his hand between my legs. "Did I buy you these?"

"Last year." I try so hard not to push against him, to deepen the contact. "Bloomingdales, w-with a bra to match."

"Are you wearing it now?"

I nod rapidly. There really is little point in hiding how eager I am.

"Darling, I'm going to need you to use your words."

"Yes." I swallow. "A matching set."

"Then we won't take them off. Not yet." His long finger curls, sliding along my slit, making my insides pulse and ache. *God, I'm so ready for this.* "We're not going to have sex in this car, Amelia." My body stills. Was I getting a little ahead of myself? "I'm going to fuck you with my fingers until you're ready to come. Would you like that?" His hand tightens when I don't immediately answer. I throb, blood rushing to greet the contact. "Your words, Amelia. I want to hear them."

"Yes." My tongue darts out to wet my parched lips. "Yes, please."

"Good girl." That should not feel like sunshine on my skin. But, gosh, it does. "How badly do you want me to finger you?"

"What?" I sound slightly worried, but my internal organs are doing a jig.

"Tell me how much you want this. If it helps, you can pretend I need persuading."

"Whit." I press my hand over his and pull it from between my legs. His eyes darken as I lift it to brush a kiss to the back of his fingers. "I've never wanted anything as much as I've wanted you." Clasping it flat to my stomach, I slide his fingers into my panties, curling my hand over his. "You were the first boy I touched myself to. The one I held all boys up against." *And they never stood a chance.* "The night I lost my virginity, you were the one I imagined." It's hardly complimentary to Adam or whatever his name was, but there really was no other way for it to play out.

"Jesus Christ." His hand tightens on my pussy as though in ownership, my hips tipping as my body wills him instinctively on.

"Every time you touch me, it's like a dream come true. Tonight, I don't want just your fingers. Tonight, I don't want to pretend."

"*Fuck.*" His breath is hot against my cheek as he flexes into me. "How did you become so perfect?"

"Touch me, Whit. Make this real." I'm so wet, I know he can feel it. Knowing what his words have done to me, I begin to paint a picture all of my own. "So many nights I've slipped into something silky. Under the covers, I'd press my hand between my legs and think of you. I'd close my eyes, and it would be your breath I could feel. You moving inside me."

"Who's seducing who?" he purrs dangerously.

"I'm just telling the truth."

"What you're doing is torturing me." His hot and reprimanding words curl around me, just as his fingers do. I stifle a whimper as his middle finger parts me, sweeping along the slick ribbon of flesh. "And enjoying it."

"Oh!"

"You prance around my office, looking like sunshine and smelling like flowers, dressed in your tight skirts and sensible blouses. But underneath, underneath you're a hot little fuck in gossamer lingerie." Gathering my arousal, he paints it across my clit. "Admit it," he demands, "you've gotten your kicks hiding all this from me."

"Oh God, yes!"

"Not good enough, Amelia." "Tell me the truth. Tell me all of it."

I thrash and cry out, as he owns my pleasure—as he owns me. "I wanted to show you. I wanted you to see."

"An inadvertent flash of a lacy bra. The outline of your thong."

"Yes, please! I wanted you to tell me to lift my skirt to show you like you did before, but you wouldn't."

"And what would happen next in this dirty scenario of yours?"

"You'd bend me over your desk and fuck me hard!" My body begins to jerk as filth pours out of my mouth.

"Good girl. I like that story. My God, you're so hot and slippery. All for me."

I almost sob, the dark reverence in his voice adding to this throbbing, needy experience overload. The sight of us in the mirror, the dark look on his face, the sound of his fingers working my wet core. "Please, Whit," I whimper, moaning a garbled plea as he pinches my swollen clit. My body twists from the delicious torture until he bands his arm across my chest, pinning me in place. Every nerve ending ignites. I'm suddenly so close to coming, I lock my knees, tilting my pelvis to deepen the contact. I almost cry in frustration as he slips out from behind me. At least until he pushes me back against the wall.

He hooks his fingers into the elastic at my hips, pulling my underwear to mid-thigh.

It feels so dirty like this. So much more dirty than being naked in front of him as his eyes fall to my pussy, his fingers opening me up to his appraisal.

"You're so fucking perfect."

His praise makes me whimper, and his mouth brushes mine as though to taste, swallowing my cries as his fingers slip through my wetness, suddenly spearing me. The intrusion is so slick and sublime and brings with it such a wave of relief as my back arches from the wall, chasing his touch. From one hand to two, he opens me and begins to strum my clit with his thumb.

"You make the hottest little moans." His lips feel hungered, his words a layer of pleasure I can barely comprehend. "Has anyone ever told you that?"

I shake my head, but I know what he's about to say by the wicked tilt of his lips. *Words, Amelia, use your words.*

"N-no one." I could give him a more accurate depiction. Hell, I could write a dissertation if he needed it. But he's going to have to stop touching me first.

"I can't wait to hear the sounds you make when I get my mouth on you."

His words turn to fragments of images in my head, those

pictures setting off a wave of reactions that I'm powerless to resist. Driven by instinct and this consuming need, my body moves with the rhythm of his fingers, the sound of my arousal almost lewd.

"You take my fingers so beautifully. Will you throb as hard around my cock?"

Oh. My. Gosh. Just when I think he can't get any filthier, he ups the ante so perfectly. Whit coaxes my climax with such attention, his thumb at my clit, his fingers a symphony of hard thrusts and delicious come-hither curls, layering sensation upon sensation, driving me senseless, driving my hips to thrust to chase his touch. Endorphins, hormones, and Whit's dark demands set off a seismic wave of pleasure. I reach out, my fingers scrambling with his jacket and shirt, this desperation crawling through me requiring he take off *all* his clothes.

"Not yet, darling." His hand is wet with my arousal as he takes my wrists, pressing them above my head. *Another layer.* I never imagined I could feel so good.

"Please, Whit." My body bows as though it would inhale him whole if it could.

His eyes seem to be lit from some light behind them, his expression as wild as any tiger. "You should thank me for fucking you with my fingers."

I try to, honestly I do, but don't get past the *"th"* sound as my body jerks. So. Many. Feelings. So many sensations unraveling the threads holding me together.

"Oh, beautiful girl, that's it. Come all over my fingers."

And like Pavlov's dog and his ringing bell, I do.

Oh, I do.

Then I think I pass out.

17

MIMI

"Don't go to sleep on me." With my lips pressed against Whit's neck, I feel the vibration of his low, rumbled words. I feel kind of boneless and melty. My arms looped loosely around his shoulders like cooked spaghetti as he carries me along the mirrored hallway, his shoes quietly echoing. Honestly, I feel like I could take a nap. I obviously won't. The man deserves better for an orgasm that literally took my legs out from under me.

"Better bring your A game."

His chest vibrates with a chuckle at my sex-slurred words, my skin seeming to buzz from the slightest brush. That's not *quite* fighting talk.

"You can put me down, you know."

"Maybe I don't want to," he replies as he adjusts his grip on me at his door. Hooking me higher against his chest, he inputs the code to the keypad with the hand under my butt. Whit pushes the door open, maneuvering my legs through first with a rumbled, "Ladies first."

"So polite."

"Ladies should always come first, Amelia."

We pass through the lounge where the treetops outside look like spindly skeletons, framed by the night sky. As Whit moves into a hallway, soft lighting automatically illuminates along the floor.

"Fancy," I murmur, plucking at the button of his dark shirt, secretly inhaling the scent of him. Dark and spicy. It suits him. "You have light *and* sex magic."

"Sex magic?" His eyes dance with amusement as he stares down at me.

"That would be the thing you pick up on."

He chuckles as he carries me into a darkened room, and my stomach swoops as I realize this must be his bedroom. It's not like I should be shocked. We've more than gone beyond the preliminaries, even if all the bases haven't been covered. Yet.

Oh my gosh, I'm here in Whit's bedroom, and we're about to do the deed unless I'm very much mistaken. Unless there's an earthquake or I suddenly drop dead, which isn't likely considering I can feel my heart tripping like a crazy thing in my chest. I'm about to get naked. With Whit! And I can't wait to see what's under that thousand-dollar shirt. I have seen him without his shirt, but it's been some time. Something tells me it's not a trick of my imagination that makes him look so much bigger now.

"What are you smiling at?" he asks as he lowers me to the end of a modern four-poster bed. It's huge, the frame charcoal and the linens the color of clouds. *Feels like a cloud, too.*

"I could ask you the same thing." Ducking my head, I fold my nervous fingers over the end of the bed, only to find my chin lifted by his finger.

"Sex magic makes me smile." His eyes sweep down my body, the look bold and possessive. "That and imagining all the things I'm going to do to you with my wand."

"You're going to keep bringing that up, aren't you?" My reply sounds so cool. Inside, I'm a pot of molten lava—a puddle of embarrassed and turned on.

"Keep bringing up my wand?" He chuckles as he presses a kiss to the top of my head, then steps back. "There's no making it go down." He slides out of his jacket, dropping it on a nearby chair. "At least you're not likely to fall asleep now. I'll be back in a minute." He strides toward the door, pausing at the doorway, but if he was about to say something, he must change his mind. Still, it gives me a moment to drink him in once more. His dark pants still have knife-sharp pleats, his thin leather belt highlights his trim waist and his shirt the flatness of his stomach. How is it he looks completely unruffled? Meanwhile... I glance down and realize my dress is still around my hips. I begin to tug it down. *At least he pulled my panties up.*

"I'd say it's a bit late for that now." He pivots, his chuckle and his steps echoing along the hallway.

Holy heck. I'm in Leif Whittington's bedroom! I must've died and gone to heaven earlier than I'm supposed to.

I take the opportunity to have a quick look around. The vast room is sparsely decorated. Like the lounge, one wall is entirely glass and overlooks the green space of Hyde Park. The bed is huge, of course, the nightstands housing nothing but space-age-looking Anglepoise lamps. The floor is dark parquet wood with a pale, fluffy rug placed between it and the bed. A massive piece of abstract artwork hangs on the wall opposite, a silver seam running down the middle. I guess it to be some sort of fancy TV cabinet. A couple of woven leather chairs, the kind you can only sit back on, or else risk tipping the chair from the front. An ottoman. A couple of chests. Doors to a bathroom and closet, at a guess. While there isn't a lot of furniture or color (monochrome of grays and black with slashes of white), there is a lot of texture. The rug, the paneled walls, woven leather, the fur-like throw draped over an ottoman. The space is masculine and very sexy.

It's also very tidy. Whit is a neat freak!

Pressing my hands under my thighs, I give a silent, excited squeal, kicking my heels back and forth like a kid. I stop abruptly, realizing he might come back in. I strain to listen but hear no footsteps. Or sound, really.

Where has he gone?

For props? Implements?

I press my fingers to my mouth, not sure if that excites me or not. Who am I kidding? We haven't yet had sex but the little experience I have with him tells me I might be in for a few more surprises. I don't have much longer to wait, for his appearance, at least, when he arrives back in the room, a bottle of water in his hand. Take away my sight and my sense of smell and I'd still recognize his presence because a million nerve endings begin to dance and shimmer whenever he's near.

"Water from Finland?" I murmur, as I take it from his outstretched hand. I glance up from the barely-there label. "Fancy."

"Very fancy. Springwater filtered through the ice layers."

"Because...?"

"Because I asked the grocery service for water, and this is what they brought."

"Should've gone to Tesco."

"Mimi," he chides. "I'm far too fancy to shop for my own groceries."

"Oh yeah. I forgot." I pinch in my smile. Too fancy to shop but not too fancy to chase his own dry cleaning. This man is complex. Fine. Grumpy and grumbly, yet too sweet for his own good

"Drink."

Bossy. The man is bossy, and I like it, my skin prickling under his attention. "Should I stretch, too? Limber up a little?" I roll my shoulders, loving how he smiles at me. Just for me.

"Do you think you're ready to stand by yourself now?"

"I'm not sure," I say, unable to control my grin. "That was, er, some experience. You're two for two, Whit." I make as though to slide my hair behind my ears before realizing I'm wearing it up. I end up toying with my earring instead.

"You say that like you're surprised." He folds his arms across his chest as though to study me. "I might've strayed from the manual a bit, but you don't seem too disappointed."

"Manual?" My brow furrows.

"The guy manual, I think you called it. Or was it something from the internet?" Reaching up, he scratches his thumb along his jaw in an action meant to convey contemplation, I think. Not for long because it's all part of the show as his eyes darken, and he swipes it against his mouth. "Sexual lore. That's what you said." Everything draws tight inside when he pushes his thumb into his mouth, the digit that was, not too many minutes ago, strumming my clit. He licks his lips as it retracts. "Your pleasure. So sticky and sweet."

"I don't think you need a manual." My words are light and wavery. I think I feel a little faint.

"No, I don't think so, either. Drink some water, Amelia," he adds, turning from me. As he disappears through one of the doors, I twist off the cap and take a few sips. Not sure what to do with the bottle, I stand to place it somewhere less impolite than his fluffy rug; the condensation can't be good for it.

Whit suddenly appears in front of me. His cuff links are gone, his shirtsleeves folded back. *Like he's about to start something. Or maybe finish it.* His feet are also bare.

"I was just—"

My words halt, my breath half in and half out as he simultaneously grasps my wrist and takes the water from my hand. He throws the bottle onto the bed behind me. Without another word spoken, he begins to wrap my ponytail around his hand.

"I'm going to take you to bed now."

"Good." I try again, this time without the squeak. "I'd like that."

"But there are one or two things we should discuss first."

"Sure." I've never touched him before, yet my fingers are drawn to his chest like iron filings to a magnet. He feels so solid under my hands, familiar yet strange, all kinds of wonderful, and not at all dream-like. *I want more*, I think. As my fingers reach to loosen the buttons of his shirt. Like a cartographer with a new land, I want to chart every valley and hill of him. Every dip and peak. "Oh." The sound is low and not at all pained, my head pulled back thanks to Whit's quick tug.

"Pay attention, Amelia."

"I am," I almost moan. Who knew my hair follicles were connected somewhere south of my torso?

"You shouldn't be here, but I've realized I've been

fighting the inevitable since you found yourself in my living room."

"Still not sorry."

"Yes. That's still apparent. It's also part of the problem. You should be sorry, and I don't know why you're not. And I shouldn't be thinking of little else but making you come again and again." Holy heck. I like confessional Whit. "I don't profess to have the answers, but I think I have the solution."

I make a noise that sounds like *do tell*. Or maybe just *do me*.

"If you're going back to Florida in six months—"

"I am." I try to nod, but *ow!* The sensation is not the same. "I am going back." I don't really have any choice. "Less than six now."

"Then I think I can teach you a few things."

"Oh?"

"Wipe the smile off your face," he says, smiling himself. "I really can't believe I'm suggesting this," he adds a little more unhappily.

"You haven't said what you're suggesting yet. Maybe I won't agree."

"Amelia." There he goes making my name a reprimand again. "I wrapped my fist in your hair while you stood as meek as a lamb, and not ten minutes, ago you let the inhabitants of this very prestigious building know you were having the orgasm of your life."

"But the elevator isn't for public use," I answer uncertainly. "There were no cameras." Were there?

"The car might've gone down. God knows I can't wait to." The first part of his answer bypasses my brain as the second twines around my insides like lustful ivy. "The doors could've opened at the foyer. Regardless, I'm sure your cries carried to the concierge and security teams."

I eye him narrowly. Is he trying to scare me off? I'd raise my chin, but I've already made that mistake once. "Why do I have to be the only one embarrassed? It took two of us to make that noise."

His mouth twitches though he masters his smile. "You're such a pretty little thorn in my side. But we're getting off track." Being on track apparently includes kissing, his hand finding my hip, his head bending to mine. Warm lips feather and tease, nipping my bottom lip before withdrawing just as quick. Thanks to how he holds my hair, I can't follow, but that doesn't stop my protest as I fasten my fingers around his bicep. He abandons his retreat, his mouth returning. His second kiss is firmer, his tongue tasting faintly of me. *The thumb he licked.* Why is that such a turn-on?

"Six months." His words skate over my jaw, and he molds his lips over my pulse point, still holding me immobile by the hair. *As though it wasn't already stuttering enough.* "Or what's left of it."

"Yes." I'd melt against him if only he'd give me the opportunity. "Six months is long enough." Six months are all I have.

"Professionalism in the office. No more tricks." His lips skate over my jaw, his tiger eyes shining as they flick up and meet my own before his lashes drop as though to veil his thoughts.

"It was a nail," I protest even as I feel the shape of his upturned lips.

"Outside of that, I'll give you what you want. I'll give you the experiences you want. But make no mistake, it can only ever be sex."

"That's all I want," I breathe, wondering how much

longer before my knees give out and my hair is yanked from the roots. That's all it can be.

"That's settled then." I feel the loss of his heat immediately when he releases my ponytail and steps back. "Take off your dress."

A cold, clinical command, contradicted by his heated expression and the proud outline of his cock in his pants. *His cock.* How many times have I imagined it? Let me put it this way: if I had a dollar for each time I closed my eyes and conjured it, I'd have a very fat piggy bank.

"If you stop trying to imagine my cock, we might get to the part where I get it out."

"Do I only get to look at it?" I ask in a soft tease.

"By the time you take that dress off, it might be too old to work."

"I'm doing it," I announce with a soft giggle as I twist one arm behind my back and the other over my shoulder.

"Turn around." His hand loops my waist as he turns me with an air of frustration.

"Whatever you say... *Daddy*." The words drip like ice cream from my tongue.

He makes the kind of sound I find hard to categorize. Pleased? Gratified? Turned on? The important thing is the way my skin heats and the stirring of the soft wisps of hair on the back of my neck the minute before his lips brush there. I feel all hot and shivery and all kinds of treasured, and I'm glad there isn't a mirror in front of me now because I'm smiling stupidly. Meanwhile, Whit makes quick work of the fastenings.

"What is it about that?" he asks as he slides my dress over my shoulders, pausing mid-bicep.

"Daddy Whit?" I glance over my shoulder, but I can't see his expression and get the sense he's avoiding my gaze. "I don't have daddy issues if that's what you're asking. You've met my dad." I turn my head back with a grimace. Why'd I have to say that?

"I find it helps if you try not to think about family when you're about to fuck."

"That's good advice." I don't want him thinking about Connor again.

"Daddy in this context is very different."

"I'll say." Again with the smiling. "I guess it just reminds me of the first time. I would never have thought back then…"

"It would've turned you on?"

That it would send a wave of excitement from my belly button to my groin. "I just found the whole thing so incredibly sexy." Understatement of the year.

"Why do you think that is?" His thumbs glide over my bare shoulders, hooking my bra straps out of the way.

"Probably because you took care of me." Which is weird because my family—nope! "I mean, you took *care* of me," I add in a *ya-know* tone. "I felt like I was the center of your world. Does that sound silly?" I glance his way again.

"No." His words are as soft as his stroking fingers. "Not silly at all. You were a gift." His lips are a warm brush against my skin. As if I could somehow preserve the sensation in my memory, my eyelids drop like the shutter of an old camera. "Your enjoyment is my prize."

"I've never felt like that," I whisper, reveling in the contact. "You made me feel so safe." A thought from my subconscious, but I realize it's true.

"You're always safe with me."

"I know." I really do.

My breath catches, my bones almost liquifying as he presses his teeth to the juncture of my shoulder and neck.

"Safe with me to explore." I'm so dazed, my whole being just lust-hazed. I almost don't notice him sliding my bra straps back in place, but there's no need to panic as my dress slips to the floor. "Let's pick up where we left off in the closet, shall we?" He takes my hand, and I turn to face him.

He is so handsome, wild-eyed, and darkly stubbled. And he's mine. Finally.

18

WHIT

HEELS. Long, shapely legs. Gossamer fine lingerie. Fuckable tits and a mouth I don't know whether I want to kiss or defile with my dick.

Both, obviously. But which first?

Amelia Valente has a body built for sin. A mind too, if I'm not mistaken. Under that very real dappling of sunshine is a curiosity for pleasure. Pleasure I can and will give her again and again. It's little wonder her parents sought to protect her for so long because she's the kind of girl men like me live to corrupt.

I curl my hand around the full curve of her hip, and it seems to rise all by itself, sliding over her waist, higher over her rib cage. My mouth waters to taste her, the scent of her lingering on my tongue. The soft sigh she releases as I cup her breast sounds like pure encouragement. As I swipe the pad of my thumb over her nipple, making it stiffen, the transparency of her bra offering me that much.

"Do you like them?"

My first instinct is to give my head a quick shake. Surely, that wasn't what she asked me, was it? Just how sheltered is she? What straight man doesn't like tits—any tits, but especially ones that are full and soft and sit so beautifully in your hand? Then the penny drops. She's talking about her underwear.

I press a kiss to the swell of cleavage with a rumbling, "Mmm, yes. I have exquisite taste." Her breath stutters as I press my teeth to one soft curve. "You really are very lovely."

"M-maybe we should lie down." There's more than a note of hope in her tone, her eyes lust hazed as her body moves pre-emptively back.

"I like where we are." Hooking my finger into the cup, I expose a rose-pink nipple to my tongue. She hesitates, the movement fully aborted as her hands grasp my shoulders. Her sharp gasp is like a lick to the underside of my cock as I suck her nipple into my mouth.

"Oh, that's…"

My reply is a sound of agreement. Of pleasure.

"I'm not sure how much longer I can stay on my feet."

"I'll catch you," I whisper against her wet, shiny nipple, and she watches with languid-eyed pleasure as I draw the taut bud back into my mouth. My eyes hold her captive over the curve of her breast when I release the hard bud to drag my tongue. Her hips buck, my arms slipping behind her, curving her into my embrace.

"Whit, please," she moans as I trail my mouth to her other breast, dragging the lacy cup down with my teeth.

"You're so sensitive," I murmur, dipping my tongue into the black lacy cup. "I want to see if you can come from just this." She makes a plaintive noise, and I chuckle. "Not tonight." No, not tonight because she's not the only one struggling. My hands are at her back because I want to hold her, touch her, but also because they're shaking—shaking like a boy with his first woman. And Amelia is *all* woman.

Her waist curves deeply as though made for my hands, her breasts full and soft, the gentle swell of her stomach and the full roundness of her arse. Soft sighs, softer skin, the velvet musk of her. She's a feast for the senses. She makes a glutton of me because I just can't get enough. So I do what I can, what I want, unhooking her bra as I move her backward toward the bed. As her thighs hit the mattress, I follow, our bodies barely touching as I bring my mouth to her ear and her hand to my aching cock.

"Feel how hard I am," I rasp, pressing it tighter. My balls tighten as the animal in me strains to take over. "You did this to me. You drive me fucking crazy." She moans, her fingers tightening over my throbbing cock. When she lifts her hips, I drop mine to grind over her.

"*Oh yes!* Right there."

"You're such a hot little fuck, Amelia. Your pussy feels like heaven. I can't wait to be inside you."

"Where are you going?" Her words sound a little desperate as I slide back, pulling to my knees above her.

"Not far." Slipping from the bed, I begin unbuttoning my shirt, when she pushes onto her elbows, her eyes smoky and avid as she watches.

She bites her lip, but the words escape anyway. "Please hurry."

"So impatient." I don't bother to hide my amusement. "There's something to be said for taking your time."

"I don't think I can wait." The platinum whisps of her hair make a halo as she shakes her head.

Truthfully, neither can I. Not this time. "Don't worry. I'm not going anywhere." As I discard my shirt, she sits up and makes a tentative gesture.

"Can I?"

Fuck, yes. "Be my guest." I step between her legs.

My abs contract as she slides a finger down the line of fine, dark hair trailing from my navel. "Earworms," she breathes as she curls her finger into my waistband.

"Ear what?" Maybe I didn't hear her right.

Something in my expression makes her mouth lift in a quick grin, though she ducks her head to hide it. "That song is going to be stuck in my head all night."

"What song is that?"

"Disney's 'Beauty and the Beast'?" Her gaze lifts hesitantly. "Don't tell me your sisters—"

I press a finger to her lips. "No talk of family." My finger drifts away, and I slide a tender kiss to that full pout. "Now, where were we?"

"Here. We were here." Her hands rise to my belt again, making swift work of the buckle as my cock strains, aching for her touch. Aching from neglect, I imagine, as I use my finger to lift her chin. It seems I can't resist the opportunity.

"Tell me what you're about to do."

"To take off your pants?" she offers hesitantly.

"And?"

Her lips twist with confusion. "Undress you?"

"You're going to get my cock out."

She blinks, then nods in the affirmative. "Yeah, I am."

"So tell me that, sweetheart. Use that pretty mouth, say the words."

"I…" She gives her head a shake. "I don't want to."

"But I want you to. And that, sweet girl, is the point."

"Then let's get to the point," she whispers, grazing her fingers over my hard length.

As quick as a flash, I grab the base of her ponytail, tugging her head back. Breath catches in her throat, her expression one of that wild place between pleasure and pain. Her teeth tug her bottom lip, the sight triggering a memory. I'd imagined this the first time she appeared in my office. I imagined working my hand into her hair to hold her in place. *I'd tease and taste.*

"Say it, Amelia." My words are silkier than a demand. "Tell me you're going to take out my cock and suck me off."

Her breasts rise and fall, lush and ripe and just beneath my attention because I can't take my eyes from hers. So gray. So intensely smoky. She might not like to use the words, but she does like to hear them, it seems.

"I want to taste you," she whispers.

Sometimes less is more, and this is definitely one of those times. I release the pressure on her ponytail, the sound of her eager breaths overlaying the slide of my zipper. The sides of my pants fall open when she seems to halt.

"Don't stop now." I brush the backs of my fingers down her neck when she seems content to stare at my boxers. "Not when you're so close." Not when my cock is so close to her mouth. She swallows, then slips her fingers into the waistband as though pulling them down for a look.

"Oh boy." The waistband snaps against my skin, the moment almost comedic as her eyes sweep up my body. "Or maybe that should be, *oh, Daddy.*"

"I'm waiting." My attention flicks down pointedly.

She licks her lips, and I swear it's not for effect as she stares at me with an intensity that makes the edges of my vision go hazy. When she glances up at me through those dark-painted lashes, I know what's coming next.

"Yes. Whatever you say, Daddy."

She is so bloody perfect.

Her fingers slide into my pants, and she takes the heft of both my cock and my balls into her hands. The experience is a tidal wave of relief that makes me moan like I'm paid to do it. Her breath is a tiny, terrible torture as she lowers her head, drawing her tongue across my slit.

The visual, the sensation, all of it—my praise delivered with a sandpapery rasp. The muscles in my thighs twitch, my hand instinctively guiding her head closer when she presses her lips to the smooth head.

"Yes, fuck, yes," I groan raggedly as she slides her lips a little lower. Nothing is more intimate than sucking pussy or swallowing cock, whichever your pleasure might be. But this? This moment is sublime. Her mouth stretched around my girth looks so fucking incredible, and the way it feels? I wouldn't be surprised to feel my soul leave my body, to see it suddenly ascend heavenward.

"Yes. Yes, like that." I slide my hand to the back of her head, and she moans her approval, the vibration turning my insides to goo. Fire runs through my veins, or maybe that's Amelia's brand of sunshine, the force of it increasing at the hot slide of her mouth. My whole being is a pool of swirling, swimming *yes, fucking yes* as I give a couple of experimental flexes of my hips. "Amelia, you take my cock so, *so* beautifully."

She makes a strangled cry, one I almost join her in as she pulls back.

"Whit!" My name sounds like amazement as she blinks up at me. "Oh my God, I never knew feedback could be so hot!"

"Debrief later," I rasp, pressing her head lower again. My cock is literally weeping, and if my balls get any tighter, they might lodge themselves in my throat.

"You first," she says with a sultry giggle. Sliding her hands into my boxer briefs at my hips, she slips the remains of my clothing down. I kick them away. "Me next?" she suggests, snapping the elastic of her knickers for good measure.

"Less talk, more sucking." Her head dips as she obliges. "*Fuck,* yes!" I groan as she inhales me deeply with a sexy little sigh. "Debrief... coming soon." Her delectable lips still wrapped around my girth, she twists the head, her wide eyes darting to mine. "Not that kind of coming." I didn't know it was possible for someone to snort while sucking cock. It turns out the raspy press of it is more than pleasant. "You're good, but..." I press my hand to the back of her head when my body bows unexpectedly forward as she paints a wet stripe of pleasure along the underside of my hard length. I growl, grabbing for her ponytail but not before she swirls her tongue around my wet crown.

So it seems Amelia likes a challenge.

"I'll come down the back of your throat any time, sweetheart." As I tighten my grip on her hair, her attention flicks my way. "I just thought it might be impolite for our first time."

Lashes lowered, she cedes control, allowing me to lazily flex into her hot mouth a few times, but the whole fucking experience is too much. I want to thrust, cram my dick down the back of her throat because she's just so fucking perfect. The half-moons of her thick lashes, her pink lips, and the velvet feel of her mouth, the hard pebble of her nipples, and the silk of her skin. Worse, my grip feels tenuous, like I'm a couple of thrusts from blowing my load. With supreme effort, I pull back, my cock leaving her mouth with a wet sucking sound. She can't suppress her small smile as she wipes the back of her hand across her mouth. She'll never truly be submissive. Just the way I like her.

Like a choreographed dance, I move forward, and Amelia

moves back, her back connecting with the bed. I press my body over hers, swiping my lips across hers in invitation. She takes it, her back arching as our mouths meet. We explore the other's rhythm in small, exploratory kisses that soon turn to something wilder. Deeper and wetter. Amelia begins to writhe under me, her hands blindly grasping—my neck, my arse—the arch of her foot a sensuous slide up my calf.

"Is this what you need?" I rasp. Dropping my hips to hers, I rock over her. The sound she makes deserves to be bottled as a rare vintage. "Use your words."

"Whit, please." Her hands tighten in the short hairs at the back of my head as she pulls my mouth to hers. A gasp, hot and desperate. "I need you inside before I burst."

My eyes close briefly at the picture she paints, a pained rumble rising from my throat. "That sounds like something I need to taste first."

She almost whimpers as I begin to slide down her body, pressing my mouth to her skin like a scattering of pearls against satin. "Please hurry."

"Oh, darling, no." She bucks as my tongue pays tribute to her nipples. "We have all night, and I plan on making the most of it." Her breath is a shallow, quivering thing as I flick my tongue over her nipple once more, then press my teeth to the soft underside of her breast. "I'm going to pin you to my bed and make your body my playground."

"Oh."

Down, down I slide until I'm on my knees like a devotee, pressed between the altar that is her pussy as her body silently begs.

"One day very soon," I whisper, hooking my thumbs into the string of her underwear, "you're going to slide your hand into these and show me how you touched yourself while thinking of me." She whimpers as I slide the scant garment down her legs. "In the daylight, where I can see every tiny reaction. Your legs spread wide and your eyes on me."

My hands on the insides of her knees, I press them wider, loving the jolt of her body as I press a kiss to the top of her slit.

"You're so lovely, Amelia." My hands skate up her inner thighs, my thumbs sliding over her pussy, exposing her glistening center. "Even your cunt is so very pretty." I hear the sharp intake of her breath as I dip my head, the hot exhalation of my words the only pleasure I'll grant her. "So pink." She shivers at the contact, her hips lifting from the bed in a silent plea. "Why don't you tell me where you need me?"

"You know where." Her words, like her body, are as taut as a bow string.

"That doesn't mean I don't want to hear. You're not the only one who likes a little *aural*."

"You just want to torment me," she says, her hands reaching for my head. She almost levitates from the bed at the next swipe of my tongue. Not from enjoyment but from anguish as I deliver a long lick to her thigh. A lick, a sucking kiss, I move to the other side, avoiding where she needs me most. "Please, Whit." She reaches for my hair when I grasp her hands, shackling her wrists with my fingers.

"Keep them here." My warning is clear as I press them to her sides. "I need you to keep still. Can you do that for me? Because if you don't, I'll eat you out all night, but you won't get to come."

"Neither will you," she says breathlessly.

Honing my tongue to a point, I press the tiniest touch to her slit. "Won't I?"

"You... you sadist."

"Fiendish at worst." My words are a tiny huff that

make her shiver. Nestling my tongue a little deeper, I deliver the tiniest flick to her clit. "At best, it's just a little payback for how you've tortured me. Are you going to keep still?"

She nods.

"I'm sorry, I didn't hear that."

"Yes. I'll try to be good for you."

"Next time, try that with a little sincerity."

Her soft laughter turns to a whimper as I spread her open, sliding a long lick along one side of her pussy, barely grazing her clit. She lifts her hips, trying to control the contact, crying out in frustration as I move lower. I deliver a series of shallow circles and tiny licks, working my tongue higher… before starting again.

Her hands ball into fists, her body taut beneath me as my mouth pays homage to her pussy.

"I'm so hard for you." *A swipe of tongue. A long, velvety groan into the center of her.* "You're so fucking delicious." *A press of lips to the soft rise of her clit.* "Like peaches and cream." My God, the musky, womanly scent of her and the sense of her pale flesh under me drives me to the fucking brink as I slip my hands under her arse, lifting her to my mouth.

"Oh God!" she cries out as I finally inhale her swollen clit. "Oh, Whit!" Her hands reach for my head again before they drop back to the bed.

Leaning on my elbow, I make a rough-sounding *tsk*. "Oh dear. You know what that means. I'll have to start again."

She cries plaintively as I press my head between her legs and begin the sweet, terrible seduction all over again, kissing her everywhere except where she really wants me, where she needs me, my tongue drawing maddeningly close to her clit before sliding away again.

"Whit, please. I'll be good, just please let me come." There's a hitch in her throat, her plea desperate.

"I don't know that I'm finished." My voice is a low rumble as I wrap my fingers around her ankle, lifting her foot to the bed. "Not when you pulse so prettily for me."

"Please," she begs as her thighs begin to shake. Her pussy contracting in a wave again.

"Maybe I'll be kind and put you out of your misery." My tone might be cool, but the knot in my belly tightens as I return my mouth to where she's wet and hot. "If you tell me what you want. Tell me properly. Use all the filthy words."

"Please, *please*, put your mouth on my clit. Suck on it— fuck me! I'll come so hard for you, I promise. Just please let me!"

Less is more sometimes. And sometimes you just want to hear her beg you.

With a growl, I engulf her clit. I suck on it. Circle and flick. I make out with her pussy until her low moans bounce from the walls of the room and her inhibitions dissolve like sugar on my tongue. The way she rides my tongue, the sound of my name on her lips. It drives me fucking wild, my tongue coated in her heavenly slickness. I'm neither able to taste enough or touch enough—*feel enough*—as she thrashes, wrapping her legs around my head. A clunk sounds as something hits the floor. The glass water bottle, I'd guess, the thought barely registering as she presses her heels between my shoulder blades, making good on her promise. Pleasure coats her thighs as I lick her again and again until her mouth is full of filth, and her climax a thing of loud, unrestrained beauty.

"That's it, darling. Ride my face. Come on my tongue."

I give her no time to come down, no soft licks or delicate tongue as I scramble from the floor, putting my knee to the mattress. Her pussy is a slick slide against my stomach as I wrap my arms around her, lifting her against me.

"What are you...?"

"Just getting us a little more comfortable." I press her down, and she whimpers at the drag of my cock when I reach across the bed to pull the nightstand drawer open. I move back, simultaneously ripping open a condom with my teeth.

"You're staring, not that I'm complaining."

"Of course you're not." Her mouth hitches in the corner.

"I wonder what it is you're trying to imply."

"Me? Nothing." The bedding rustles as she gives her head a tiny shake. "You're just being you, and why wouldn't you be. But..." She worries her lip a little as though hesitant to go on.

"Tell me." Her breath hitches, her eyes glued to where I take my cock in my hand.

"Do you ever think of me when you touch yourself?" she asks, her gaze lifting warily.

I give my cock a thorough tug, for her benefit mostly, my smile spilling as slow as molasses. "Since you appeared and decided to torture me, my right hand and my cock have never been quite so intimately acquainted. Not since I was a teenager, at any rate."

"Really?"

"Don't look so pleased. That wasn't a compliment." It absolutely was. "It's all on you. And it will be *all on you* if I don't get this on." I raise the open condom packet between my forefinger and middle finger.

"I'd like to see what that looks like sometime."

"Yeah?"

"I've seen it before, you know. In porn."

"Then I might show you the real thing. Some other time."

"If I'm a good girl?"

My gaze flicks over her. "Let's not make goals unobtainable."

"What's that supposed to mean?" she ask, faux aggrieved.

"I'm not sure being good is your forte. You're like that rhyme about the girl with the pearl. When she's good she's very, *very* good. But when she's bad, she's fucking delightful. Oh look," I add, bending and swiping my thumb over the rise of her clit. "You are the girl with the pearl."

She laughs, flashing that gorgeous gap as she lifts her wrists above her head, stretching out in a supple line of attitude and wanton need. "You don't think I can be good?"

"Not without incentive."

Suddenly, she looks like the cat that licked the cream. She draws her foot up the bed and drops her knee provocatively. "I can be good, Whit. In fact, I think I can be really good. Ditch the condom, *Daddy*. I have the implant."

I don't answer, at least, not immediately. I think my heart might've stopped working for a second. *Skipped a few beats?* Fuck her bare; did I just hear that right?

"I mean, not that you have to." Her knee begins to close, the insecurity in her tone penetrating my lustful stupor. It's all I can do not to fall on her to fuck her immediately. I manage not to do the latter, but the former happens before I even realize. She is a gift. A fucking gift.

"You're sure?" I press my lips to the juncture of her neck and shoulder to hide what her offer does to me. The way I feel right now, I'd fuck her while wearing a rubber kitchen glove. "Because if you're not—"

"You would never put me at risk," she says, pressing her hand to my cheek.

Her breath hitches as I turn my head, and my lips graze her hand. "Your trust undoes me." Taking her hand in mine, I lift it once more above her head, then push up onto my palms.

"I can't believe we're really going to do this." Her voice trembles with emotion, but I can no longer speak, so I press my lips to hers. It's a small kiss, but one that seems to take on a life all of its own. Passionate lips and teeth and tongue, the slide of her hot breath across my lips making my abs tense with need, endorphins and chemical lust rushing through my veins.

"Does this not feel real to you?" Do I think it or say it as I drop my hips, sliding the crown of my cock to where she's so open.

Her reply is all gasp as I breach her so slowly, I know it's hurting us both. *Pain in the best kind of way.* "It feels unreal." Her voice is a delicate slide across my cheek as I stare down the channel between our bodies, past the sacred dips and valleys of her to where her body accepts mine. "My God. Oh, Whit."

I am bathed in her bliss as I push in fully.

She's so—Jesus! I'm not sure a word has been invented for how her body feels wrapped around me. Hot. Tight. Silky. All those words and more. Buried to my hilt, inside her, she pulses around me. Her hands scrabble at my back as I withdraw, her fingers almost piercing as, with a snap of my hips I drive into her again, my grunt countering her cry.

"You're so big," she pants beneath me.

"And you're perfect. Feel how we fit." As though I need to prove the point, I cradle her jaw in my hand as I thrust slowly inside her. My eyes dare hers to look away as I fuck her slowly, steadily. Her gaze never wavers when I pull back and drive deep inside her, though the movement would be reason enough.

So fucking perfect. It's all so fucking perfect.

"You feel like you were made for me." Her whimpers turn to cries as I deliver a series of deep, punishing thrusts, our mouths meeting messily on my grunting upthrust.

"Oh, darling." I tighten my grip as I begin to flex and pump, grinding against her as her body coaxes me on. "That's right," I rasp as she goes silent. Goes rigid. "Come for me."

She gasps. I feel it on my face. I feel her pulsing around me.

I groan, undulating above her, not daring to move. "Amelia, I can feel you coming around my cock."

Her body milks mine for all that it's worth—and she can have me because right now, there is nothing to stop this from happening. Fire rushes through my veins, white-hot and intense, as my own climax begins to build. I'm unable to stop, unable to process the waves of pleasure drowning me as I hammer myself home one final time.

A pulsing rush of sensation overcomes me. I see lights and stars, my mind punching out as my body takes over.

19

MIMI

I WAKE like I've been shaken violently, my body trembling under the sheets. I'm alone, and the room is silent. There are no sounds of children kicking a ball in the neighbor's yard. No hum of the radio playing downstairs in the kitchen. Just the sound of my heart hammering in my ears. It's disturbingly still, the air around me pitchblack.

Like a coffin.

I jerk upright with a sick sense of panic, pressing my hand over my tripping heart.

I can't be dead, I think as I glance down, feeling a slight breeze of central air. *Dead people aren't naked*. Well, maybe they are at some point, but not in heaven, surely. But then I realize heavenly bodies probably aren't wrapped in sheets that reek of sex. They don't smell like masculine shower products.

I rub my cheek against my shoulder and stretch like a cat. I smell like Whit. And rightly so. His bed. His bath. His bathing products he used to wash me with in middle of the night. I shiver as I recall the soapy slide of him. I can still feel the press of him between my legs.

I fumble for the bedside lamp, then pad across the vast bedroom floor toward the bathroom. Air brushes my skin, a sensation I wouldn't ordinarily recognize. I feel wholly sensual as I stride across the floor, uninhibited by my nakedness. Am I changed? Has one night with Whit altered me so much? According to the mirror, not so much. I look a fright. My hair looks like a huge tumbleweed, my skin marked and reddened in places my own mouth couldn't reach. But I am stupidly happy—I mean, who isn't not to be dead—my smile so ridiculously goofy as I brush my fingers through my hair.

While I might not be dead, I'm pretty sure I got a glimpse of heaven last night during orgasm number two. *The first time I felt Whit move inside me.* I reach out, gripping the cold stone vanity, screwing my eyes tight as my body undergoes a ripple of sensory memory. It was everything I ever imagined and a thousand times more. His shoulders over me, blocking out the light, made me feel so small. The way he'd moved inside me, he owned me in those moments. The taut length of his neck, his expression almost pained as he'd pressed himself to me, undulating as he'd reached his climax.

It wasn't sex. It was a communion. A mind-bending, thigh-shaking, religious experience. And I will never feel the same about sex again. Except I will—I'll feel like this over and over for what's left of my not-quite six-month hiatus from my real life. And if that thought doesn't make me smile, I don't know what's responsible for this ridiculous happy dance!

Back in the bedroom, I exchange the towel I'd wrapped around myself for Whit's shirt from last night. As I pull it from the chair, I note my dress and underwear, wavering for a moment in my decision. Should I get dressed properly? Or take a clean shirt from his closet? But then it wouldn't smell of him, I decide as I slide it on, pressing my nose into the collar as I inhale. His scent makes my insides turn all gooey again.

"You seem deep in thought."

I press my hand to my chest as I spin to the doorway. "Oh my gosh, you scared me!"

"Sorry," he says, not sorry at all, judging by his expression and the way his eyes flit over my bare legs. He's already dressed in dark jeans and a gray fine knit sweater that clings to the flat of his stomach and molds to his biceps. He slides his hands into his pockets, resting his shoulder against the doorframe.

"How long have you been standing there?"

"It's too early for confession. Breakfast?" he asks, his expression turning purposely bland.

"What's on offer?"

"Keep looking at me like that and you'll be breakfast." His lips curl, part seduction, part amused.

That is *totally* where my mind went, but is it any wonder when he looks so delicious? "Who says I'm looking at you like anything?" I answer instead.

"You think I have an overactive imagination?"

I affect a slight shrug.

"Pity." The way his eyes slide over me feels like the brush of silk against my skin.

"How's your lip?" It looks better than last night. It's just a little swollen, and there's barely a hint of bruising.

His finger lifts as though to touch it. "Why don't you come and take a look at it yourself?"

I can't believe he went for that asshole, and I can't believe I find physical violence such a turn-on. "Looks good from here." I slide the sides of his shirt a little closer, feeling as though my naughty thoughts are exposed.

"Are you coming?" he asks with a tiny smirk, as tempting as the devil himself. "I have coffee."

"The prospect is exciting, but..." I tamp down my ridiculousness even though he does chuckle. "Coffee would be lovely. Caffeine might help pull me from this sex haze."

"That would be a shame."

My cheeks start to burn. Why aren't my brain and mouth friends?

"Coffee it is." He straightens, pushing from the doorframe. "Breakfast has just arrived."

"Just give me a minute to put on some clothes?"

Whit sort of pauses as though considering something, then says, "What you're wearing looks good."

I glance down at his shirt. The buttons aren't yet fastened, but I'm not flashing anything. Nothing he hasn't already seen, anyway. *Touched. Kissed.* "Yeah?" I say as I glance up.

"Yes, definitely. If it was up to me, I'd tell you to wear the shirt." He gives his head a shake as though rousing himself from some thought. "Seeing you in it is all kinds of hot."

My nerve endings begin to flicker and flash like a pinball machine. I've read about this. How men like to see women dressed in their clothes, that it gives them a kick. Some sense of ownership.

"The shirt and nothing else." He laughs as he delivers his verdict.

"That's a surprise. Not."

"I'm just saying, underwear is optional." He turns, his footsteps echoing along the hall.

You're a hot little fuck in lingerie.

With an unsteady breath, I reach out and catch the back

of the chair as the echo of his words come from nowhere. What the man can do to my body with one look is nobody's business. But the things he says create an actual visceral reaction within me. And the things he does... well, I'm not sure words have been created to describe that.

My stomach decides at that moment to gurgle. It's ready for breakfast, even if the rest of me is ready to *be* breakfast. I hurriedly braid my hair. The next few months are going to be such an experience. An experience of a lifetime, I think with an internal *squee*. Winding my hair tie around the ends, I practically hop, skip, and jump out into the living room.

"...think that's the stupidest idea in the history of ideas."

I hear Whit's voice before I see him. His back is turned to me, his phone pressed to his ear, the bulk of his bicep visible under his sweater thanks to the way he holds it.

"Well, because I said so."

I pause. I can't hear who's on the other end of the phone and maybe I shouldn't want to. Should I excuse myself and let the man take his call in private? I don't, mainly because the cadence of the other person's voice seems female. It could be one of his sisters? I liked meeting Heather last night, not that I get the sense that this is who he's talking to. I don't think she'd stand for Whit taking that highhanded tone with her. She was way too cool.

"I don't have to give you a reason," he adds, the words spluttery with laughter. "I don't!" The knot in my stomach eases, thanks to his demeanor. It could definitely be one of his sisters. "Because it's fucking inconvenient, that's why."

Note to self: learn to swear in British. It sounds so much less offensive.

"Tell them what you like. It's not a public pool. You can't traipse in with all and sundry when you feel like it. Yes, I know your friend's names aren't *all* and *sundry*." Pressing his phone between his shoulder and ear, he pulls a couple of cups from the top of a fancy-looking coffee machine. "Yeah, maybe. I said maybe next weekend." He's smiling as he turns, the wattage turning up as he spots me, moving his phone to his other ear. "No... and even if I did, it would have nothing to do with you. Yeah, well, maybe I have. So? Maybe I like them dirty." He gives me a heavy-lidded glance, the kind that makes my insides thrum as a muffled parrot-like shriek sounds down the line. Whit grimaces, pulling the phone back from his ear. "If you didn't want to know, you shouldn't have asked."

I pull a tall stool out from under the island counter, muffling my own shriek as my bare thighs touch the cold leather seat.

"I've got to go, Primrose. Yes," he adds in the vein of one being worn down. "I said I'd think about it. Okay, see you tomorrow." He hangs up and places his phone on the countertop between us. "Sorry about that."

"Martinis?" I suggest with an unrepentant grin.

"It's a bit early for me."

"Your phone call," I add with a laugh as he very obviously misunderstands me. "I'm guessing you like them dirty."

"James Bond can keep them. I'm not a fan. It wasn't martinis Primrose was squawking about. According to her, I prefer dirty girls to her company."

"Excuse me?" I splutter.

He begins to laugh, the sound deep and rich. "She didn't say *you* were dirty. Not exactly. Her nose is out of joint because I wouldn't let her and her friends hang out at the residents' spa and pool. She accused me of preferring the company of dirty women to that of my baby sister."

"And do you?"

"I prefer your company," he says, leaning his elbow on the marble. "And dirty, like underwear, is always optional."

I'm not touching that. Not with a ten foot pole. "She doesn't know I'm here, does she?"

He pushes up again. "She was just guessing. As well as trying to wear me down. Probably because she doesn't hear the word *no* often enough."

"In general?"

"Probably just from me," he adds with a shrug. "Habits are hard to kill."

"So long as she doesn't know I'm here. It's just, I haven't been here long, Whit. You're the boss and—"

"You don't want to be that cliché?"

I frown. "I'm not sure anyone does."

"Can we just ignore that my sister called? Go back to how things were a few minutes ago." He scoops up the coffee cups by the handles with one hand. "I'm assuming you like your coffee the same way as you like your men?"

"I'm almost afraid to ask."

"Hot, dark, and in your lap." He gives a comically suggestive wiggle of his brows.

"That was so bad." But I love this side of him. "I get the sneaking suspicion that you're a morning person."

"That sounded like an insult," he says over his shoulder.

"People who get out of bed with a smile on their face are to be treated with suspicion."

Putting the cups down, he turns and presses his palm to the countertop behind, muscles and tendons standing to attention as he levels me with a look that's nothing short of searing. "You're not telling me you haven't caught yourself smiling this morning, that your mind hasn't wandered to last night?"

"That would be telling," I demur, *floving* seeing this side to him. He's thought about last night, and it's making him smile!

Turning his back to me, he shoves one cup under the coffee machine spout and the other to the top. Cuffing his wrist with his free fingers, he shoves the sleeves of his sweater up his forearm, highlighting toned and tan forearms. "Latte?" he asks over his shoulder.

"Please." Sliding one of the cups under the spout thingy, he presses a button, and the grinder begins to whir. He heats the cup, taps something, fits something into the right hole, and all the while, the fine knit of his sweater moves like a second skin, molding to the strong muscles in his back and shoulders. If he was my local barista, I know I'd develop an addiction. "Total coffee shop porn."

"What was that?" He twists his head over his shoulder.

"Your fancy-looking machine."

"I'm a bit of a coffee snob thanks to working as a barista when I came back from the States."

"I bet the place you worked was like Abercrombie and Fitch, but for coffee."

"What?"

"Nothing." I smile and shake my head as though he must've been hearing things. But as an idea, a business plan, it would totally work. "Was this before you got the job at the bank?"

"My first job was as an analyst at an investment bank. Then I moved into trading derivatives." My face must reflect my lack of knowledge as he adds, "Derivatives are financial securities and, as a trader, you buy and sell them on behalf of financial institutions, hedge funds, and the like."

"Like a stock broker?"

"Yeah." His finger rasps against the stubble on his jaw. "I had a knack." He shrugs. "And a lot of luck. I made a lot of money and a lot of connections, and it set me on the path to this." He flicks out a hand, indicating the multimillion-dollar bachelor pad. "I hit the big time."

Then he hit the big time. Or rather, worked very hard to get where he is today. Whit comes from a regular family, not from a monied background. Boy done good. Boy done *really* good.

"I suspect your success has a lot more to do with the person you are than a bunch of random luck." Connor always said Whit was a math whizz and I already know he's the kind of man people gravitate to. *Women especially.*

"It keeps me out of trouble," he says with the kind of gleam that makes my stomach flip.

"Can I do anything to help?" *Before we end up having sex in your stylish kitchen?*

"You could move some of the containers over to the table." He gestures to the fancy boxes and bags from some French-sounding patisserie.

That I can do.

"Is this a usual Saturday morning breakfast for you?" I ask as I loop a finger under the delicate ribbon of a couple of pink cake boxes and carry them over to the large dining table where two place settings have already been set. Plates, glasses, and silverware. There's a half-filled pastry platter, a tropical fruit salad, and a carafe of juice, and that's just the start of it.

"Is that your way of asking if I regularly have women overnight?" I pretend not to hear that over the noise of the coffee machine. "I'm usually in the office by now."

That's not really an answer to my or, rather his, question. His question and now my piqued curiosity.

"You work weekends?" I begin to pull out croissants and

containers of berries, tiny cakes that look more like works of art.

"I work whenever I'm not sleeping."

"You sure you're not expecting more people?" I ask as I put the contents of the second box on a platter.

"You got me. Because I don't do this very often, I thought I'd invite all the women I've slept with this year over for brunch."

"Looks like we're expecting a lot of women," I say, my eyes sliding over all the goodies. "I hope they're hungry." Weird, but I've only just taken in that this is food and I'm not really hungry. How is that even possible? I guess my mind is on other things as I lean over the back of a chair to deposit a couple of linen napkins on a table mat. I'm so lost in my own thoughts that I don't realize Whit's behind me until his hand curls around my hip as he sets both coffee cups down. My skin reacts like tinder to his touch, wildfire spreading across my skin.

"You're the first woman I've had stay over in a long time."

"That seems almost a shame." My answer is barely a whisper, my fingers grasping the back of the chair as his lips brush against my hair. "Maybe gifts like yours ought to be shared."

His laughter is dark and velvety, and his hand doesn't move, almost as though he's forgotten it's there. "Like a public service?"

"For the good of womankind."

"I didn't say I was a saint."

"I think I've already gathered that." I don't think he's forgotten he's holding me, not as his fingers tighten and his lips slide down my neck. "Leif Whittington, Patron saint of wayward women."

"Are you wayward, Amelia?" His lips tighten in a sucking

bite, my resulting sigh a taut, needy thing. I close my eyes and swallow as his hand slides from my hip to my stomach, pulling me against him. As he sucks at my skin, blood rushes to the surface as though in greeting.

"I wasn't. I think I might be getting there."

"You're so lovely to rile." His words are a hot breath against my neck as his other hand rises, wrapping around me in a nothing short of a full-body hug as he says, "Let's get some food inside you."

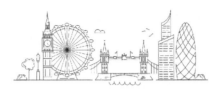

20

MIMI

WHIT PULLS out a chair for me and I slide a decorous hand under my butt to pull down his shirt, not wanting to repeat the stool situation. If he notices, he politely doesn't say so.

"Champagne?" I ask sheen he suddenly produces a bottle of the fancy French looking stuff.

"Let's call it brunch rather than breakfast. No one ever complains about alcohol at brunch." He splashes some into a couple of tulip flutes.

"Just call me a heathen," I say, topping mine up with orange juice. Old habits die hard. Plus, I'm not really a fan of champagne. But a mimosa... "This really is a lot of food for two people," I murmur, shaking out my napkin with unsteady fingers.

Whit slides into his seat at the head of the table, the morning sunlight cresting his head, turning the tiny strands of gray at his temples silver. "You haven't seen my appetite yet."

"Haven't I?" Reaching out, I pluck the clear top from a tub of berries, popping a raspberry between my lips.

"Tip of the iceberg," he replies with a slight narrowing of

his gaze. Something tells me we're not talking about breakfast preferences. "And stop staring at my graying hair."

I burst out laughing. "I wasn't!" His lips twist in some show of distrust. But that's all it is, a show. "I think it makes you look very distinguished," I say, trying for sincerity.

"Yes, just what every thirty-six-year-old man wants to hear." He slides me an unimpressed look.

"You should because I dig it."

"Oh good. I'll take the Grecian 2000 out of my virtual shopping cart," he deadpans as he lifts his coffee to his lips.

"Yes, do." I catch myself the moment before I add, *Daddy*.

"You know, since you arrived," he adds over the rim, "I'm sure I find another dozen every morning."

"You don't even have a dozen now," I scoff. "It's not even gray. It's just a little salt in with the pepper."

"Eat your breakfast," comes his mock-stern reply.

"You must have a very sweet tooth," I say, reaching for a miniature croissant and tearing off a chunk. "Oh, chocolate." What's better than a croissant? One with a chocolatey surprise.

"I might've gone a bit overboard," he admits.

"Maybe you were hungry when you ordered and got a little carried away?" He watches as I pop the flaky pastry into my mouth, his eyes darkening as I cast my eyes heavenward. "Oh, my gosh, these are good." I press my knuckle to my lips as I speak. "Sorry." My shoulders move with a sneeze-like laugh.

"What for?"

"Speaking with my mouth full. It can't be a good look."

"That all depends on what you have in your mouth."

"You're so bad!" I point the remains of my croissant at him when he leans over the table and snatches it with his teeth. Those tiger eyes level on me, his jaw working as he chews. I find myself swallowing along with the powerful movements in his throat while imagining myself pressing my mouth there to feel the movement.

Picking up my fork, I spear a piece of mango from a bowl of fruit salad.

"And you have such an appetite. A lust for life."

I feel suddenly exposed, more so than for just sitting at the dining table in nothing but his shirt.

"If I go for groceries when I'm hungry," I begin to babble, conscious of the sudden silence, "I seem to buy all kinds of cake."

His expression remains mild as I pop it between my teeth. "That must be what happened to me."

"You were hungry?"

"Obviously." But he's not looking at the feast before him. He's looking at me.

I purse my lips, mainly to hide my pleasure. "Are you going to tell me why we're sitting down to a breakfast that would make Marie Antoinette orgasm?"

"Only Marie Antoinette?"

"I bet you're more the disgusting protein shake kind of breakfast, aren't you?" I say, changing the subject. He doesn't need to hear how, if I were here by myself, I'd struggle not to fill my plate with one of everything. My name is Mimi, and I'm a sugar fiend.

"You're wrong." He presses his forearm to the table, leaning in as though to part with a secret. "This morning, the only thing I was hungry for was you. It was get out of bed or devour you."

"I wouldn't have minded," I answer quietly.

"I kept you awake a long time last night."

"I think we kept each other awake." Because every time

we'd settle, skin flushed and a little breathless, Whit might throw his arm around me or maybe my leg would be over his thigh. We'd snuggle—yeah, snuggle. There'd be whispers in the dark, then tiny strokes that would ignite. Before long, we'd be back to that rolling, raging inferno of can't get enough.

"Yes, that's true enough."

"So come on. What's with all the cake?"

"Not just cake," he protests. "Fruit and fancy yogurt." Y-o-gt; I just love the cute way he says that.

"And cake. A lot of cake." I find my fingers reaching for a tart.

"I might've heard someone say she liked cake."

My hand stills in midair. "When?"

"And she'd better like cake," he says, watching me like I'm the cake and he's the binge eater.

Oh, Lord, he can binge on me any day of the week.

"She does," I admit shyly, not quite able to look at him as I pick up the tiny piece of lemon deliciousness. He ordered this feast for me and that kind of robs me of breath. I mean, what am I supposed to say? Thank you? Also, do I get to take home what I don't finish? "What are these?" I find myself asking instead as I point at three bronzed cakes that look like they were made in Jell-O molds. They're kind of the ugly ducklings of this culinary feast.

"The things that look like inverted nipples?" At Whit's unimpressed description, I snort and clap a hand to my mouth. "And Heather thinks that's normal," he says with a disparaging shake of his head.

"Normal is overrated. I happen to think Heather is a very good judge of character."

"You might be onto something there. She thinks El is a tosser," he adds conversationally.

"I'm guess that's something not very complimentary." I fold forward a little as my shoulders sag. "Please don't make this a thing." I don't want to come between him and his brother. "Don't be angry with him. He was just trying to be friendly."

"Friendly." He quirks a brow as he reaches for his champagne.

"Yeah, I think so."

"I think not so. You need to make it very clear to him that you're not interested. I suggest you use plain words with short syllables."

"He's not stupid, Whit."

"I mean it, Amelia. Make it crystal clear."

"I'm not interested in your brother. I made it clear enough to him last night—and he didn't seem to take the news badly. Remember the server?" More than ever it's apparent that this thing between us needs to be secret. El isn't hung up on me but Whit seems intent on laboring over the point. I refuse to come between them, though it seems only one of them has a problem.

He points at the cakes. "Those ugly little tits are what Brin plans to feed you tomorrow when he takes you for coffee."

"You got me canelés?"

"Not very impressive, are they? For all his waxing lyrical. Though they were a pain in the arse to track down."

"Why did you?"

"The café El was talking about is closed on Sunday. I thought I would have to get them flown in from Bordeaux."

"That doesn't answer my question. Why would you go to the effort?"

"Because I can. Because I wanted to. Because you have a

sweet tooth and because you sounded so interested when he was banging on about them."

"I was just being polite," I say with a laugh. "He brought me coffee!"

"Yeah, well, so did I, so you'd better drink it," he grumbles.

"It's not a competition." I reach for my mimosa. "And even if it was," I say, putting it back down. "You've already won."

"Yeah?"

"You won before he'd even set eyes on me. You won again when you ordered me lunch that day, and when you made sure I got home when my skirt split. I'm not interested in your brother, Whit. There is no competition."

"It doesn't hurt to hear it."

"I'm glad you're listening. Don't make this a thing. You're a good man, and you love your brother. Not to mention, you're one hell of a screw."

"Amelia!" He says my name with the cadence of a Southern aunt spotting someone wearing white after Labor Day.

"Those years of practice obviously paid off." I allow my gaze to slide over him as though he were a sweet treat. He's certainly delectable.

"All those years and I didn't realize you were a little voyeur."

I'm saved from answering as his phone buzzes in the kitchen.

"I should've turned it off," he mutters, pushing back his chair. He pauses as he passes, curling his hands around my shoulders and tracing his lips around my ear. "Eat some sugar. Hydrate."

"Why?" I call after he pulls away.

"You'll need the energy."

I try to contain my smile by nibbling at the tart. I don't need to try for long because the citrusy flavors meld so well with that of the butter case, I take a proper bite. I really ought to try the canelés, given the trouble he went to get them, right?

"Dan, how are you, mate?"

That must be his brother Dan judging by the effusive happiness that seeps into his greeting. I take a mouthful of my cooling coffee, then pour a little more vivid orange pulp-rich juice into my champagne. It's tart and sweet in an odd contrast to the dry champagne, plus the sugary cakes I need to stop gorging on.

"No, no worries at all," Whit says into his phone. I can almost feel his eyes burning into the back of my head as I look out over the park. It looks like a nice day for a walk. The sky is so blue and the sun vivid, its warmth seeping through the glass.

It feels like a layer of sheer bliss.

"Yeah, of course I have time." Whit falls quiet, presumably as Dan fills him in on his news. I guess Dan must be the adventurous type, given he's trekking around Thailand. I'm not cut out for living out of a backpack, not that I could put my parents through it, either, I guess. Coming to London is one thing. Jungles and questionable medical facilities would push them right over the edge.

"Well, that's great, Dan, but I don't know what to tell you except go with your gut."

My gut says stop feeding me cake, so I finish my coffee while trying not to listen to Whit's conversation while he doles out cautious advice that sounds like it might be about his brother's love life.

"Sorry about that." He touches my shoulder as he passes.

"No problem. Everything okay?"

"Dan has met a girl." His smile leaks through his explanation. "He wanted some advice, though why from me is anyone's guess. He should've rung Heather. She's the only one of us who has a successful relationship."

"Are you looking for a relationship?" I ask, half hopeful, half horrified.

"Fuck no." He laughs unhappily. "I don't have time. Besides, who'd want to take me on? I'd barely be around."

"I'm sure lots of women would take that chance."

"And then regret it," he replies seriously. "VirTu takes up so much of my life and my headspace, I just don't have it within me to commit to a relationship."

"But you have sex."

He doesn't reply but for a secretive kind of smile.

"Is it more the case that you don't want to take on anything else?" As the words leave my mouth, a sudden sense of foreboding washes over me.

"Yeah, I suppose. I have work, and I have my family. Sex is more like working out, taking care of myself. It's not an emotional drain."

"Drain?"

"Commitment," he amends. "A relationship is a commitment."

"So who do you normally have sex with? If you don't mind me asking?"

"Did I say I didn't mind?"

"No, but you know you're going to tell me anyway." I slide a piece of pineapple into my mouth as a way to keep myself from talking. I want to crawl into this man's brain and poke around. Learn all his deliciously dirty secrets and feast on them for a little while.

"You're talking about that night, aren't you?"

"And the girl who looked like me. Do you have a type?"

"Yes. Girls who do as they're told."

"You lie," I say with a chuckle, actually feeling a blush move across my skin. My gaze falls to the table again. If we're just having sex, what's with the banquet? I paint on a bright smile again, unable to ignore the thoughts beginning to swim through my head. This is what Whit does. He takes care of those he cares for. No matter what he says, this isn't going to be just sex. He's going to see me as one of those he needs to take care of.

I won't let that happen. I refuse to become one of his responsibilities.

"You've gone quiet." My head jerks up at his words. "And not the good kind of quiet. You're not worried, are you?"

Yes. Very worried. Thanks, fluttering heart, for pointing out what a bad bet I am. He can't be responsible for me. I won't let him. "What would I be worried about?"

"We had sex without protection, and now you're thinking of the women I've slept with."

I shake my head. "I know you wouldn't put me at risk." That realization should've been my first warning sign. "Do all of your siblings come to you for advice?" I rush on, desperate to change the subject.

"Mainly the younger ones." His fingers twitch on the napkin. "When Dad died, that side of things just sort of fell to me."

Along with a million others, I'd guess. "Death leaves such a hole."

We both fall quiet to our respective thoughts, our own

missing loved ones before he seems to shrug off the memories. "I'm nearly through it now. Lavender is out of her teens as of this month, so maybe she'll grow up a bit. Or pigs might fly. Anyway, she'll be finished with university soon and out in the big, wide world. In theory," he adds under his breath. "Which just leaves the baby of the family, Primrose. And then I'm all done."

He sounds more like a dad and less like a daddy.

"Do you want some water?" Heat spreads across my cheeks as I reach for the fancy ice cap filtered water, which is sitting in a pool of its own condensation. But it's not my table, so I shouldn't complain. I guess someone doesn't like their water room temperature, judging by the ice dancing in my water glass as I fill it up.

"Juice, please." I pass over the OJ as he murmurs his thanks, taking the fancy glass carafe from my hands. I think for a moment he doesn't want me to pour when he leans back, setting the bottle on the credenza. I watch as he tops up his champagne and places that out of reach, too.

Okay, a little weird.

"Is Dan the baby?"

"No. He's next to Heather. Older than Lavender and Primrose. He's had a bit of a rough time."

"Don't they ever go to your mom when they need advice?"

"When it suits them," he says a little darkly.

"Death really does change the family dynamic. It must be hard on you." The weight of the family balanced on your shoulders, siblings squawking like baby birds.

"I think the harder thing has been the change in our lifestyles."

"How do you mean?"

"VirTu," he answers simply. He runs his finger down his

glass, pressing a line through the condensation. "Money changes everything, attitudes first and foremost."

"But it's your money."

"And I've spoiled them with it," he adds with an unhappy laugh. "Brin, El, and Heather are okay. They'd already made their own way in the world before I... well, before I had all this." He makes a gesture with his hand to indicate the space, a testament to his success. His money, yeah, but by the sound of things, he thinks the way his younger siblings behave is down to him. *His responsibility.*

"You worry about them."

"It's hard not to," he admits softly, "especially when you know Dan is off trying to find himself after a stint in rehab."

"Oh, Whit. I'm sorry." I don't say anymore as his body language refutes my sympathy.

"The girls." He sighs. "What happened the other night with Lavender is the least of it. Primrose is all right so far, just a bit overindulged."

"But they're not kids." Reaching out, I press my hand over his. "They're old enough to make their own decisions."

"It would be easier if they didn't." Though he smiles, I know he means it. I guess I can see why control is his thing.

"I don't want to overstep, but your mom is so lovely. Can't she step in?"

"That's probably my fault, too." As he leans back in his chair, his hand slides out from under mine. "She was a mess when Dad died. You know what it's like," he says as his gaze slides to mine.

"Yeah, I do."

"There's just this void where that person used to be. But when Dad went, the void was two people wide because Polly just... disappeared. She retreated into herself. She couldn't cope. That's such a stupid phrase," he mutters. "To cope is to survive, and we're all here. We got through it."

"But nothing is the same."

"Yeah." He rakes both hands through his hair, leaving furrows where his fingers were. "I mean, Polly is better now. More present. But, let's face it, when you get picked up drunk in the street and the police shove you in a cell to sober you up, are you going to call your hardheaded brother to come pick you up, knowing the only price you'll pay is listening to him rant and rave as he drives you home? Or will you call your tenderhearted mother, the woman you don't want to hurt but that you know will weep and see your failings as her own. The woman who might, if you're unlucky enough, book you both a place at a weekend retreat where there is nothing to do but talk about your *feelings*. That's not a rhetorical question, by the way. If you want to know the answer, ask Daniel."

"He went to Thailand to get over the bonding session?"

"So he says."

"If you don't mind me asking, why does Daniel... why does he..."

"Have a normal name?" The corner of Whit's mouth quirks with amusement. "He chooses to go by his middle name. His actual name is Orion."

"Oh. Sorry."

"What for? You didn't give us ridiculous names."

"Leif isn't ridiculous," I demur.

"No, not if you're a tree."

I giggle softly. I love that he can laugh at himself. "A tree or maybe someone Scandinavian." Or maybe just a wonderfully gorgeous man.

"Which clearly I'm not," he says, holding out his hands. Look at me in all my glory. I stifle a sigh because oh, I do.

"Anyway, we all became very good with our fists, thanks to our ridiculous names."

"That I know to be true."

"Come here."

"What?" His sultry purr catches me off guard.

"Come here," he repeats as he pushes back his chair and pats his knee.

This man. He has a heart as big as a house.

Oh my God. I'm a monster. How could I do this to him?

The thoughts come from nowhere, they just sort of drop into my head, the implications of my actions suddenly crystalline. I feel weighted to the spot where before, I'd felt nothing but free. Fearless and reckless, drunk on the power I seemed to wield.

But now, now I feel ill.

I shouldn't be here. I should've left last night. Left after sex. This feels like we might've set a precedent. Hell, we shouldn't even have had sex! Just look at all this food! I mean, what's it all for? What is this about? Because I like cake? Because Whit likes me?

He is worth so much more than this, worth more than being used by me. Though I guess if I asked him, he'd argue strongly for the opposite. He'd probably insist he's quite happy to be used. *As hard and as often as I like.* But that would only be because he doesn't know the whole of it. And more than that, I now see that he won't be able to resist adding me to the list of his responsibilities. This is why he was so dead against us. This is what he was trying to do for my brother— to do what he does for his own family. He guides them. Looks after them. And now he'll want to do that for me.

Maybe even after I go home.

He deserves better than that, better than me.

Even if he's not the one living on borrowed time?

Especially so.

The guilt weighs like a stone on my chest, but I push it all away at the same time as I scoot back my chair. He wants to hold me and despite what I now know, I want to be held. Because I'm selfish and shallow and because the truth is painful.

I could lose my heart to him but what good would come of it? That piddling thing would be no good for him.

Another step closer, the shame and remorse swimming through my head.

What if he fell for me? What a catastrophe that would be.

Do my eyes leak regret as I stand by the side of his chair?

Whatever happens between us, he won't let me walk out of his life. The realization makes my stomach hurt; the truth feels sickening. I think too much of him to make myself another weight on his chain.

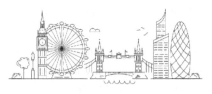

21

WHIT

"Did you eat enough?" I ask as she distractedly, rather than obediently, comes to stand next to my chair. My shirt hangs a little from one shoulder, her silver bangle disappearing under the length of a folded sleeve. I'm surprised I haven't passed out from a lack of blood flow. She looks so hot in the thing.

But one question remains. Underwear: did she forgo or no?

"No canelés," she states with a tiny moue.

"Good." Even if they were a pain in the arse to source, they were El's thing.

"I nibbled on other things."

"Nibbled," I repeat, though not in the same vein as I press my hands to her waist and maneuver her between me and the table.

"I thought you wanted me to sit on your knee."

"I want to look at you first." I clasp my hands to her hips and allow my gaze to crawl up from her pink-painted toenails to where her legs disappear under the hem of my shirt. But as I sit forward, I realize something isn't quite right. "What's wrong?"

"I feel like we should talk about what happened."

"Oh?" Her body moves with my hands as I adjust my grip a little, my thumbs pulling the sides of my shirt apart from the last button down. "I see you went *with* underwear."

"What?"

I lift my head, unperturbed by how serious she looks. "Underwear optional?"

"Ah, yeah. It seemed like the best option."

"For whom?" I can't stop the quirk to my lips. "Next time, I'll just have to remember not to give you the option."

"About next time."

Dark amusement skitters up my chest. No. That's *not* what this is. "You're having second thoughts?" Even as the words leave my mouth, my brain contradicts the possibility. I made her come so hard she lost the power of speech. She went to sleep at least once on my chest, her expression one of bliss.

"Well." She pauses, conflicting emotions coming into existence in her expression before fading again. "You said yourself we should have parameters, that we should have—"

She's in the middle of one such confliction when I lean in and kiss her. I feel her startle for a second before she sighs, and her mouth begins to work in tandem with mine. The pressure in my chest begins to dissipate. She still wants this.

"Guidelines." Her arms slide around my neck, her words a warm whisper against my lips. Toothpaste, sugar, and coffee. Who'd want breakfast when such a feast is within reach. "Whit, are you listening?"

"Hmm." With this woman in my arms, serotonin and dopamine flooding my system? Probably not.

"Whit." Her hands slide into my hair where they tighten, the pleasure-pain dichotomy pulling a growl from my throat. "Are you paying attention?" Her hands move to my face, my lips pulling from hers in small increments.

"To you. Always." Since she arrived, thoughts of her have dominated my waking hours. "I know you were talking." My voice sounds rough as I press my hand over hers where it rests on my sandpapery cheek. I rub like a cat demanding attention. "That's why I kissed you."

"Because you didn't want to listen?"

"Because I was watching the way your lips move." I close the space between us, my mouth a teasing slide against hers. "I can't seem to resist your mouth."

"You managed pretty well up until yesterday." She sighs as I bury my nose between her shoulder and neck, inhaling the scent of woman and skin, wanting to touch her everywhere, pull her apart and see what makes her tick. I slide my lips up her throat and press my teeth to her erratic pulse.

"*Oh God.*" Her whisper sounds like submission. "Oh God." And that one not quite so much.

"What is it?" I pull back, my hands clamped once more to her hips.

"I think we need to talk."

I inhale through my teeth. "Now, there's a passion killer."

"Postponer, maybe." Her frown says otherwise. "We need to talk about last night."

"I thought we'd covered last night *last night.*" At length.

"We agreed this would be temporary," she says carefully.

"Yes," I say, using her serious tone. Those words seem to have been said long ago now, but yes, temporary was—*is*—the plan.

"You said you'd give me what I want."

A faintly wicked-feeling smile creeps across my mouth. "I did, didn't I?" As my fingers tighten, she clamps her hands over my wrists.

"The experiences I want," she qualifies.

"And probably some you don't realize you want."

"But it can only be sex, though, right?"

It's never just sex. The thought rises unbidden, but I push it away. I've been fucking women without the entanglement of relationships since my late twenties. It's worked out okay so far. "That's what we agreed. Are you having doubts about that?" And if she is, how I'd feel about that prospect feels like quietly pleased.

"Well," she begins hesitantly, "don't take this the wrong way, but I want more." I don't know about the wrong way but I don't quite know how to take that. I'm even more confused when she adds, "Please don't look at me like I just murdered your puppy. I'm not asking you to put a ring on it."

Cock ring? my ridiculous mind supplies now.

"...because that's not the kind of more I'm looking for."

"Puppy killing?" Maybe I need electrolytes. My brain is obviously struggling.

"I want different," she adds a little desperately, "not necessarily more."

I feel my eyebrows rise because I can do different. Fuck yes, I can.

"But I don't want monogamy." Her words seem to startle Mimi as much as they do me.

"You want to fuck other people?" My demand is low and rough. "Was last night..." Too much? Too intense? Not enough? Fuck that, last night was amazing. At one point, she came like that chick from *The Exorcist*, thrashing and cursing. Thankfully, no green goo.

"Last night was amazing. It was…" She licks her lips, and I just about manage not to kiss her again because she's so fucking gorgeous, but also I don't think I want to hear what she has to say. "I guess I just don't have the vocabulary to describe everything it was."

"What about perfect."

She smiles. It's fleeting but sincere, a flash of white teeth and gap and everything.

"Yes, perfect. That about sums it up. But this morning I've realized you have so much more going on in your life. You're married to VirTu, and you have your family. You're not going to have time to take me dancing, or for coffee, or for a trip to the London Eye."

"That tourist trap is literally ten minutes' walk from the office." A lock of her hair falls forward. She swipes it before I can do it for her.

"You gonna walk me there? Go up with me for a ride."

I resist the low-hanging fruit in that question. "What are you trying to say, Amelia?" Spit it out. Get to the point.

"I'm not here for long and want to cram about five years of experiences into what little time I have. I want to see the sights and experience all that London has to offer." I'm about to suggest she books some tours or maybe take a look at TripAdvisor when her next words flay me. "I think I want to date."

"Fucking Sorrel," I grate out, my hands falling away.

"No!" she snaps. "What do you take me for?"

"At this minute, I'm not sure I know."

"I want to go for coffee, mooch around museums. Go to clubs and sit in pubs with a glass of beer with a name I can't pronounce. I want to hang out. See things. Do… stuff."

"So go with a friend."

"I don't have any." Her hands rise and fall, slapping her thighs with futility.

"Then make some."

"Oh sure. I'll get right on it now."

"Define monogamy for me, Amelia. I'm beginning to think our understanding might not be the same."

She swallows, her eyes filling with tears. Is this some trick of hers I don't know about? Tears on command must be useful. "I just want to live and breathe London, Whit. I don't want to do it alone, and I don't have any friends here." That might be true, but it's not the whole truth because she can barely look at me.

"What if I make time for you? Make time to take you out." Fuck, what am I saying? This could get messy.

She gives her head another shake. "No, I won't ask you to."

"And if I offered?"

"If you want to take me out, then sure." Her shoulder flicks in a way meant to convey inconsequence. But she still hasn't raised her eyes.

"You mean I can take you out if you're not already otherwise engaged. With a date." The hard *t* seems to echo between us.

"Don't make a hole in your life for me. I'm not going to be here long enough to fill it."

"Do you intend to fuck these dates?" I verbally hold the word up by the scruff of its distasteful neck. That's not happening. If I have to tie her to her desk. If I have to cuff her to my bed.

"Will you be sleeping with other women?" she demands just as sharply.

"I think that depends on how you answer." I didn't think

it was a good idea to fuck her, and now it's all I can think about.

"I've never slept around." Her hair swishes as she shakes her head. "If you want the truth, I've never had another man make me feel the way you do." She inhales deeply, as though fortifying herself, her gaze lifting to mine. "I've never had another man make me come."

The lizard part of my brain gobbles up that insight like an ouroboros eating its own tail. But I can't ignore the rest of what she means or even fathom it. I try not to feel pacified, but it's hard when she's looking at me with those big gray eyes.

"And if you change your mind?"

She's already shaking her head. "I won't. Not when I have the best. If you still want me on these terms..."

I hook my finger under her chin, lifting her eyes to mine. "What is this about, Amelia? Tell me where this has come from."

"I have to keep things casual, Whit. Can't you see that?"

"You're frightened." Beneath my fingers and my gaze, she freezes. "But frightened of what?" Last night was a lot, especially for the inexperienced. It was more than the collision of flesh, but I feel like there's something she's not saying. "Did I frighten you?" Did the strength of her own reactions catch her off guard?

"No, of course not. Please don't try to complicate this." Her breath hitches as her eyes take on the appearance of smoked glass. No, not tears summoned at will. This is genuine regret. I won't get to the bottom of those fears right now, so what can I do but play along?

"I don't like it," I growl, taking her face in my hands.

"I don't think you have to." And I don't think you'll be

going on any dates, I fail to add. Mainly because I'm not an idiot. "Please let's not make things complicated."

"Do I have to remind you that you pursued me? Doggedly." At least she has the decency to lower her eyes at this. "I don't like playing games, Amelia."

"I'm not playing." Her eyes are wet when they rise once again. "I'm just trying not to get hurt."

If not you, someone else. The memory of her words are brought to life like the strike of a match, Connor's voice echoing them. *She's too innocent for her own good. Make sure she doesn't end up with some dick.*

Innocent? Try a contradiction.

"Only I get to touch you," I add with meaning, pushing the recollections away because it's not about what her brother wanted. Not anymore. It's about her. It's about how much I want her. "Only I get to fuck you."

I expect her to recoil or make some protest. Instead, she answers, "If you still want me."

Another dark chuckle escapes my chest as a quote I'd read drifts through my head. *Women are fickle. And men are idiots.* I'm missing something. I just don't know what.

"And kissing?" I take her hips in my hands, brushing my lips over hers, forcing her to give. To bend. "Who gets to kiss you?"

"Only you," she whispers, her lips chasing mine until I sever the connection between us when I pull back. Her eyes seem suddenly so solemn, but maybe I only see what she wants me to see. "It takes courage to be vulnerable." My hand seems to lift of its own accord, the backs of my fingers stroking down her neck.

"Are you talking about you or me?" A smile catches at the corner of her mouth. A second later, it's gone.

"The strengths of reactions, of feelings can be frightening."

"I know. I've never wanted anyone like I want you." She shakes her head almost ruefully.

"That's something, at least."

"But I think you might be too much for me." She angles her glance away.

"*Amelia*." I say her name the way she likes to hear it. Part chastisement, part wonder. "You took me *so, so well*." My hand ghosts down her front, snagging on the first of the fastened buttons before my finger and thumb make quick work of it.

"What are you doing?" she asks nervously.

"I would've thought that was obvious." Another button, and again. "But in case it's not, I'm about to remind you why you'll only come for me." Parting the sides of the shirt a little wider, I press my lips to the warm skin of her breastbone. "You can tell me to stop, and I will."

My gaze lifts, her eyes turning languid, her hands trembling as they fold under the edge of the tabletop.

"Don't stop. Please."

With each button, I expose a little more skin, my lips moving incrementally, tasting her dips and valleys, worshipping her body. The morning sun turns her hair golden, washing her skin in its rays as I drag the sides of my shirt over her hardening nipples.

"You look like you're made of sunshine." Her skin dappled with gold, her fine hairs on her arms shimmer.

"I feel kind of exposed." Her eyes slide to the wall of windows behind me.

"No one can see you from up here," I whisper, tightening my hands on the cotton to slide it across and back, letting her soak in my attention. Revel in the sensations. Such secrets I could show her, layers of sensuality she could barely guess.

"No one but you."

"As it should be. Your body is mine when it's before me."

The sound she makes is almost plaintive as I slide my hands under the shirt, curling them once more around her hips. My thumbs caress the protrusion of bones there. I want to bend her until she feels hollow. Until she's weeping with need to be filled. I reach behind her and drag a container of fruit closer. Selecting a wedge of mango, I lift it to my mouth. Bright orange and pulpy, the juice drips down my fingers.

"This reminds me of something," I murmur, sliding it between my lips.

"Of what?" She swallows thickly, prompting me to run my fingers over her bottom lip. Her tongue darts out, licking the sticky juice. I take the opportunity to slide my fingers inside her hot, wet mouth.

"You tell me." She doesn't need the instruction, already swirling her tongue.

Selecting another piece, I slide the sticky flesh between her breasts, following it with my tongue.

"Are you going to eat it or torment me?" It doesn't sound at all like a complaint.

"Eat it or eat you, should be the question."

She releases a delicate moan as I glide the fruit around one of her nipples. "It's so chilly," she whimpers, her body an elegant arc at the contact.

"Not for long." Bending my head, I suck her wet nipple into my mouth. I make a rough sound of appreciation as I draw on the tight bud, feeling it stiffen against my tongue. Soft swipes and wicked flicks, my actions are oh-so controlled until she's panting, wordless beneath me.

"Tasty." The word slides into a groan as I move to her other breast, repeating the process until her hands are in my hair and she's convulsing under me, dry fucking my thigh.

"You eat it." I bring what's left of the wedge to her mouth, painting the juice across her lips, teasing her with it. "Do you want it?" She makes to bite as I move it back.

"Yes." One hand lifts to capture my wrist. "I want it."

"How much do you want it?" The mango falls, my voice husky as I take her mouth. She tastes like mango and looks like an invitation to ruin. *But for which of us?*

"I want it however you want to give it to me."

"Good answer." I bite back a grin. "Open wide, sweetheart." I slide my fingers into her mouth, my cock aching as she sucks on them. Licks them clean.

A dark, captivating ache washes through me as I wrap my hand behind her, pushing the plates and containers away. Some slide the length of the table, some hit the floor. I don't really pay attention as I don't care; all I can think about is the woman in front of me. How I crave her. How I'll take her right here and right now.

I can make her fears disappear.

Or make them worse, something dark whispers.

22

MIMI

"You're smiling," Whit's low voice rumbles. One palm flat to the table, his other bands my back.

"Better than tears." I feel his mouth curve against mine as his hands slide under me, lifting me to the tabletop.

"Different to tears," he says on a sigh.

I tip my head back as his hot breath slides down my neck as though testing where his lips might like to land. But I'm not really smiling, and there are tears, the bittersweet kind that I'm blinking back. What have I done? Why couldn't I have just said, *thanks for the memories, but I think I might become a slut someplace else now.*

Because I can't resist him.

Because I don't want to hurt him.

Because I'm not cut out to play these games, would be my guess.

His teeth grip the tendon between my shoulder and neck, his hand resting at the base of my throat to gently press me back. My palms fall to the tabletop behind me, his shirt sliding from one shoulder like a slattern. His chest rises and falls in a steady rhythm, but he doesn't speak or touch me except where his hands rest.

"You're looking at me like I'm a bottle of wine you're about to taste."

His laughter is dark, hot, and velvet. "Hope springs eternal, my darling?"

My cheeks burn at how suggestive I'd sounded. "I didn't mean..." My words trail off as his hand slides down my body, his palm pressing against my pussy.

"Fine wine, Amelia, should always be given time to breathe as a prelude to taste."

His fiery gaze travels over me, lingering on my face. His appraisal feels like hot syrup sinking into all the secret places of me.

I am so in trouble.

Best make the most of it, a little voice says.

God, I love that little voice.

"Lift up." He hooks his fingers into the sides of my panties before pulling them down my legs. "You are entirely too lovely," he says as he slips his thumb inside and presses it to my clit. "And it's a little too early for wine."

Leaning closer, his lips brush mine, his tongue skimming my bottom lip. He swallows my cry, my body bowing as something ice cold and wet flows down my body.

"Oh, *oh!*" Champagne cascades down my chest, spilling over my hips and between my thighs. "What was—" Sensation rushes to the surface of my skin like a greeting as Whit licks at the rivulets with the flat of his tongue.

"Too early for wine, but not champagne." He looks faintly wicked as he puts down his glass, and his tongue swipes my nipple, lapping the cold sting. The contrast of his hot mouth following the shock of ice-cold bubbles makes me shiver and moan.

"You might've warned me." My complaint is halfhearted as he slips his tongue over the equally sensitive curve of my breast.

"And spoil the surprise?" He yanks the shirt down my arms, simultaneously hooking the chair leg with his foot to drag it closer. He drops to the seat and presses his palms to my knees, spreading my legs wider. Electricity pulses through me in jagged, silvery jolts as his tongue licks the inside of my thigh. "Take off the shirt," he suggests oh-so reasonably. "Let the sun dry your skin."

That's true. It's also true his suggestion is a ruse as I find myself twisting at the cold, cold pull of his fingers at my nipple. Fingers cold from the bottle—no, the glass of ice. Ice that's now on his tongue.

"No!" I press my knees together as best I can, considering Whit's hand is still between them. Along with my warning, I hold out my finger the way you would to still an unruly child.

Ice cube balanced on the tip of his tongue, he almost shrugs an innocent, *what? Me?*

"No," I repeat firmly. "I'm a Florida girl. I don't do—"

A cold thumb presses to my clit. I open my mouth, but no sound comes out.

"It's not so bad, see?" Husky voiced, Whit begins to circle his thumb, massaging that tight bundle of nerves. "It'll be even better when you let me..."

"Oh God, yes..." My legs fall wide, his dark head bending to my lap, the touch of his lips cool but warmer than his thumb. Less of an invasion. And getting warmer by the second.

"I'm starving, darling." The sound vibrates through me as he deepens the contact, beginning to make out with my pussy.

My head tips back between my shoulder blades, the sight too erotic for my brain to process.

"Watch me, Amelia." My name on his lips is whisper soft. "Watch me feast on you." He owns me with his tiger's gaze, the hungry longing there echoed in the way my body responds. "I don't know if I want to lick you dry..." I close my eyes at the sight of the flat of his tongue licking the length of me.

"Yes," I moan, pressing into his mouth.

"Or swallow you whole. Who makes you come like this, Amelia?"

"Only you," I whimper. Literally only you. I chance another look, and our eyes connect, the sensation of him watching me like a jolt of pleasure shooting through my whole body. "Please, touch me..." The final word draws off into a plaintive cry as something ice cold swirls around my clit. Ice—he has ice in his mouth. I try to pull away, but Whit's hands are like manacles around my wrists, his body keeping my knees spread wide.

Panic strikes at the very core of me, self-preservation causing me to thrash. My reactions have nothing to do with the cold press of his mouth and everything to do with my desire for the man he is.

Oh Lord. This was supposed to be easy—my poor heart can't take anything more.

"That's right," he says, his glance up my body nothing short of commanding. "No one will ever make you come like I do." He trails his ice-cold lips across my thigh, warming them in a sucking bite. "Ever."

This is what I deserve. To be forced. Held. I don't need tender touches or sensual brushes. I don't fight him when his mouth returns or when his cold fingers fill me. My body bows, my muscles taut like wire, my movements chasing his punishment as he licks me again and again, cold becoming warm, warm becoming cold again. It hurts, oh God, it hurts. It hurts to know I don't deserve him as I submit to this sweet, intense torture.

The clink of his belt. The susurrus of his zipper, the head of his cock, hot and ruddy, pressed to my center. My body offers him no resistance as he pushes inside, the heat and feel of him sending my thoughts spinning.

"Look at me." I hadn't realized, but he's right, my eyes were screwed tight. He slides my damp hair from my face and presses a kiss to my temple, his next words pitched so softly. "Let me in, darling."

With a mewl, I rock against him and gasp as his pelvis brushes my clit. Whit grunts his approval, sliding his hands under my ass. He drives into me then, so hard and so deep, that the heavy table moves, shrieking a protest against the wooden floor.

"Please, again," I pant, sliding my hands into his hair. Pulling him closer, I clasp him to me, not wanting him to see my face, to see what this is doing to me. My heart beats so hard it feels like it's trying to get to his.

"This arse," he growls as he lifts me to him. I cry out as the angle changes, and his big hands tighten on my cheeks. "The things I could do to this arse."

I whimper as he licks my neck. Bites. "Oh!" It's such a tiny sound to be so full of encouragement.

"I'm going to send you off on each of your little dates with my cum dripping between your legs."

I cry out, not just from the possessive picture he paints but because I'm suddenly *so* full—impossibly so—as he drops to the chair behind him. My hands fall to his shoulders as I adjust to the sensation, pulsing around him. My brain short-circuits as his hands find the curve of my hips, pressing me deeper, impaling me. My body seems to move of its own volition, undulating over him.

"Yeah, like that." I rise in response to his coaxing hands, riding him. "You were made for this."

You were made for him. I screw my eyes shut at the invasive thought.

"Sweetheart." Whit's hand cups my cheek. "Open your eyes, look at how you take me." The awe in his voice prompts my gaze to follow his to where my body accepts him. Holds him.

Oh, that's too much.

"No, it's perfect." I don't pause to wonder if he read my mind as I rise over him to reveal his glistening cock inch by slow inch before he rocks my body into his again.

"Yes, that's it." His thumb swipes my cheek so tenderly. "You're so beautiful, Amelia. Your cunt feels like velvet." That word—the bass, coarseness of it causes a cascade of sensation through me, the effect written in the pleasured pain response on his face. "Oh Jesus, yes!" His hands coast down my body, his fingers sudden manacles against my wrists. He pulls them to the small of my back, adjusting his hold to one hand. With the other, he slides the tangled hair from my face, cradling my cheek, all dark, tender eyed.

"Move for me, darling." His words drip through me like honey. "That's it," he encourages, moving with me. "Ride me."

"You're so big this way," I choke out a garbled compliment, my insides throbbing at the thick slide of him. "I can't—" I can't think. Not as he grips my breast, lavishing my nipple with his tongue, leaving it hard and shining rudely in the daylight.

"Yes, you can. It's okay to take what you want."

I begin to rock, tentatively at first, then harder, buoyed

on by the way he watches me, watches my face, watches my breasts as they move, observes how my body accepts him.

"You look so beautiful riding me." My tempo increases with his compliments, my thighs beginning to sting as I work myself over him. "Fuck yes, fuck me harder. Like that. Fuck me until I tell you to stop."

"Oh God, stop—stop talking before my head explodes."

"Don't stop until Daddy tells you to," he adds with an unrepentant grin. "*Fuck!*" He draws the expletive out on a groan as my body bows, my walls contracting around him. "No denying how much you love the sound of that."

"Stop talking and kiss me."

With the slightest resistance, he releases my wrists, allowing me to slide my hands around his neck as I devour him. His lips are faintly sticky from the mango, his breath hot and sweet as I work myself over him again and again.

"Oh God!" The brush of his pelvis is like the cherry on this sexual sundae.

I've never felt this way. My skin feels alive to his touch. So alive, so sexual.

His hands slide up my back, curling around my shoulders, his grunt countering my cry as he thrusts up into me. "Come on, Amelia. Fuck Daddy like you want to."

Pleasure radiates through every inch of me, our mouths meeting, messily tongued and panting as we rock and surge like one entity, our moans filling the room.

"I'm so fucking close." Tense-jawed, he draws his brows together as though desperate to delay the inevitable, and if that doesn't give me a sense of power, I'm not riding Whit's cock like my life depends on it. *And I am.*

"I want it," I whisper. Knowing he's close somehow heightens my pleasure, makes me rock harder, makes those pulses stronger. "Give it to me." I begin to ride him, it's the only way to describe my body's motion as I impale myself on him over and over again. From one breath to another, I suck in a sharp gasp, my whole being suddenly electrified. My skin is on fire as Whit chokes out a curse, undulating into his climax. Lost to the pull, lost to his expression, so beautiful and true, my fall follows his.

23

MIMI

PARTING IS SUCH SWEET SORROW?

I never thought I'd say it, but I can't wait to put a little distance between myself and Whit. It's not that I want to leave him, but I just can't stop being awkward, swinging between *I'm going to climb you like a tree* and *you deserve better than me.*

I need to regroup—I need a day to decompress. I'll be fine by Monday morning. Equilibrium restored, all *grab-life-while-you-can* cylinders set to go. But for today, I find I need to hate myself.

"You're sure you're okay?" Whit's tone is concerned as he glances briefly my way.

"Of course." I want to say *it's not you, it's me,* but that would require an explanation I can't give. I'm not even sure I can make sense of my feelings. I just know I thought being with Whit would be uncomplicated and now I realize there's no such thing. "I just wish you'd let me make my own way home," I add when I notice he's staring at me again.

"Give it up," he murmurs as the lights change and he merges into the traffic. "Not happening."

A glimpse of last night flashes in my head and my belly, the thoughts a pleasurable undertow impossible to resist. The thatch of his midnight ink hair between my legs and the rasp of his cheek against my inner thigh as his gaze rose to meet mine. His devilish grin as he—

"Have you got any plans for the rest of the weekend?"

"No." My insides pulse and pound and I duck my head as though the sensation might show on my face. I absently pluck a thread at the hem of my dress, and as it begins to unravel, I make a frustrated huff. I shove my hands under my thighs against the temptation to pull it. To ruin it like I've ruined my plan. I wasn't supposed to feel like this about him. It was just supposed to be sex—his heart and his feelings weren't supposed to be my concern. No, that's not right. I'm not so callous. I just saw Whit as I remembered him. A man irresistible to women. A man always down for a little no-strings tryst. And I suppose he is, but it doesn't stop me from hating myself a little bit. Turning my head to the side window, I watch the London streets spin by. Well, crawl, maybe. Knightsbridge traffic is no joke, even on Saturday.

"Next time, you should bring a bag?"

"Sorry?" My head spins back. "What was that?"

"Next time we get together, you should bring a bag." He does that thing men everywhere seem to have perfected— you know the thing where it seems like they barely glance your way but take you *all* in.

"To save me looking like I'm doing the walk of shame?" I adjust my definitely not for daytime sparkly clutch on my knee.

"I'd say last night deserves a victory lap." He swipes his thumb at the corner of his mouth, but it doesn't hide the way his lips tip.

"Thanks for the loan of the cardigan, anyway." I

tighten the navy fisherman's knit tighter over my dress. It's long enough to hide the way my dress splits. And its length, I guess. My sparkly bag, heels, and sex hair, not so much. At least Aunt Doreen won't make a fuss. *Her being a woman of the world and all.* "I'll bring it into the office on Monday."

"There's no hurry. It's been at my place for weeks."

"Well, thanks to whoever it belongs to." I have no business sounding snippy about who he spends time with (read: bangs) when I've told him I want to date half of London. I mean, who does that? Tries to solve a man problem by throwing a few more fictitious ones into the mix?

This idiot. Even if it is for the right reasons.

"Prim." The accusation seems to hang in the air between us.

"I am not!" Just because I don't have your kind of experience—" His lips tip kind of ironically. "Just because I want to see more of London doesn't mean I'll be banging men indiscriminately!"

"Primrose, my sister. That's her cardigan."

"Oh. Good. I mean, God. I mean, thanks to Primrose," I say... primly.

"She hasn't missed it yet. And I haven't missed that this isn't about you playing tourist."

"Don't, Whit," I say plead softly.

"I'll play along. For now."

We fall quiet, the low hum of the radio filling the space between us.

"Well. That didn't go as planned."

"What didn't?" The words fall from my mouth before I can stop them, and I frantically scan my mind for something else to say. "What kind of car did you say this was again?" I ask as he flicks on the turning signal, expertly feeding the leather steering wheel through his fingers.

"A Bugatti. Why, do you like it?"

"It's cool." And expensive, at a guess.

"Would you like to drive it sometime?"

"In London?" I ask, aghast. "Thanks, but no. Some of the streets look like they belong on a *Harry Potter* set. Ye olde world tiny," I add when he doesn't seem to follow my meaning.

"We could go out of the city. Find a quiet country lane."

I shake my head. "I'm no good with a stick." His laughter fills the space between us, deep and rich and so... *him*. "You know what I mean."

"We don't have to drive. We could always try that other thing you haven't done in a car yet. Maybe you should make a list."

"Like a bucket list?" Why does that feel like a sudden weight on my chest?

"A fuck-it list," he amends. "Put car sex at the top of it, if you like."

"I haven't had sex in a car. I also haven't eaten octopus. Doesn't mean I'm gonna do either."

"I have. Truthfully?" he adds, his attention sliding my way. "Vastly overrated."

"Octopus?"

"Both. But if it's on your fuck-it list, I'll give it another go."

"I'm not a fan of seafood," I say, turning my smile from him. At least, not octopus.

"And the other."

"I'm not having sex with you in a country lane."

"Can't blame a man for trying," he replies, unrepentant. "Next time, bring a bag when you come to stay."

"Okay." The word comes out small, my stomach a mess of knots. Pleasurable knots mixed in with the conflicted ones.

"You're not going to ask, are you?" he says, sounding mildly annoyed.

"What is it you want me to ask?"

"When we'll see each other again."

Of course, it would be right now that the lights up ahead change to red. Meaning he turns to me with *that* expression. The one that seems to say: *give it up, you know you're going to.*

"I mean, I'll see you at work on Monday."

"*Amelia.*"

The sound of my name in that tone makes me want to shimmy and sigh. "I just meant I assumed we'd talk about it then."

"We've got time to talk about it now, given you're staying in the arse end of London." The latter he adds in a mutter.

"Which is why I wanted to take the Tube home."

"Give it up, blondie." Reaching out, he pulls on the end of my braid.

"Blondie?" A pet name shouldn't feel mildly thrilling. I mean, it's not even a pet name yet. Just because he said it once doesn't mean it'll stick. Anyway, I'm not supposed to be simp-ing after him.

"Have you got a problem with that?"

I shrug. Whatever. Secretly, I'm thrilled.

"You're like sunshine, you know."

"Bright and cheerful?" I reply with a tiny preen.

"Deceptively dangerous. Something tells me if I'm not careful, you'll leave me burned."

"Don't say that," I whisper. "This is supposed to be fun, not painful."

"You didn't answer my question. *When?*"

"I guess, one weekend—"

"Not *one* weekend, Amelia. Multiple weekends. Don't tell me you've had your fill because I've barely scratched the surface."

Interested is the least of what I am. Whit might be an obsession in the making, and that's exactly why I need to be careful.

"Interested *and* that you can find time to fit me into your busy dating schedule," he adds caustically.

Someone upstairs must think I need a break as the driver behind us leans on his horn, shifting Whit's attention to the now green light. "All right, wanker," Whit mutters, glaring in the rearview mirror as the car glides forward.

I find myself sounding the word out silently. I like Brit speak.

"I hope that wasn't meant for me." I turn my head and watch mild amusement flit over Whit's face.

"I would never presume to call you anything so insulting." But fun. "London swearing feels so... continental. Tell me, is a cheeky wank the same as a cheeky wanker?"

"What?" He barks out the word, amused.

"Isn't it?" My shoulders move with bemusement. "*Are* they the same thing?

"Who've you been listening to?"

"El." That wipes the smile from his face. "Well, I overheard him calling someone a cheeky wanker, and the other I heard on the Tube last week."

"In what context?" he asks. "Because the mind boggles."

"I was eavesdropping. One girl was describing to another how she'd given her boyfriend a cheeky wank. She made it sound like she was doing him a favor."

"Well, a cheeky wank can be fun," he offers, trying hard to fight a smile. "Especially if there's another party involved and they're into it. But an appeasement wank sounds pretty sad." His chest rises and falls as though to prepare himself, his eyes sliding briefly my way. "You sure you're not having me on?"

"That means teasing you, right?" I give my head a shake. "Definitely not *winding you up,*" I say with the authenticity of the chimney sweep in *Mary Poppins.*

He laughs again and, *ah me,* I love making his mouth tip up and that chest heave with amusement. It's addictive—like love crack, without the illicit connotations or actual love. Romantic love, I mean. I'm totally prepped against that.

"So come on. Explain!" I literally bounce in my seat.

"I can't believe we're having this conversation," he mutters as he signals left and begins to turn.

"A conversation is two way thing. Spill!"

"Fine." He blows the word out on a long breath. "A cheeky wank is an impromptu act of self-love."

"A what?" I feel my brow pucker.

"Meeting Mrs. Palm and her five lovely daughters." Holding up his left hand, he wiggles his fingers before making a cylinder of them and, well, you know.

"Ohh." The graphic gesture totally makes sense.

"So a cheeky wanker is someone who's having a cheeky wank?"

"No, that one is more like a mild insult. Like someone is taking the piss, annoying you? Like calling someone a jerk-off, but less venomous."

"You are so educational. I know you said you'd teach me, but…"

This time, the amusement that flitters across his face is a mite darker. "Tip of the iceberg, little fly. Tip of the iceberg."

I dip my head to my lap and the loose thread again. "Flies are so..."

"'So handsome are your gauzy wings, how brilliant are your eyes.'"

"Do you know the whole poem?" I ask softly.

"I might've googled it recently," he admits with a touch of amusement.

Danger. Danger! This is the kind of man a girl could easily fall for.

"And speaking of the internet," I say with a forced brightness as I pull out my phone, "what are the popular dating apps in London?"

"And you suppose I'd know." His tone is suddenly gruff.

"Come on, Whit. You're not a monk. The girl you were expecting a few weeks ago when I turned up didn't just materialize. She came from somewhere."

"Not a dating app." The phrase "brooks no opposition" springs to mind. "I take it that means you haven't changed your mind." Something unpleasant flits over his face, but a passive mask soon resumes.

"About dating?" Serious about making you think I am, anyway. I need to put more thought into this than letting knee-jerk ridiculousness spill from my mouth. Why the hell did I think asking would help?

"Forget it," he mutters, grumpy CEO Whit taking over.

I wish I could forget. I wish I could take myself back to the moment I realized Whit deserved to do better because then I'd make sure to gloss over it. I'd think of only me and be greedy about my fill.

"I don't think it would be a good idea to change my mind. That's why I asked about dating apps," I say calmly. Much calmer than I feel, anyway. It strikes me that I'm going to need to put more effort into my little ruse than I anticipated. It's not like I have to date. I can just pretend. I'll just download an app or two. Whit won't need to know I'm swiping left (or is it right for refusal?) all the time. Because really, who wants to date in real life? Only masochists and people who can take a risk on love.

"So where do you meet the women you…"

"Fuck?" he finishes for me, all hard fricatives. "Nowhere suitable for you, little fly."

Way to point out I'm one of the training-wheel brigade. "Too niche for my tastes, huh?"

"Have you ever used dating apps before?"

"Have you?"

"You do know there isn't an app to meet people as friends, that most people out there are looking to hook up? Which you won't need," he adds with a sharp look my way.

"That might be the rule, but there are always exceptions to every rule."

"Yes, I'm sure. Those looking for that special unicorn also known as *the one*."

"There has to be more than that," I mutter, swiping Google open as I begin to type.

Dating apps in London for Friendship.

"What about Feeld?" I announce, bringing up an article about the app.

"That's mostly couples looking for a casual third."

"How do you know that?" He slides me a look that's hard to decipher. "But it has a tag for friendship," I add defensively.

"I'm sure I read somewhere that it was created by a couple looking to introduce others into their sexual experiences. I might be wrong," he adds with the confidence of someone who knows they aren't. "You can do your own due diligence, I'm sure."

I scan the text and, yup. I find something to that effect in the sales pitch. "What about Hinge?" I say, flicking back to Google and picking the second from my search.

"A bit like Tinder." My brows pinch, and my mouth falls open, ready to protest when he adds, "Sign up. See how many people you match with, people who are looking for friendship and not a casual fuck."

"Fine." I go back to my search. "Bumble BFF," I announce excitedly. "It says a simplified way to make meaningful connections—I can date women!"

"Women?" he says in *that* tone.

"Urgh! For friendship. For coffee dates and things." On second thought, maybe I should stick to fictitious men. I don't want him getting too comfortable. "Although, in my experience, women can be harder to befriend."

"They're certainly hard to fathom," he mutters.

We leave the conversation there, the rest of our journey to Edgeware silent, slightly tense, and very awkward.

"What in the world..." Before we get to the red-bricked street I currently call home, we're flagged to a stop by a policeman. The road ahead is cordoned off with blue tape. Beyond it stands a couple of fire trucks, police cars, and people in reflective jackets.

"No access to the road ahead, folks," the policeman says, bending as Whit opens his window.

"What's going on, officer?" I ask, ducking down to see him better.

"Unexploded ordinance was found in a garden in Barnaby Street."

"Oh no. That's Aunt Doreen's street." I glance at Whit,

then back at the officer. "Unexploded ordinance? You mean, like a bomb?"

"Probably left over from the war," he says. "The army's bomb squad are on their way."

"The bomb squad?" My heart begins to flutter rapidly. I press my hand to it, willing it to settle.

"Don't worry. Your aunt will be safe," Whit offers. "She will have been evacuated."

"Yep." The policeman stands. "The houses are all empty. Reverse at the corner when you can," he directs Whit as he turns.

"Don't worry," Whit says, taking my hand. "They do this all the time."

"They do?"

"Well, relatively speaking," he amends. Pressing his arm across the back of my seat, he twists his head over his shoulder as he begins to reverse.

"The camera." I point at the image that flashes up on the dash. "Wouldn't that be easier?"

"It would also be cheating," he says with a small grin.

Maybe there's a class they teach somewhere. Driving: How to Make it Look Hot. It shouldn't be sexy watching him reverse. "No one finds it sexy when I do it!"

"Finds what sexy?"

Damn. "Nothing," I mutter, glancing out of the side window.

"You think it's sexy when I reverse?" he asks, driving back the way we came.

"*Shut up*," I plead.

"Sure you don't want to give this a drive?"

I expect to find innuendo painted across his face when I look. But no. "No thanks."

"The offer stands. And you can back yourself up on me any day of the week."

"Funny."

"I wasn't joking." When I don't answer, he adds, "So where to now?"

"Oh, pull over! There's my aunt." Doreen is holding court, sitting on a low garden wall. She has a teacup in her hand and a bag and cat carrier by her feet. "Oh, good. She has moggy."

"Her cat is called cat?"

"No, his name is Moggy."

"Moggy means cat. Like mutt means dog."

"Oh. Then I guess Aunt Doreen is unimaginative." Which can't be the case at all.

"There she is!" Doreen announces as we make our way toward her. "I was just talking about you."

"I hope it was all good."

"What a thing to say," she scoffs. "You're an angel. Didn't I say she was an angel?" she says, turning to the woman on her left. "This is Sadie. She lives here." She gestures to the house behind her. "She was kind enough to put the kettle on while we wait."

A chorus of "lovely cuppa, this is," starts up from the china cup holding brigade of elderly women.

"How long before you get to go back?" As Doreen's eyes widen, then flick slowly up then down, I realize how rude I'm being. "Oh, sorry. Where are my manners? This is Whit, Aunt Doreen. You remember I told you about Connor's friend?"

"I remember you mentioning him, dear," she says, suddenly patting the back of her hair. "And now the picture is becoming very clear. He's her *boss*," she announces, all wide-eyed and nodding head.

"Oh!" clucks the chorus.

I don't quite know what that means, but anyway... "Whit, this is Aunt Doreen."

"Pleased to meet you," he says, holding out his hand. His voice sounds deep and gravelly, like a fox in a house full of hens. Quite aggressive hens, actually, judging by the appraising looks he's getting.

"Sorry, how long do you think?"

"Before we get back?" I nod, and Doreen shrugs. "How long is a piece of string? They're talking about taking the thing away for detonation."

"It's that big?" Whit asks.

"What does that mean?" I ask, my head swinging back and forth between the two. "Isn't anyone freaked out by this?"

"Of course we are, love. But they've been finding bombs in London since the Luftwaffe buggered off home. We just take it in our stride, don't we, girls?"

Again with the agreeing chorus.

"So will we be allowed back, do you think?"

"Once they've moved the thing."

"Can I offer you a nice cuppa tea, loves?" Sadie, the owner of the garden wall, asks Whit and me.

"We'll budge up," Doreen says, already moving the women along the wall with her butt. "Sit yourselves down. It won't be long."

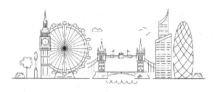

24

WHIT

AUNT DOREEN. She's truly an unreliable narrator because it was long—very long—before we found out what was going on. While Amelia insisted I go home, suggesting I must have better things to do, I didn't leave. I'm sure I have better things to do, more important things at any rate, but I find I can't leave her out in some random street, facing such uncertainty.

So I stay. I drink countless cups of weak-as-piss tea and eat more rich tea biscuits than I've had in a decade. I listen to the oldies gossip and almost choke on a mouthful of tea when one of Doreen's lesser fans takes me aside to tell me I ought to protect "young Amelia's impressionable mind" because Doreen is a "goer" and a "man stealer." Apparently, all the men of a certain age in this borough know Doreen can "suck a golf ball through a garden hose."

Might it be a family trait?

More tea drinking. More gossip. More worried looks from Amelia.

I let Sadie's grandson sit in the driver's seat of my car to pretend he's Batman and agree with the oldies that it's a good thing it's not raining. There are definitely better uses of my time, but I just can't get my feet to take me.

A little after four in the afternoon, news is brought to us by means of a community police officer. She's wearing a high viz jacket about ten sizes too big, which makes her look like a little girl wearing her father's coat. But she has the appropriate amount of authority in her tone to get the older ladies to pay attention. We're told that the houses on Doreen's street, plus three others, are off-limits until the almost eighty-year-old bomb, that is likely highly volatile, is moved off-site for a controlled detonation.

Cries of dismay go up, but it's not the young WPC's fault, so no one gives her a second look as she moves along to deliver the news elsewhere.

"But we don't have any of our things." Amelia looks genuinely dismayed.

"Well, I did think ahead," Doreen says, reaching for a blue, white, and red checkered shopping bag. Large and square, you could probably fold a dead body in it. "Not much, of course. Just a few things. Here." She thrusts a phone charger Amelia's way.

Amelia blinks. "Anything else?"

"I thought there was more," Doreen says, digging deeper into the bag, "but this is all my stuff. My makeup bag...I wouldn't go anywhere without that."

"Too right," strikes up one of the chorus.

"Me either," agrees another.

"I have my good shoes and a change of undies, my slippers, plus my nightie and face cream. And my vibrator, of course."

"Aunt Doreen!" Amelia declares, her face a picture—a picture of a thousand burning suns.

"What's wrong with you?" the older woman demands.

"I'm sorry I didn't get more of your things, but by the time I'd chased Brian around the house—"

"Who's Brian? Actually, you know what?" Mimi holds up her hand. "Don't answer that." She also seems to be resisting a shiver of discomfort.

"The cat." Doreen gestures to the pet carrier on the floor. "The ginger tom cat you've become such friends with."

"I thought his name *was* moggy."

"I did tell you," I murmur, which earns me a frown from both women. "It sounds like Doreen's vibrator was just at hand. As far as packing goes."

Mimi scrunches her nose in distaste.

"Well, yes, it was," Doreen begins, making Mimi look like she might pass out from embarrassment. "I keep it on my armchair next to the fire. You know I do," she says, turning to Mimi. "I asked you to switch it on the other night." That squeak? That might've been from me as I try not to lose my ever-loving shit. This is hilarious! "Remember I said it helps with my lumbago?"

"The vibrating seat pad with the infrared heat!" Mimi says in a moment of relieved *eureka!*

"What did you think I was talking about?" Mimi shakes her head, but it doesn't stop the older woman from barrelling on. "For goodness' sakes, did you think I was talking about a dildol?"

"Dil*do*," one of the senior sisterhood helpfully puts in. Mimi is now puce, and I think I might not be far behind. This is the most entertaining conversation I've heard in forever, and it's seriously taking some effort not to give in to a belly laugh, the kind that makes you bend forward because you feel like you can't breathe. Oh, man. Talk about entertaining.

"Dildo," Doreen corrects.

"*Aunt Doreen*," Mimi pleads, pressing her face into her hands.

"I'm no prude." She glances between Mimi and me. "I doubt he is, either. But I don't own a dildol—a dildo," she amends with an annoyed shake of her head. "I don't need one, not when I have Frank!"

The woman of the garden hose comment looks like she's just swallowed a brick. Geriatric jealousy in the suburbs? This would make a hilarious TV show.

"Give over," heckles another woman. "The man is seventy-five if he's a day!"

"And I'm older than that," she says, puffing out her chest. "Let me tell you, Barb, many a good tune is played on an old fiddle."

"Or a garden hose," I find myself barking out, unable to help myself this time as I bend at the waist and give in to a shoulder-shaking, belly-aching roar.

"What's up with him?"

"If you don't stop snickering, I'm going to scream."

"I can't help it," I protest, flicking the indicator, or turn signal, according to Mimi, before turning right. "You'll have to distract me if you don't want me thinking about this afternoon. God, I hope I have half as much life in me when I'm Doreen's age."

Mimi harrumphs and folds her arms, turning her gaze to the passenger window. It's only there a beat before she turns to me again. "Do you think I'll be able to get back to the house tomorrow?"

Of course I insisted she stay with me until given the all clear to return to the house. I'm hardly a knight in shining armor, whisking her away from a perilous situation on my white steed. I'm more like a selfish knight up to no good. I also want to know what's going on in that head of hers.

Doreen offered to take Mimi to Frank's house, who I understand is Doreen's boyfriend. Though this seems a silly bit of terminology, given he's no boy and they're both well into their senior years. Anyway, she'd said Mimi was welcome to stay there, too. Oddly enough, Mimi looked like she'd been offered the choice between the devil and the deep-blue sea—death by wolves or lions—when I'd suggested, as an alternative, she come home with me. It seemed the logical explanation. A win-win situation. She gets to avoid the senior citizen love-in and gain the pleasure of my company. I didn't put it quite like that, obviously. I just suggested if she did decide not to come with me, she might have to endure Doreen and Frank's monkey noises. The low-hanging fruit is always the easiest to grab.

"Hmm," I ponder. "It's hard to tell. Sometimes these things can take a couple of days, so I've read. If you're uncomfortable"—though why would you be—"I could give Polly a call. See if you can stay with her."

Mimi's brows dip, and she gives an adamant shake of her head. "That would involve telling her why I'm with you in the first place. It's not a conversation I really want to have."

"Agreed." Best not to give Poll any ideas.

"Should I be insulted or flattered?" she asks, now looking amused.

"Relieved. You should definitely be relieved."

"You know you're gonna need to explain why."

"Right, well, when we all had lunch together, I could actually see her mentally shopping for tiny baby clothes."

Mimi barks out a laugh as I knew she would. "You're paranoid. Your mom *so* isn't the type."

"What type would that be?"

"Controlling, I guess." Her expression falls a touch, no doubt remembering her own situation.

"Oh, she absolutely would be, if I let her." I glance away. "She's just good at hiding it."

"I still can't see it."

"That's because she's so good at it. A silent assassin—a steel fist in a velvet glove."

"You're paranoid."

"You've known her for only a little while. Take my word for it. She's a mother of three sons in their thirties and has one daughter happily married. Yet—" I hold my forefinger aloft—"there isn't a sniff of a grandchild on the horizon."

"No!" Mimi scoffs.

"She might play the game well. *I just want to see you happy,*" I intone, pitching my voice a little softer. "But what she means is she wants us all to be knee-deep in nappies—diapers," I amend, "and in need of a rescue visit from gorgeous grabby granny." I make a snapping claw with my hand.

"Well, let's definitely not call her," Mimi replies easily.

"I'm glad were on the same page." About babies and her accommodations. We just have to get rid of those ridiculous dating ambitions. "What about Heather? I could call her. She and Archer have a spare room." I'm nothing if not reasonable, though I always have an angle.

"I've only met her once. I couldn't impose like that."

"Well, that leaves my place or a hotel. And the downside of a hotel is—"

"Turning up looking like a refugee?"

"I was going to say a hotel doesn't have me."

"Is that supposed to be a plus or a minus?" she asks cheekily. "I'm not sure."

"Come on, Mimi. You enjoy my company."

"Oh, so I'm back to being Mimi now?" She quirks a teasing brow, enjoying our exchange.

"Until you misbehave again."

"Misbehave? Who do you think you are? Don't answer that," she adds quickly, blood rushing to her cheeks.

"Don't remind you that I'm Daddy?" I murmur sultrily.

"Stop," she whispers, her eyes dropping to her lap. "Damn." When I my gaze skims her way, she seems to have unraveled the hem of her dress. "It's not like I could wear it to work anyway," she mutters. "What the heck am I going to do for clothes?"

"Naked works for me." She scowls at my offer. "I'll join you if it'll make you more comfortable."

"And for work? What if I can't get into the house tomorrow? What will I wear to work on Monday?"

"I'm sure we'll figure something out."

"Does your sister have more clothes at your place?"

Perfect timing. "I was thinking more about this," I say, silently thanking the parking gods as I pull up right in front of a boutique just off Brompton Road.

"If we're going shopping for Lavender's gift, this look won't be well received in a place like this." She adds a flourish of her hand down her torso.

"A black Amex gets well received everywhere."

"Can't we do it another time? I don't much feel like shopping."

"Whoever does?"

"Then why are we here?" she asks wearily.

"Because sometimes you have to suck it up."

"Shopping is fun, Whit." She eyes me with disbelief.

"It's an afternoon in purgatory."

Disbelief turns to dismay. "Whit, I love shopping! It's like my vocation in life. Nothing is more fun than picking out accessories or treating yourself to a new dress, then taking the goodies home to see how they work with the rest of your wardrobe."

"Sounds like you should work in retail, maybe become a visual merchandiser. A personal shopper. A buyer. Surely a job you enjoy is better than admin."

"I guess I just allowed my parents to choose a path for me."

"But none of those avenues are high octane or dangerous." What the hell has gone on in her life? What have I missed?

She gives an awkward shrug that doesn't make me feel better.

"Why don't you look into retraining?"

"You're just trying to get rid of me." Her brightness is false, more brittle than genuine.

"No, that's not it. I feel fucking awful I wasn't more present."

"Stop." The word seems ironclad. "You're not my brother, Whit. You aren't responsible for me."

"No, you're right, but Connor—"

"You know, I think I might ask you to call Heather," she says, swiftly turning her gaze out the windshield. "Maybe she can loan me sweats or something." The jut of her chin; was she always this stubborn?

"I'll call if you want me to." Reaching over the console, I curl my fingers over her unresponsive hand. "But if it means anything to you, I'd much rather you stay with me."

"I don't need anyone to look after me."

"I get that. I don't mean to come across as overbearing. I suppose I'm just trying to understand what I've missed. "

"Let it go," she says, turning to me now. "I'm living my life the way I want. That's all you need to know."

I sense that isn't the case, but I'll let it go for now as my attention is tweaked by movement in the shop's window. "Should we go?" I make a gesture with my head to the boutique.

"I guess," she replies, unimpressed. "I can't believe they're still open." She cracks the passenger door open.

"Yes, strange that."

"You must be a generous brother." Mimi's words carry over the roof of the car. "That place looks pretty pricey."

"I forget you haven't met Lavender yet." My eyes briefly turn to the boutique's window display. "Lavender's tastes run a bit more gothic." Though just as expensive I don't bother adding.

"Then why are we here?" she asks, clearly confused.

"Come on inside, and I'll show you."

She mutters something unintelligible as she rounds the car, and I make sure her hand is in mine before we even get to the door. Which is probably just as well as the manager of the boutique has the door open before we even reach it.

"Mr. Whittington, welcome. Please, come in," decrees a manager of indeterminable age and lots of filler, I'd guess, dressed in a three-piece suit and a pink tie.

"Thank you." My fingers tighten on Mimi's as I pre-empt her surprise.

"As I said on the phone, the entire store is yours." Is it odd that the manager is a man? I don't think I'm qualified to know, given I don't think I've ever been in a woman's clothing boutique before. "Please do let us know if there's anything we can help you with."

He holds the door open as, with a nod of acknowledgment, I pull Mimi past him.

"Can I get you anything?" he asks, his hands pressed together as though in prayer. I suppose he's giving thanks, considering the eye-watering amount I'd guaranteed to spend here this evening in exchange for keeping the place open. "Madam? Could I perhaps bring you a glass of champagne?"

"No, thank you," Mimi answers stiffly. I give my head a brief shake.

"Then I shall leave you in the very capable hands of Charlotte, our best sales associate." The manager tips his hand to indicate a dark-haired woman around Mimi's age.

"What have you done?" Mimi whisper-hisses, turning from the obsequious manager. I've found money makes people very weird. I should be allowed to treat those I like and love without them making a big song and dance about it.

"Just roll with it." My reply sounds like a bored sigh.

"I am *not* having a Julia Robert's moment with you," she says, trying to snatch back her hand.

"Is that the one where she gets fucked on the piano?"

"Whit!" she castigates in a shocked whisper.

"I thought I was Daddy?" My own volume carries.

"No—no it's not. You are *not* my daddy—"

"You say that now but..."

She doesn't bite though she adds, "And you are certainly not my sugar daddy!"

"Of course I'm not," I answer reasonably, then glance over her head. "Mimi here has had a bit of trouble with an unexploded bomb from the early nineteen forties," I say, directing my explanation to Charlotte, the dark-haired sales associate standing close enough to have heard everything passed between us. Which Mimi has belatedly realized.

"Oh, I'm terribly sorry," the woman says, her accent

decidedly plummy. "I did hear about that on the radio." I give her points for not scrunching her nose at Doreen's Edgeware address.

Meanwhile, Mimi is putting a lot of energy in her evil-eyed narrow glare. *You're going to pay for this*, the look seems to suggest.

"I do love promises," I murmur with a tiny smirk. She probably considers kicking me before, painting on a bland smile, she turns to the sales associate.

"I can't get in to the house to get my clothes. I have work tomorrow, and well, I'm stuck." She gives a tiny yet adorable shrug. The kind that makes me want to pick her up and spin her around.

"How frightful," the woman drawls as though Mimi had just said a pack of hyenas recently devoured her entire family. At Camden market. "We *absolutely* can help."

"Fond of a superlative, this one," I mutter, earning me an elbow in the gut from Mimi.

"Maybe just a skirt and a shirt," Mimi suggests, glancing warily over her shoulder at me.

"Great! Sounds like a naked Sunday." I rub my hands together with relish.

"And maybe something a little more casual for tomorrow," Mimi amends through gritted teeth.

"Underwear?" Charlotte suggests, but Mimi shakes her head.

"Commando also works for me."

"I'll wash what I have," she snipes before turning back to the sales associate all smiles. "But maybe something to sleep in."

"Something silky," I suggest.

"I was thinking more flannel pj's. Maybe a onesie?"

"And a chastity belt."

Mimi swings around, her gray eyes stormy. "Would you like to wait outside? It's not like you need to be here."

"I could." I shove my hands in the pockets of my jeans and affect a shrug. "I'm just not going to." With that, I spy something blue and slinky on a minimalist rack to Mimi's left. "This," I say, reaching for it. "You should definitely try this."

"No," she says.

At the same time, the sales associate says, "Oh yes. That color would look beautiful on you."

"Agreed."

"What do you know?" Mimi's hand slides to her cocked hip.

"You already know I have excellent taste." My gaze flickers over her heatedly.

"And a big head."

"Massive," I enunciate with exaggeration. "It's one of the things she loves about me." The sales associate actually blushes as I send a wink her way. "My huge, massive—"

"I don't even like you." With that mutter, she snatches the dress out of my hand, pivoting to the rack behind her.

"You like at least one bit of me." She inhales a tiny gasp as my hand deliberately brushes her waist, taking the hanger from her hand. "If you could hang that in the dressing room."

"Of course, sir." Charlotte takes it from my hand and hurries off.

"I don't know why you're doing this," Mimi whispers as she skims through the items on the rack in front of her.

"I think this is called payback." If I was an artist and I painted her current expression, I'd title it *what the hell are you on about*. "You've been goading me since you appeared in my office."

"I'm talking about the clothes!" Her hands slap her thighs as though exasperated.

"Oh. Don't make it a thing," I mutter.

"I don't need you to do this."

"What if I want to?" I answer honestly. "Because it's not about you." My lips curve into a smile as I take a step toward her, pressing my entire body against hers. My hands lift to her hips, my mouth pressed to her hair. "This is purely about me and what I want."

"What is it you want?" I hear the tiny waver in her voice. See it in her hand.

"You say I've been buying you lingerie for years. I want a taste of that."

As she opens her mouth to respond, I press my teeth to her neck in reprimand, or maybe encouragement as she makes the kind of breathy moan that makes my dick rock hard.

"Let me do this. Let me watch you dress."

"Whit's own Barbie Doll?" She ducks her head, but I see the smile she's trying to suppress.

"If you were my Barbie Doll, you'd always be naked."

"And my hair a mess?" I make a low sound of agreement. "Sounds like you've seen inside my toy box."

"I would *love* to see inside your toy box sometime."

Her laughter vibrates against me. "Honestly, it's not even as exciting as Doreen's."

"Are you trying to tell me you don't own a vibrator?" She doesn't answer, though the sweep of her dark-blond lashes lower. "Not even a little bullet you press to your clit when you think of me?"

"I dread to think what nefariousness dwells in your toy box," she whispers instead.

"Why is that?"

"Your mind is inventive enough already."

"Oh, you have *no* idea."

"I don't think I'll ever be able to look at a mango again without blushing. Drink champagne, or even watch the condensation on a cold glass."

I could just eat her up, she's so fucking open and adorable. I can't resist wrapping my arms around her waist and hugging her to me. "Come on, Mimi." Spinning her in the direction of the dressing room, I slap her delectable arse, making her squeal. "Let's go play dress-up."

She slides me an arch look over her shoulder. "Putting clothes on?"

"The novelty feels like payment itself."

"Well, this is kind of cute," she says, pulling a sweater from a nearby rack. "It's the same as the one hanging in the window. I noticed it when we—holy Moses! How much?"

"That's not for consideration," I say, taking it from her hands. "What about pants?"

"Whit, no!" She turns, her expression shocked.

"No pants? Works for me."

"Be serious!"

"How can I be serious when we're playing dress-up." Reaching out, I grab the first thing my hand falls to. "I'd like to see you in this."

"A jumpsuit?"

I examine the garment and resist saying I thought it was a pair of really long pants. "Don't you like it?" I say instead.

"Well, it is cute."

"Look, they have it in miniature, too." I slide another hanger from the rack.

"That one's a playsuit," she informs me.

"Is it indeed? Doesn't look like it'd be much fun to get into."

"Or out of."

Holding it out, I examine the thing. "I'd just use scissors."

"Not in a public bathroom!"

"Is it, indeed," she repeats with a less than patient expression. "You sound like you're one hundred and three. All you need is a moustache to twirl."

"How about I twirl you instead?" One hand still holding the hangers, I reach for Mimi's hand. As I lift it, she twirls gracefully under it. "And an evening gown."

"What? No!" She laughs as though that's the most ridiculous thing she's ever heard. "I don't need an evening gown."

"Surely, every woman needs a posh frock." I can't believe the nonsense that's coming out of my mouth. "Right..." I turn to, what was her name again? Ah, "Charlotte." According to her name tag.

"Absolutely! You never know where one might be invited."

"Well, *this one* has never been invited anywhere."

"Give it up, Cinderella. Someone else needs the pumpkin."

"What?"

I turn to Charlotte. It's either that or laugh at Mimi's expression. "Can you give us a few options?"

"Oh, absolutely." Charlotte twirls away. All she's missing is a wand, and she'd be a very posh fairy godmother.

"What has gotten into you?" Hand on her hips, Mimi eyes me warily. "I don't need an evening dress. I just need something to schlep around in and maybe something to get me to work on Monday."

"What if one of your upcoming dates invites you somewhere fancy?" I ask a little caustically. There's no way she's going to date anyone, not if I have my way, but the idea is like a scab I keep picking. She gives a tiny shake of her head as though she can't believe what she's hearing. Fair enough. I can't believe it, either. Except when I add, "What if I want to take you somewhere special?"

"Like where?"

"That would be telling." The event that springs to mind is the one that got me into trouble in the first place. It was after such a *gathering* that I'd found I was pleasuring—fingering?—the sister of my deceased best friend instead of the woman I'd anticipated.

"Yeah, and this," she says, pointing at her still moving mouth, "would be asking."

"I'm always getting invited to things. Galas and art shows, gallery openings, the opera."

"Those are the kind of places you take a date," she says carefully.

"You did say I could ask you out."

"Are you asking me out?"

"Are you angling for me to ask you out?"

"Are you going to answer the question?" she says, fighting a smile.

"I've taken the liberty to hang a couple of *gorgeous* gowns in the dressing room," Charlotte announces, oblivious to the charge bouncing between Mimi and me.

"Thank you." Mimi turns her attention my way. "I'll try them on, but that's all I'm promising."

"That's fine."

The rest I can work with.

25

MIMI

"YES, THAT'S MUCH BETTER," Charlotte decrees, fastening the last hook on the most beautiful evening gown I've ever seen. Black lace over a sheer under dress, the fabric clings to me like a second skin to my knees where it flares gently. It even has a train! It's grown-up and sexy and, in truth, makes a person take a second look because it looks like I'm naked underneath. I'm not naked. I'm also not wearing my own underwear. "Infinitely better," she adds. "This bra doesn't interfere with the corseting or the flow of the dress."

Apparently, my own bra did. It was also an unsightly slash across the backless element. I said my imagination worked just fine, that I didn't need to try the "correct" underwear. But because Charlotte is very thorough and likely working on commission, she insisted. She also brought matching panties with an obscene price tag considering the tiny amount of fabric, along with a pair of shoes with heels as high as a skyscraper.

"Surely, it doesn't take that long to put on a dress."

My stomach flips. There's something kind of wicked about dressing and undressing knowing Whit is just on the other side of the door, listening to the sound of zippers and the low hum of our conversation. Conversation, I'll admit, I've been hamming up. I'm not sure Charlotte gets what I'm trying to achieve, but she's played her part well. We've chatted. We've giggled. We've admired, making low *oohs* and *aahs* before opening the dressing room door with a *ta-da!* kind of reveal for Whit's perusal.

He wanted to play dress-up, so I get to play the character I want.

"I love the way this one feels," I murmur sultrily as I slide my hand over my hip as though he could see.

"Yes, it really is rather beautiful on you." Bending, Charlotte adjusts the train like a lady-in-waiting.

"Thank you, Charlotte. You're such a doll."

"*Come on,*" Whit mutters in complaint. If I'm not mistaken, that was his forehead hitting the door.

"When was the last time you wore a dress?" I ask, not bothering to hide the smile from my words.

"I remember taking a few of them off." Charlotte giggles quietly, like he needs the encouragement. "And it never took this long."

"You probably used scissors," I call back. Then a little lower but still loud enough for him to hear, I add, "He has to hurry on account of his *little problem*." Charlotte's expression is a picture—a picture reflected back at me from all angles, thanks to the excess of mirrors in here.

"My little problem," he purrs. "That's not what you called it this morning. Not when your mouth was stretched wide—"

"In shock? Yeah, sorry. That was unfortunate. I didn't mean to make you feel—"

"What's unfortunate is the fact that I'll need a walking

frame before I get to see this dress," he grumbles. "Charlotte, the phone is ringing in the other room."

"Thank you, but that's fine. It'll go to voicebank."

"I think you ought to answer it," he adds pointedly.

A pause follows where Charlotte seems torn.

"Maybe you should check," I suggest.

"Perhaps." Her expression conflicted, she adds, "I'll be back in a jiffy."

"No problem."

Unlocking the door, she slides silently out. I make as though to lock it, just for fun, when I'm prevented by Whit's foot.

"It took you long enough..." His words trail away as I pull the door open fully. His shoulder pressed to the doorframe, his stance is utterly casual, though his gaze tells another story as it wanders down my body. The sensation it causes is like his fingers had traveled the same path.

"A sight worth waiting a dozen hours for," he says, husky voiced with approval.

I pause to unknot my clumsy tongue, my attention on my hand as I smooth it down the front of my thigh. "It is a beautiful dress, but—"

His finger at my chin, Whit lifts my gaze to his. "*You* are beautiful, Amelia."

"But this dress..."

"Is perfect."

"It's too much, Whit. I can see by your face what you're going to say, and the answer is no."

His chest moves with a chuckle. "How did you guess I was about to promise I'd fuck you in it?"

"Funny," I deadpan. "But you're not buying this for me."

"I think you'll find that has nothing to do with you."

"No!"

"Yes. I'm also going to take you out on a date while you're wearing it."

"Whit—"

"Yes. If you can date other men, you can be my arm candy from time to time." I narrow my gaze, not sure if I believe his flippant tone. "And if you're a good little date, I might even kiss you on the doorstep. Of course, I'll be on my knees, under the hem."

"Come on, stop it," I whisper-hiss. "She'll be back any minute."

"We'd better make this fast then, I suppose." As quick as those words are spoken, he's inside the dressing room, clicking the lock closed on the door.

"Not even!" I say with stuttering chuckle.

"Why, whatever do you mean?" His answer is the embodiment of an elderly aunt with a hand pressed to her chest. *Not Doreen, obviously.*

"You and me." I waggle my finger in the air between us. "In here?" I make a circle to indicate the space. "Not happening."

He chuckles as he curls his hand around my shoulder. "You have a dirty mind." He turns me to face the mirror, the mirror I'm currently pulling a *you wish* face in. His sly smile feels like a bolt of current as, without moving his gaze, he brings his lips to my ear. "You've been so easy to corrupt."

Were truer words ever spoken?

"I'm serious." As serious as a girl can be when her nipples are rubbing against the lace of her dress at the illicitness of his suggestion. He hasn't suggested it, but something tells me it's only a matter of time. And God help me, for obvious reasons, I'm gonna have to buy these panties myself.

"So am I. I'm buying you this dress."

"No." I turn my head over my shoulder, finding his lips impossibly close.

"Yes." His answer is a bare breath that caresses my lips. "If I can buy you lingerie without knowing it, I can buy you an evening dress for the pleasure of seeing you in it."

"I seem to remember you've had the pleasure of seeing me in the underwear, too."

"I'll see more than you just wearing it before we're through."

"Except, technically, these panties don't belong to you."

"You can't make me harder than I already am." His hands slip to my hips, pulling me against him as though to prove the point.

"That's such a weird thing to say." Instead of the giggle I'd anticipated, I find myself exhaling a breathless sort of trembling thing. It's a breath that belies the riotous feelings simmering under my skin. *God, I want him.*

"You should leave." I don't sound convinced. "She could be back any minute."

His fingers slip over my hip bones, the firmer press reminding me of how empty my body feels right now. How it could be if I just give in. My mind hops to all the ways Whit can satisfy this hollowness. How many ways he could take me.

Lord, my insides begin to throb like a bruise.

"She could turn up, or the very astute and practical Charlotte could stay on the shop floor for a very long time."

"What did you do?" I turn my head over my shoulder as though his dark-eyed reflection is too much.

"That would be telling," he murmurs as his lips feather mine teasingly. "I think we should get you out of this dress." The huskiness in his voice makes his meaning more than clear. I might be a fool, a fool for him, but I go with it.

"Unfasten me?" I slide my hand under my hair as Whit's fingers lift to the nape of my neck. One hook undone, he presses his lips to the bared skin. Another hook and he repeats the action, causing tiny shivers of anticipation to shimmer down my spine.

His hands slide over my shoulder, the sounds of cloth sliding before the weighty dress drops like a theater curtain to the floor. "Show's over," I find myself whispering.

"No, sweetheart." In the mirror, his gaze sweeps over my body, the look bold and possessive. "It's just beginning."

His body gracefully folds behind me, his fingers making a loop around my left ankle. As he lifts it, I reach forward, my palms pressing to the mirror for balance. He repeats the action, throwing the exquisite dress to the chair behind him.

"Careful," I protest, but I have nothing else to offer as he stands, his palms sliding along my calves, my knees, up my thighs. I make as though to move when he stills me with a hand to my hip.

"You have a freckle here." His thumb sweeps over my shoulder blade before slipping down my spine. "And here. So many freckles to trace."

"Sounds like a good game."

"Yes." The way he looks at me feels like a tongue licking my belly from the inside. "Yes, I think it could be."

My body seems to register what he's about to do, excitement rippling through me in anticipation a second before his arms engulf me.

"We can't—not here." I turn my head over my shoulder, maybe because I don't want to see the lies leave my lips.

"We can." His whisper is hot against my ear, his palm like a brand as he presses it flat to my stomach, sparks of pleasure radiating under my skin. "We just have to be quiet."

My thoughts scatter as his fingers dip into my panties, my body melting against him like soft wax as he cups me.

"Open your eyes, Amelia."

My insides ignite at his words and how his middle finger slips through my wetness. His thumb finds my clit, and all doubts—thoughts—disappear.

"You're so fucking beautiful," Whit whispers, his body moving with mine as I chase his touch. The mirror fogs with my fevered breaths as his mouth trails my shoulder, the nape of my neck, his free hand sliding higher to mold to my breast. "If only I'd known what fun shopping could be before."

"You've never done this before?"

"Never have I ever taken a woman shopping." His fingers gather my arousal, painting it across my clit.

"That feels…"

"Never have I ever fucked a girl in a dressing room." I cry out at the almost reprimanding press of his teeth. My spine arches, my breasts thrusting out in the direction of the mirror as my body yields. "Oh, but I'm about to."

His finger slips wetly from between my legs, the press of him fading. My pulse begins to go haywire at the metallic *click* of his zipper, and I watch in the mirror as, from behind, he slips my panties to the side.

"Open up for me, Amelia." My thighs begin to tremble, but I do as he bids. His knees dip, the satin-smooth head of his cock a stroke against my wet ribbon of flesh. "Wider." His foot slides against mine, his open mouth a wet press to my shoulder. He sucks, drawing a sound from my throat as he coats his crown in my wetness.

Our eyes lock, but he doesn't smile, the moment too dark for flippancy as he pushes inside. Whit grates out a sound, though it might've easily been me, the shock of being so full of him is so sinfully delicious.

He rolls his hips, then thrusts harder, pleasure radiating through me, my body clenching a greeting around him.

"Oh Jesus," he groans in a plea for mercy. "Do that again."

But my consciousness is too feverish to heed his words. My knees almost buckle but for where he holds me, where he fills me, stretched and full to his hilt. With a flex of his hips, he continues the torment. Long, punishing thrusts, shallow teasing jabs as his fingers curl around my shoulder to hold me in place—to hold me for his pleasure as he gives and I take.

"Oh God!" I cry out, my breath clouding the mirror again and again as he fucks me with something that looks like vengeance, those dark, feral eyes watching and his body take, take, taking.

"Louder, darling," he demands in the spaces between his thrusts. "I want the walls to shake with your sounds."

I begin to thrust backward, my body in charge, driven by an all-consuming need as hot liquid pleasure spreads through me.

He groans, thrusting firmly, changing tempo at once. This time, he offers me no mercy, which is just the way I want it as I meet him cry for thrust. An exquisite tension builds inside, the intensity mounting and twisting with the collision of skin. Higher and higher it spirals, pushing all the air from my chest until I come loudly, my mind fragmenting, my body flexing and arching through its chemical release.

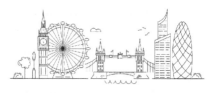

26

MIMI

"Morning."

A tiny shiver of anticipation runs down my spine at his voice. I don't turn around, instead giving my mind a moment to revel, a moment to pretend this is my everyday reality. Whit greeting me in the kitchen, pressing a kiss to my head as he reaches for the Lucky Charms. Not that he either kisses me or reaches for something as fun as Lucky Charms, but a girl can pretend for a moment or two. Even if said girl isn't destined for such a future, a fact reinforced when I'd found myself relegated to another bedroom overnight. On the one hand, it feels kind of weird, given I slept *with* Whit in his bed the night before. Yet on the other hand, why should it be weird. It's not like we're even a thing. Maybe I snore, and no one has thought to tell me.

"Good morning." I lift my head from where it's pressed against the cooling coffee cup in my hand, turning a brief smile Whit's way. The rasp of his fingers against the dark scruff on his cheek makes my insides bloom and heat. I shouldn't feel like this but can't seem to prevent it.

"You worked out how to use the machine, then."

"I found a jar of instant," I say, pressing the cup back to my cheek. "The coffee machine was too intimidating to contemplate." Surely, a Keurig would be easier. Something with pods?

"Want me to show you how it works?" he asks, pulling the milk from the fridge. "Latte, right?"

"No, thank you." I kind of jiggle my cup. "This is good." Too much caffeine gives me fluttery palpitations, which lately makes me feel anxious. Or maybe it just makes my parents feel anxious? The line is so blurred it's hard to remember who has the problem.

"What about breakfast?" he says, putting the milk back.

I will myself not to blush as my mind slips to yesterday morning's cake-and-mango fest. It feels like such a long time ago somehow. Realizing he's waiting for an answer, I give my head a belated shake. "I'm not hungry yet."

"You're sure I can't tempt you?" he says, jiggling an espresso cup. I don't answer and barely look up. Not until he begins to busy himself with the machine, his back facing me. Then I do indulge in a little temptation. He is a study in London grays this morning, though the sun is uncharacteristically bright and shiny this April morning. Shorts that look to have been sweatpants in a previous life hang from his narrow hips, a well-worn gray T-shirt clinging to the architecture of his broad back. His hair is slightly bed mussed, making him look sleep-rumpled and warm and all kinds of sexy.

Sure I can't tempt you? I play the words in his accent back in my head. I'd jump on his back like a clingy spider monkey if I thought it would do me any good. Why am I so crabby this morning?

"Did you sleep well?" he asks as the coffee grinder powers down as part of his morning coffee ritual.

"Like a baby." A confused, neglected baby who wondered what she'd done wrong because the difference between Friday and Saturday night was like night and day. *Ah, that's why.* Saturday began with such sweet promise, pardon the pun. Then he'd sex'd me so hard in a dressing room of a high-end boutique that not only did the sale associate hear us but probably the patrons of a nearby restaurant, too. Poor Charlotte. She could barely look at us when we emerged from the dressing room. Although Whit did take great joy in pointing out she wasn't the only one with an avid interest in her shoes. I hope her commission makes up for the awkwardness.

By the time we'd gotten back to the apartment, our messy breakfast had been cleared away and the apartment looked as pristine as a showhouse. Whit had ordered dinner in—a Lebanese mezze plater with enough food to feed half a dozen—and we'd sat cross-legged on the living room floor, eating and talking and laughing. Sharing stories. Though we were careful to avoid the topic of the past, glossing over any cracks in the conversation for fear of invoking Connor.

I miss my brother, and I always will. But I refuse to let him sit like a wall between us. All in all, the evening had been so good. Warm. Fun. Intimate. At least until it was time for bed.

Salty? Moi?

You bet.

"Nice pajamas."

I hear the smirk in Whit's voice and angle my gaze his way. I'm not wearing pajamas but one of his T-shirts. I've also borrowed a pair of his sweatpants, rolled at the waist and ankle, though he probably can't see those from this angle. I'd found them in a neatly folded pile in the laundry room last night and thought to borrow them. The pants are maybe a bit unnecessary given the air in this temperature-controlled haven, but I kind of feel like he set the tone when he showed me into a different bedroom last night.

"Thanks for the loaner."

"Anytime."

He turns back to the machine as I mutter, "It's just a temporary measure."

He turns fully then and leans back against the countertop. His fingers looped around the ridiculously tiny handle on the espresso cup, he watches as I gently pluck the cotton between my thumb and finger.

"I'll obviously wash this."

"Weren't there pajamas in…"

"The whole new wardrobe you paid for?" I probably shouldn't sound so ungracious. A red-cheeked Charlotte said she'd arrange for delivery of "our purchases" and shortly after we got back last night, a guy from concierge arrived at Whit's door with one of those brass hotel trolleys. It was laden with bags and boxes branded with the boutique's name, literally spilling with stuff I didn't try on—or need! I'll probably be back at Doreen's later today, and there is literally no space in my tiny closet. But my protests fell on deaf ears. I can't help but secretly love it. Not only that he'd buy me stuff but that he'd choose it. Such a bossy attitude.

"Who knew shopping could be so much fun." His words trail off as his eyes move over me heatedly. "Not that I don't like to see you wearing my clothes."

Especially when I'm not wearing a bra, I think cynically. With that thought, I put down my cup and fold my arms against the countertop, leaning against them. No one needs to see nipples like doorknobs this early, least of all him.

He probably doesn't even want to see them, or else why did I sleep alone last night.

"There were pajamas." One pair I'd chosen. Three pairs I had not. "Along with some seriously slinky nightgowns that I think Charlotte must've boxed by mistake."

"Oh?"

"Yeah. They aren't the kind of things I would've chosen for myself."

"How so?"

"High-end fripperies in silk and lace? That's not me at all."

"You forget, I've seen your underwear." After bringing the cup to his lips, he moves his neck with a swallow.

"Yeah." I squirm slightly in my seat because he's got me there. He can have me too, right here, right now. I just don't know how to bridge the gap. "I'm more practically minded when it comes to sleepwear."

"The way I see it, some clothing is meant to be worn just for the joy of taking off."

"Sounds like you know what it's like to wear a bra."

"What?" The word bubbles with laughter before he brings his cup to his lips for a leisurely sip.

"The joy of sliding off your bra after a day at work?" I give a blissful sigh before giving in to a smirk. "But I take it that's *not* what you meant?"

"No, but I'm happy to relieve you of your bra anytime."

"You don't happen to know how I come to be the owner of so many clothes, do you?" Unable to hold his tiger-bright gaze, I fasten my fingers to the rim of my cup, rotating it against the counter.

"You know who's responsible," he murmurs as though I'd just asked him to put the trash cans out.

"Can we shoot for *why*, instead?"

"Can I want to see you in them?" I watch as he pivots from the waist to put his cup down.

"You can want, yeah," I find myself answering with just a hint of taunt. His expression doesn't waver; he still looks mildly amused. So I go with the truth over my failed brand of flirting. "But you can't see me in them this morning." *Because you didn't want to last night,* a huffy-sounding voice says from somewhere deep inside. "Can't wear clothes that haven't been washed." I shrug. "Especially not underwear and nightwear." It's not sanitary.

"Very sensible."

"Yeah, sensible is *such* a turn-on."

"Oh, you have no idea. Did you sleep in my T-shirt last night?"

I give my head a quick shake, biting my bottom lip against the notion of admitting I slept naked because it seems too obvious a ploy, even if it is the truth. "I found the washing machine last night," I say, changing the conversation's direction. "So I'm good to go this morning."

"Feel free to wear my clothes anytime."

"You might want to rethink that offer." Because your clothes smell like you, and I literally want to roll in your scent like a puppy finding a new smell. "Especially as you look like you might be a little short on T-shirts." Short literally, I think as I gesture to his current outfit. Not only is his T-shirt well worn, but it also looks to have shrunk in the wash. It barely meets the waistband of his shorts, which isn't—

Heat blossoms deep inside as he slides his palm to the flat of his stomach. He lifts the cotton a touch to revel a fleeting glimpse of dark, fine hair that trails from his navel down. My lips twitch because it's not called a happy trail for no reason.

"What's wrong with my T-shirt?" he asks, hooking his thumb into the soft elastic of his shorts. Tendons and muscles flex in his forearm and it makes me want to ask if he does that on purpose, but then I realize the whole motion wasn't to treat me to a little arm porn but for me to feast my eyes on that tiny strip revealed lower. A dip of muscle and the hint of that V-shaped groove along his hip.

Is it on purpose or am I imagining it?

"It's too small." My eyes snap up to his, his expression showing no sign of amusement. *Like he didn't set me up. Like he didn't just catch me perving.*

"I can take it off." My stomach tenses as he makes to do so, reaching a hand over his shoulder, grabbing the fabric between his shoulder blades. "I will if you will."

"Funny." Is he being funny? It's hard to tell, but that sounded more like teasing, more provocative than jokey. Not that it matters as Whit shrugs, aborting the maneuver, his dark eyes still watching me, seeing through me, anyway.

"There's no news yet on Doreen's place." I find myself filling the gap in our conversation. Or is this banter? The Brits love a *bit of bants*.

Stop overthinking—you're being really weird.

Well, he should've taken me to bed and then I wouldn't feel like the ends of a loaf of bread. You know, the bits that get touched but that no one ultimately wants.

"You look like you're having a very intense conversation with yourself."

"I was just thinking maybe I should call Aunt Doreen." My gaze slides to the right where my phone is charging behind him. "I was leaving it for a little while. It's still early."

"Does she often stay at Frank's?"

"No. It's usually the other way around."

"That must be fun for you."

"I have earplugs."

Whit barks out a laugh and ruffles a hand through his very bed-head hair. *Very sexy hair.* "You're probably right. It is a little early to call the morning after the night before."

"At least one of us is having a good time," I mutter.

"What was that?"

"I said I hope she's having a good time."

"With *lover boy* Frank?"

"Try Thursday boy Frank."

"No way," he says with a chuckle.

"Doreen has a colorful love life. A different man for each day of the week. Not that there's anything wrong with that," I add quickly. *Kettle, meet imaginary pot,* I guess.

"Hm." His expression turns thoughtful. "That explains the sour grapes from her friend with the green cardigan yesterday." I pull a quizzical face, not sure what he's talking about. "Frank must be quite the boy because green cardi wasn't impressed that Doreen had gotten her claws into him first."

"It's like a soap opera for senior citizens," I say, propping my chin to my fist.

"Maybe Doreen can lend the other woman her dildol." He pulls a ridiculously funny face, and I giggle against my better instincts.

"It makes me wonder where Doreen gets the energy from."

"I thought for a minute you were taking a leaf out of her book. All those dates you're planning on going on."

"I didn't say—"

"London might be a small city, but it's jam-packed with things to see," he adds, about as unconcerned as he could be about my so-called dating life. I shouldn't feel disappointed about his response, yet I do. But feelings don't have to make sense, and the whole point of this dating misdirection is to protect him. Well, him and me. We're just two people who have casual sex. And work together. Two people who have casual sex who have a history. I'm probably overthinking things. It's not like Whit is complaining. I bet he's had a dozen arrangements like this. So maybe who I'm trying to protect is not him but me.

His hand appears in front of me, and I realize he's passing over my phone.

"It's fully charged. I see you decided."

"Decided?" My attention dips, and I see a notification from the dating app I'd downloaded this morning. "Oh."

"Don't sound so enthusiastic," he says without an ounce of disapproval in his tone. My insides flutter as he negligently leans against the end of the island instead of moving back.

"I only just signed up this morning." My gaze dips, and I find myself stumbling over my explanation.

"What photographs did you use? Hinge has three, right?"

"Just ones from home." This is disturbing, not to mention uncomfortable. "You've used the platform before?"

"Let's see them," he says, ignoring my question.

What the heck? I absently input my password. And get it wrong twice.

"You're all fingers and thumbs this morning." Now he's just trying to make me feel worse. The third time's a charm. I flick open the notification.

"I got a rose?" My voice sounds uncertain, my brow scrunching in a frown. As part of the account process, I had to upload three images of me and pick three prompts to answer. The photographs I loaded weren't great, and I put the least effort into answering the prompts. Who the hell is trawling for dates on Sunday morning?

"That means someone really likes you."

"That's not true." I glance up at his amused expression. "It's not—you can't get to know someone over that tiny amount of information."

"I've known less about women I've fucked," he murmurs so quietly. It still stings. "Let's see which prompts you chose." He reaches for my phone.

"No!" I press it to my chest in two-handed protection.

"Why not?" His eyes tighten at the corners.

"Because it's none of your business. And, by the way, I see you're already familiar with the interface." This comes out way more snipe-y than I anticipated, but there's no denying how I feel, which is annoyed at his blasé attitude. I'm also oddly irritated by the fact he's been on Hinge.

Hypocritical? Absolutely. But I didn't say it made sense.

"Come on, Mimi. I'll show you my prompts, if you like?"

"You're still on there?" Oh my. That was a little shrill.

"Nope," he says so, so amused. "Not for ages, but it's easy enough to reinstall the app."

"There's no need for that," I mutter mulishly as I pull my phone away from my chest. Just a hint of threat is all it takes. "I'll let you look, but you're not allowed to laugh."

"Why would I laugh?" he asks, still loving this exchange as I input my phone's password which, thankfully, only takes me one attempt this time. I hand it over and my stomach somersaults with nervousness.

"I'm looking for," Whit begins, reading aloud the first prompt I've chosen. "Someone who loves our Lord and Savior, Jesus Christ, and is down to show me what London has to offer." His attention slides to me, his mouth turned down.

"What? What's wrong with that?"

"I didn't know you were religious."

"I'm not particularly. I just thought it might set the right tone."

"Because every man wants to corrupt a good girl?" he grates out.

It's my turn to pull a face. "No!" Unless they do, because how would I know? "Wait, is that really true?"

"I'm sorry to break it to you, but men don't operate from one massive hive mind."

"I know that." Because it wouldn't need to be massive to support the majority of them. "Look, I used the religious line because the tone I wanted to set was I'm not interested in any funny business. You know, not DTF."

"What's DTF?" Whit gives a tiny, confused shake of his head as he stares down at me.

"It's an acronym."

"Yes, but for what?"

"You know."

"If I did, would I be asking?"

"It means down to... fudge. But the other word."

"I don't know what the other word is," he says. But then his mouth quirks and it makes me want to hit him. "I'm just pulling your fudging leg."

"Well, be careful. That leg has a donkey's kick."

"Good," he says, leaning his forearm down against the island countertop. "Because the God-fearing, good girl Christian angle could go both ways. It might send the right signal to some, but to others, it might make you more of a challenge."

"Urgh!" I drop my head back like my neck is a flexible joint. "This is *hard!*"

"Let's look at the rose sender's prompts," he says, swiping my phone out of my hand.

"Hey!"

"Greg?" He glances up from the screen, brows riding high on his head.

"What's wrong with Greg?"

"What's right with him?"

"You can't object to a name."

"I think you'll find I can object to whatever the fuck I like."

"Let me see." I reach out when Whit twists his upper body, holding my phone out of reach.

"Ah-ah!" he mouths as though talking to a toddler. "Now, where were we?" Still holding the phone over my head, he taps the screen and begins to read the first prompt. "'Something about me that surprises people is... I'm still single.'" Whit's phone-holding arm drops, along with his expression. "What a complete twat."

"You don't think that's cute?"

"I'm beginning to think you're the kind of person who, when faced with a red flag, just sprinkles glitter on it."

"I am not!"

"For God's sake, it's borderline narcissistic," he says, rubbing his hand down his face. I just love how he does that. Big hands, big... never mind.

"Let's hope it was him trying too hard, and he redeems himself with the second." He lifts the phone, his lips twisting a second later. "Dear, oh dear. Greg is a worry."

"Oh, come on, it can't be that bad." Can it?

"Prompt number two says, 'dating me is like... taking a mouthful of water and finding out it's actually vodka. Surprise!' *Anal*," he adds in a low murmur.

"What? It does not say... say that!" I make to grab my

phone when he holds it out of my reach again.

"If Greg is the kind of bloke to give you vodka when you ask for water, he's definitely not going to think twice about trying to shove his dick up your arse with an 'oops, wrong hole!'"

"Ew, Whit!" Does that even happen? "Just give me that back." I stretch out my arms as I stand on the stool's foot bar, but I'm nowhere near high enough to reach.

"Keep your knickers on." His eyes flick down. "Ah, I forgot. You haven't got any on."

"I'm hardly naked," I protest. "I borrowed your sweats!"

He grins like the devil, and his eyes drop. "Doesn't look like they're going to stay on very long."

I glance down and realize how low the waistband has sagged. "Dammit." I grab it in one hand, and with the other, I make a hand gesture like I'm in a Lucy Lui action movie. *Bring it.* Only more like a whiny, "Just give it to me."

"What's it worth to you?" Devilment flits across his face.

I drop back to the stool, suddenly defeated.

"What's wrong?"

"I give up."

"No, you don't," he says, putting my phone down next to him. "You never give up."

He's thinking about the fake Mimi, not the real one. The real Mimi gave up and let her parents rule her life. It was probably a good thing that she did because she's really making a mess of things.

"Mimi, come on. What is it?"

My chin jerks up, and I do this weird *pfft* sound, disputing his perceptiveness. "I was just thinking I have no idea where I'll put all my new clothes," I say, plucking the first topic out of my head. "I mean, I am grateful, but I only have a tiny room and no closet space to speak of."

"You can leave them here. Some of them. Most? Whatever you like. You'll be here often enough to wear them."

"I will?"

"You were the one who demanded the full experience. Unless you've changed your mind and think Greg is a better choice."

I hate that he's being so blasé. "No, I don't think that."

There the real Mimi goes again, making a mess and complicating things when the man just gave her a very reasonable out. An out from danger, from her feelings.

"Good." He leans his hip deeper against the counter as those tiger eyes slide over me. "Though I'm not sure there's enough time left before you leave to do all the things I want to do to you."

"That makes last night a waste, then." The words escape my mouth without my say so.

"Last night?" Doubt flashes across his brow, lightening almost immediately, his mouth hooking up in one corner as though tugged by a string. "Well, it's taken you a while, but at least you've said what you mean."

"I always say what I mean," I retort like the liar pants I am.

"Last night." He sighs and rubs his right hand up and down the back of his head. "I suppose I was giving you space. Trying not to come on too strong."

"You might've said."

"You might've said you were unhappy," he says, looking the opposite of that state. "You were the one who said you wanted to date other men. Maybe my sensitive little feelings were tweaked." He reaches out and pinches my nose gently.

This is so strange. How have we gone from growly denials and sex that feels like he's trying to imprint on me—

or at least imprint the shape and sensation of his penis in me—to this? To flippancy. But before I have a chance to pull away in protest, his thumb slips to my bottom lip.

"I thought you would've understood." His eyes turn golden as he lowers his head, meeting mine. "You have a standing invitation to my bedroom."

"I didn't want to presume," I whisper, breathing in his scent.

"Oh, Mimi." His thumb drifts away, his lips brushing mine. "I find that hard to believe."

"It's true," I say, twisting my mouth from under his.

He pulls back with an amused chuckle. "You know, if I looked up unsubtle in a dictionary, I'm sure I'd see your picture there—"

"Is that supposed to be flattering?" I ask, speaking louder and over the top of him. "Is that how you woo women?"

"You've been the absolute opposite of subtle since you whirled yourself into my life. Happy or not, horny or not, I assumed you'd be sure to tell me where you were on those scales. Whenever you were on those scales."

"How about cuddly?" I ask a little aggressively. "Am I allowed to demand affection?" Maybe I'm trying to frighten him off.

"Why the fuck not?" he says, leaning his weight onto his hip. "Have I missed something?"

"No." I tilt my chin, my reply prickly. "I'm just checking."

"Are you feeling cuddly right now?" His expression? It says quite clearly *you know you want me. It. I mean, you know you want a hug.* And dammit, I do.

"I might be," I answer, slightly mollified.

"Bring it in." He straightens, curling his finger in a *come-hither* motion.

I duck my head to hide my smile, knot my hand in the

waistband of his pants and hop down from my stool. My happiness is easier to hide as he wraps his arms around me. My insides turn to goo at the low "*hmmm*" he makes as I bury my nose in his T-shirt.

"Are you sniffing me?"

"You have a very vivid imagination, Leif Whittington."

"That's true. However, you'll have a very red bottom if we have to undergo anything like this again." His finger slides between us, lifting my chin to reveal my *I'd like to see you try it, buster,* face. "If you're unhappy, you say so."

"I'm pretty unhappy about being threatened." My hands fasten around his forearm.

"It's not a threat."

"Oh, so it's a promise? You *promise* you'll spank me?" A derisive noise shoots from the back of my throat as I push his arm away.

"I promise you won't always feel this way about it."

"Ah!" The sound is short and sharp. "*Right.*"

"You'll change your mind."

"See, you're still making it sound like you think there's a spanking in my future."

He grins though tries to rub it away, but it's too stubborn. "If I'm honest, I'm counting on it."

"Lord knows why."

His expression? So, *so* smug. "Because, while I like it when people do as they're told, I also secretly like it sometimes when they don't."

"People?"

"You."

"You want to spank me?" My tone is lower than I'd anticipated, but I put that down to his expression. No way I like the sound of being spanked.

"I want to possess you for a little while. Hear your gasp

as you anticipate the contact. Make you moan when you push back onto my fingers, demanding more."

Heat and light shoot though me, my insides as hot and as wild as a summer storm. "Sorry, I can't see that happening." My voice sounds wavery. I'm not lying. I can't see it, but I can feel it viscerally.

"You'll come around."

"Wanna bet?" I demand, jutting out my chin. This is so confusing. Do I want to fight him or do I want him to *make me?*

"It would be unfair of me to take advantage of you when you're obviously so... het up."

"Who's het up? And who says spanking is taking advantage. Unless you win, fair and square."

"It's more like giving."

I make another *pfft* sound. "Still sounds like you don't want risk it. In fact, it sounds to me like someone's a *itty bit chicken*." I make chicken wings with my elbows.

"Are you... clucking?" he says, trying not to be amused.

"If the feathers fit."

"Fine, have it your way. I'll take your bet."

"I bet you a *cool* one hundred you won't ever get to spank me. Not without my permission."

"I'd give you a much cooler thousand right here and right now just to try it."

I don't know which is the bigger shock. The money he's offering or the fact that I'm thinking about it—not even for the money but because he's so sure about it. So sure about me.

"No." I rub my lips together. Meanwhile, Whit begins to make his own impersonation of a chicken. *Or a cock.*

I begin to turn, not for any other reason than I think I

might want him to make me. "I don't like being manipulated."

"Is that why your cheeks are pink?"

"I think I should leave—" I half turn to deliver my edict, but the next sound out of my mouth is an inhaled gasp as Whit catches my hand, spinning me into him. His thick thigh presses between mine, and his hand connects lightning fast with my ass. His arm slides around me, and he grabs a handful of my ass, then presses my body tightly to his.

"According to the Metropolitan Police's Twitter account, you're not going home anytime soon." His head dips, his lips a whisper from my ear. "There's still an unexploded bomb in a nearby garden. Nowhere to run, little fly. Nowhere to hide."

I heard *bomb,* and my insides bloom, probably because his hands have slipped down the back of the sweatpants I'm wearing and are kneading my bare butt. "Are you ready to earn that cool five thousand?"

"You said one."

"I'll pay you ten times that."

"Not for money," I whisper. "Think of something more fun."

"Fun for which of us?"

"You're really weird."

"No, gorgeous, I'm hard." His hand covers mine, sliding it between us to where his sweatpants already leave little to the imagination.

"Commando," I whisper, rubbing my palm against the head.

"Great minds think alike."

Before he's finished speaking, I find myself twirled and bent over the island. The marble is cool under my palms,

Whit's hands hot on the cheeks of my ass, sliding the loose sweatpants down before his hands drag liquid fire up the back of my legs.

"This arse." He spreads his fingers wide as though to maximize the contact. "This arse was made to be fucked by me." I guess I must squeak as he adds, "Yes, fucked, Amelia. I'll worship this arse when you give it to me."

It feels entirely natural to stretch out beneath him as I elongate my spine like a housecat. "That wasn't what I meant by fun." And that sounded way more sultry than I was aiming for. It earns me a dark chuckle and a foot between mine that slides my feet farther apart.

"Have you ever been taken like that, Amelia?" His words sound dragged over gravel.

"That's not something I've ever *given*," I retort. My breath halts as I feel him lift the hem of his T-shirt with both hands, folding it delicately to my lower back. I'm impressed how unaffected I sound as he slides his fingertips along the crease of my right butt cheek.

"It's not something you can rush." My whole body is jarred as his hand slips between my legs. "Even if you are wet just thinking about it."

"And you're hard at the thought of it. Which of us is the bigger deviant?"

"Do we have to be deviants? So judge-y, judge-y, *judge-y*!"

I swear I feel the *whoosh* of air before his palm lands on my right cheek. I make a noise that's not exactly a complaint, the low *ungh* much closer to an encouragement.

"All right?" His palm slides over the sharp sting, the path agonizingly deliberate.

I nod, too... *something* to speak. Puzzled, is what I am. Embarrassed? Turned on? It didn't hurt, but I am standing in his kitchen, naked from the waist down. Not to mention bent over with my ass in the air. That's not sexy, is it? I lie —I lie, *and* I moan as he pushes two fingers slickly inside me.

"Oh!" I hear the evidence of my enjoyment, feel it in the slippery twist of his fingers. Hear it in my mewls and sighs as he thrust them inside me this way and that, working me into a wet frenzy. "Whit. Oh God, that feels—"

"Just think, we could've been doing this last night if you'd been honest." His fingers curl and stroke, reaching that point inside me that turns my mind to mush and makes my thighs twitch. "You understand that now, don't you?" he says darkly, his fingers beckoning me on.

I make a noise in response. I hope it sounds like a yes. *God, yes.*

"Use your mouth for something other than back talk, Amelia. Tell me you understand that if you want me to fuck you, you just have to ask."

I make an inarticulate protest as his fingers slide wetly away, my body twisting to turn when he presses his palm low on my back.

"What's more fun than a spanking?" His words are almost pondering as he touches my ass like it belongs to him.

"What?" I ask, confused.

"Is it more fun pretending you won't be into it." His hand comes down again. Flesh meets flesh a little more thuddy this time. *Less of a sting.* I cry out all the same, but the noise is somehow different. "Forcing my hand?" he almost crows. Then *thwack!* Again. And again.

It's not pain I feel, not exactly—he isn't hurting me. It's more like a delivery of sensation. Solid thwacks interspersed with light strokes. Teasing taps. A squeeze of my flesh followed by a dirty compliment.

"Look how wet this makes you." A brush. A promise. The sight of his fingers, silky with my arousal.

"Stop talking."

"I don't think I will. In fact, I have an idea." His hand strokes as though painting art on a canvas. "I'll send you out on your little dates with my cum dripping between your legs, and I'll—"

It's almost as though I hear the sound of his hand moving through the air the second before it impacts.

"Oh!"

"Spank you for deserting me when you get home."

Another thud. Another sharp sting. The experience feels like a release because, with each strike, I feel somehow unburdened. Lighter, maybe? My mind is certainly free of noise and chatter. Free to just feel. There's no rhyme, no reason, no agenda. Just Whit and me and sweet, sweet relief.

"Such a lovely pink color," he says with an admiring stroke over each curve.

My cheeks smart. Both sets of them. I'm not crying, am I? My eyes are wet, yet I feel warm and fuzzy. My chest heaves a little, my breath rapid and shallow as though I've been running.

"This was worth more than five thousand."

"We're finished?" I sound a little panicked as I turn my head over my shoulder, his dark eyes meeting mine.

"That's up to you. What is it you want, Amelia? Use your words, beautiful."

I want more sensation. More pleasure than pain. I want this to be a prelude more than anything, but I can't find the words. How do you form words for something you can't comprehend? Instead, I fall back on what I know works for us as I turn and press my aching breasts against the marble. Lowering my head, I stretch my arms out in front of me like a supplicant. Or someone who'd just offered herself on a platter as I whisper, "Please, Daddy. I need you."

"What do you need? Be more specific."

"I need you to fuck me."

"That wasn't hard now, was it?"

"It had better be—*oh!*" I stretch under him like a cat as he presses the head of his cock against me. In one long thrust, he's inside me, hot and thick.

"That hard enough for you?" His dark words curl around my ear, his body pressed to mine. He slides the hair from my face and the tears from my cheek. He doesn't need my answer. It's in my whimper as he slides back, leaving me empty, and it's in my cry as he thrusts into me once again.

"Yes, oh God!" I push back against him as a lightning storm of need burns to life inside me.

"Fuck!"

He fills me again and again, his hand curled around my shoulder to keep me in place as he gives and gives. As my body receives. My pleasure registers somewhere outside of me, sounds that are hardly feminine, rough sighs and sharp gasps, whispered encouragements that overlay Whit's masculine grunts.

And then it happens—I shouldn't be surprised, but I am because there is no soft buildup, just a burst dam of sensation that fractures through me as my fingers scrabble against the counter as though it could keep me from falling.

It doesn't.

"Fuck, yes. That's it," Whit growls, his body pressed tight and undulating against mine. "Who gets to fuck you, Amelia? Who is it that fucks you so well?"

"Y-you!" I whimper as this liquid, hot climax drowns me.

I'm aware of nothing else but the soft grunt of his own release against my neck.

27

WHIT

I LIFT my hand and wave at old Mr. Maqsood as he stands in the doorway of the newsagents. Polly says his eyesight isn't great, but he never fails to spot the Bugatti. Or frown at me.

"Did you upset that man?" Mimi turns her head to stare at him as we pass him by.

"Yeah, when I was about seven. He caught me trying to steal a Mars Bar from the confectionary counter."

"Wow. And he still bears a grudge?" She turns to face the front again. "That's some commitment." This is probably the most she's spoken since we left the apartment.

"Spite more like. It's probably the only thing keeping him alive."

"So these are the mean streets you grew up on?"

"Something like that."

She smiles. It's not one of her regular smiles. More a vague, professional tip of her lips that reveals no hint to what had passed between us just a couple of hours ago. Is she upset? Regretting it? Fuck knows I didn't spank her as hard as I wanted to. The thought of her being with someone else made me want to paddle her arse hard. Which would make me sadistic as well as an idiot for forgetting how young she is. How inexperienced. In my defense, she's been so self-assured. So forthright.

I thought I was annoyed on Friday when she told me my brother was taking her out. The thought of her dating random men makes my head feel like it's about to explode. And all twisted up inside.

No matter what she says about her reasons for dating, I know it's her way of reminding us both of the fleeting nature of our time together. I get that's the whole point of joining Hinge, and I can tell her heart isn't in it. She's not punishing me, and while a part of me wants to punish *her*, the more human part of me, a more sensible part, knows he should be thanking her for her efforts.

Thanks for taking my cock like a champ, Mimi.

Oh, and thanks for making sure neither of us gets too attached.

But I don't want to thank her. The jealous part of me, the animal part, wants to lock her away and never let her out of my sight again. And, yeah, I wanted her in my bed last night —of course I did. I guess I was just being a bit of a dick. But I also thought she'd come storming in at some point to call me out. I didn't think it would make her feel so wrong-footed. She was so spiky over her vulnerability.

I find myself glancing her way. She looks so fucking perfect wearing black pants and a slinky cashmere sweater that keeps sliding off her shoulder. It's meant to hang that way, but she keeps sliding it back like a flash of shoulder might give me ideas. If only she knew. I don't need to see her bare skin to get ideas—dressed for the office, in my sweatpants, or in a bloody burka and I'll still be thinking where my mouth has been. The places I've licked and sucked. The noises she makes when I discover something new that she likes. The experience kept me awake well into the night. Maybe it's little wonder I continued being an arsehole this morning.

Fucking Hinge. I wonder if I can persuade the board to buy the company just so I can close it down.

"What's funny?"

I realize she's looking at me, and the scoff in my chest turns to a sigh. She is so fucking lovely. "I was just thinking about my Mars Bar stealing days. I was terrified the old bloke would chop my hand off."

"Oh wow!"

"Luckily, his wife intervened and said she'd just tell my mum."

"What did your mom have to say?"

"Put it this way, it might've been easier to have my hand chopped off." I shake my head. "Polly was like a water fountain. She couldn't believe she'd raised such a deviant."

"If only she knew, huh?" This time, her smile is more like her own. I tighten my fingers around the steering wheel because I almost reached out for her hand.

She's not dating anyone. Fuck that idea. *But we both entered this with our own agendas,* comes my next unwelcome thought.

Mimi wants to experience a side of life that was unavailable to her before. She wants to explore her sexuality. She might want to cuddle, even sleep in my bed, but she's trying to limit the potential for being hurt. She's going back to Florida. I have to remember that.

"That's the park," I find myself saying, desperate to keep the strained silence at bay.

"Trees. Climbing frame. Swing." Her cheeky gaze slides my way. "Your story checks out."

"All right, smart arse. I was just making conversation," I say, biting back my grin.

"Brin and I used to ride our skateboards at the skate park until Heather wanted to tag along with us."

"And you didn't want that?" She turns her body toward me, her left foot hooking behind her right calf.

"It's not cool to have your little sister tagging along after you."

"Just what every little sister wants to hear." She laughs at my expression. "You must've been kinder to other people's little sisters because you were nothing but nice to me."

"I'm still nothing but nice to you," I say in a low purr. "Very nice. In fact, I seem to remember you paying me a lot of compliments this morning." I realize, maybe for the first time, that reference to our joined pasts no longer raises the specter of Connor. Guilt, I guess.

"You weren't very nice to my ass."

"And you loved it."

"You can't say things like that," she says, succumbing to a beautiful blush.

"I want to feast on your arse. Can I say that?"

"Stop!"

"The way it moves when I smack it—"

"Oh nice!" she splutters. "Tell me I have a fat ass, why don't you?"

In response, I slide down the window and much to her mortification, belt out a few discordant lines of Sir Mix-A-Lot's 'Baby got Back.'"

"You are something else." She gives a disparaging shake of her head.

"And you have an arse that's a dream."

"Are you sure this is a good idea?" she asks a few minutes later, her tone now unsure. "Sunday lunch with your family. I feel like I might be intruding." Her answer is a variation on a theme. I could type up her list of attempts to get out of coming today and have enough words for a dissertation. Or I could paint the excuses to canvas and make a show out of them. Bottom line? She's tried really hard to get out of this.

"It's not intruding when you're invited."

"Come on, this is awkward. You know it is. You only have to glance my way, and I blush today!"

This time, I give in to the urge to grin. "I know. I love it."

"Your brothers are going to love it too," she mutters.

"What?"

Her lips twist. "Really? That's what you picked up on?"

"Can't help you bring out the caveman in me," I mutter. I stretch back in my seat. For the first time since I bought this car, it feels uncomfortable. Too close. Too confined.

"Just don't go trying to drag me around by my ponytail," she says, touching the top of it."

"Don't worry. I've left my club back at the cave." I don't need it. Threats are usually enough to deal with my brothers.

"I can't believe we're actually doing this." She folds her arms, turning her attention back to the windshield.

"You saw Polly's text. She doesn't take *no* very well."

"I know, but after what you said about her desperation to become a grandma, do you really want me there?"

"She's not going to hold you down while I impregnate you on the dining table. She's not that unsubtle."

"Neither of us wants your brothers to know about us, though."

Weird. I find I'm not opposed to them getting the hint somehow. I don't think she'd appreciate my attempts because I wouldn't be too delicate about it.

"Maybe I should just text and say I can't make it, last minute. You could drop me at a bus stop, and I'll—"

"No chance. Besides, it's no good texting back with an excuse. Polly's notoriously bad for paying attention to her phone." On purpose, mostly. "She will have already started cooking."

"With three grown men at the table, I'm sure her efforts wouldn't go to waste."

"Five. Archer, Heather's husband, will be there. Not that it matters because you couldn't possibly put me in the situation of turning up empty-handed."

"I'm not a bottle of wine. Oh gosh." Her expression is suddenly stricken. "Wine. Or flowers? Whit, you have to pull over somewhere so I can get some chocolates or something."

"There's really no need. It's just Sunday lunch. She does it at least once a month."

"I'm not going to your mother's house empty-handed!"

"Fine," I mutter. "There's a florist back the way we came. I'll just..." I flick the turn signal and pull over.

"Thank you."

I realize she's twisting her hands, so I press mine over them. "Are you really that uncomfortable?"

"I feel like it's a test I'm going to fail. You said your mom has... ideas."

"Of me settling down, you mean?"

"Yes. It's freaking me out. What if she picks up on something? Aren't you worried Heather or El might say something to her?"

"Like what?" I give her hands a reassuring squeeze. Is the prospect of being tied to me so awful? "That I took you home because my idiot brother took a fancy to the waitress?"

"Server," she corrects. "And Heather knows it didn't go down like that."

"Heather is a vault." I move my hand back to the steering wheel. I don't know who she thinks she's kidding. How can she want to date other men when she was in such a strop this morning because she didn't sleep in my bed? "Just don't think you can get out of lunch. Polly will send out the flying monkeys to find you."

"The flying monkeys? Like the Wicked Witch of the West? That's an awful thing to call someone as lovely as your mom!"

"She's certainly got some kind of witchy magic, but it's me you should have pity for."

"Because she wants—horror upon horrors—for you to be happy?"

"You won't be singing that tune when she pulls out the baby photographs."

"Oh, I will," she scoffs. "I'd love to see some of baby Whit's cutey patootie."

"Why, when you have access to his grown-up... one of those?" Whatever a patootie is, chances are, I've still got one. "As for Polly being a witch, who do you think that makes captain of her flying monkeys?"

Hooking one hand into my armpit, I begin a terrible impersonation of an ape. Totally worth it to see her smile again.

"You're crazy!"

I'm crazy something all right.

"Remember, don't sit next to me," Mimi says as I push open the garden gate. "And don't sit across from me, either."

I half lift my arm and sniff my armpit. "Why? Do I smell?"

She stills me with a soft hand to my forearm. "Please be serious."

She turns toward the red-painted front door when I slip my fingers into hers with a reassuring squeeze... and a dirty whisper in her ear. "Think they'll be able to smell you on me?"

Her tentative smile is snuffed from her expression like a candle blown out.

"Mimi, come on." I glance at the large bay window of my parents' terrace house. "It's just my lot in there." I note the twitch of the curtain and think better of pointing it out. It might be weird, but I find I don't give a fuck if we're being watched. *Maybe I should just kiss her and be done with all speculation.* I stifle a sigh at the idiotic thought. She's really not down for that.

"Exactly. Your family. Your mom was so lovely when I called her when I was looking for work. And Heather was so cool on Friday. They can't find out, Whit. I don't want them to think badly of me."

I tilt my head to the side, almost floored by the needy words that shoot from my mouth. "Am I important to you, too?"

"You will always be important to me," she says soberly as her hand falls away. "More than you'll ever know." She slides the soft sweater over her bared shoulder which is probably a good move because I want to kiss her there. Let's face it, I want to kiss her everywhere. "I don't want them to pick up on any vibe between us. It wouldn't do for them to get ahead of themselves."

Mimi is more astute than I've given her credit for. I'm beginning to think it's me—that I'm a great big fucking idiot.

Why would I have a lump in my throat the size of a golf ball? How did this get so complicated over the space of a weekend?

She accused me of possessing sexual voodoo, but maybe it's more a case of her magical pussy? I'm a fucking idiot because Mimi is way more than that.

"Look, don't worry." I ease out a careful breath. "I can behave myself."

She slides me a look that's hard to decipher. "Ah hell, the flowers!" She pivots, then pivots back. "Open the car, would you, please?"

I pull out my keys, but before I can offer to get them, she's already off down the garden path. I slide them back into my pocket at the same time as the front door creaks open.

"That all looked very cozy."

I turn to the sound of El's voice and find him leaning against the doorjamb, arms folded, like a cheap soap opera villain.

"I didn't know you like to watch." He frowns at my words. "I saw the curtains twitching."

His expression twists before his mild answer carries across the space between us. "What am I supposed to be watching?"

I glance at the flower bed. Purple crocuses and daffodils, ornamental grasses waking from a long winter slumber. I inhale a deep breath and paste on my *do I give a fuck* face. "You've been panting after Mimi since she got here," I say, very obviously misunderstanding his meaning.

"Hey, Mimi."

"Oh, hey, El." Mimi's happy expression peeks above an explosion of flowers. "Good to see you."

No, it's a fucking ball ache.

"You, too. Where'd you go Friday night?"

"Are we allowed in, or what?" I mutter pugnaciously, remembering about a second too late that I'm not supposed to reach for Mimi's hand. She shoves the bouquet at me as though that's what I'm after. I almost take them, too. "You give them to Polly."

"But you paid for them."

"I'll dock the money out of your pay," I grumble, turning away.

Of course, El clocks the entire exchange. Tough shit he doesn't look too happy about it.

28

WHIT

"OH, MY GOODNESS!" Polly's enthusiasm knows no bounds as she takes the proffered bouquet. "How beautiful, but you really shouldn't have."

The sun streams through the bifold doors sparking off the stone countertops and white shaker kitchen units. The kitchen had a makeover a year ago and a big extension. I offered to buy Mum a new place, but she said somewhere else wouldn't be the same because the walls wouldn't be filled with so many memories. If you ask me, that's reason enough to want to move, but not for her. At least she let me pay to renovate the place. When Dad died, it was half home, half building site. The man was always tinkering with something.

"They're just a little something," Mimi replies, "to say thank you for the invite."

"The summons, more like," I mutter, resisting the monkey noises I thought to make as I lift the carving knife from the chopping board. Whacking off the end of the beef joint resting on it, I tear into it with my teeth. "'S good," I mouth around the tender piece.

"Honestly, you lot are like a plague of locust." Putting the bouquet on the countertop, Poll plucks the remainder of the beef between my fingers and sets it to the side. "Elvis can have that when he gets here."

"The dog gets beef, but I don't?"

"Yes, because he doesn't help himself," she says, exasperated. She turns to Mimi. "I've already had to hit Brin with the wooden spoon for stealing one of the Yorkshires." She rolls her eyes as though she doesn't secretly love that we all fall into old roles when we walk through the front door.

"Brin deserves it," I say, eyeing the beef again. Polly slides the chopping board farther away as if that would even stop me.

Suddenly, her hand darts out and captures my chin. "What's this?" she asks, turning my head sideways so my profile catches the light.

"An accident." My lip is a little swollen, though nothing too bad. I think Mimi kissing it better a dozen times probably helped.

"What's a Yorkshire?" Mimi's gaze bounces between us.

"Yorkshire pud. Pudding," I amend.

"Like dessert?"

Fuck, she looks like a dessert. Like a crème brulée. Sweet-scented and sugary, but deliciously decadent underneath. She makes me want to roll my tongue over every inch of her. Her pussy is the bowl of cake batter I want to lick clean.

"Yorkshire puddings are savory." I realize Polly is trying to explain while my mind had checked into gutter town. "Though you can have them with treacle and cream, and they're quite nice like that." Mimi nods like she knows what Mum is talking about. "But not as good as when you have them with a roast. They're a staple of a roast beef dinner,"

Poll adds, "unless my mother made them. No one likes a soggy bottom."

"Oh, I'm sure." Mimi blinks, almost straight-faced.

"The problem is..." Mum swipes up a teatowel and begins to vigorously rub a plate from the drainer. "You can't rightly tell until their bottoms are exposed."

"Sounds plausible." Mimi nods, though I notice how her lips twitch.

"What you're aiming for is something rigid." Mum makes a fist around the towel, her expression deadly serious. "It's got to be hard before you put it in your mouth. Otherwise, it's just not as satisfying." I slide her a look, wondering if she's been on the cooking sherry when her blue gaze catches mine. "Isn't that right, Leif?"

"Your satisfaction at mouthing hard things isn't any of my business, Mum."

I've barely finished the taunting sentence when she's whacking me with the teatowel. "Filthy animal!"

"If I have a dirty mind, it's hereditary." That earns me another whack. When I turn to Mimi, laughter dances in her eyes. "How do you think my parents had seven children?"

"The usual way!" Polly butts in.

"With an awful lot of practice in between."

"Oh boy. You are in trouble." Mimi presses her hand to her mouth, but it doesn't hide the amusement from her eyes.

"I don't know where I got you from!" Poll protests, throwing her hands up.

"Well, it wasn't the cabbage patch, that's for sure." I don't normally bring up the topic of her and Dad's sex life in company. When just us kids are about, it's fair game because we were the ones who had to live through those years of free and often loving. Free with each other, at least. As teenagers, we'd pretty much announce our imminent appearance in a room just to make sure we weren't walking in on something. I saw my dad's arse more times than I will ever admit. But it's good we can tease her about it these days because for a while, there was no joy to be found in reminiscing. These days, Poll's grief isn't so sharp-edged. It's become a little easier for all of us, I suppose. Not that you'd think she's happy about it right now.

"Your father would turn in his grave to hear you," she fake-wails.

"Difficult," I retort, "considering he was cremated. Besides, you know he'd be encouraging me right now. Squeezing your bum and insisting he can't help himself on account of you being so irresistible." Mum's expression softens, and she presses her hand to her cheek, almost as though she can feel the phantom press of his lips.

"I miss him," she whispers.

"We all do." Stepping into her, I press a brief kiss on the crown of her head. "Oof!" I feign a cracked rib as she pokes me in them.

"And if you've got a dirty mind, it's all your father's fault, the randy old sod. Has he?" My stomach tightens when, as quick as a flash, Mum's attention slides like a knife to Mimi.

"Has he what?" Mimi blinks back innocently, and surprisingly, there isn't even a hint of pink to her cheeks.

"Oh, she's good," Polly says, her attention turning my way.

"A good PA? Yeah, Mimi's great."

Mum makes a noise in the back of her throat, cutting off any further comment. "Definitely your father's son," she says in a tone none too complimentary.

"Leif's not as bad as El." Primrose comes to my defense as she appears in the kitchen.

"That was a compliment, Primrose, dear."

"Oh. I thought you must be heading down the *randy old sod* route."

"Takes two to tango," I offer up. "And in our parents' case—"

"Eww!" Prim protests, scrunching her nose. "Maybe you are as bad as El."

"Why, what's he done?" I fold my arms and lean against the fridge.

"Just the usual. Honestly, I'm not sure if he thinks I'm an idiot or a kid. He believes he's speaking in code, but I know what a nosh job is," Prim protests, slightly aggrieved.

I press a snicker into my hand, my eyes catching Mimi's. She's no idiot, and she's no kid, but by her expression, she doesn't know what that is.

"So what is it?" Polly's attention swings back and forth between my sister and me. "I don't know. Is someone going to tell me?"

"I've no idea," I say, painting on a bland expression. We're an open family, but there's no way I'm discussing blow job terminology with my mother.

"Prim?" she demands. "Nosh is food, so what is a nosh job?"

"I'm not falling for that one," Primrose answers. "Last time you threatened to wash my mouth out with soap. Just so you know," she says, turning to our guest, "there's no swearing at the dinner table."

"Most people aren't heathens who need to be told that," I point out.

"You must be Mimi," Prim says, ignoring me. "Are your ears burning?"

"Hi, yes." Mimi's hands half lift to her ears before she catches herself. "I mean, no. Should they be burning?"

"Yeah, who's talking about her?" I grumble.

"Everyone except Lavender. She's talking to some boy on her phone." Prim angles her head in the direction of the lounge.

Nosh jobs and Mimi? That had better not be the conversational flow in there.

"That thing will need to be surgically removed from her hand," Polly mutters.

"Anyway, I'm Primrose," she offers. "The sister whose personality is as sunny as her name."

"And as you've probably guessed, she is *so* modest," I put in.

"The glue that keeps this family together," she counteroffers, her arms held wide.

"We could use some of that glue for your mouth."

True to her cheeky personality, Prim sticks out her tongue.

"Make yourself useful," Mum says, swiping Mimi's bouquet up again. "Put these gorgeous flowers in Grandma's vase."

"That's *vase*," I say, ducking my lips to Mimi's ear. From the outside, I'm sure it looks like I'm teasing her about her accent, mainly because no one can see the way I have my hand on her arse. The way I'm squeezing it.

"*Vase*—vase," she says, almost springing away.

"Why don't you take Mimi into the living room and get her a drink?" Poll suggests. "Dinner won't be long."

"Can't I help?" Mimi asks, staying clear of my hands.

"Want me to lay the table?" I ask, eyeing the mostly bare kitchen table.

"I already did it," Primrose says. "We're eating in the

dining room today because we have a guest." She dips an ironic curtsey.

"There's just not enough room at the kitchen table," Poll says, shooing us out of the door with her hands and into the darker hallway. "Go and open the wine or something." With a weird flash of her teeth, she closes the kitchen door behind us.

"The dining room and wine. You should come more often."

"I shouldn't be here at all," she says, trailing me into the formal dining room.

This time, I do make monkey noises, making her smile. She walks to the French doors overlooking the back garden as I decant a couple of bottles of Pinot Noir into the flat bottomed carafe. Mum has gone all out with the best china and silverware. The posh glasses she and Dad bought at some French antique fair.

"You have a tree house." Is it weird that I know she's smiling?

"Technically, it's a tree fort. Tree house was far too emasculating for our young minds."

"Except you have sisters."

"It became a house when they got their hands on it. They even hung curtains."

"The height of domesticity," she teases.

"Here." She startles a little as I slide my hand to her jean-covered hip and hold out a glass for her in my other hand.

"Shouldn't we wait for everyone else?" she says, still reaching for the stem.

"No one will know." Her hand lowers as she intuits my intentions, allowing me to tip the glass to her lovely bottom lip. "Open wider." I can't help the sandpapery rasp to my tone or the way my cock perks up as she does, leaning her head back until it's resting against my shoulder. I tip the glass, quietly pleased that she trusts me. Her tongue chases the taste from her lips as her attention returns to the garden and a sparrow hopping around the lawn.

"It's like the secret garden." Her hands crossed loosely at the waist, she continues to rest against me.

"It's not that overgrown," I say with a low chuckle. In fact, it's in a better state than it was when Dad or me or even El and Brin were responsible for the garden chores, thanks to the gardener I employ.

"Like the book," she says, angling her head to look up at me. "Kind of idyllic."

It's just a suburban London terraced house, but I suppose I know where she's coming from. The house was built in the early eighteen hundreds and has all the charm of the Victorian period. Slightly gothic yet at the same time quite frivolous; ceiling roses and chandeliers, scalloped coving like a heavily iced wedding cake. The garden isn't big, but it's charming, I suppose. The vined arbor just coming into flower. The loveseat and the little wooden summer house where Polly can often be found sitting in the summer.

Her sigh sounds happy, and for a fleeting moment, I get a flash of a future that isn't ours. Snow in the garden, ice laced on the windows, Mimi leaning against me just as she is now, her hair shot with silver, her face softened with age but still so fucking beautiful.

"I can imagine you all running about the place, the girls in smocked dresses with pigtails and the boys in boater hats and sailor suits." Her body moves with mine as I find myself stepping back in shock, I suppose.

"You've a very vivid imagination," I say gruffly. I throw

back the remaining inch of wine, putting the glass on the table behind me.

She rocks forward before turning on her heel to face me, her lips tipping mischievously. "Oh, but not as vivid as yours."

"This might be true." Despite my previous movement, I lean in, pressing my lips to hers. She tastes like wine and her skin is warmed like sunshine as I slide my hand under her sweater, gripping her waist as I deepen the kiss.

"Not here," she protests in the spaces between our kisses. I trace a circle on her skin with my thumb, pulling her hips against mine as I grab a handful of her bum. "Whit, I don't want..." Her soft sigh and her body's response deny her words, my mind spinning through the possibilities of where I could take her. *To take her?* To fuck her. To scratch this near-constant itch.

This isn't right. She deserves better than a quick fumble in the downstairs loo. Plus, there'd be no hiding it from the truffle hounds I have for brothers. I slow my kiss, then press my head to her shoulder. "Sorry."

"Don't be. I really like how you are with me."

"How am I with you?" I pull back and note how her eyes look like hazy, smoked glass.

"Demanding. Spontaneous. You make my head dizzy and my insides kind of fizzy when you're near."

"And that's why I'm not really sorry at all." Even if I should be. "In fact, if I still had a bedroom in this place, I'd be dragging you up there and putting on some really loud music."

"Like a teenage fantasy."

"If I'd known you when I was a teenager—"

"Oh, honey," she splutters, pressing her hands to my

cheeks. "When you were a teenager, I was a little girl with skinned knees and pigtails."

With a groan, I wipe my hand down my face. *Connor, mate. I didn't mean for it to feel this way.*

"But if it helps, I can relate. Because when I was a little older, you were my ultimate teenage fantasy."

If I'm going to hell, I might as well make it worth it as I slide my hand to the nape of her neck, registering her wide eyes the second before I press my lips to her ear. "I really want to see you touch yourself." I want to taste that little gasp and swallow her soft moan. "I want a replay of those moments when you bought yourself lingerie in my name."

"I don't know—"

"Yes, you can, darling. You'll do it for Daddy."

"You are a wicked, wicked man."

"And you are slut for the *d*-word."

"I just don't get it. It's not like anyone would look at us and think *is he her dad or her daddy?* It's not like you're that much older than me."

"Daddy is a mindset, darling. It doesn't come with age restrictions."

"Daddy is..." Her eyes slide over me avariciously. "So hot on you."

Is it any wonder I want to bend her over every surface I see? But I don't have time to dwell, not as the front door bangs open and the scratch of nails on floorboards heralds the arrival of Heather. *And Heather already knows too much.*

"That'll be Ambrosius and Heather."

"Your sister is married to someone named Ambrosius?"

"No, that's the dog. Or one of them, at least. Archer is her husband, and—" I pull open the dining room door and nearly bump into a life-sized, scowling Tinker Bell. "Jesus Christ!"

"He would've been easier," Heather mutters. "A white sheet, sandals, and a stick-on beard. Sadly, no one ever requests JC. Hello, Mimi," she tags on before trudging in the direction of the kitchen.

"I thought you were done with dressing up," I call after her. She waves her hand without turning, signifying an answer is either unwarranted or that she can't be arsed.

"Don't get her started." Archer, Heather's husband, appears at the end of the hallway with his faithful mutt, Elvis, trotting alongside him. "Or she'll bang on for an hour about the feckless nature of theater kids and why hiring them always causes her grief. Who's this, then?" he tags on, spotting Mimi. Despite his friendly tone and mild expression, I find myself bristling. Archer used to be a model, though he denies it whenever the topic comes up. And while I haven't exactly got a face like a bag full of smashed hammers, Archer has cheekbones you can hang your shirt on. More to the point, women blush and fall over themselves when he's near.

"This is Mimi," I say. "She's covering for Jody while she's on maternity leave."

"Ah." So many meanings in that one tiny sound. I suppose it was too much to expect Heather not to tell him. "Nice to meet you." Before Archer can proffer his hand, Mimi hunkers down to lavish the dog in a greeting.

"And who do we have here?" she says in an adorable baby voice.

"This is Elvis," Archer beams.

"You are *such* a handsome boy."

Archer's gaze meets mine, thoroughly won over, but also amused. Elvis is anything but handsome. He's got a head like a masonry brick that's far too big for the foundation and is getting on in years, hence the gray muzzle. And don't get me started on his slobbery death breath.

"Oh my!" One minute, Mimi is on her heels; the next, she's on her arse and the recipient of Elvis's doggy halitosis. "I love you, too!"

"Elvis, get off." Archer hauls the mutt back by his pink collar.

"Should we open champagne?" Heather suddenly appears behind Archer. "To welcome Mimi to the family. I think it's the least we can do, given she's been tongued by two members of it."

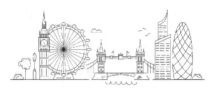

29

MIMI

"Your father would be turning in his grave!" Polly exclaims, passing Whit another bottle of French red for him to open.

Just when I think my cheeks have begun to return to their natural color, Polly's expression sets me off again. My sides hurt from laughing, and if I were wearing mascara, I'd look like a panda right about now. This family is hilarious and irreverent and silly and just so darned lovely! And oh, man. The thing that Heather said about me being tongued? I don't know which of us was most embarrassed. She totally didn't mean it that way, not that it stopped everyone else from rolling around laughing.

"Given Dad was cremated, do you reckon that would make him a snow globe," Brin asks, glancing across the table to El.

"Whatever will Mimi think of us!" Polly says, throwing up her hands. Not just for theatrics, because she also throws a little beef Ambrosius's way.

"No table scraps," Heather complains.

"Darling, I can't give one without the other," she retorts as she slips Elvis a little beef under the table.

"Elvis likes to sit next to the weakest link," Heather says, leaning into me. She's no longer dressed as Tinker Bell but in black pants and a chambray shirt, her red hair tumbling about her shoulders. She runs the children's side of a large event company that caters mainly to the offspring of the rich's party needs. These days, she only dresses up as Tinker Bell, a pirate, or a Disney princess when there are staff shortages, she explained. *She's still hanging out for Jesus.* "Wherever we go, I watch the four-legged fiend, weighing up who is most likely to be taken in by his puppy dog eyes."

"Rheumy, more like," Whit mutters from across the table. Despite my request that he not sit next to me or across from me, there he is! Polly sits at the head of the table to my left, and Whit is seated to her other side. "Though, with Elvis, it's probably more like who can he hypnotize with his halitosis."

"You leave my baby alone!"

"I thought I was your baby?" Archer says, popping a roast potato into his mouth.

"No, you're my husbot," she says reasonably.

"That's not what you called me last night."

"*Archer.*" Whit draws out his brother-in-law's name in a groan. "I really don't want to hear what goes on in my sister's private life."

"Oh, but it's okay to keep upcasting mine?" Polly complains.

"Yes, because people who fornicate in glass houses..."

"Once! It only happened once in the greenhouse!"

"Once was enough," Brin says with a full-body shudder. His eyes catch mine. "Should I be thankful she still had her gardening gloves on?"

"And my wellies!" Polly retorts indignantly.

I press my hand to my mouth, trying hard not to laugh. This afternoon has been the best. Sure, I've had to loosen the button to my jeans because I've eaten way more than I ordinarily would, but it was all so delicious, I couldn't help myself! Tender, pink roast beef with a dollop of a horseradish condiment hot enough to clear anyone's sinuses. Honey-glazed carrots and parsnips and crispy roast potatoes with insides so fluffy they sort of melted in my mouth. Sprouts are usually a big no thanks for me, but cooked with pancetta, chestnuts, and parmesan? So yum! I'm fit to burst—who even knew cauliflower cheese was a thing? It's like a gooey, cheesy religious experience.

Whit's siblings are such a hoot. The dynamic is so cool to watch. Like how his mom just handed him the wine without even looking at him? Things obviously just get deferred to him. Must be that Daddy energy. They all tease Polly mercilessly, but no one seems to think to dish any nonsense Whit's way. Well, I guess that's not strictly true, but they seem to respect him. Though I get the impression they'd rather swallow glass than admit it. I'm so glad I came, even if I don't exactly feel good lying to these lovely people.

It's been a big weekend. A great weekend, but a lot to take in. *Literally, in some aspects.* But tomorrow, we all go back to work. Noses to the grindstone, back to everyday life. Whit already made his feelings clear; work is work, he said. No shenanigans in the office. Maybe. Who knows? I might contrive to get him in the supply closet again. But at least we'll both have our own space soon enough, once this crazy bomb business is over. Meanwhile, I'm just loving seeing this relaxed, slightly goofy, family side of him.

"Let he who is without sin cast the first stone," Primrose announces dramatically before grinning in Brin's direction.

"Don't forget how Lavender and I caught you snogging Priya from next door in the tree house."

"My God," Lavender huffs. She seems to be the only family member who hasn't warmed to me. Then again, she doesn't seem to have a preference for anyone. Slumped in her chair, she twirls the stem of her barely touched glass of wine. "Don't remind me. I think I should've had therapy after that."

"What?" Brin protests. "We were just kids. There was no inappropriate groping. Well, it was all over the shirt, not under."

"What base is that, Mimi?" I find Whit's eyes on me, dancing darkly.

"Base?" I don't dare look, but I'm pretty sure Primrose's gaze darts between him and me. "Like teenagers on American TV shows, you mean?"

"Asinine," Lavender mutters, slinking farther down in her chair.

"Yes, let's not ever be entertained." Prim's reply sounds like the rolling of eyes. "First base is snogging, right, Mimi?"

"Go on, Mimi," Brin encourages. "You're our resident expert."

"Snogging is kissing, right?" prompts Prim.

I can literally feel my shoulders folding inward with embarrassment. This is not the kind of attention I like.

"Yeah, snogging, necking," El says, joining in.

"Copping off," is Brin's inclusion.

"Tonsil tennis." Now it's Primrose's turn.

"I always liked smooching myself," Polly offers.

"No need to tell us that," Whit murmurs, earning him a slap to his arm. "Go on, Lavender, you have a go."

Lavender's eyes flick up, and just when I think she's about to tell him where to go, she utters, "Sucking face."

"Eww, but also, good one!" Primrose could literally out sunshine me!

"I suppose that just leaves me and you," Heather says, turning to her husband.

"We could always go for a demonstration," he answers, leaning closer only to find the meat of Heather's palm in the middle of his forehead.

"Not happening," she sing-songs. "Canoodling," she adds, turning to the gallery of her siblings. "Your turn, husbot."

"Swapping spit," he answers with an unrepentant grin.

"Well, they all sound like making out," I agree, then give a tiny shrug. "Some nicer than others, but all are first base, I guess."

"What base constitutes a little over the shirt action, then?" Whit toys with the stem of his wineglass and the look he's wearing makes me want to melt in my chair.

"I feel like they've had this conversation before," Prim says with a quiet chuckle.

"Purely in the interests of US-British relations, right, Mimi?" *If you'd just stop purring your words, Whit, people might not be so suspicious.*

"Second base," I rush on, finding I have to swallow over my suddenly swollen tonsils, "is action all above the waist."

"Under the shirt or over?" Brin asks. "See, snogging Priya was strictly over." He makes a grabbing motion with his hand, throwing in a honking sound just for laughs.

Lavender isn't so amused and makes a disgusted noise. "No wonder Priya changed her pronouns."

"She did?" Brin seems surprised.

"Yes, they're now *they slash them*," Lavender murmurs. "I wonder if the experience with you left its mark."

"Is that Lavender cracking a funny?" El presses a

pondering finger to his chin. "It's amazing what life you find when you put your phone down, eh?"

"Leave her alone," Whit mutters, topping up his mother's glass. His very happy mother's glass who has made so many references to how wonderful it is to have almost all her children around her. "More wine, Mimi?" He holds the bottle over my glass in anticipation. I rest my hand over it with a shake of my head.

"But you've only had a glass," El protests.

"It is lovely, but I'm not a big drinker." I reach for my water glass instead as my mother's voice echoes in my head. *Everything in moderation, Mimi.* I'm pretty sure an overload of meat and veggies won't kill me this once.

"Think she's nodded off with her eyes open?"

El's joking tone brings me back to the moment. "Food coma," I say, lifting my water. "Just a mini one."

Thankfully, the Whittington clan seem to have lost interest in any explanation regarding the rest of the bases, though I'm not done myself as I slip off my shoe and stretch my foot out. I can't quite reach third base, but I can run my toes up Whit's leg. Why? Because I have had so much fun today. I'm so happy he ignored my arguments and persuaded me to tag along.

I don't need wine to make me feel warm and fuzzy because the way Whit keeps glancing at me makes me feel like that anyway. He wants me. And I want him, always, but seeing him here with his family just makes him all the more perfect.

And who doesn't want perfect, even if just for a little while?

"...honestly, El. She wasn't interested!"

I come back to the conversation at Heather's giggled words.

"She was totally into me." Elbow on the table, El does the chair-based equivalent of a swagger.

"Really?" Heather scrunches her nose unconvincingly. "And you could tell that just from looking at her in that chainmail bikini?" Oh, they're talking about Friday night. His exploits with the server? "Because your eyes weren't exactly on her face."

"Of course I looked at her face," he complains. "Eventually." His siblings all chuckle.

"She gave you her number, then?" Brin throws his napkin across the table at him.

"Not exactly." Balling it up, he volleys it back.

"But you asked her out?"

"Yeah."

"And?"

"Well, her lips might've said no, but her eyes said—"

"Read my lips," Heather butts in, making everyone laugh again.

The conversation goes on. El taunts Brin with a story from one of his old girlfriends. Apparently, El was dating one of her friends (the term used loosely, I gather, for Polly's benefit) when she revealed that Brin is nicknamed *Noodles* within their friend group. Why? Because according to Brin's old conquest, he thinks foreplay only takes two minutes.

Gasps and splutters break out, Polly wading to the conversation when she comments he didn't get *that* from his father. I'm paying attention and laughing along, of course I am, but I'm also watching Whit as he portrays not one hint of what my toes are doing to his leg. The man is supremely cool about my silly seduction.

I make an exaggerated *oh, my goodness, I am so full* kind of motion as I slink a little farther down my chair. It gives me an inch more leverage.

But still, nothing

Because that's the table leg. I curl my toes around definite edges. *Yep.* I chuckle to myself. *I'm trying to get the table leg off.*

"Be careful what you wish for," Whit murmurs, and I startle, thinking he's talking to me. I breathe easy again when Lavender answers.

"I don't make wishes because wishes are for suckers."

"I'm with you on that one," I find myself agreeing.

"You don't believe in wishes?" Primrose asks, perplexed. She's looking at me like she thought I was one of her people. Optimistic, maybe. Bright and cheerful, definitely. I am—I still believe in good over bad and think that most people would be happier if they just smiled a bit more. But wishes? I grew out of that concept not so long ago.

"I thought you believed in magic," Whit asks from across the table.

"Hmm." I press my index finger to my lips and cast my eyes to the ceiling a little theatrically. "I think I said voodoo." Because I believe in Whit magic, in his sexual voodoo. I'm also a devotee of what his wand can do.

"I knew it was something like that." Whit's mouth quirks, those striking eyes weaving their spell.

"A shop on Camden Road will sell you voodoo dolls." Lavender looks at her older brother almost as though she's trying to goad him. "And chicken's blood for spells and stuff."

"I hope they've got a license."

She looks mildly disappointed by his answer. Meanwhile, I drag my toes up the inside of a human leg this time. Whit's leg, definitely.

"Are you thinking of getting a part-time job there?" he asks airily.

"No. My exams are coming up soon, so I don't have time for work."

Whit just smiles. At least he knows he's responsible for spoiling her.

"You okay?" Heather asks as my body suddenly jolts.

"Yeah, fine." I paste on a smile. Whit just grabbed my foot. I should've thought this through because my feet are really ticklish, and I think he's about to find that out. "I was just thinking about my very first job."

"I've had jobs before," Lavender puts in, taking offense to God knows what.

"Hanging around festivals isn't a job," Brin teases.

"I handed out leaflets—and water and stuff!"

"You look like you're about to cry." Heather frowns my way, ignoring them.

"Just a sneeze," I say, scrunching my nose ridiculously as Whit draws his thumbnail along the sole of my foot. "Oh!" I give my nose a rub when what I really want to do is yank my foot back and kick him with the other one because the cause for violence is real!

"You can sneeze," Heather says next. "I know Mr. Moneybags over there thinks he's posh, but the rest of us aren't."

"Mr. Moneybags objects to that," Whit answers as he plays *this little piggy* with my ticklish toes. I don't like it, not one bit! But the way he's watching me, I dig. "You object to it too," he adds, tilting his head like an inquisitive terrier. "Don't you."

"Yes!" I peep. "Just a little bit." I turn to Heather and hope my wild eyes seem at least a little apologetic. "I knew your brother when he was a poor, ramen-eating student. He hasn't changed." I shake my head, less to convince her and more *no, no, no, just stop!*

"I worked while I was at college." Whit seems determined to involve me in this conversation. Or make me scream. One of the two. "Do you know what I did, Mimi?"

"Sperm donor?" El suggests, allowing me a reason to bark out a laugh. Oh, that felt so good to get out. Maybe it was a little loud but it's too late to do anything about it now. I try to twitch my foot away again, but no dice. And when Whit presses his thumb to the middle of my arch, I'm pretty sure my eyes almost roll back in my head. A hot deliciousness begins to pulse along my leg, getting higher and higher until it quivers in a place it has no business being at the dinner table.

The breakfast table, however...

"A donor." That sounded way more sexual than I intended. "Your brother donated freely and regularly when he was on vacation." His fingers still, and the room goes deathly quiet. "Not like that," I add quickly. "I didn't mean professionally."

A collective sigh seems to be released, and El pipes up, "Thank the Lord! The world can only take one of that bossy ba—bar steward."

"I told you there was no swearing at the dinner table." Primrose laughs.

"What I want to know is where you gathered this intel," Heather says, sending me a sly look.

"Purely observational," I answer. "I was just a kid."

She looks disappointed when Whit says, "Let's return to the topic of jobs. Brin had a job while he was at university, didn't you?"

I angle my attention Brin's way, and he nods. "I had a job in a sandwich place. I got fired for putting my finger in the pickle slicer." He shrugs. "She got fired, too."

A groan goes around the table, though Whit and El

laugh. They also get bombarded with left over sprouts, much to their disgust.

"No phones at the table!" Polly protests. Brin looks up sheepishly from glancing at his phone under the tabletop, I guess. His attention doubles back comically, though.

"Mimi, aren't you staying with an aunt in Edgeware?"

I nod. "Mm-hmm."

"Did you hear about that World War 2 bomb they found?"

"Yeah. How crazy is that?" I'm not sure I'd make a very good actress.

"You know what's even crazier? It's just gone off."

"Off?" I give my head a little shake. "What do you mean?"

"It's just exploded in someone's back garden."

Oh man. This is not good.

30

MIMI

"I'm a big girl. I don't have to stay here."

I blow out a breath as I pause in my pacing the living room, catching my worried frown in the mirror above the modern, oversized fireplace. "And I can also talk to myself without feeling like a complete idiot."

Or at least I can try.

I turn to the window and watch the sun's rays dapple the blossoming treetops. It's amazing what a difference a day or two can make. And I'm not just talking about spring. I've discovered that my life is becoming way too complicated, and after getting off the phone with Doreen, it's not about to become any easier. I guess I know what the little pig in the straw house felt like. Not that a wolf has blown down Aunt Doreen's house. It's still standing, but half the street has been declared unsafe for the foreseeable future. Doreen mentioned something about structural engineers being called in by her home insurance company. Apparently, the streets around the garden with the EOD, or whatever it's called, are still crawling with police and army personnel.

The good news is no one was hurt. But when I asked

her if there was a timeline for when the street might be deemed habitable, she said no, before adding how lucky we both were to be staying in the homes of "our lovely men."

Just a couple of weeks ago, she was cautioning me against getting involved with Whit, but now she thinks he's "just gorgeous!"

And he is gorgeous. He's sweet yet spicy and all the good kinds of wrong. And his family is so lovely, it'll be so hard to keep lying to them. But I really feel like I shouldn't be exposed to this lifestyle for too long. I might not want to stop, and that's just not feasible.

Whit didn't understand when I said I'd have to ask Doreen not to mention to my parents what had happened or where I'd be staying.

"You're twenty-four, Mimi. You can do what you want."

And he's right. But I haven't given him the whole story.

"It's not about doing what I want, it's about protecting them."

"Protecting them from understanding they have a grown-up daughter?"

"It must be nice to live the kind of life where you don't have to take other people's feelings into account," I'd tried not to snipe. *"But sometimes you have to do the wrong thing for the right reasons. This would be one of those times."*

And sometimes you do the wrong thing for entirely selfish reasons, but that's a different story.

Meanwhile, here I am, wandering around Whit's gorgeous apartment, living my very own version of *Pretty Woman*, without the sex worker aspect. Although the kind of sex we have is likely to melt my brain. Anyway, Doreen had ended the call with a cheery, *be good!* before adding, *but if you can't be good, be careful!*

What kind of advice is that? And be careful of what? My

DONNA ALAM

hips? My sanity. Maybe the current state of my fertility? Two out of three I don't need to worry about.

Before we left Whit's mom's house yesterday, she offered to make up the spare room for me. Heather offered me a room at her place, too. I felt so awful lying to them both, but I could hardly tell them Whit had taken care of me already. *On lots of fronts.*

But I didn't need to lie because, in front of everyone, Whit casually suggested I stay with him. It would make the most sense, he'd said. We're both going to the same office most days, and it wouldn't be for long. Besides, he had space, he'd offered magnanimously. So much for not encouraging his mom because I don't think we were fooling her. I also think we both know we're fooling ourselves. I have a feeling this won't end well.

I rest my butt on the arm of the tactile velvet sofa and slide over it like a sloth, my new black pants aiding my descent. Whit was already gone when I woke this morning. He had a flight to Zurich to make. He'll be gone a few days, which will give me time to devise a plan. Maybe Doreen's place will be given the okay, or perhaps I could look for a temporary flat share? Or I could just stay here and gorge myself on all that Whit has to offer. *All those bedroom delights,* my mind supplies, making my insides flutter.

My phone begins to ring next to my morning cup of coffee, flashing with Whit's name. I consider ignoring it, but I don't have the willpower.

Will I ever learn what's good for me?

"Hello, gorgeous."

"How are you there already?"

"It's only an hour and a half away. Plus, no airport loitering when you fly private."

"Oh fancy."

"It is a bit. But don't be too impressed. It's a company jet."

"Yeah. It's not like you own a huge chunk of the company or anything." Leaning forward, I straighten a pile of artsy-looking books on the coffee table until square, smiling at the sound of his carefree laughter.

"Sometimes I think I should pinch myself."

"You definitely shouldn't," I reply. "You should ask me to do it."

"I told you last night I wasn't ticklish."

"I'm not sure I believe you. If you truly weren't, you would've let me try to tickle *you*."

"Hmm, but that's not how the game goes."

"Why do the games always have to go your way?" I almost whine. Can you complain while smiling? Picking up my coffee cup, I realize it's gone cold. And that I'd forgotten to use a coaster. Oops!

"Because I'm in charge and that's the way we both like it."

"I'm not sure I do," I lie.

When we got back last night, Whit said he had work to do, but I eventually persuaded him to watch a movie with me. I might've implied there could be a little action under the cashmere throw I'd pulled over our legs. When it didn't happen quick enough for him, he'd pulled me down on the couch and began ruthlessly tickling me. I blame him discovering my ticklish feet.

Anyway, it wasn't a random act of deviance but a premeditated undertaking to get what he wanted. His demand? That I'd run my choice of "friendly dates" by him. There might've been some mention of a veto vote, but that was in the heat of the moment.

I mean, how can he choose when I'm only planning on playing pretend?

"You're a lovely little liar." How does this sound like a compliment? "You like the sense of being powerless."

"Do I?"

"The vulnerability. Feeling helpless in the face of my dominance."

"Sounds like something *you* like."

"I'm not going to lie," he answers reasonably.

"Really?" I draw the word out, kind of, *tell me* as between my legs throbs at the recollection.

"I like that you laugh, whether you mean to or not. I love the fight you put up. Your hips between my knees. The way your wide, wild eyes stared up at me when you realized you wouldn't be able to wriggle away."

"I must've looked like a crazy person." A crazy person being tortured by the devil.

"You looked beautiful, balanced between panic and pleasure and pain. Laughing and begging and all breathless, your skin still so sensitive when I slipped my tongue between your legs."

I release a tremulous breath. "It's way too early to be having these conversations." It's way too early in this non-relationship for me to be feeling like this.

"You're saying it's a good thing I didn't wake you before I left this morning?"

"You couldn't possibly have—"

"Next time, I'll be sure to wake you up to show you the evidence for yourself. I had to take care of myself in the shower."

"Oh."

"Yes. *Oh.*"

"It hardly seems fair."

"We're not keeping score, darling."

"No, I just mean you might've woken me. I would've liked to have seen that."

"Amelia, you make it so hard—"

"Just how I like it." Gosh, listen to me, living my best life, giving as good as I get.

"Make it so *hard* to stay coherent. I have a very busy day today, and all I'm going to be thinking of is the many and varied ways I intend to own your delectable arse."

"Sounds like you're saying I make you a little crazy."

"You sound entertained by the prospect. Make the most of your alone time, darling."

"That sounded like a threat."

"Good."

The phone goes dead. I find myself staring at it. Staring and smiling.

George picks me up for work not long after our call ends, and I spend the ride in scanning the dating app on my phone, making "connections" that I'm really not interested in. But if Whit's going to start vetting my dates—like, did I even agree to that?—then I'll need to be prepared.

Prepared to tell more lies.

It's like, the more I tread carefully, the more the universe conspires against me. Urgh.

At least no one seems to realize that I arrive on the executive floor by means not available to mere PA's. Or that my security swipe card gives me access pretty much everywhere.

It's crazy how far Whit has come since our Tampa days, though I'm not sure which is crazier; that he owns his own plane or elevator. It makes him sound like some kind of control freak when he's really just a regular guy with lots of money.

I prep the file Whit wanted last Friday, the one that led to our fumble in the supply closet, which seems to have happened a lifetime ago. I whip a few tasks off the Monday list of Jody's PA bible, do a little filing, and organize Whit's expense reports.

Finding myself with a whole hour on my hands for lunch, I grab a sandwich from Sainsbury's Metro, along with a couple of ridiculous items that I think will make Whit smile and find a bench to soak up some spring sunshine as I eat my New York-inspired (maybe squinted at over a great distance?) pastrami on rye.

When I return to the building, I pull out my purchases and line them across my desk.

"Nice cactuses," someone says as they pass.

"Thank you." It's cacti, but I forgive you, little philistine. There are also succulents. I bought ten of the tiny little suckers, all in bright pink and yellow pots. One pot is even pink with yellow spots! I think I'll keep that one for my desk, but the rest are going in Whit's office. The place could do with a bit of brightening!

Oh, the satisfaction I feel as I peel off a pair of googly eyes from their sticky backing before pressing them carefully to one of the plants. That one gets pride of place on his desk. I can't wait to hear what he thinks of them.

———

"How has your day been?"

My stomach does a little flip at the sound of Whit's deep, smooth tones. That voice should come with a warning label.

This isn't the first time he's been away from the office since I started to work at VirTu, and it isn't the first time he's checked in, either. But it feels different. It could be the silky tone he uses.

"It's been busy. I've got lots to do. Lots of work to get through. You see, the boss man likes to keep me busy."

"Does he now?"

"Yes, he's very demanding."

"That doesn't sound like a complaint."

"I can't help that I like to impress him."

"And how are you aiming to do that?"

"Well, I had this report he wanted me to prepare, and I have," I say, straightening the perfectly bound, brightly colored report on my desk. "But you know what? He's not even in the building today."

"What an idiot. How could he not be there?"

"Well, he is quite important. Lots of people want his time, but I guess I'm just not at the top of the list of his priorities." I don't know where I'm spinning this stuff from.

"It sounds like he doesn't deserve you. In fact, if I were you, I'd go and sit in his chair right now."

My stomach flips pleasurably. "But what would that achieve?" I ask innocently.

"I'm sure I'll think of something before you get in there."

"It sounds like you're trying to get me fired because my boss specifically said there was to be no shenanigans in the office."

"And that was the word he used?" he asks, sounding amused.

"It was something like that. But the bottom line is I've got to be a good girl while I'm here."

"Because he's keeping an eye on you?"

I sit a little straighter. "How?"

Whit chuckles, breaking character. "There are no cameras in the office." His gaze narrows. "What have you been getting up to?"

"What about at home. I mean, your apartment?"

"It could be arranged if you want to try."

"Try—? Sure," I add, full of snark.

"It was just a suggestion. There's a camera in the hallway between the elevator and the front door but that's the extent of my current depravities."

"What about Friday night?" My heart skips a beat. "When we came back from the club."

"You're asking if it recorded our elevator shenanigans?" he asks in a terrible Irish accent.

"Be serious. Is there footage somewhere?"

"No, the camera is motion activated once you step into the hallway."

"Oh."

"You sound disappointed."

But it's not that. It's the implication of what I'm about to say next.

"I'm going out this evening." I close my eyes, my shoulders hunching as though expecting a blow and press my hand to my head. "I'll give it a wave as I pass by."

"Going anywhere nice?"

"Out for coffee."

"One of your dates?" he says as though he's been expecting this. Expecting it and is totally okay about it. Unbothered, even.

"Yeah."

"So you decided to go out with Greg, after all?"

"Gosh, you're invested," I reply lightheartedly. Because his tone isn't the same as it was. Where's the snark? The vitriol?

"I thought I'd made my feelings crystal clear last night."

Oh, there it is...

"You don't really mean that. You can't want to help me pick my dates."

"We agreed you'd run them by me."

My expression kind of twists. "I don't think I did."

"It looks like we'll be revisiting last night's conversation," he says, his tone suddenly dark.

"That wasn't a conversation. It was more like you were waging war on my body."

"Look, Mimi, I don't want you going out with any old creep. I also don't want you going out with anyone you might prefer over me."

I actually laugh because he doesn't even bother to sound serious. That wasn't a chink in his armor, more a man throwing me a bone.

"I don't agree with your methods, but I know why you're doing this."

"Of course you know why," I retort as my stomach flips unpleasantly. "I told you why."

"I know what you said. I also know you want to make me insanely jealous."

"You're ridiculous," I say flatly.

"So insanely jealous that I'll kidnap you and drag you to my lair, spank your arse, tickle you until you can't breathe, and then fuck you over and over again."

"So basically, a repeat of this weekend?" Now I'm amused, mainly because he sounds like he is, even if this conversation is really weird.

And the prospect strangely tempting...

"For me, yes. For them, they'd better not even look at you in that way."

"That's not what this is about."

"As long as no one else gets to fuck you. You do want me to fuck you, don't you, Amelia?"

That sounds so nasty. It shouldn't make me feel good, and I shouldn't agree with him, but I do.

"What was that, sweetheart? I don't think I quite heard."

"I said yes, I only want you to..." I turn my head so I'm facing away from any passing foot traffic, not that we get much on this floor, but it wouldn't do to be caught dirty talking on the company dime. Even if it is to the boss. "I only want you."

"Want me to what?" he whispers back. *Asshole.*

"I'm not saying it." I shake my head in denial. "I'm seriously ruined."

"Oh not yet, you're not."

"Ruined that I would allow you to sexually Svengali me during office hours." There's more than a hint of grievance in my tone.

"It might take me a minute to dissect that. Meanwhile, you're missing the point. I'm just looking out for you."

"What, like you're my dad?"

"No, darling, like your daddy. You want Daddy to fill your aching pussy, don't you?"

"Stop," I say without conviction.

"We'll do this my way because Daddy knows best."

"Again, that's not how I remember the conversation going down."

"I'm sure you remember me going down. The rest is probably a blur. Who is it you're going out with? Not the idiot from Hinge, I hope."

"Who?"

"The rose bloke, Garrett, wasn't it?"

"Yeah, that's it." My stomach plummets off a cliff. He is way more invested than I've given him credit for. "Garrett.

That's who I'm going out for coffee with. I know you didn't like his profile or his prompts but—"

"He probably isn't that bad."

"No?" Talk about a change of direction.

"Just don't let him buy you any lemonade."

"Okay. Wait, why?"

"Remember his profile. Surprise anal!"

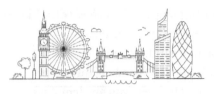

31

WHIT

His name is Greg, not Garrett...

After ending the call, I quickly type out a text but then delete it before I hit send. Why is she doing this? That she can't even remember the arsehole's name means she's not going out with him. She's probably not going out with anyone. Or is that just wishful thinking?

"Fuck!" Slamming my phone down on the table, I spin away from it because I want to smash it off the wall, and I'm not that arsehole. I mean, I am. I can be bad tempered and surly, but I'm not the kind of prick who'd smash a perfectly good phone and then insist someone lower down the food chain pop to the Apple store to pick me up a new one.

Even if I really do want to.

I should've known it wasn't going to be as cut-and-dried as I'd told myself. I would've been better off letting her run wild through London and learning for herself how fucking brutal it is out there. But then, that would've required some kind of mental fortitude, not to mention lots of keeping my hands to myself. And where Amelia Valente is concerned, it seems I just can't help myself.

Why am I twisting myself in knots over a woman who has no intention of hanging around longer than a few months? I should be elated, shouldn't I? Not looking for reasons she wants to keep things casual between us.

But as I'd held her under me last night, her pulse wild against my thumb and the air between our lips, swirling and somehow elemental, I'd experienced some inexplicable shift. I didn't mean or expect it to happen, but I suddenly knew without a doubt that I'd drifted out from a safe harbor without realizing, beyond the breakers that buffer my ordinary life. I wasn't looking outward, and I wasn't looking back. I was looking down, and Amelia seemed so soft-eyed and compliant, yet I asked myself how I'd ever missed the depths of her. My fathomless need for her.

"Fuck!" I slide my phone from the table, stare at it, then hurl it at the wall as hard as I can. The back ricochets off, the screen cracking like ice on a pond.

Worse, it doesn't make me feel one fucking iota better.

But it does encourage a slow, sarcastic round of applause from behind me.

"Well done," Beckett murmurs in that annoyingly modulate tone Englishmen of a certain age and station seem to have perfected. "I'm assuming it had offended you in some way?" His expression bland, he glances behind me at the wall. "Or perhaps it was the bearer of bad news."

"Nothing like that," I mutter as I trudge across the conference room to retrieve the pieces like a naughty schoolboy. "I'm just a bad-tempered arsehole today."

By the time I turn, Beckett has pulled out a seat at the contemporary conference table. He loosens the button on his bespoke suit jacket before lowering himself to sit at the head of the table. "Only today?"

"What?"

"You're bad tempered only today?"

"Yeah?" I feel myself frown.

"It seems to me that you've been out of sorts since your very capable PA left to give birth. Joanne, I think?"

"Jody." Beckett is a stickler for details but only when they pertain to him.

"And the new girl?" He pulls a small case from the inside pocket of his Savile Row suit, opens it, then begins to clean the lenses of a pair of rimless spectacles I know he has no intention of wearing. They're new, according to Olivia, his wife. Also, according to her, he's far too vain and stubborn to wear them. "What's her name again?"

"Mimi."

He tsks and lowers the specs to the table. "No."

"No?"

"Mimi is the name of a Pekinese or something equally as fluffy and yappy."

"Amelia. Her name is Amelia," I say, dropping the broken bits of my phone to the table.

"She's a friend of the family, I think."

I've no idea how he knows. Or why he even cares. "Yeah. I was friends with her brother. He died a few years ago. What's this about, Beckett?"

"It just strikes me that you've been a little distracted since she arrived."

"Bullshit. How am I distracted? I'm here, playing good cop to your bad one. We've raised the capital and support we needed today, haven't we?"

"Yes," he agrees, "we have."

"And I was there with leading counsel last week when we had that sit-down with the FCA."

"You mean when the Financial Conduct Authority handed us our metaphoric backsides?"

"Teething problems," I insist. He waves my words away.

"Yes, that's all fine," he says as though I'm boring him. "But this person stood in front of me? Do sit down. I detest being looked down upon."

With a snort, I pull out the chair to his right. "Better?" I mutter pointedly.

"Much. Thank you."

As I lean back in my chair, I wonder how he makes that sound like *get fucked*. "You could be lying on your back in the gutter, and you'd still find a way to look down your nose imperiously at people."

"Imperiously." He mouths the word as though he's never heard it before. I bet it's mentioned somewhere on his birth certificate. "Obviously, I wouldn't look that way at you." Which is true, but only because I've made him a lot of money. "But the point I'm trying to make is you're not the person you were a month ago. Even Olivia agrees."

"I have a lot on my mind."

"No more than usual, if you're referring to work. This business has never been healthier. It has weathered storms and is now coming out on the other side. Your face should be wreathed in smiles, not full of dark looks."

"Dark looks?" I scoff.

"Yes, I'm familiar with how that looks. I've seen the expression before."

"On a hound?"

"In the bathroom mirror, actually."

I start a little. My conversations with Beckett are always about business. We don't share personal stuff. I don't know what his angle is, which is why I say, "I have no idea what you're talking about."

"Missing meetings—"

"One-half of a missed meeting last week." The day I

decided I'd rather watch my brother hit on Mimi than leave my office. Then Friday night, I was supposed to be on the other side of London, wining and dining investors. Instead, I blew the evening off consumed by the thought that Mimi might bang my brother. And here we are, a few days later, but instead of El or Brin, she's going to go out on a string of dates with some of London's finest fuckwits. And I have to be all right about it or pretend, at least. When what I want to do is carry her to my bedroom and tie her to my bed until she tells me what's going on in her head. Until she tells me—

No, that's ridiculous.

I don't want her to say that she loves me.

Do I?

I'm losing the plot, I think as tension suddenly tightens my shoulders. It's just jealousy talking. But the thing is, I don't do jealousy. I don't do monogamy, so how can I be jealous?

Because you want that from her. Because you've demanded it from her.

How did I not even realize?

"I have just the thing for that."

"What?" I look up, suddenly self-conscious. Did I mutter some confessional?

"The thing with your shoulders."

"There's nothing wrong with my shoulders."

"Nothing Kerry couldn't work out, at any rate," he says, reaching for a nearby newspaper. *Le Figaro*, a French morning paper. Slipping his hand inside his jacket, he pulls out a gold Montblanc, scribbling something in the outer margin before sliding the paper my way.

"What's this?" I stare down at the scrawled UK mobile number, glancing up. "Who's Kerry?"

"The best you'll ever have. One hour of absolute torture where you'll feel like you'd sell your soul to the devil just to get those hands to stop, but by the end of the experience, you'll feel like you can take on the world."

"Does Olivia know you engage the services of a dominatrix?"

"Kerry is an Australian massage therapist. Not a *she*, but a he," he replies witheringly. "And if I were to hire a dominatrix, Olivia would only want to watch. Actually, she'd probably supply implements."

"Ever heard of TMI?"

"Knowing my wife, she'd probably buy some awful mediaeval torture device. Thigh-high boots, too. She's nothing if not committed."

I chuckle because the pair argue more than any couple I've ever known. But the way they look at each other is what Primrose would no doubt describe as *#couplegoals.*

I make as though to pick up my phone to take down the number, just for the sake of politeness, when I remember what a tit I was a few minutes ago.

"Take the paper," he says. "There's a very interesting article in it about Sergei Asmalov's new venture."

"Right." *Le Figaro* is a French newspaper. Beckett probably speaks fluent French. These posh public schoolboy types always do.

"But getting back to the matter in hand, I guarantee there will be more in your future."

"Missed meetings? No, there won't. I haven't come this far to piss it all away."

"Shoulder problems. Tension. Bad moods. Idiotic conduct and destructive behaviors."

"You've lost me."

"The bank will be fine. It'll weather any oncoming

storms. You, on the other hand, look like a man who's about to find out what ruin looks like."

"I enjoy these little conversations, but I must be slow today because I literally have no idea what you're saying."

"I'm saying love is like an illness."

"Love of money?" I clarify. I'm not driven by money especially, and I'm not sure I want to know what makes Beckett tick.

"Love of the heart," he says as though speaking to an idiot. "You can only ignore the illness itself for so long. And there is only one cure."

"Death?"

"The love of a good woman," he enunciates. I open my mouth to protest when he cuts me off. "Or a bad one, though I recommend the former. It's much easier on the heart and head. Though there are times when…" He seems to catch himself. "Well, never mind."

I'm so confused. Beckett and I don't have this sort of relationship. "Deny it all you like," he continues. "I won't be the one to suffer. Prolong the agony. Fight the tide, but the bastard will be waiting for you when your arms tire."

"Swimming metaphors?"

"The best I could come up with on short notice. And what I'm about to tell you, I know you won't repeat. I also know that if you do, Olivia will eat your liver. Which she'll probably extract from your arsehole or some other ingeniously nefarious way."

"You don't have to tell me anything," I say, rubbing my chin. "The mention of her in thigh-high boots was scary enough."

"I forced Olivia to marry me."

I chuckle. "Good one. That's funny." I nod my head as I consider how handling Mimi sometimes feels like juggling a bag of cats. Handling Olivia would be like juggling a bag of piranhas.

"It's true," he replies, amused.

"With the greatest respect," I begin, "but fuck off. I can't imagine anyone being able to force Olivia to do something she doesn't want to do."

"And you're assuming she didn't want to marry me?"

"Well, yeah. On account of you saying you forced her."

"Persuaded might be a better word."

"Blackmailed," I say flatly.

"Not pretty but perhaps more than accurate." Beckett tips his hand in a gesture that seems to say *I couldn't help it.* "I discovered her weakness. It was her business, of course. I used it as leverage."

I always thought Beckett had the capacity for ruthlessness. Now I know he has. Olivia made a shit ton of money when her start-up went public a few years ago. If I put myself in her shoes, faced with the prospect of losing VirTu, there isn't much I wouldn't have done to save it. Not for the money but because it's your baby, your life's work. In the early days, it's all excitement and *can do*, but the next thing you know, you can't sleep for worry, you're graying prematurely, your dentist tells you you're grinding your molars to dust, and your family looks at you like you're crazy for bothering. Meanwhile, you continue to bleed sweat and tears just to keep your dream afloat. And that's difficult enough, but then throwing a spot of blackmail into the mix?

So yeah, I can imagine her marrying the ruthless bastard to save her company. But she's still married to him. And I know that beneath the combative exchanges volleyed across the boardroom table, there's a fuck-ton of heat simmering.

"The waves of your disapproval emanate across the table, Whit."

I shoot the unrepentant bastard a grin. "I was just thinking, blackmailed to love sounds like the title of a terrible romance book."

"A book that will never see the light of day. And the thing you must remember is that we're still married."

"Don't tell me—because you're holding her family hostage now."

"Very droll." Folding his fingers into his palm, he appears to examine his highly buffed fingernails. "We're still married because she loves me. I don't know what I've done to earn that honor, but I don't take her love lightly—and God knows I made it hard enough for her—but I'll spend the rest of my life making sure she remembers I treasure her."

"I'm pleased it worked out for you, but I can't see how blackmailing Mimi would help."

"Oh, so you admit it is Amelia."

I don't like to hear her name on his lips. "It's complicated," I say with a frown.

"These things generally are."

"She works for me."

"That's one issue. A minor one. The company is big enough. She could go to another department, I'm sure. If you wanted her to. If you needed her to."

He means if I find her a distraction. There has never been a more distracting distraction than Mimi Valente, not that I'm about to admit it.

"And she's going back to Florida later this year." *Don't make a hole in your life for me. I'm not going to be here long enough to fill it.* The echo of her words makes my chest feel tight.

"Plans change." His hands fall open, his tone reasonable.

"She's pretty adamant about it, and my life is here. Anyway, I'm too busy for a relationship," I find myself saying.

"And so we tell ourselves. Of course, you have your siblings as well."

I slant him a look. I don't think I've ever mentioned my family dynamics to him. We aren't friends. He's a major investor—a mentor, even—but that's it.

"Don't look so worried. Olivia tends to know these kinds of things, things that then come into the sphere of my existence whether I'd like them to or not."

"Well, my family is fine. The only issue is their sheer number." It makes for more opinions and more drama. If I take Polly's perspective, it also means more love.

"I hear it won't be long before you become an empty nester."

"I don't know where you're getting your information from, but I live alone," I say with a hint of amusement. "They don't live with me." Because my apartment is the only place I get any peace in the world. Except when Mimi's there, and that's more than all right with me. Maybe I need to blow up her aunt's house for definite so she's stuck with me. Then tie her to the bed to stop her from going on a fucking date tonight.

"Squeeze that phone any harder, and it will become a permanent part of your hand."

Sure enough, a shard of hard plastic has already pierced my skin. *This is ridiculous*, I think as I drop it back on the table. This isn't me. This isn't how I operate. It's all just so fucked up. I know the reasons she's given me, but I'm not buying them. I know she's scared. Scared of getting too involved? Scared of falling for me, but guess what? She's not the only one. But it doesn't stop me from wanting to be with her. *Just the opposite.*

"You take your responsibilities as the eldest sibling very seriously. There's no getting away from that. It's in your genetic makeup." He folds up a forestalling hand as I begin to speak. "But what I meant to say is your responsibilities are coming to an end, I understand. The chicks will fly the coop, as they do."

I shake my head. He has no fucking idea. "They might leave and they might not, but it doesn't matter because my life, my job, my life's work, if you will, is in London. And Mimi fully intends on going back to Florida. In fact, as of this evening, she'll be out on a date with someone else, some other fuck who isn't me, just to prove it." I snap my mouth shut. I can't believe I fucking told Beckett—of all people! This is not the type of relationship we have.

"And you're just going to take it?" He quirks a brow that might as well spell out *you're an idiot* across his forehead.

"I suppose I could take a leaf out of your book."

"What do you have for leverage?"

"I was fucking joking!" I say with a laugh. "And no, I don't want to sit here and just take it. But short of a possible kidnap and false imprisonment charge, what can I do?"

I want to lock her up. Of course I do. It's what the caveman in me wants—to throw her down on my bed and show her in no uncertain terms what she was built for. I want to bind her to my side and demonstrate over and over again how right we are together. Instead, I've played my reactions down and shown little response to her plans and even less in her reasons. The only part of her I've shown interest in is her pussy, I realize belatedly.

"What can you do? Let me see... off the top of my head?" He actually taps the top of his head. "Tell her not to? Or what about, now here's a revolutionary idea," he adds with much sarcasm, "show her you're a better option. A better bet. A better man. One worth risking her heart on. Because if you let her do this, if you let her go, you will regret it," he says, all stiff upper lipped once more. And a little nihilistic. "Go home, Whit. Sort this idiocy out."

"Tomorrow we've got—"

"Frankly, I don't need you here. Your good cop requires a glass of scotch and a couple of Xanax."

"That's not fair."

"Your usual diplomacy and aplomb are shot to fuck. You're no use to the negotiations in your current mood."

"That's not true," I grate out, refusing to sit here like a scolded kid.

"And if tomorrow you go back to London and find that she's involved herself with another man, would there be any coming back from it for you? Would it aid your performance?"

"That's not fair."

"Spare me the platitudes. I only require you understand that, once she leaves, you will find, as trite as it sounds, that you will function differently. Possibly not at all for a little while. And if you're as foolish as I was, you won't discover this until she's already gone. Second, when you find yourself having this mental breakdown, I will have you removed from the board."

Now, there's the Beckett I know. Blackmailed his wife into marriage? I can well believe it.

"Close the door on your way out," he says in a final act of dismissal. Picking up his spectacles again, he adds, "Don't forget to take the newspaper. Kerry will sort out your shoulders."

But I don't need a massage. What I need is Mimi.

32

MIMI

WEIRD, weird, weird. That conversation with Whit was freakin' weird!

How did we get from hot promises and growly declarations of *I don't like it* to apathy? How did we go from *I'll send you on your dates with my cum dripping between your legs* to *careful you don't drink the anal lemonade!*

He isn't acting like my lover. Or my big brother. More like my pimp. My nonsexual pimp. I mean, *he's* sexual, but—

Urgh! This makes no sense.

The afternoon passes quickly. I check in with Jody again and listen to her complain about her being the size of a bus. Brin calls but doesn't mention our missed lunch date to the canelés place. I can't say I'm surprised or disappointed, and while Sunday lunch was great, I could do without feeling like I'm undertaking a deposition. I don't think we're fooling anyone about being strictly employee and boss. Not that I won't insist on the charade still playing out.

I'm really not looking forward to going back to Whit's to get dressed for my fictitious date. Worse, I'll have to leave and find a coffee shop to sit sad sack and alone in. So I'm pretty happy when I'm hit by a wave of genius.

That might be overstating it a little, but it works for me.

I don't go home. Well, not until it's gone eight in the evening. My grand plan? I didn't have to go through the motions—my fake date could be straight from work! And so it is—a date with myself! No preening or primping, no effort at all, in fact!

I'd called George and told him I didn't need a ride home, then I caught the bus into town and spent some time wandering around Liberty London, which is this funky department store that isn't like a department store at all. It looks like something out of the Tudor period with its black and white façade, and while I'm sure there are buildings in London that *are* from the Tudor reign, I'm guessing Liberty's isn't. It's still pretty old, though. And I love it. I'd sprayed myself in different perfumes, wandered along the cosmetics counters, and drooled over a couple of ridiculously priced purses. Then I wandered up and down the ornate staircases and perused the shelves at my leisure, but ultimately, I'd left the place empty-handed. I didn't need anything after Whit's spontaneous shopping extravaganza.

I spent another hour soaking up the atmosphere as I'd strolled around the theater district. As the light begins to change, the evening rolling on, the theaters began to shimmer and shine, and it was wonderful.

It feels freaking awesome to be in London. I'm so buzzed to be here and went on to congratulate myself on my good life choices by treating myself to a bowl of katsu fries and a fancy lemonade (minus the occurrence of surprise anal) at a nearby cocktail bar. I even got hit on, but that wasn't the highlight of my day because that comes when I'd keyed in the code to get back into Whit's apartment, finding him already at home...

My smile literally stretches across my face when I see his fancy Rimowa cabin bag in the hallway. Slipping off my coat, I practically skip into the living room. Doesn't seem to matter what the head says, the heart (and libido) want what they want. And what they—I—want is standing in the middle of his living room, dressed more like someone who robs banks for a living than the CEO of one.

"You're back!"

"I am." My heart feels like an elevator that drops a floor as I notice the lack of warmth in his tone. Oh, yeah. I've been on a so-called date. I guess that's why his gaze falls over me, like he's looking for some change.

"If I'd known, I would've come straight home."

"What about your date?"

I shrug. I would've fake cancelled my fake date, I don't say, relieved when he doesn't demand more. "How come you're home early?"

"Things got sorted quicker than I thought they would." He pulls out a black beanie from the back pocket of his tight running pants, throwing it to the couch. Judging by the color in his cheeks, he's recently come back from a run, rather than about to head out for one.

"Cool." God, this is awkward. As excited as I was to open the door and find Whit home, it's not like I could've launched myself into his arms. None of this *hi, honey, I'm home!* So what do I do now? Just stand here, making it more awkward than it already is, apparently.

"How was Garrett?" Despite his mild tone, his eyes glitter heatedly.

"Meh. He was okay." *I can do this*, I tell myself. I can sell it. I sold him on the idea of us in the first place, didn't I?

"Well, that's nice."

"Nice. That about sums my evening up." It's time to get this show on the road, I decide, as my feet begin to move again. Whit tracks my steps across the living room, and I drop into an armchair with a sigh. "But you know what no one ever told me?"

"That you make the hottest sounds when I'm balls deep inside you?"

My mouth drops open in shock, and my insides seem set to *throb*. That wasn't the direction I was going in. Shouldn't I be used to his smutty segues by now?

Apparently, I'm not.

"Was that not it?" he asks, all innocent eyes as he crosses his arms at the hem of his fleece sweater.

"No, it was not."

"Then I give in." He gives a quick shrug before quickly pulling the sweater up his torso then over his head. "Sorry for interrupting, but you were saying?"

"I was saying..." Something before this dizzying visual assault. Does the man not own T-shirts? But I guess that's the point, like his words, the whole tan, toned and lickable sight of him meant to provoke. And it does. It provokes all kinds of sensations as pleasure spirals its way through me, his muscles rippling and flexing as he sets his water bottle on the floor next to a rolled towel.

"Something that that no one ever told you," he prompts as he gracefully lowers himself to the floor. He swipes a hand through his ruffled hair before resting his wrists on his bent knees. "Now that I think about it, it couldn't have been the conversation we had about the noises you make."

"What's wrong with me?" I give my head a tiny shake. It can be hard to follow Whit's conversations at the best of times, but when he's shirtless... "I mean, what's wrong with the noises I make?"

"There's nothing wrong with them." He reaches for what I thought was a wrapped towel but is actually a foam cylinder. "Quite the opposite."

I startle a little as, in one fluid motion, he drops to the floor in a push-up position, swiping his legs behind him.

"What are you doing?" My voice is a little high as I watch him readjust the foam thing under the front of his left thigh.

"Stretching my quads." His explanation sounds so reasonable as he slides the opposite knee to hip level. But the way he's poised is *not* so reasonable—he looks like he's about to show the foam a really good time. I startle as he suddenly glances up at me. "They're a little taut."

I know that feeling.

"I've never..." Seen him *deliver* from this angle. Positioned over the roller on his palms, veins, tendons, and muscles pop in his toned arms. And his ass? Is it any wonder my thoughts go straight to the gutter?

"Never what?"

I give my head a sharp shake as though to rouse myself. Was I even speaking? I thought I was just perving. Whit's response to my non-response is a ripple of motion as his hips dip and he grinds—yeah, grinds—working himself over the foam cylinder.

Absolutely like he was *doing* it.

He flexes and the thing rolls forward and back with his movements. But that's not the important part to note because this vantage point must be the reason people install mirrored ceilings.

"You seem deep in thought," he says without lifting his head.

"Yeah. Thinking," I answer like a lady Neanderthal. Where is there a club and a cave when you need one?

"Thinking about what?"

Thinking about how this must be what you look like doing me. "Sorry, what?"

"Maybe this will refresh your memory." His words are a groan of pleasured agony as he slowly undulates as though intent on hitting the roller's pleasure spots. Lord knows he's certainly hitting mine. I'm not sure about my memory, but I might need to refresh my panties.

What in the world and, "How?"

He lifts his head, his teeth tugging at his bottom lip. My insides begin to pulse and tighten, reacting as though *I* was that roller.

"I was doing something a little like this when I said 'you make *the hottest* little moans, has anyone ever told you that?' And you said—"

"We weren't doing that." My words fall quickly, a snapshot of memory flashing overwhelming me suddenly. "We were in the elevator, and you were—" I roll my lips inward, catching the words just in time.

"Oh, that's right," he says with a faintly evil-looking grin. "My mistake. I wasn't inside you. My cock wasn't, at least." He drops lower to the ground, his golden eyes still focused on mine. "I suppose it can't be classified as a conversation unless you count *ungh...*"—he gives the earthiest, most porn-worthy moan as his body surges over the roller—"as a coherent response."

I blink. Swallow. Then the denials begin. "I'm not sure I've ever made that noise."

"I'll have to record you next time. Do you have a preference between audio and video?" he asks with so much incitement, my cheeks heat hotter than the sun.

"That's not happening." I reach out and swipe up the newspaper, unfolding it with a decisive *thwap*. I stare at it. Through it. Okay, I peek over the top just in time to see Whit lower his head, giving me a stellar view of the muscles in his shoulders, back, and lats. He laughs softly, the gorgeous, horrible man. I shake the newspaper again, turn the page and stare unseeingly as I try to calm my riotous insides.

"Amelia?"

"Yeah?"

"What is it you're doing?" he purrs.

Trying not to watch you giving that roller a *really* good time. "What, you've never seen anyone read a newspaper before?"

"I didn't know you were interested in current affairs. *French* current affairs."

"What?" A sinking feeling seeps through me.

"When did you learn to speak French?"

WHIT

I'm still chuckling to myself as I strip off my track pants. The roller was a stroke of genius—the way her arms had dropped as though they'd suddenly turned to concrete, crushing the newspaper. The priceless look on her face.

She was so fucking riled watching my incitement—so ready to go. I know if I'd slipped my hand into her underwear, she'd be dripping wet. It's like a sign from the heavens that this is what I need to do. Seduce her. Not just sexually. I need to get her to let her guard down, to step away from whatever fears she's clinging to, and I'm going to do that by delivering the woo. Big time.

I'd left Zurich full of plans for a confessional. I was going to tell her that the thought of her wandering around museums and art galleries with some other fuck was driving me insane. That I wanted to be the one next to her, carrying the program, reaching for her hand. Stealing kisses in secluded corners. But then George has picked me up from the airport and mentioned how Miss Mimi hadn't needed a ride home from work. She'd told him she was "going out."

My heart sank like a rock from a thirty-story building. Then came the venom. She'd done it. She was out with another man, and I had no one to blame but myself for allowing that to happen. I wasn't sure of my plans when Beckett booted me from the afternoon meeting, but I was certain they would involve making sure she didn't go on her date. *By any means at my disposal.* But she was already out.

The apartment felt strangely hollow without her. I'd found myself wandering around it, looking for signs of her existence. Her duffel coat hanging in the cloaks closet. A half-eaten bar of Godiva chocolate in the fridge, not with squares snapped off, but with teeth marks. The scent of her perfume in the hallway drifting all the way to the spare room. A wave of displeasure roiled up my body as I'd spotted bags and boxes with the name of Sunday's boutique stashed in the room. She'd slept in my bed last night, but her shit was still in this room. I'd stalked to the closet, summarily squashing a bunch of hanging garments together, swiping them up before hanging them in my walk-in robe. I'd made a couple of trips before I'd whipped out drawers full of underwear and the slinky bits of nightwear I'd chosen for her, before dumping them to my bed.

Fuck the idea of her sleeping and getting dressed elsewhere.

And then, as I didn't have another phone to smash, I decided a run through Hyde Park might get rid of this churning, pent-up displeasure. It turned out to be a long run, and I'd ended up passing by Serpentine Lake. I usually avoid that stretch of the park thanks to the heavier foot traffic, both tourists and the webbed-feet kind. Flocks of swans and geese that make their home on the lake and can be a little unpredictable to navigate. But finding myself there, my strides had begun to slow as I'd watched people out on the water in bright-blue pedalos, or paddle boats. Tourists, probably. It struck me that Mimi would enjoy the experience. It would probably appeal to her sense of fun and ridiculousness. I couldn't quite see myself pedaling through the water, but a rowing boat might be an option. It might even be a little romantic. It would hardly rival a gondola on a Venice canal, but it could still be a possibility. I'd set off once again, a plan forming in my head, and by the time I'd gotten back to my apartment, I didn't want to smash my phone anymore. I felt resolved. I had a plan. I was ready to pull out all the stops, whether she was ready for it or not.

And then I'd dug out the roller. My quads were stiff after my punishing run, but I'd usually just do a few stretches. The fact that I'd pulled it out of the gym feels like a form of divine intervention, I think with a smug-feeling grin.

She doesn't want to date me but looks at me like I'm the juiciest piece of mango, the most decadent piece of cake.

I drop my track pants to my bed, on top of the piles of underwear and nightclothes I'd dumped there earlier, then pad naked to the bathroom. How long before she finds them there? Before she asks why?

Switching on the shower, I relish the burst of cold water against my chest as I step under it. The water heats instantly as I press my hands to the tiles and tip my head under the spray, allowing the water to sluice over me. I am going to woo Mimi, woo her so fucking hard she won't know what's coming for her. I'm going to kill her with kindness—render her helpless by orgasm overload. I'll make her beg for it, beg for me. And then? I suppose we'll see what truth comes out. *For both of us.* We'll see what the future holds, because the way I feel right now, fuck six months. Sixty years won't give me my fill.

Suitably soaked, I slick my hair back from my face and reach for the bodywash, slicking it to my hand. I smear it down my chest, then farther to where my cock is still semihard at the thought of her watching earlier. Her mouth softly open, her eyes dark. I bet she's wet after my filthy little show.

"Fuck." I abandon all thoughts of washing and make a soapy stroke along the hard length. It feels so good. Better still when I close my eyes and imagine her in front of me. On her knees. Her pink-painted nails digging into my thigh muscles, her full lips stretched wide around my girth.

"*Ungh.*" As with any kind of pleasure, the first touch is sublime and melts through my body like sugar on the tongue. *A sugar addiction isn't a thing for no reason.* I swipe my fist over my thick crown, one touch blending into another. The weight of my cock is a comfort, hard and slick against my palm, and the soapy upstroke a satisfying second best to her mouth.

I want to come. To come in her. Come on her. Have her on her knees in front of me. I find myself smiling at all the ways I'm going to have her as I indulge in this little prelude.

She'll be so wet for me.

Fuck, I want it. I want to feel her on my tongue, feel her squirming to get away as I make her drip between her legs.

I swirl my palm over my glans as I let the water fall

down my body in a teasing cascade. Another layer of
sensation. Another flicker of memory as I tip my head back
and groan her name. The rough sound echoes over the
noise of the shower, but there follows a tiny gap—a divine
interference or a tiny stutter in the flow, I'm not sure. What's
important is how I hear that feminine gasp. Fisting my cock,
I turn my head and spot the object of my obsession on the
other side of the bathroom. Her golden hair is piled on top
of her head, her slim fingers clutching a downy towel at her
chest.

"Have you come to join me?"

Her head moves from side to side. "My drawers were
empty."

"What was that? You'll have to come closer," I taunt. "I
can't hear you."

"My pajamas have been dumped on your bed," she says
a little louder as though this is reason enough for her to be
standing in here. Her eyes dart between my face and my
hand as I give my cock another experimental tug.

She releases a physical, shivering breath, then ducks her
head. "I was looking for my clothes."

"In my bathroom?" I throw back my head as I force
myself to keep my hand light. "Fuck, yes. This feels so much
better now that you're watching."

"I—" She looks frantic for a moment as her fight-or-
flight instinct kicks in, but when I groan her name again,
she releases a stuttering breath.

"You're thinking of me?"

"Like you're on your knees in front of me."

"You are so bad." She shakes her head again as though
denying my words.

"You say that like it doesn't turn you on. Your clothes are
on my bed, which is where you should be. Get in it or get in

here," I growl, still working my cock. My abs flex, my thigh muscles as hard as steel. "Then I won't have to imagine."

She hesitates but ultimately responds to my goading by dropping the towel where she stands. Her hand slowly rises to her hip, her expression suddenly full of incitement.

"*Amelia.*"

"What? I'm just giving you a little something to work with."

"Get. The. Fuck. In here."

Her smile rises slowly, then she turns on her heel as over her shoulder she mouths, "Make me." And then she's gone.

I flick off the water, grabbing my towel with a grumbled, "This is how accidents fucking happen," as I hurriedly step onto it so as not to break my neck. "You'd better make good use of your head start," I yell, whipping the cotton up to wrap around my waist. "Because I'm coming for you." In response, there comes a peal of giggles and the patter of fast feet out of my bedroom. "And when I get you, there's no mercy."

The giggle turns to a shriek as I stalk out into the hallway, a blur of skin and blond disappearing around the corner.

Tension and exhilaration expand in my chest as I follow her, my tone very *fee-fi-fo-fum* as I call after her. "Amelia..."

"Ha, that's not gonna work today." She laughs, her bare feet pattering against the wooden floor.

"What do you think you're doing?" I can barely keep a straight face as I round the corner and spot her on the other side of the open-plan space. In the kitchen, her back is to me, the island blocking the rest of my view. As I get closer, the sight of her takes my breath away. Long and lithe through the leg, her arse is shaped like a heart and her hips softly flared like an instrument begging to be played.

"Looking for protection." Her head swings briefly over her shoulder, her eyes a bright flash before she returns to hurriedly opening and closing drawers.

"You're out of luck if you're looking for a shower cap."

"I can totally see you wearing one." She giggles her answer, letting out a small "Eep!" as she slides another look my way before returning to rummage again. As I reach the island, she pivots to face me, her hair coming loose in wispy blond waves. "Don't come any closer," she warns. She slides the hair out of her face with the back of her hand, and in the other, she brandishes a copper spatula.

"How can I not, Amelia? How can I resist so much temptation." My gaze roams over her. She doesn't miss my meaning.

"Rude!" She presses her left arm across her breasts, her fingers curling inward.

"Need a hand?" I take a step closer, and another, Amelia matching each for another backward.

"Not even." She brandishes the spatula my way again.

"That's an interesting choice of weapon," I say, ignoring her warning.

"I mean it—don't come any closer!"

"I mean it too, my maddeningly sexy brat." Exhilaration floods my chest as I dash forward and make a grab for her. Squealing, she pivots and runs in the direction of the dining table. Chasing Mimi would be a pleasurable experience any day of the week, but a naked Mimi? It's fucking awesome.

"Stay away!" From the other side of the table, she laughingly wields her spatula. "Oh, my gosh, I can't believe you're chasing me!"

"I can't believe you'd defy me in such a brazen manner." I glance at the wall of windows. "Not to mention giving the good people of Kensington such a show."

Her gaze follows mine. "But this is privacy glass, right? No one can see in—we're high up!"

"Hussy," I say with a frown I won't hold. "Can't hold weapons and hide everything." My gaze dips pointedly. "Not that I'm complaining. Come over here and let me see that pussy better."

"Hey!" She presses the spatula over the area in question. "No fair—you have a towel."

"Because you dropped yours like a checkered flag."

"It's only fair you drop yours, too," she demands laughingly.

"I'm all for equality, but do you know how hard it is to run with a hard-on?"

"Why don't you show me." She tilts her head provocatively, her lips a tempting little moue.

"I'll show you my hard-on any time." I put a little swagger into my step as I make my way to the end of the table, refusing to give in to the anticipatory thrill rolling through me. "But not when you're armed."

"I would never!" She enunciates her denial like the most puritanical teacher in the school.

"It's a pity you don't like the rest of me as much as you like my cock." My tone is taunting and silky as I slip my thumb into the towel at my waist as though to loosen it.

"I like you more than I should," she answers, her avid eyes not sure what to watch first.

She feints left, and I follow, our stalemate a game of who dares wins as I lunge around the table after her. She shrieks and whirls away, but in a few steps, I've caught her elbow.

"Gotcha," I rasp, pulling her against me, wrapping my arm around her waist. Her excited squeal vibrates through me as I lift her feet from the floor as she kicks and flails ineffectually, her bones turning to jelly at the shock of being caught.

Shock and excitement, I'm sure.

"What are you going to do?" Her words are panting and breathless.

"Do?" I shake my head like a wet dog, shaking off the droplets of water dripping from my hair to my face, making her laugh. I use the opportunity to wrestle the spatula from her hand.

"What are you going to do with *it*?" Is she excited or worried? Probably a bit of both.

"That's two questions," I murmur, pressing my mouth to her ear. Her breath hitches as I graze my teeth along the shell. "Which do you want the answer to?"

"Both, of course."

"So greedy." I can feel her heart beating as I carry her over to the sofa. The fight having drained from her body, she's compliant as I bend her over the back of it.

"You won't—"

Her words halt as I slide the copper edge up the back of her thigh. "Won't what, Blondie? What do you think I'm not capable of?"

"Cruelty," she whispers as her fingers curl over the sofa, and she presses her temptation of an arse out.

"Do you think I should punish you?" I purr as the edge of the copper implement reaches the crease between her thigh and her buttock. I notice the tremor in my hand. My heart hammers in my chest. There's exhilaration and excitement, yes. But that's not all I feel. I won't say love is a stranger to me because I've felt love and I have love for my family. But the romantic kind of love? I'm not entirely sure what that is. And while I won't say I'm in love now, whatever this is, its will is stronger than my own.

A droplet of water rolls around my bicep, dropping to the floor as I lift my arm. I swing my arm wide and bring the spatula down on the right buttock.

"That's for defying me," I growl as she cries out a needy sound. For going out on a date when she knows I can give her everything she needs. The next swipe comes from underneath and without the same kind of intensity. "And that's because you drive me to the brink of insanity." Copper thuds against the wood as I drop it, bending to paint a wet stripe along the offended cheek. She moans as I slide my tongue along the crease.

"And that one?" Her words are a slide into hope as she tips up onto her toes.

"Because I fucking need it," I rasp, dropping to my knees like a penitent before burying my face in her pussy.

She cries out, her desperation sending a prickle of sensation across my skin. I make an anklet of my fingers, sliding her leg wider, burying my tongue into her very center.

"Oh God. Whit, no. It's too much." She squirms as though trying to get away when I bring my hand down on her backside. "Oh!"

"Stop wriggling."

"It feels so dirty."

"Stop wriggling." I spank her again, one stinging swipe that makes her pussy pulse. "Before I bury my tongue in your arse."

"No!" But there's a hint of something there to explore later as her clit throbs around my fingers, as I drive my tongue against her again and again. I feel like a starving man let loose at a feast, not sure where he wants to start, only that he wants to gorge.

"You're so wet for me, Amelia. So shiny and your arousal sweet."

She whimpers, the anticipation of her falling like a tiny explosion of delight deep in my chest. Her honied whispers turn to cries, her knees locking as the waves of her orgasm begin to pull her under. I don't let up because I can't touch enough, kiss enough, be enough. I want to taste every inch of her silky skin. Make her see that she was made for me.

Shit.

Shit. Oh shit!

I lean back on my heels, the thoughts in my head running free now, unable to be ignored. I love her. I love her, and I'm so screwed.

What the fuck am I going to do?

I look up as she begins to turn; it might be minutes or an hour after she's come. It's hard to tell.

"Wow. I feel like a foal," she says, her limbs slightly uncoordinated. Meanwhile, I just sit there, staring at the woman who ought to belong to me.

Who will belong to me. I've just got to figure out how.

"Whit? Are you okay?"

My mouth hooks up in one corner as my gaze slides over her. "Yeah. I'm good." I'm terrified but, "Actually, I'm amazing."

"Oh yes, you are." She tilts her head to hide her smile as I push up from the floor.

"Can I?" Her words are tentative as she gestures to the towel. Without waiting for an answer, she pulls the edge free.

She stares at me, I stare at her, and my cock between us grows impossibly hard.

One minute, Mimi is pressed against the sofa, and the next, I am. The downy towel is around my ankles, and my brain is melting down the back of my neck as her eyes and her fingers trail over my chest. My abs react under the tips of her fingers as she follows the trail of dark hair to where my cock juts between us—hard, ruddy, and so ready. She stares for a moment, watching as it jumps in response to her touch, my thighs tight, my balls tightening, my whole being ready to explode.

"I want to kiss you." Her eyes rise, following the line of my bicep until they meet mine.

"Want to kiss me where?" I ask with more wit and feeling than I currently possess because my wits are blown at the prospect. As for feeling, every inch of my skin cries out for her touch. When she wraps her hand around the base of my shaft, I almost combust.

"Here." Her whisper is tremulous as she leans closer, licking at a trail of shower water that drips from my hair down my chest. "And here." I groan and tip my head back as she circles the flat of my nipple with her tongue. As good as it feels, it's not quite as special as the way her hand gravitates to my cock. She slides her fingers along the length, palming the crown the way she'd watched me hold myself in the shower. I growl a little as the point of her tongue flicks the hardened bud of my nipple like a kitten lapping milk. I press my hand to the back of her head, encouraging her closer with one whispered word.

"*Bite.*"

She presses her teeth to my chest at the same time as I press my hand between her legs and swipe my middle finger through her wetness. I feel her startled gasp against my skin, her fingers tightening on my cock.

"I love kissing you here." My thumb slides over the soft rise of her still swollen clit. "I'd crawl between your legs and make your pussy my home."

"You have…" But that's all she manages as I slide another finger inside her. Her free hand finds my bicep, her fingers almost piercing. And there we stand for breathless beats, my fingers inside her, my thumb petting and sliding over and over again as I force her onto her tiptoes to feel the full effect, our mouths all hot slides and breathlessness.

"I want…"

"Tell me. I'll give it to you." Again and again.

"I want to taste you." She rocks against me, breasts pressed to my chest, so lewd and so lush as a chuckle rises from my chest, dark and sort of frantic.

"Then get on your knees, darling."

"First, tell me who Kerry is."

"What?" I pull back a little to better see her face, not quite sure of her meaning.

"Kerry," she purrs as her hand slides between us, wrapping her dainty fingers around my cock in a surprisingly firm hold.

"The number on the newspaper," I murmur, trying to keep a straight face.

"Yeah. Who is she?" Mimi repeats as she begins to slowly and methodically jerk me off.

"Beckett," I almost grunt, the rest of the explanation leaving my mouth in a rush. "Gave me the number."

"Oh. Right." She angles her face away, but not before I see a flash of disquiet.

"A massage therapist." I'm a bastard, but what's good for the goose is definitely good for the gander as her tongue returns to my nipple and her free hand cups my balls. Her hot breath pools against me, and I'm glad I have something to lean against as she works me. This feels so good.

"Oh, look. You're a little wet."

I glance down at her words. Her thumb pressed to my

slit, she pulls it away, pre-cum suspended like a tiny spider's web between us. Until she brings her thumb to her mouth, where she sucks.

"Wet just for me." Her gaze lingers almost speculatively before I bring my hand to the back of her head.

"Just for you. All for you, and nothing will be left of me when you're through." I add a little pressure when her knees bend, her body bowing gracefully before me. "That's right, little fly. Get on your knees for me."

"Yes, Daddy."

Her smoky eyes watch my reaction as she paints a wet stripe of pleasure across my cock head, making me groan.

"You're so silky here," she whispers, wrapping her fingers around the base and her lips to my crown. Breath halts in my chest as she tongues the glans, licking and swirling like I'm an ice cream on a hot summer's day. "And here." Her solemn gaze watches as she licks along my length, making my toes curl against the towel, my hands finding themselves in her hair.

"Put me in your mouth, darling. Suck me off."

Her eyes sweep up, her look bold. "You can't put bad things in my mouth."

My laughter, fuck, it's loud. At least until she presses her lips to my crown. "This isn't bad." She swirls her tongue. "This is you, and I have wanted you for a very long time."

"And now you have me. I'm all yours." In more ways than I'm prepared to admit. In more ways than you're prepared to hear.

"Not Kerry's?"

"No more than you are Garrett's."

She seems satisfied by my answer, putting her lips to me in a tight kiss, her lips widening as she slides her way down. It's some show, watching my cock disappear into her mouth.

"Fuck, yeah. That's it." My head drops back, the sight of her dark-painted lashes like the sweep of an angel's wing. Her lips, pink and full. The remains of her messy bun. She looks like an angel but she sucks cock like a professional as she holds me there, deep in her mouth, hollowing her cheeks for a slow return.

I hiss out a curse at her next return, my hands encouraging her as I cradle her head.

"Fuck, yes." My compliment is a shallow moan as I ease her closer. "Deeper, darling. Take me all the way in." My fingers tangled in her hair, I give a couple of tentative thrusts, power seeping deep into my bones. To my surprise and delight, she presses her fingers to my thighs, offering me her mouth, and ceding control.

Her eyes are penetrating, her lips sensuous, and her mouth like velvet as I slide myself deeper. My thighs tremble, and my brain turns to porridge as she moans soft encouragements.

"You're so beautiful on your knees for me."

She moans softly as I tell her how beautiful she looks, and tears fall from her eyes as I press against the channel of her throat. She doesn't fight me as I hold her there. She just stares up at me with such trust.

"I fucking love—" My heart feels like it's about to burst, and not just because of the blow job of the year. The way she trusts me. The way she bends. This shit she's doing so we can pretend. It's her—it's all her. We're fighting the inevitable, can't she see that? When will she realise?

I'm trembling as I withdraw from the wet confines of her mouth, my emotions a heavy layer over this ecstasy. I have to control this. I can't fall apart. So I give her another experience, one she's said she'd like to see.

"—*this.*"

My insides light like fireworks as I use her saliva as lube, my fist slipping wetly up and down my length, my other still tangled in her hair. And her expression? I want to kiss it. Fuck it. Come on it. Which is fortunate, because that's what I'm about to do as I angle my cock down and with an almost plaintive sounding curse, I lash her neck and her chest in hot, wet bursts.

33

MIMI

"You all right?"

I blink up from my dirty daydreaming. *Whit's fingers making a bracelet against my wrist, his attention a tender stroke to the underside as he's lifted me back onto my feet.*

"Love?"

"Sorry. Super busy!" I announce with a bright smile, holding out my hands for the shoebox-sized parcel the man in a security uniform is holding in his hands.

"Looked like you've gone to sleep with your eyes open," he says, smirking as he hands it over.

"It was all internal work," I answer briskly, placing the box to the left of my desk. "Do I need to sign for it?"

"Nah. The courier will have gotten that when it was left at reception. I just said I'd drop it off on my rounds."

"Well, thanks!"

The security guard can't have taken more than a few steps before I find my finger caressing my breastbone as though I were still on my knees, Whit's body bent over me. It was so hot watching him work himself. Seeing him fall apart. Being the object of his desire, then the focus of his tenderness as he'd helped me up from the floor and swiped up the towel.

"*You okay?*" he'd asked carefully, his thumb on my pulse.

I'd nodded. I didn't have the words. It was like my mind checked out and my body took over and, just, hell, it was so good.

"*That was better than any kind of porn,*" I found myself whispering. Laughter had burst from his chest, and he'd taken my face in his hands when I'd added, "*That was amazing. When can you do it again?*"

"*You want me to come on you again?*"

"*Yes, no. All of it. Whit, you make me want to do things I've never even thought of. You turn me on so much. I'm not just aroused with you, but I'm safe. I know I can do or say what I think and feel, and—*"

He'd pressed his finger to my lips. "*Don't date anyone else,*" he'd said softly. "*Just be with me. I promise not to fall in love with you.*"

I fell. That was all it took.

I give in. I surrender to this thing that's bigger than me. That's bigger than him. But that doesn't mean I have to admit to it. As far as Whit is concerned, I'm just making up for lost time. He doesn't need to know that I'm in love with him. What would that knowledge even do? It might frighten him off. Or worse, it might not.

No, it's better that he thinks this is just sex. There's no future for us.

But, gosh, I need to get it together because when my phone rings in the afternoon, and Whit's name flashes up, my hand shakes like maracas.

"I've been expecting your call," he says smoothly.

"But you called me." Okay, so I'm a little slow this afternoon. "Aren't you supposed to be in meetings all afternoon?"

"Yeah, but I would've excused myself to take a call from you."

"Did you used to skip meetings to take Jody's calls?" I ask, trying to bring the conversation back to work.

"I wasn't getting a stiff cock under the boardroom table thinking of Jody naked. Oh, what do you know. It looks like I've discovered the cure-all."

"What are you talking about?" I half say, half giggle.

"The words *Jody* and *naked* in the same sentence is an erection killer. It might've been helpful if I'd realized that earlier, but better late than never, I suppose."

"That's not very complimentary." I fill my tone with more disapproval than this silly conversation warrants.

"But it's better for my health this way."

"Yeah." My agreement hits the air in a chuckle. "Jody would probably unman you for that two-word sentence alone. She told me last week that the third trimester of a pregnancy should be called the *I will cut you* stage." The first is the *I want a glass of chardonnay more than my next breath* stage, and the second, *get your hand off my bump before I snap your wrist*. Being pregnant doesn't sound like much fun.

"I can't tell if you're playing this really cool or you just haven't opened the box sitting on your desk."

"I usually lean more toward dorky, I'm not sure if you've realized. Second, there isn't a box sitting on my desk."

"According to the tracking information, it's already been delivered. You'd better get your delicious arse down to reception," he suggests softly. "Track down your gift before someone else opens it."

"You bought me a gift?" It's hard to sound excited and disapproving at the same time.

"Just a little something. Something we both might enjoy."

The soft hairs on the back of my neck begin to prickle. "I hope whatever it is, it doesn't look suspicious. If I go to reception and they hand me a banana-shaped package, I won't be happy."

"It's not a banana."

"You know what I mean."

"So suspicious."

Our call ends to the sound of his laughter. Of course, I know the parcel isn't in reception because it's sitting on *his* desk. I'd been distracted this morning and assumed it was for him.

I close the door to his office behind me because there is no way I'm opening that box at *my* desk. Who knows what might fall out. I snicker a little as I round his behemoth of a desk and pull out his chair. Sure enough, the parcel is addressed to me. *I must've missed it*, I think, as I swipe up a fancy silver letter opener that looks like it belongs on a *Bridgerton* set and slice the tape. Dropping the cardboard to the floor, I pull out a gift box wrapped in pink ribbon. The box reveals sheets of white tissue paper and a tiny envelope containing a spiky, handwritten note.

> *Amelia,*
> *Please accept these gifts as a token of my ardent desire.*
> *I can't wait to see you use them.*
> *Wx*
> *PS You're a little too old and a lot too lovely*

to have only balding Barbie dolls in your
toy box

I shiver, the sense of excitement and trepidation causing a wave of goose bumps to spread across my skin as I peel away the rest of the tissue to find Whit has gone a little overboard in a high-end sex shop. I pull out sex toy after sex toy, laying them on his desk in a row. After a moment of just staring at them, I order them from smallest to largest, scattering the, erm, *accouterments* around the very expensive-looking phallic display. Blacks and golds, each comes in a velvety bag and a fancy name tag.

The Luna.

Aphrodite

Venus

The Blessed Bullet and—

"*Whoa.*"

I hold what I'm pretty sure is known as a *wand* in my hand. I might not have owned sex toys because I shared a room at college, then later, my parents never once knocked before stepping into my tiny above-the-garage apartment. Not to mention Mom insisted on popping in to *run the vacuum across the floor* or *help me out with laundry* whenever I was at work. Heaven forbid I do anything that might cause me to break out in a sweat!

She'd have a fit if she saw how sex with Whit leaves me.

No, my living arrangements were not conducive to any sex toy but my hand, meaning my fingers and I are very intimately acquainted.

Where was I? Oh right. The massive, powered schlong

weighing my arm down. The wand named *The Pandora*, I assume because of the havoc it could wreak on your box.

Placing it down on the desk, I swipe my phone out from my dress pocket and take a quick snap. I quickly send it to Whit, along with a text, as my chest moves with a burbling giggle.

> Are you expanding the business? VirTu banking and sex toy parties?

> Party for two?

There are enough to share, but I don't think I'll mention that, not on the back of our tentative agreement. *Just be with me. I promise I won't fall in love with you.*

Is it too early or too late for this heart pang of regret?

He won't fall for me, which was the point of my fake dating schtick. Maybe not the whole point, but it's too late to try to protect myself. If I'm honest with myself, which, as a rule, I try to be, I was already fooling myself Sunday morning when I told him of my stupid plans.

But what's done is done, and I've proven to myself this year that I'm a lot stronger than I look. I was strong enough to come here, to stand in the face of my parents' fear and disappointment. I was strong enough to fight for Whit. When the time comes, I know I'll be strong enough to walk away. My heart might break, but at that point, what difference will it make?

I forcibly push away the thoughts (compartmentalizing is my jam) as my phone vibrates. *It's in good company*, I think with a snicker.

I pull it from the pocket of my shirt dress sparing a glance at all the vibratory things. Plus lube and cleaning wipes and... I'm momentarily distracted by a black satin mask.

> I hope you're not trying to find a polite way of telling me you play well with others...

What? Oh, sex toy parties. Or maybe plain old sex parties would be more Whit's lane.

> I was thought maybe you sent these to me as some kind of trial incentive. Sort of: sign up to the VirTu banking app and we'll make sure your banking goes with a bang!

> Each one of those toys is an incentive itself, chosen to give you pleasure. Solo or otherwise.

My poor heart, my poor panties, I think as I use my index finger to straighten the tiniest of the toys as a fragment of memory flickers in my head. *A little bullet for you to press to your clit when you think of me.*

> Also, maybe I should move you to the marketing department.

> Would it be a promotion?

My phone vibrates with a call in my hand.

"You're going nowhere." His voice takes on a husky edge. "Unless you count riding my cock as some kind of promotion."

"It sure is an incentive." I find myself matching his tone.

"Bad timing," he utters unhappily. "I was hoping to be there when your new toy box arrived."

"Oh no." My answer is wavery with amusement when it should be full of warning. "Between office hours, ours is a professional relationship." Whit begins to grumble, but I just talk over him. "It's no good complaining, these are your rules."

"Rules are made to be broken."

"Such a bad example to set, Mr. CEO," I reply, picking up one of the more ergonomic sex toys. It sort of looks like a pebble and fits into the palm of my hand.

"As is my prerogative, Miss Sexy Secretary." His stern voice sends a zing of something down my spine.

"That's Miss Executive PA to you. Miss Sexy Executive PA, even."

"You're such a hot piece, Miss Sexy Secretary. I wonder, what would you take down for me if I was there?" My body reacts viscerally to his base suggestion, a throbbing pulse running through me like the beat of a sensual drum. "And I don't mean a memo."

"What *do* you mean?"

"Oh, I think you know," he purrs in return. "In fact, why don't you do it now?"

"What?" Is it me, or has someone turned off the air in here?

"Take down your underwear."

"That sounds suspiciously like it falls under the category of shenanigans." My voice sounds a little reedy as I drop into his extremely comfortable leather chair and literally fan my face. Vibrators and sexy talk on a weekday afternoon? The man has no boundaries. *And I like it.* "And as I've already explained, Mr. Bad Boy CEO, I'm a good girl who doesn't like to break the rules."

"You lie because you're most certainly sitting in my chair."

"Ha! You can see all the way from across the city, can you?"

"No, but I can hear the creak of the leather."

"So I'm not allowed to sit in your chair?" In an act of unseen defiance, I kick up my legs, placing my heels on the edge of his desk.

"Only if you promise to get the seat wet."

"That also falls under office shenanigans." Closing my eyes, I let the thought possess me for a beat. It's hardly the first time I've imagined him bending me over his desk, only now I have a lot more to work with. I know how my name sounds groaned from his tongue, and I'm intimately acquainted with the hum of his body as he comes. I know how deliriously happy it makes me when he stiffens above me, his body shaking as though he hasn't another ounce to give. I know how it feels to have him inside me. Oh yes. I'm intimately acquainted with Whit's sexual voodoo.

"Live a little," he chides. "How many times will you get to say you got yourself off in the boss's chair?"

"If it's up to you, probably plenty."

His laughter is as dirty as a drain. "Seriously, though. I'm about to head back into a meeting. You must have something a little sweet to share with me. I won't even ask you to choose your weapon." His words trail off as the penny drops.

"You can't mean—"

"Just use your hand for me."

"Why don't you just use your imagination?" I retort.

"You mean like you did when you watched me fuck my own fist in the bathroom?"

The images his words paint, the fragments of memory rising like steam. "It's not even as if I'll get to watch. I'll just get to enjoy a little audio."

"I am not masturbating in your office." I'm not. Then why is my hand inching toward the hem of my dress?

"Start slow. Just loosen a couple of buttons on your dress. Maybe two at the top and two at the bottom."

"I should've known you were up to no good this morning when you suggested I wear this."

"When I said your tits looked wonderful, you mean? You could wear a rice sack and still look totally fuckable. Just a taste, darling. I bet the door is closed."

"Be reasonable, Whit." But there's little protest in my tone.

"Let me hear those sweet moans. I'll talk, you just listen. And play."

"I could just pretend," I retort in a last-minute half-assed attempt. I don't know why I'm fighting him.

"Open your legs for me, Amelia." He uses that tone, causing a shiver to roll down my spine. "Open your legs and take your fingers for me like a good girl."

"This is madness," I whisper, lifting my heels to slide my legs farther apart.

"Don't fight it. Slide your hand inside your underwear. Are you wet?"

"Of course I'm wet," I mutter as though I've been given a chore, but I'm still doing it.

"It was a rhetorical question, my love. I know you're always so ready for me. Slide your fingers farther down. Feel how soft you are. How wet. Slide them inside, Amelia. Feel yourself pulse around them."

"Whit stop," I beg a little breathlessly. "I can't, not here. Not in the office."

"I know you want me to bend you over my desk. You're a good girl who loves to be made to be bad. Be bad for me, Amelia. Slide those fingers into your pretty little cunt." His words slide into a groan and everything inside me pulls tight at the sound.

"Are you…" Do I dare? "Are you touching yourself?"

"I'm at the far end of a room full of people, but all I can think about is you."

I both love and hate that I can't resist him as I drive my fingers hard inside. I gasp, my body bowing from the chair, making the forgotten vibrator slip to the floor.

"What was that?"

"I dropped something." My heart hammers in my chest, the throb of it echoing between my legs.

"Better pick it up, little girl. Now," he adds when I don't answer. "Then slip off your knickers."

Knickers. The name sounds so ridiculous, but I can't help how delicious it feels growled against my skin. "Maybe I'm not wearing any."

"You'd better be," he says, the warning clear in his tone. "Especially as I watched you slide them on this morning."

"Maybe I couldn't wait for you to be bad. Maybe I started without you."

"Fuck." The hard fricative is all frustration. "Just wait until I get my hands on you."

Pressing my palm against my clit, I moan. "Sounds like I'm just gonna have to use my own for now."

But then the door opens and there Whit stands, looking like a cat that's about to play with a juicy mouse.

WHIT

As I wrap my fingers around the handle of my office door and push, the muscles in my chest and shoulders grow taut. There's every possibility Mimi will be doing something other than what I'm imagining, like scanning her socials while pretending to indulge me. But then she wouldn't be the most perfect girl I've ever had the pleasure of knowing. I promised I wouldn't fall in love with her, and I wasn't lying. On a technicality only. I'd already fallen for her at the point I'd said that. Fallen hook, line, and painful sinker. I can't think what comes after this. How things will work out beyond her six-month mark. I only know that I have to be with her—to try to make her see there is a chance for us. That love is worthy of that chance. The details, the who will live where and how we'll navigate the obstacles, can come later. Even if it means bailing on more meetings and blowing up Doreen's house.

Meanwhile, I play my part well. I'm just here to fuck her. That's my cover. I just need to figure out how to steal her heart like a thief.

As I push the door open, my aching muscles relax as I find her seated in my chair, her heels on my desk... and her hand pressed between her legs. She jerks upright, instinctually closing her legs.

Probably because you've still got the door open, dickhead.

"Stay where you are." I slip into the room, closing it behind me before sliding the lock. "Well, Miss Valente. What have we here?" Despite sounding like I'm a truncheon and a funny helmet away from a bobby on the beat, the sight of her almost takes my breath away. Such a stunning vignette, one hot enough to make any police officer's truncheon ache.

"Whit—"

Her panic feels like a blessing and gives me an idea.

"That's Mr. Boss Man to you, Miss Valente." I drop my voice an octave, making my tone very stern.

"Oh." She catches on to my direction quickly, her smile so brief it would've been easy to miss... say, if you were staring at her tits. The top two buttons of her shirt dress have come loose, unless she unbuttoned them. The second prospect is much hotter, but I don't mind which is the culprit.

"So this is what you do when left to your own devices." My stance wide, I fold my arms across my chest as I stare at her with a severe expression. "I'm afraid I'll have to report you to HR."

"Oh, please, no," she says breathily as her feet slide from my desk. "Please don't report me." She tilts her head demurely as she slides her phone into her pocket, unable to hide the amusement in her gaze. "I can't lose my position here."

So much emphasis on the word *position.* So many options.

"What sort of boss would I be if I allowed you to squander company time, Miss Valente?"

"A kind one. Compassionate?"

"Kindness doesn't keep us in business."

"Please, sir. Don't report me."

Fuck, she pleads so beautifully. I wonder how many times she's watched something similar in porn.

"It goes against everything I stand for." I bring my hand to my chin as though torn. "Despite the very hard case you're making."

"Hard. Yes, of course it is." Her eyes dip pointedly. "Only, I'm so desperate for this... position."

My mouth tips. I can't help it. Such innuendo. Such fluttery subservience.

"I'll do anything."

"Anything?" The word comes out in a low rumble as though she's caught me off guard—as though we haven't both been waiting for this since I stepped through the door.

"Yes, sir." She nods, her gaze rain filled. "Just tell me what I can do to make this better. To make it up to you."

Fuck, yes. "You know what I'm going to say." I stalk across the office, shedding my jacket and dumping it on the sofa as I pass.

"No, I don't." She shakes her head in denial, her chest rising and falling in tight little breaths as I draw to a stop in front of her.

"No, *sir*." Along with the correction, I slide the backs of my knuckles over her breast. "You've done something wrong, and you need to be punished. Doubly so." My gaze drops to the floor, where one of the vibrators seems to have been dropped. "Mistreatment of merchandise. Pick it up."

Her gray eyes flare, wide and expectant, and she laughs a little. Nervousness mixed with anticipation. But she swipes it up.

"Take out one of the wipes and clean it."

Confusion ripples across her face as she reaches for the packet and tears it open.

"Clearly, you don't deserve nice things."

"No, sir." She holds out the vibrator, cradled in her palm.

"Put it on the desk with the others, then take off your underwear."

"Here?" She pauses in the act of setting it down next to the others, her big, innocent eyes blinking back at me. "While you watch?"

In answer, I hold out my right hand.

"I'm sorry, sir." She angles her gaze away as I notice she's lined up the vibrators in order of size. "I don't understand. Specifically which bit of my underwear?" As she turns back to face me, her hand already a teasing slide into the open neck of her dress.

"The tiny strip of lace barely covering your delicious

pussy." But I know what she's angling for as I lean closer, my answer a rough whisper in her ear. "Take off your knickers, you naughty girl."

"Oh, shivers!" She gives a little shimmy, and her smile reins free.

"Hurry now, Miss Valente. Slip them off and hand them over. Phone," I add in a bark. Hand outstretched, I curl my fingers inward. *Give.* "No doubt you were using it to talk filth to someone."

"Yes, I was." She ducks her head as she reaches for her pocket, but I see her amusement anyway. "I think maybe he needs punishing, too."

"Not my concern," I mutter, glancing at her dress pointedly. "Do I have to strip you myself?"

Her hands immediately slip under the hem of her dress, and I spot a flash of pink lace.

"An unproductive worker and a liar to boot."

She lifts her gaze but not her head as she realizes what I mean. "You didn't really expect to find me walking around bared-assed, did you?"

Catching her chin in my hand, I raise her head. "What I didn't expect to find was you sitting in my chair, rubbing your pussy." A blush immediately tints her cheeks. "But now that I have, I hope to see it again. Maybe from a closer vantage point."

"You are so bad."

"No, Miss Valente. You're the one in trouble here. Surely a man of my position shouldn't be required to supervise you every minute of your day."

"You'd like that, wouldn't you? To watch me." There's so much encouragement in her reply, but I don't break character.

"You can't even pretend to be contrite. It's obvious I'll

need to punish you for your behavior. Make you see the error of your ways."

"I—"

"No need to answer." I release her chin. "Take off your underwear." I hold out my hand. "Hurry, Miss Valente. Hand them over."

I spot the ghost of her smile as she ducks her head, slipping her hands under the hem of her dress. A moment and a suggestive wiggle later, something pink and lacy slides down her legs.

"Sir." She passes the warm fabric to my hand, a spark of electricity passing between us as our fingers inadvertently touch.

"Bend over the desk, Miss Valente."

"What?" Is it nerves or excitement that makes her voice wobble?

"Press your palms on the desk and bend over this end." I point at a spot away from my chair.

She does this without a word of complaint, bringing the vibrators into her immediate line of sight. "I feel so..."

"Vulnerable?"

"Now that you mention it." She swallows audibly.

"Do you think you'll have a favorite?"

"I guess I won't know until I try them out."

"Yes, all of them," I agree. "But not all at once." I lean closer without allowing our bodies to touch. "I think it'll be this one." Placing her phone down, I rest my finger on the bag containing the wand. Mimi immediately begins to giggle and splutter her denials.

"It looks like something to work the kinks out of your shoulders."

"Oh, I think there's no working the kinks out of you." I

pull away, and the soles of my shoes scrape against the floor as I study her from several vantage points.

"What are you doing?" She glances over her shoulder, her gaze skating down my body, bold and possessive. I fucking love the way her eyes stick on the way my pants tent. I palm myself as I step closer.

"I'm staring at your delectable arse." I lift the back of her dress higher with a deliberate gentleness. Folding it across her back, I run my hand over the roundness as she gasps. Her tension unfurls in a long sigh as I slide them along her bare pussy. "Wondering when you'll let me fuck it." I almost feel her flutter against my hand. "Open wider for me, Miss Valente. Let me see what I have to work with."

"This is a strange punishment," she whispers as she steps her feet wider.

"This part is just for my enjoyment." My hand slices through the air, the connection of my palm making her flesh quiver. "That was part of yours."

"Oh!"

"Say thank you."

"For what—"

I slide two fingers inside her pussy, and the way she groans feels like a lick to the underside of my balls.

"I've barely touched you, and you're making such a mess of my fingers. It looks like I'll have to work harder to make you more contrite." I press my fingers deeper, twisting my hand at the wrist. She begins to whimper and thrusts back against my hand. "What was that?"

"I said I'm s-sorry, sir. Please don't stop."

"This." My fingers slip wetly away as I lean over her a second time, pulling a notepad and pencil from across my desk. My fingers glisten with her silky pleasure as I scratch out a note. "Read it," I instruct, sliding it to face her. For all my formal commands, I can't help but graze my mouth over the corner of hers. She smiles shyly, and the flash of that gap between her teeth makes me feel like I could climb inside her. I've had a lot of sex, fucked a lot of women in a lot of places (holes and otherwise), but I've never wanted anyone the way I want her. It's like I can feel it in my guts and bones, the gnawing sensation that I'll never have enough of her. She feels like home. She feels like she belongs to me.

And she will, but I turn down the volume on my consciousness for now.

"Go on, little fly. Read."

"I must not touch myself when I'm at work." I hear her swallow. Imagine her licking her lips. It makes me wonder which part of that turns her on—the doing or the getting caught? It makes me wonder if her pussy is pulsing emptily. "Not without permission."

"Well done." I bring my hand down on her right bum cheek, hard and fast.

"Oh!"

"Read it again."

"I must not... *jeez!*" My second slap turns her skin a fresh pink. "I must not t-touch myself when I'm at work." My third a slightly sharper sting and causes her to suck in sharply. I don't worry that it might've been too much as she picks up where she left off in a breathy tone. "Without an audience."

"Without permission," I correct, taking her flesh in both my hands. I squeeze and knead, relishing her moans as she drops her head. And that answers my earlier question. "Freudian slip, my love?"

"Without my boss as an audience." Her words are muffled as she drops her forehead to the desk, pressing back into my hands.

"And anyone in the vicinity who might happen to use a telescope."

"What?" Her head jerks up, her worried glance sliding over her shoulder.

I use my hand to turn her head. "Keep going."

"I must not..."

I know she hears the soft *zvvt* of my zipper, the rest of her words slightly garbled as I press the head to the very center of her.

"I must not—"

It's as far as she gets before I drive myself home with a lust-soaked groan.

"Oh yes!" Her hips rock back, chasing my retreat, and I don't fucking know where to put my hands. The curve of her hip? The swell of her arse. I want it all. I want to touch, own, devour as I begin to fuck her solidly.

"Read," I growl, slapping her arse again, making her internal walls greedy.

"I must not... oh, you feel so big."

"Compliments are unnecessary. This isn't about your enjoyment."

She stretches like a cat beneath me, the paper still held between her two hands. I pull back at the sight of her, my cock hard and glistening between us.

"*Fuck!*" With a snap of my hips, I drive myself inside her, my fingers leaving red marks on her hips. "The words, Amelia. Read the fucking words."

"I must not... I must not... Oh, I think I'm going to."

I press my palm flat next to her head and cover her body with mine. "Your position here depends on you coming only when I tell you to."

"Oh God, Whit. I don't think I can."

"Yes. Yes, you can. Concentrate," I grate out.

In profile, her gaze seems to turn inward, her teeth digging into her bottom lip as I continue to fuck her, slow and steadily.

"That's it, good girl. I knew you could do it." God, that fucking blush will be the end of me. "But can you do it like this?" Reaching for the clitoral vibe she's just cleaned, I flick it on, and cradling it in my palm, I press it between her legs.

"Fuck!" she cries, crumpling the paper as she almost collapses under me.

I actually laugh out loud, the sound breaking free from my chest with absolutely pure fucking delight. "So that's what it takes to get you to curse?" I drive myself inside her again. "Fucking technology."

"L... l... literally?"

"Clitorally," I amend, slipping the softly pointed end deeper.

"Oh. Oh. Oh!"

"No coming. Not until I say so."

"Can't... fuck! Sh... shiver my timbers!"

I laugh again. Laugh and fuck and pressure her joyously. This is the best way ever to spend a weekday afternoon. Of course, as though the thought summons reality, her phone dances across the desk. As a name I know flashes up on screen, an evil thought skitters from my brain. Reaching out, I accept the call and flick it to loudspeaker.

"No!" Amelia whines, dropping her head.

"Mimi?" Brin's voice drifts out from the speaker. "Are you okay?"

"I'm f-f *finnne*." Her answer stutters with my thrusts. *I'll say she is.* "I just dropped something."

"Yeah," I whisper in her ear. "The f-bomb."

"Oh, okay," Brin answers. "How are you?"

DONNA ALAM

Using my middle finger, I press the clit vibrator hard against her and give another flex of my hips.

"Mimi, you still there?"

"Mm-hmm." The noise carries, despite how she seems to be biting her forearm.

"I was going to pick you up one of those cakes."

The hostility drops out of me because I've already beat him to it. I've beat him to *all* the things.

"No!" She squeaks. "No, thank you. Sorry, I have to go now. I'm kind of in the middle of something *big!*"

"Yeah, you are," I assert as her finger ends the call. "You're such a *good* girl."

"Can I? Please," she begs desperately.

"Come for me, sexy little secretary."

With that, she arches her back and very thoroughly begins to milk my cock for all it's worth.

Turns out, it's not worth much more as white heat barrels down my spine. I give a strangled moan that sounds like her name as heat jets from my cock. It's a good thing my brain and mouth are uncoordinated as I pitch forward and almost collapse on top of her because all I can think is *mine.*

She's mine. All mine. She just doesn't know it.

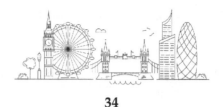

34

MIMI

I CAN'T STOP BLUSHING. Every time I glance his way, I can feel my cheeks heating. I'm not even a blusher, per se, yet here I go again. It's not even nine in the morning, and I must be on blush number six, at least.

"Kissing your hand makes you blush?" Whit's gaze shines approvingly as he peers over the top of our linked fingers. The Bentley then goes over a bump in the road and our knuckles inadvertently catch him under the nose.

"Oh, ouch!" I say yet can't stop my giggle as he, then stares at me through one narrowed eye. "What's that look for? If you hadn't been holding my hand—"

"And I can't help that I can't stop touching you."

Ah, me. With each passing day, I turn a little more into Romeo's lovesick girlfriend. But it can't go on forever, can it? It's just all that new relationship energy. And that's what we've agreed on—a relationship—even if it will be temporary. I don't know. Maybe it's that factor that makes things seem so much more joyful and brighter—because we have an end date in sight and we're either consciously or unconsciously trying to cram all those moments in. It would explain Whit's insatiable sexual appetite, I guess. *Mine, too.* We just can't keep our hands off each other. It's no wonder I blush.

"Then I guess you'll just have to take those knocks." Leaning over the center console, I press my free hand to his cheek and bend in for a kiss. But again, the Bentley goes over a pothole, and I miss my intended target, my lips grazing the divot above his finely carved top lip. He gives a satisfied little hum at the contact, and I find myself murmuring, "That answers that question."

"What question?" Amusement seeps into his reply. "I said nothing."

And there I go, blushing again. "You didn't ask the question. It was a question I asked myself. Before." Before we'd even kissed. Not that kissing was our first act of intimacy. "I just wondered what noise you'd make if I kissed you here." I press my finger to the space. It fits perfectly. "I liked it," I add softly. Taking my hand, I pull a face as I land a tiny punch to his arm.

"What was that for?"

"For making me a total simp."

"I hope that's a good thing."

"Depends which angle you're looking from," I grumble.

"You don't have a bad angle." Dropping his voice, he adds, "I especially liked the rear aspect last night when you were on all fours."

I inhale a tiny gasp, angling my gaze George's way.

"Don't worry. He can't hear."

"How can you tell?"

"Because I pay him enough not to."

"I don't think that's how hearing works. Good Lord." My plea to the heavens comes out on a quiet breath. "This can't go on forever," I then mutter to myself.

"What can't?"

"This..." I make a gesture back and forth between us, kind of manically waving my hand. "How we are." I lower my voice to a whisper. "It can't be normal to have this much sex."

Whit's peal of laughter fills the car, loud and unrepentant. "Is there a prescribed number of times, do you think?"

I slide him a look because, really. What kind of question is that? Neither of us can get enough, which is only part of the reason I haven't moved back to Doreen's place. But then, she hasn't gone back, either. The house was declared structurally sound last week, though Doreen has taken Frank up on his sudden offer to make his house slippers a permanent fixture under her bed. They're even talking about getting married. Of course, I'd asked her not to mention where I was sleeping to my parents.

"*Us girls can stick together,*" she'd said. "*A little white lie won't hurt them.*"

Them, no. Me? I guess eventually.

Meanwhile, I'm just enjoying the benefits of having a man like Whit around. And enjoying those benefits repeatedly. It's a good thing Whit is so busy during the day, or I'd never get any work done. Because when he is there, oh boy. Yesterday, for instance, he called me into his office to ask me to pick up a dropped pencil. Next thing, his hand is on my ass and from there, our clothes just seemed to disappear. Then there was the spanking I got for trying to redecorate his office (that monument to the love of monotone) when all I did was place a cactus no bigger than a bar of soap on his desk. It was in a pink and yellow pot, and had googly eyes, but still. I also might've dotted a few more of them around the place.

But that spanking led to other things.

Last week, in an effort to do something normal, I bought tickets to a local movie theater. Whit was so amused when I insisted on paying for his popcorn too and made some comment that it would cost me more than a movie and a bucket of popcorn to get him to put out. This was a blatant mistruth given we were forced to leave before the movie had reached the halfway point. It was either that or face a potential public indecency charge. Then there was the drive out to the countryside when it began to rain unexpectedly. We'd taken a picnic but didn't make it that far, gorging on each other instead. And in a car the size of the Bugatti, it called for some inventive moves, let me tell you.

I could go on. Netflix and chill where we never got beyond the home screen. A glass of wine after dinner where the bottle ended up being used indecently. Scrambled eggs for breakfast where the only thing scrambled was my brain. It doesn't seem to matter what we set out to do, we invariably end up doing the same thing.

Each other.

I'm not complaining. Not really. But in my quiet moments, I worry what's on the other side of this. Heartbreak is my guess, but what's one more issue to the pile?

"Are you worried it might fall off?"

"Worried what might fall..." *Urgh.* I catch on belatedly.

Whit laughs again before, to my mortification, he brings George into the conversation. "Hey, George. Have you ever heard of anyone having sex so much their todger falls off?"

George scoffs as I whisper, "Todger?"

"Another Brit word to add to your vocabulary."

"No, thank you."

Whit leans closer, his lips a whisper from my ear. "Store

it in your dirty *dick*tionary, between *bellend* and *cheeky wank*."

"Todger would come after cheeky—" I halt, noting the gleam in his eye. "Good try," I say, eyeing him stonily.

"Do you reckon todger comes after or before cheeky wank? I suppose you need a todger before you can have the other." As he speaks, Whit's gaze remains fixed on me.

"Good grief." With a groan, I drop forward and briefly bury my face in my hands.

"My eldest girl, Della," George pipes up, "is a nurse at St. Barts. She told me that a fella once came with a broken whatsit."

Whit sucks in a sharp breath, almost as though he can feel the unknown man's pain.

"I mean, your old fella doesn't have any bones in it, 'scuse me for saying so, Miss Mimi." *I manage not to snicker. No bones for the boner.* "But it can still break, particularly if you have vigorous intimate relations."

Nope, can't keep *that* giggle in. Whit, meanwhile, still looks like he's in pain.

"Right you are then, we're here," George then announces, maneuvering the car to the side of the road.

"Here?" My head bounces left, then right. We haven't been in the car long enough to be at the office. "Here where?"

"We've taken a minor detour," Whit adds.

"But your schedule is full today?" No time to take detours or mess around.

"And now it's not. Well, mostly just this morning."

Oh, my poor little heart. As if excellent sex wasn't enough, if laughter, good company, thoughtful gifts, and new experiences weren't enough, now he's clearing his schedule for me?

"Come on." He shoos me to turn to where George is already opening the passenger door.

I slide on my purse, crossbody style, as I wait on the sidewalk for Whit, wondering why I'm standing at Hyde Park Corner. Which is just a stone's throw from Buckingham Palace, but also basically just along the street from Whit's place.

"Have we just driven around the park?" I ask as he draws closer.

"Might have."

"But you live just down... there." I point in the general direction of his swanky building. Whit just grins. "*Okay.*" The word seems to draw out over several syllables, all of its own accord. "I guess Marble Arch seems pretty in the morning." I shrug, kind of. I have no idea what we're doing here, and honestly, Marble Arch looks like a piece of history that was picked up, then put down in the wrong place. An anachronism plonked in front of a sandwich shop chain. "What are we doing here?"

"Well, the sun is shining, and I thought, why don't we have a walk through the park before work?"

"Hyde Park?"

"Yep."

"The fact that we drove around it doesn't seem odd to you?" I make a circle in the air with my index finger.

"Sunshine." He points at the sky. "Birds singing." He then points at the trees, and I notice how some are heavy with spring blossoms, like spring has sprung overnight. "And fabulous company." He thumbs his chest. "Where's your sense of adventure?"

"Adventure in a park?"

"Not like that," he says with a dirty gleam. "It's the wrong park for it."

"I'm not even going to ask what that means."

"It's much too nice to be cooped up in the office," he says, hooking out his elbow. "Shall we?"

I feed my hand through the loop he's made. It's a little different, but I can roll with it. "Why not?"

"Have you walked through here yet?" he asks as we stroll.

"No, but I've looked out your living room window and thought about it."

"You won't have seen Speakers' Corner," he says as we pass through a nondescript path flanked by railings. Black cabs, buses, and all kinds of commuters whiz by on the other side.

"Can't hear any speaking." Not over the traffic noise. "Is it supposed to be some kind of phenomenon?" I glance up at the treetops, wondering if the name has something to do with the wind. Maybe on days when people aren't rushing to work?

"No." He chuckles, amused, as though it isn't odd enough that a corner of a London park is named for speakers. "It's a spot you often find people saying stuff they feel others need to hear. Sometimes it's controversial and there's a bit of a debate. Sometimes they just get heckled."

"*No*," I full of false disbelief answer. "Here in London? People wouldn't be so rude."

"I know, right? But it can be mayhem along here some Sunday mornings, especially if the weather is like this." He tilts his head, the sun's rays catching his cheekbones and making a golden living god out of him for a beat.

"Looks like Wednesdays at eight in the morning is a good time to get a slot."

"Yeah. Have you got anything you want to say?" he asks, slanting his gaze my way.

I love you. I think I've always loved you. I think I will always *love you.*

I paint on a bland expression and give my head a quick shake. "Can't think of anything. How about you?"

"Morning." It takes a split second to process he's not speaking to me as he inclines his head, and a passerby returns his greeting.

"What's with the stepladder?" I whisper once she's passed by and is no longer in earshot.

"Her version of a soapbox would be my guess. Want to stay and listen to what she has to say?"

"No thanks. I get enough of being lectured in Florida."

His expression falters, my home state a sudden, stark reminder between us.

"Why here?" I babble. "Debates in a park seem a little odd. Wouldn't they be more at home, say, in a pub?"

His shoes scuff against the path, our footsteps slowing before he turns to face the way we came. "Over there, just outside of the park, there's a spot marked with a plaque that shows where the Tyburn hanging tree stood."

"I'm guessing that wasn't a garden."

"It wasn't even a tree, I don't think. For centuries, that spot was used for public executions. Criminals, heretics, that sort of thing. I suppose Speakers' Corner sprang out of that. Spectators probably made a day of it. Pack a bag with a bottle of beer, add a couple of pies, then head off to watch some criminals swing. Maybe later, pop over here to listen to the dissenters of the realm."

"I think I'll stick to Netflix."

"And I'll provide the chill," he says in that velvety tone of his.

"You have zero chill." I tighten my grip on his arm. "You're more like the frenetic frenzy of f—"

He's a frenetic frenzy of the f-word. And I'm a frenetic frenzy of feelings.

"Nearly," he says with a gleam. "Frenetic, eh?" His gaze slices my way. "We can try tantric, if you want. In fact, we can try whatever you want."

"Are you trying to make my heart stop?" It seems the universe does not like this invocation, throwing up pebbles in my way, making me stumble.

"Are you trying to make mine stop?" he says, catching me before I face-plant. "I should've thought about those." He glowers down at my heels as though they just cursed his lineage.

"And spoil the surprise?" Of a walk around the park, which is way better than work.

"Exactly." Instead of straightening, Whit sweeps me up off my feet, bridal style.

"Hey, no! Whit, put me down!" I demand as my purse flops against my hip.

"I will, just not yet. Morning." He greets another passerby with a wide grin. A dog walker, I notice as they pass by.

"Good morning," I add in a much smaller voice, then whack Whit again with a demand he put me down before I flash the world my *knickers*. He does put me down, but not for a while when we walk hand in hand toward a...

"A lake?"

"Yeah." His expression turns almost bashful. "It seems stupid now that we're here, but I thought you said you wanted to do touristy stuff. I was out for a run, and I saw the boats, and I sort of convinced myself you'd like to go out on one."

Oh, my heart. An unsure Leif Whittington is adorable. "I

would—I would love to!" Now. Five minutes ago, I would've been ambivalent.

"Then the day started so well, sunshine and blue skies, and I thought, fuck it, let's do it. But now that we're here," he says, bringing a hand to his mouth to hide his grin, "I feel like a bit of a tit."

"Why? It's a great idea. I love it!"

"Yeah? You wouldn't prefer afternoon tea at The Ritz or an evening of cocktails at the top of The Shard?"

"No, I want to row a boat," I say, taking his hand. I *love* that he thought of me, and I love how sweet and awkward he's being right now.

"Yeah?" His answer seems filled with doubt.

"I love, *love* it!" I insist, practically jumping up and down on the spot. "Come on, let's get on a boat! I mean, if it's even open." I turn to where two men in matching polo shirts line up a row of blue paddle boats. Few people are looking to hire boats this morning, the passersby mostly dog walkers and commuters taking shortcuts.

"It's not officially open…"

"Then how can we—"

He shrugs, a little more confident now. "It's just open for us."

"Have you been using your influence, Mr. Sexy CEO?"

"Not unduly, Miss Valente. Not the way I do with you." He slides his arm around my shoulder, pulling me against him as we stroll toward the men in polo shirts. "Not everyone is interested in my cock the way you are."

"Hush! You'll offend the swans."

The shorter of the two boat attendants has either met Whit or senses he's this morning's special customer. It's not a huge leap, I guess, given the choice between Whit in his sharp suit and the man in jeans being pulled along by a Labrador.

"Mr. Whittington?" the man hedges.

"Just Whit," he corrects, holding out his hand.

The man looks surprised but smothers it well. The pair shake before he directs us behind him. "We have your rowboat ready over there."

"You mean we're not going on one of the blue paddleboats?"

"We can, but that means you'll have to pedal." Whit glances doubtfully at my shoes.

"Or I could just watch you row, I guess." My gaze slides over him suggestively. "You're gonna need to take off the jacket, though."

"Yeah?"

"At the very least."

"We should go to Venice one weekend. I'll get you on a gondola."

"They don't have public indecency charges in Italy?"

"Get your mind out of the gutter, Miss Valente."

Polo-shirt guy clears his throat. As we turn to him, he ducks his head sideways, his face as pink as mine right now. "This one's yours."

Ours is apparently a little wooden rowboat with extras! The plank benches are covered with brightly colored blankets and cushions, and there's an honest-to-goodness picnic basket placed between them. The kind that Yogi has, though Yogi's stolen booty wasn't from the food hall of Fortnum and Mason. Yum.

"You went all out!"

"Second best to a gondola in Venice," Whit asserts, holding my hand to allow me to clamber in. "Hang on." He drops to his

heels, and before I know what he's doing, his fingers make an
anklet as he lifts my foot to slip off my shoes. This time, my
mind definitely does roll into the gutter as a fragment of
memory flashes in my head. We're in his office and my cheek is
resting on his desk. One minute, Whit is looking over at me,
and the next, he's sliding my ankles wider. "Okay?" Our eyes
meet as he stands, and I just know he's thinking the same.

He takes my hand again, and this time, I step into the
tiny rocking boat. A moment later, his jacket comes off, and
he throws it my way. I place it over the cushion next to me.

Polo-shirt guy gives him the safety rundown without any
great enthusiasm as Whit loosens his cuffs and folds them
back. He catches me watching, and one of his brows lift,
seeming to speak a language all its own.

"You're staring," he murmurs as he steps into the boat,
settling himself on the wooden bench opposite me.

"I know." Just banking the memories for the rainy days
ahead. "I should've taken a picture, right? It'd last longer."

"You can if you like."

"I can what?"

"Take pictures. Film video."

The suggestions feel like some kind of sensual jackpot.
Or a trap as he takes the oars in each of his hands, his eyes
sliding past me as he uses one oar to maneuver the boat
away from the dock.

"Pictures of you?" My voice sounds a little high. "Or us?"

He doesn't immediately answer, but once satisfied with
the course, he begins to row, his arms moving
simultaneously, the strength in his back and abs powering
the bow smoothly through the water.

"What would you have me do?"

"Touch yourself." My answer is instinctual.

"While you settle back and enjoy the show?"

"A bit like now," I agree, allowing my gaze to meander over him. Watching him row is worth taking a video.

"I think you should open your legs for me."

"No way." My denial, like my will around him, is wobbly. "We're not getting freaky out in the water." My gaze darts to the boat ramp. "Don't come a-knocking when the boat is rocking? People will see. We'd probably fall in!"

"I just meant if you widen your legs, it'd make it easier for me to row."

I glance down and realize he's right. It's all abs, arms, and thighs, and his are planted wide. "Fine." Instead of sliding them wider, I bring them together, bent at the knee.

"I can still see your knickers," he taunts.

"No, you can't. I like this pastime," I add, not bothering to move my eyes from him as his shirt tightens around his shoulders and biceps, the muscles in his forearms springing to prominence with the movement.

"But you know what would make this better? If you were shirtless. Maybe even in your underwear."

"You want to play Cleopatra and her slave?" My laughter fills the air. "You know that means I oil you up and feed you grapes."

"Come for the oil, stay for the grapes?"

"Oh, you'd definitely come."

"The longer I know you, the worse you get."

"That's because the longer I know you, the more I want you."

"Isn't that the opposite of how this is supposed to work? Isn't the glow supposed to dim?" Which is what I was asking myself earlier.

"I don't know. I've never experienced anything like this."

"Same," I whisper, satisfied to let the creak of the oars and the swish of the water fill the silence.

"It never dimmed for my parents," he eventually says, pulling smoothly on the oars, his thighs flexing. "They were always so happy together." He pulls a face. "So, so... naked." He seems to shake off the thought as my reply shoots out of my mouth.

"Sounds like us."

"It does, doesn't it?" He smiles sweetly, so I keep the rest to myself. *Without the happy ending.*

We go once around the lake, Whit pointing out places of interest. During the warmer months, a section is cordoned off for swimming. Whit tells me his mom would sometimes bring the brood during the summer vacation where they'd swim in the icy water, then sun themselves on the banks.

In the middle of the water, Whit brings the oars in to rest.

"What's in the basket?" he asks.

"Have you worked up an appetite?"

"My appetite is constant when near you." Pressing his hands behind him, he tips his face to the sun. He looks like a giant house cat, much loved and at home in his own skin. In his own lovability. A house cat with a tiger's gaze, I realize with a pleasurable jolt when his attention moves abruptly back.

"I'd let you film me," he says, picking up the thread of our earlier conversation. "But you'd have to give me an incentive."

With a chuckle, I lean forward and lift the lid on the basket. "You're incorrigible."

"So you might've mentioned once or twice."

As it turns out, there are grapes in the basket. I pluck one from out and throw it at him. Of course, Mr. Almost Perfect Sexy CEO catches it in his mouth. Even the way he chews is inciting.

"I'm not like this with everyone, you know. Women, I mean." I don't know how to answer that, selecting and abandoning responses before he speaks again. "I'm not short of partners, but I've never met anyone who I want to spend this much time with outside of the bedroom."

"Or the office." My flippant words fall flat.

"You're a one-off, Mimi Valente."

"I'd say that's a good thing," I answer, picking at a thread on my skirt.

"Agreed. I couldn't cope with two of you. Though I'd give it a really good try." When I look up, all trace of seriousness has gone. I almost breathe out a happy sigh.

"I say again, incorrigible."

"And you love it."

And that's a problem because I really do.

We drift for a while, talking about nothing, picking at food neither of us seems hungry for. There's champagne in the hamper, but I say I'd rather not, so we stick to bottled water from the Scottish Highlands.

"Are you having fun?" Whit asks suddenly. Somehow, it feels like he's been waiting for the opportunity to bring the conversation around.

"Of course. What's not to be happy about?"

"I've noticed that about you. Your happiness doesn't depend on stuff." I frown, and he adds, "Things. Deeds. You don't require a lot." Maybe he's comparing me to his family. It would be an unfair comparison.

"I don't need a lot, but you keep giving."

"That's what you do for people you like, though, right?"

"I guess."

"You buy them a cactus to decorate their desk."

"What can I say? I saw it and thought of you."

"I bet you did," he murmurs, leaning back again. "Do you enjoy your work?"

"Is this where I'm supposed to say I have a really great boss?"

He transfers his weight onto one palm to scratch his cheek, making the boat rock the tiniest bit. "That's a given, isn't it?"

"I don't know. You were a hard-ass in the beginning." And I kind of loved it. I loved how he made me work for him, and though in some ways I feel like it was a role I'd stepped in to, I feel like, being with him, has made me that girl.

"And you were relentless." His head moves from side to side as though he can't quite believe he gave in.

"I've never wanted anything the way I want you." Want you still.

"I know the feeling." His expression turns soft, and my heart flutters in my chest. Despite being out in the open, maybe unreachable in this small body of water, the moment feels intimate, the air between us suddenly heavy and expectant.

As those flutters turn to panicked wings beating in my chest, I turn my head. "Whit." *Please don't. Please don't make me deny this because I don't think I can.* A sudden gust of wind whips the hair out of my face, and I turn my head to slide it away. Like a sign from above, I notice a woman at the side of the lake. "Whit, is that your mom?"

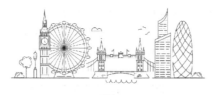

35

WHIT

It's not like I was going to propose, but I was about to suggest she stay. It's fine, though. There will be other opportunities. And that morning, I got to go home freezing cold, covered in pond scum, and soaked to the bone, to find that Mimi *ardently admired* my wet shirt Mr. Darcy moment. She'd helped me strip out of my wet things, led me to the shower, and then I wasn't cold anymore.

It's all good and that things devolve—evolve?—into sex frequently is just a symptom of how much we're into each other. I see the way she looks at me when she thinks I'm not looking. When she's curled on the sofa watching some ridiculous makeover program or a movie. I know there's more to this than just sex. We get along well, even if she has dubious viewing tastes. Her favorite movie? Pretty Woman.

She likes me. She always has. And I've always said those two factors alone have to be enough to take a chance on us.

I have other plans up my sleeve, including a private ride on the London Eye booked for next week. That's thirty whole minutes by ourselves where, because of CCTV, there won't be any hanky-panky. I'm sure I could get them to make it malfunction for our ride, but my plans might be better served if I used my mouth for something other than pleasure during that time.

I want her to have fun, but more than that, I want her to start to see herself living here. Being here. With me. I think that was the point of this morning's expedition, no matter how idiotic the idea seems right now.

"Hello, darlings!" My mother waves manically from the boat ramp as I use one oar to maneuver the boat to the edge of the ramp. What the fuck is she doing here? "What a coincidence!" The rowboat attendant barely has time to tie up the boat before Polly crowds him like a dog eager to hump a visitor's leg.

"Oops!" Realizing she's in the way, she steps aside, and the bloke holds out his hand to help Mimi climb out. "Fancy seeing you two here," Polly announces.

"Yeah, fancy." I don't know where she gets her intel from, but that gleam in her eye isn't exactly subtle. I'd very briefly considered calling her to get her on my side this week. I'd thought about confessing my feelings and plans for Mimi, before abandoning the thought. She'd be all for it, snapping at the chance of me settling down like a tourist eating crocodile but she'd probably do more harm than good. Polly isn't exactly known for her subtlety.

"So, come on then." She practically bounces on the spot. "What's brought you here? What's the occasion?"

Calm down, Polly. We're nowhere near the proposal stage yet. Like I'd row Mimi out on The Serpentine to ask her to marry me anyway. It's so weird how just thinking that doesn't freak me out—not even a little.

"The occasion was the boat ride itself," I mutter as Polly's attention bounces back and forth between Mimi and me. "It just seemed like the day for it. Cheers," I add as the attendant hands me my forgotten suit jacket. "Maybe we're celebrating the arrival of spring." I hook my forefinger in the collar and sling it over my shoulder conscious of looking like a menswear catalog model. "What are you doing here?"

My mother's fleeting expression suggests we'll be circling back to this point in just a minute. "My dear friend Deb has taken it upon herself to give a little talk at Speakers' Corner this morning."

"She doesn't happen to have a little stepladder with her, does she?" Mimi asks, no doubt thinking of the woman who passed us earlier.

"I don't know, dear. I'm supposed to be meeting her for a coffee beforehand so I shouldn't think so."

"What is it she has to say?" Mimi seems genuinely curious.

"Goodness knows." Polly gives a roll of her eyes. "She's been militant about so many things since menopause. But she's a good friend, and she was there for me when Whit's father passed."

"Oh." That one little sound holds a world of understanding. I only just manage to stop myself from hugging her to me. It's bad enough to lose a parent, but a sibling? I can't imagine it. My lot drive me round the twist sometimes it would be like losing part of myself, I'm sure. Then it seems she also lost her liberty. All because she's too caring a person to fight for what she deserves.

"I like to show my support where I can." Polly's eyes slide my way. "No office today, darling?"

"You know how it goes, Mum. No rest for the wicked." I slide my free hand into my pocket as I add, "This is causing me a bit of déjà vu. It feels a lot like the time you caught me skiving from school." She was just as amused, at any rate.

"Skiving?" Mimi repeats.

"Playing hooky. I was in my uniform and coming out of McDonald's when she caught me."

"Yes, I remember. You should've been in geography, I think."

"You've got some memory."

"I've got eyes in my head, too," Polly sort of mutters as she tidies the back of her hair. "Primrose tells me you haven't been home the past couple of weekends."

Mimi's attention slides my way reproachfully.

"I just said I didn't want her and her friends hanging around the pool every weekend. It's not as though she lives there."

"And you, Mimi? How are your accommodations these days? You were able to move back into your aunt's house?"

"Yes, the house was given the all clear," she says, sidestepping the actual answer, though not before turning the color of her underwear. Pink this morning. I love watching her get dressed, that sensual reverse striptease. There's something so voyeuristic about it, like seeing something you're not meant to see.

"Oh." I'm not sure old Polly is fooled. I like that Mimi's not a skillful liar.

"Well, we better get back to work," I say, arching my back a little to stretch it.

"We came out to the boating lake for a brainstorming session." This weirdness is expelled from Mimi's mouth at the approximate speed of a hail of bullets.

"Did you, now?" Polly looks delighted. The thing about Mum is the less information you give her, the better. I've known since I was fifteen that if you're in the shit, you close your mouth and you take what she has to give. You don't keep trying to dig yourself out of the mire because you'll just find yourself sunk even deeper. Before you even realize it,

Polly has wheedled all of your secrets out, and then you're pretty much screwed. Of course, Mimi doesn't know that. *Bless her.*

"Yeah. Brainstorming," she adds with a bright-looking smile.

My mouth ticks up in one corner; it's a capitulation. A white flag of sorts. Polly and I both know the jig is up. I've been rumbled. Outed. Hung by my own petard. Or maybe hung by Mimi's petard. Anyway, it really is that simple, even if poor Mimi hasn't cottoned on.

"Whit just happened to mention a new marketing scheme and that he wasn't happy with the direction the department has taken it, were you?" Mimi's head whips my way. Her expression, like her words, is a little frantic.

I'm not the type to micromanage, and I have no fucking idea what constitutes a marketing campaign, not that I say any of that.

"Not happy at all," I answer, pressing a reassuring hand to her shoulder. I give it a sympathetic squeeze because she won't know what's hit her. Mimi turns back to my mother when the old girl's eyes meet mine over her head. They remind me of the heart-eye emoji on my phone. The weird thing is, I'm not even bothered.

"Well, that seems like an excellent idea. A break from the office to get the old juices flowing." And if that's not bad enough, she makes a weird sort of sailor gesture with her arm. I shake my head quickly; you're trying too hard, Poll. "Anyway, I must be off before Deb thinks I've deserted her. Lovely to see you again, Mimi." She steps into her, pulling Mimi in for a hug, whether she likes it or not.

"And you, Mrs. Whittington."

"Polly!" she chastises. "You and I are friends, darling.

We're going to get on fabulously," she adds, laying it on thick.

I chuckle as Mimi's eyes find mine. She looks so unsure. I mean, is that a smile or a grimace?

"And you." Suddenly, Polly is in front of me, her arms a tight squeeze around my waist. "It's about bloody time," she mutters into my chest before she glances up at me, all teary-eyed.

Bloody hell, I think. *You'll frighten her away.*

Polly's nose scrunches as she pulls very slightly away and theatrically announces, "I must be off," before adding, "Oh dear!"

It all happens so quickly, but I'm not fooled because I distinctly feel her hand sliding up my arm. She whips my jacket from my finger, her other hand planted suddenly and firmly against my chest. "Oh no!" she adds as she pushes— pushes me—very fucking hard.

I hear Mimi's sharp intake of breath and see the blurred motion of her movement, but that was a solid shove and I'm moving backward far too quickly for anyone to stop the momentum. The only thing to wait for is the splash.

"Fuck!" The water is the kind of ball-shrinking cold. Only a few months ago, this body of water was partially frozen over. "Jesus Christ, Polly!"

"Oh no! Darling! I'm so sorry," the culprit calls back. She looks sorry, too. She's a good actress, my mother.

"Are you okay?" Mimi's worried face joins my mum's at the edge of the boat ramp. I stand up because the water isn't that deep at the edge. Still deep enough to make me feel like my nipples might fall off, though.

"It's fucking freezing," I say, wading to the edge as I glower Polly's way.

"I don't know what happened," she says, turning a

troubled expression to Mimi. "I think I was about to trip, and I must've pushed poor Whit in confusion."

Utter bullshit.

"Are you okay, mate?" The boat worker appears next to Polly.

"Yeah." My teeth begin to chatter, forcing me to clamp them together. It's easier to scowl that way. "Just about."

"Well, look on the bright side," Polly says as the bloke holds out his hand to help me out of the drink.

"And what bright side would that be?" I grunt through the exertion of climbing out.

"I have your jacket, so your phone and wallet are intact." She smiles brightly. "Also, Mimi just had a Mr. Darcy moment." With her back turned to the woman in question, she mouths, *"You're welcome."*

Like I needed the help.

WHIT

"Jeans and sneakers?"

"Yeah." I give her a quick once-over. "What you've got on is fine. More than fine." Black jeans and a long-sleeved T-shirt slashed at the neck. Cute little sneakers, I mean, trainers, and a jacket. Mimi looks as cute as fuck.

"And you're not going to tell me where we're going?"

"Nope," I repeat. "Because then I wouldn't be able to call it a surprise."

"Man, I hate surprises," she lies, doing this cute little dance on the spot.

"That's a shame because I love dishing them out. You ready?"

"Yeah. No, wait. I'm gonna put on the boots."

"The new ones?" The ones from the boutique, she means. Can I just say Mimi is the best Barbie Doll ever. I've never had an interest in buying a woman clothes before. The odd posh purse, maybe. Wave something with a designer label under a girl's nose, and they're usually very grateful. *And their thanks muffled when they drop to their knees.* But buying Mimi clothes has been very, very different. I find

I want to treat her because it's a pleasure all on its own. And I love the little fashion shows she's treated me to, especially the lingerie.

"Yeah, the ankle boots," she says, her gaze flicking down to her feet.

"Stick to the sneakers," I suggest.

"Comfort over cuteness?"

"Comfort with cute. Now, come on."

"Hey, George. Where are we off to?" Mimi bounces out of the door of the building thinking she's being the cunning kind of cute as she bounds up to the driver, who's waiting by the car.

"I just go where I'm told," George says with a blank expression. The man is a vault and has been sworn to secrecy.

"Dammit!" She gives an adorable pout before climbing into the back of the Bentley.

I feel kind of nervous as I slide in on the other side, though not about the first part of what I've dubbed "Surprise Saturday" in my head. I think I'll blame the dream I had last night for these jitters. I dreamed of Connor. He was at the pearly gates of heaven in silver gym gear and heavy white wings, which is just crazy. Crazier still, Saint Peter was spotting Connor as he bench pressed, his wings folded around him. Well, Connor wasn't exactly happy to see me, and Saint Peter was all for him landing me on my arse as I tried to explain how I'd fallen for Mimi.

"*Connor, mate, I was trying to protect her,*" I'd pleaded. "*Like you said I should.*"

"*By fucking her yourself?*" he'd demanded with such disgust.

"*You said to make sure she didn't end up with someone like us.*" I tried so hard to make him understand, my tone beseeching.

"*I'm pretty sure I said someone like* you," Connor growled, his wings beginning to flap like an angry swan. I probably have the boat trip to The Serpentine to thank for that.

"*Yeah.*" Saint Peter sounded like a wheedling, snot-nosed kid from a teen movie, not like heaven's doorman or all-powerful security detail. "*Connor has already made the right side of the gates. Meanwhile, you're out here,*" he'd taunted. "*What do you think that means?*"

"*That I'm dead?*"

"*If you're not, you will be,*" Connor snarled. "*You were supposed to protect her, not fuck her.*"

"*That's what I'm trying to tell you,*" I pleaded. *"I'm not like me anymore. She makes me want to be a better man."*

Then he punched me.

To be honest, I would've punched me too for that line. In my dream, I'd tumbled from heaven like the devil himself. I could feel myself falling, falling, before coming back to myself in my bed with a hypnic jerk, my heart pounding, my eyes on stalks and straining to see in the dark. But then Mimi had snuffled next to me, murmuring something about cupcakes being under the fridge. I'd wrapped her in my arms and ease had returned to me almost immediately. God, Saint Peter, Old Nick, Connor. They can all go fuck themselves as long as I get to keep this girl.

"The airport?" Mimi makes what feels like her tenth guess as George takes the turning for London City Airport.

"Yep, you got me. You've heard of train spotters, right? Well, I'm a plane spotter."

"Do you spot them from the skies? You know, when you're up there in your private jet."

"The bank's private jet."

"The bank you're the major shareholder of? So kind of, sort of your private jet?"

"I'm not sure the rest of the shareholders would see it like that," I say, turning my attention to the window. It's pretty miserable out there. I hope the weather is nicer where we're headed.

"Did you tell the front desk that Primrose and her friends were visiting today?"

"Yep," I reply, popping the p. Mimi had given me a hard time about keeping my family from visiting. I hadn't the heart to tell her most of them seem to have already guessed she's staying with me. *And more.* Only Primrose and Lavender don't seem to be aware, and Lavender only turns up when she wants something. She must have a new boyfriend, given I haven't been called to pick her up from any police stations for a while.

At Mimi's gasp, I turn my head.

"We *are* at the airport! Where are we going?"

"I'll tell you." Her smile widens. "When we get there."

"*Super* swanky," Mimi says as she wiggles her delectable bum in the cream leather upholstery.

"It beats the bus, right?"

"Oh, Mr. CEO, I think it's been a while since you rode *any* bus."

"True, but I still remember how they work. I also remember what it's like not to be rolling in it." I think that helps to keep me grounded.

"Well, I don't know many rich people, but for what it's worth, you're my favorite."

I laugh. "Such high praise."

"I know, right? Oh, hello." Mimi turns her face to the purser.

"Miss Valente, Mr. Whittington. Can I get you any refreshments this morning?"

"No thanks, Gwen," I reply.

"I could go for a juice," Mimi says.

Gwen runs through the juices available on the in-flight menu, providing me with the opportunity to watch Mimi. To observe the tiniest flickers of enjoyment across her face. She is so fucking beautiful, but it's not just in her looks. She radiates joy—is sunshine personified. And while I'm sure she has her dark moments, like everyone, she never seems to let them get her down. But I hope there's a time in the not-too-distant future when she'll let me share those moments with her. When she'll lean on me as part of her team. I'll introduce her to people by saying *this is Mimi, my better half.* And she'll laugh like she's amused, but we'll secretly know it's true because we'll both be part of the other, the way all the best couples are.

"Six types of juice is some kind of fancy," she says as Gwen retreats. "And that's not even including the tomato juice, which, although technically made from a fruit, should not be included in a selection of juices."

"It has seeds. Therefore, it's a juice."

"You would think, right?"

"Know so."

"Then you'd be wrong. Tomato juice should be something you reserve for spaghetti sauce."

"I'm sure there's a little bit of logic in there somewhere."

"Don't hate me because you're wrong."

"Mimi," I say with a chuckle, "hell would freeze over before I could ever hate you."

She stares at me for a beat, and I swear whatever I see turns the blood in my veins into ice water. It's like a switch has gone off, dimming the light inside her. It's just a fleeting moment that lasts as long as a blink. A heartbeat. It's gone in a second, though the residual energy seems to linger between us.

I want to ask, *what was that? What were you thinking there*, but it turns out, I'm a chickenshit when Gwen reappears.

"One pineapple juice," she announces.

I glance at the glass of opaque juice balanced on a napkin on her silver tray. "I've changed my mind, Gwen. Could you rustle me up a Bloody Mary when you have a minute, please?"

"Certainly, Mr. Whittington."

Mimi pulls a distasteful face. "If you think I'm kissing you after you drink spaghetti sauce—"

"I'd be right?"

She shrugs. "Probably."

"Definitely. You know you can't resist me."

She turns her head to the window with a melancholy-sounding sigh. "Yeah, that's true."

My drink arrives, and I stare at it. I'm not the sort to try to numb the pain, but I drink the fucker anyway. Not that I'm in pain, but I don't know. I suppose I just want to chase away this sense of foreboding.

"We've been in the air a little over an hour, and the plane is beginning to descend."

"Good deducing, Miss Marple."

"So I'm gonna guess Scotland."

"We'd already be on the ground if that were the case."

"Northern Ireland? Not the other part because I don't have my passport."

"Don't you?" I pull an *oh shit* face.

"Do you carry your passport around with you?" She scoffs, unfolding her legs from beneath her and turning to face me fully.

"What? You mean Americans don't?" I frown in confusion as I slip my hand into the top pocket of my shirt and, "Ta-da!"

"You don't carry your passport around with you."

"So what's this?" I give it a little shake.

"Well, mine is with HR," she says, flopping back in her seat. "They asked me to bring it in during the week. Something about my visa and the biometric reading."

"Oh, dear. Sounds like you've been scammed. It's probably been sold on and an Albanian nana somewhere is at this moment opening a bank account in your name."

"Don't joke about that." She folds her arms across her chest and scowls in my direction. After a beat, she adds, "Are we really going somewhere I'll need it because I really don't have it."

"No, but I do," I say, pulling it out of my jacket pocket.

"You sneak!" She immediately follows this up with, "So where are we going?"

But I just laugh.

"Paris!" she squeals.

"Steady on," I faux-complain, sticking my finger in my ear. "These eardrums have got to last me another fifty years, at least."

"You brought me to Paris!"

"Happy?"

"Try ecstatic!" Mimi practically bounces her way to immigration at Le Bourget private terminal. One of the better perks of flying private, especially into Paris, is avoiding the immigration queues. Charles de Gaulle Airport makes you feel like you need a break just to get over the experience.

Why Paris? It's the city of love, right? If I can't make her love me here, what chance have I got? And I will be pulling out all the stops. But also, Mimi had become engrossed in a travel program on TV recently, so I knew it was somewhere she'd like to visit. And then there's the matter of her favorite movie, which I think I might be able to incorporate.

"Bonjour!" She greets the immigration officer with such enthusiasm, complimenting the woman on her lipstick and generally peppering her with thoughtful questions.

"How to win friends and influence people," I say, taking her hand as we step out of the terminal. I bring our linked fingers to my lips. "I should've taken you with me when I had to meet the FCA."

"What do you mean?"

"You've missed your calling. If you can make a Parisienne immigration officer smile, you should go into hostage negotiations."

"It costs nothing to be nice."

Nothing. Just my heart.

We climb into the Mercedes Town Car I'd arranged.

"Where to first?" she asks, still vibrating with excitement.

"I think it would be rude not to eat a croissant first." My laughter fills the back of the Mercedes as she wraps her fist in my sweater, pulling my lips down to hers.

37

MIMI

DESPITE WHAT WHIT SAYS, the way to my heart is not through my stomach. And whatever his assertion, he's embedded himself in there. *My heart, not my stomach.*

He is the best of men, not because he planned a secret trip to Paris, but because he pays attention. Because he listens and he watches, and then he offers not just material things and experiences but thoughts and ideas. Conversation and silliness. It's all so subtle; the way he treats people is almost by sleight of hand. What you see on the outside is this quite upright, slightly austere, successful man, and I'd bet that's where most people's observations end. Maybe my history with him makes me see beyond this facade. I'm not sure what it is because it's hard to see past all this love.

I'm so doomed.

We eat flaky croissants in a tiny café away from the tourist track, as recommended by the driver, Jacques, who has nerves of steel because driving in the center of Paris is not for the fainthearted! *See a space and squeeze into it* is how I'd describe the Parisienne driving style.

Anyhoo, at the café, I order, *"deux cafés au lait et deux pains au chocolat, s'il vous plait,"* in my best (but still terrible) French.

"You want lattes?" the unimpressed bearded hipster answers from behind the counter, but he doesn't dampen my enthusiasm.

"No thanks, when in Rome!" I say, but he's already turned.

I've read that French people dip their croissant in coffee for breakfast, but after trying, I wouldn't recommend it. It's a perfect way to ruin a perfectly good breakfast. But the experience provides the perfect excuse for us to stop at one of the more traditional cafés an hour or so later, where the servers wear long white aprons and are old, grouchy, and rude. It's exactly the experience I imagined it would be!

And then? Well, Paris is my oyster.

"Twenty-four hours," Whit tells me. "One whole day and night to make Paris your own."

"We're staying overnight? But I haven't packed a bag."

"Don't sweat it. It's all been taken care of. All that's left for you to do is decide what you want to do." He presses a guidebook in my hand, and I start to laugh.

"They still make these? Google is everyone's go to these days."

"Don't be a smart arse," he says, spinning me around and swatting my *smart arse*. "Get choosing before we waste the day."

"Are the touristy places open in the evening, too?"

"It's like this," he says, lifting his wrist to see his watch better. "I should've said you've a whole seven hours to fill with what you'd like to do because there are a couple of places I'd like you to see this evening."

"Would that be... things inside of a hotel room?"

"What do you take me for?"

"The best." I throw myself at him, sliding my hands around his waist to hug him.

I'm so glad Whit suggested I wear tennis shoes because we walk everywhere for the rest of the day! We walk hand in hand along the Seine and take a million photographs with the Eiffel Tower as the backdrop. When we make it to the base, I decide I prefer looking *at* the structure over visiting it. I'm not a fan of crowds, and the queues are huge. Instead, we munch on an unimpressive yet overpriced crepe from a vendor on the other side of the road, then I insist on haggling with the guys selling cheap touristy knickknacks. No way I'm overpaying for that Eiffel Tower on a keychain! A man tries to sell us cigarettes, another champagne from a bucket, and the third a poorly made I LOVE PARIS hat. Refusing all of the above, I splash out a few Euros (withdrawn from an ATM) on a cartoon caricature of us on our day in Paris.

"I'll treasure it forever," I say, hugging it to my chest.

"Is my chin really that big?"

In answer, I tip up onto my toes and press my lips there. "It's perfect." Just like the rest of him. My head does a double take. "Look, Whit! It's a Soiree Bus!" I watch in delight as the sleek vehicle passes by.

"I'd rather queue three hours to get to the top of the Eiffel Tower," Whit grumbles, unimpressed. "I'm a bit long in the tooth for disco buses and cheap shots of vodka."

"I don't want to go on it. I just think the name is amazing. Party Bus is so lame. The Soiree Bus? That's where it's at."

A day isn't long enough to see all that Paris has to offer, and while I'd love to wander around Le Louvre, the queue wait times aren't the best use of our time. Instead, we call Jacques, and he takes us to the Montmartre area of Paris, where we eat lunch in a tiny café where the decor looks unchanged since the nineteen thirties. When Whit orders escargot and I pull a face, he and the server laugh. And he points out when I place my order (mussels in white wine) that we basically ordered the same, the only difference being he'll eat snails from the land and I'll eat snails from the sea. I get over myself when the food arrives, and the aromas hit my olfactory system.

"This is the best bread ever," I say around a hunk of heavenly bread that's crispy on the outside and oh-so fluffy in the middle. The food is delicious, and the champagne is sold by the glass. And when we leave the café, I realize why Parisiennes are not overweight. It's all the walking they do. But, oh my gosh, is Montmartre perfect! We wander through cobblestone streets, each corner turned revealing a pretty vista or a piece of historic statuary. We find ourselves in the Place du Tetre and watch the oh-so-talented street artists before taking in the Sacré Coeur Basilica vista. Before the evening begins, we stumble across a blue-tiled piece of wall art called *Le Mur des Je T'aime*. The wall of I love yous.

We stand for a while, each of us lost to our own thoughts as our eyes scan the many ways to say I love you. The wall speaks of language. *Je t'aime. Te amo. Rakastan sinua. Aroha i a koutou*. But the language of love is more than words. As we stand, holding hands, I think of Whit and the many ways he shows affection. His love. I hope his family know how lucky they are to have him looking after them. I think of how he'd stepped up to fill his father's shoes when so many men in his place would've been consumed with their own grief. I think of the time he devotes and how his loved one's needs are his priority. I think of his thoughtfulness, and I think about the person he is.

Whit tugs on my hand, and as I turn, he's wearing this expression that I find really hard to place.

"You okay?"

"Yeah," he says softly. "You?"

I glance back at the wall. *Je t'aime*, I think to myself. "It's just really lovely, isn't it?"

"Yeah." He nods, gaze dipping to his shoes. His phone buzzes as he slides it out of his pocket. "Jacques is at the end of the street. Are you ready?"

"Where shall we go next?"

"Well, this is that part of the day that isn't up to you." He fights a smile and loses, and as though he doesn't want to admit it, he pulls me in and presses a kiss to the top of my head. I take the opportunity to breathe him in.

"So we're off to the hotel?" I wiggle my brows suggestively.

"You know what I'm going to say, don't you?"

"Get my mind out of the gutter?"

Whit slides his arm over my shoulder, and we turn from the wall of love. "I feel like I've created a monster."

"And what would that make you?"

"What kind of a question is that?"

"A reasonable one," I retort.

"Amelia, whether in London, Paris, or whatever, I will always be your daddy!" And with that, his hand slips down my back, his fingers digging into my (recently discovered) sensitive sides. I squeal and jump from his reach, not wanting to be tickled as adrenaline begins to pump through my bloodstream. I might not be a fan of tickling, but being chased by *Daddy* gives me the shivers.

"This looks exactly like the exact kind of place you arrive at with no luggage," I whisper as we follow a twentysomething woman up a grand staircase, feeling very conspicuous about our lack of bags.

"You think this looks like the kind of place that rents rooms by the hour?" Whit angles his amused gaze my way.

"More like the kind of place I couldn't afford to rent an hour in." When we'd arrived at the hotel, I almost walked by the entrance because it was so unassuming. It looked like a house, though the hanging Moroccan lanterns on either side of the door seemed a bit odd. Once the door opened, we moved into a space of such fabulousness. The color scheme is dark and sensual, the decor opulent, all marble floors and crystal chandeliers. To put it another way, I felt like Alice in Wonderland, stepping into another world.

"It's a good thing you've got a wealthy patron then, isn't it?"

"Patron?"

"A better title than a john, I think."

"What?" If the first explanation had poked at me, the second stopped me in my tracks, my steps grinding to a halt at a small landing. My ears must be playing up because there is no way he just insinuated *that.*

"That didn't come out very well." He pulls a face, kind of abashed. "This place," he adds with a flick of his fingers. "It used to be a high-class brothel a hundred years or so ago."

"I guess they haven't changed the decor," I answer, staring up at a life-sized nude on the wall in front of us. A painting on canvas, old or made to look so. The model faces away, her head turned coyly over her shoulder as though startled but not unhappy at being caught in a state of undress.

"*C'est magnifique, non?*" The hotel employee showing us

to our room pauses from a few steps away. I don't need to speak French to understand what she's referring to, especially the way she's staring up at the painting.

"Yes, it's very beautiful. *She's* very beautiful."

"We think this is one of the women who worked here when the 'otel was a bordello," she continues. "Her patron would've been very rich to have commissioned something of this scale.

"So you don't know her name?"

"Non," she says sadly. "The women would want to keep their anonymity, hoping to move on to better or different things."

"That makes sense."

"But each of our suites is named for a famous courtesan," she adds. "Come, let me show you to *La Pompadour*. I think you'll be very happy there."

I turn to Whit as the door to the room closes, not quite believing what I'm seeing. It's beautiful, and though quite spacious for a city hotel, there's something cocoon-like about the whole suite. Dark silk in a handsome shade of blue I can't even name covers the walls, the bed a huge ornate four poster with a canopy that draws toward the ceiling like an Arabian-style tent. A velvet chaise in front of a working fireplace, ornate gilt mirrors, and sensual artwork adorn the walls. Heavily fringed lamps provide the suite with a sultry glow and vases of orchids the rooms heady scent. There's a small lounge where I can totally see a courtesan serving her gentleman champagne before bringing him into the bedroom for a small slice of heaven.

In short, it looks like a suite built for the purpose of pleasure.

"It's a bit over the top, isn't it?" Whit murmurs as I make my way to the French windows. *French windows in France. Fancy that.*

"Not if you were planning on seducing me." I turn my head over my shoulder in some semblance of the painting in the stairwell. "Oh, monsieur," I say, fluttering my lashes. "'Av you brought me 'ere to have your wicked way wiz me?"

"Who seduces who in a brothel, do you think?"

"You want me to work for it?" I ask, pulling back the heavy voiles. I gasp. Beyond the doors is a tiny terrace with views all the way to the Eiffel Tower. "Come look at the view."

"Do you like it?" His question is a purr in my ears, his broad palms sliding around my waist, pulling me against his chest.

"It's so perfect."

"Next time, we'll come for longer." My heart gives a little pang. I could almost kid myself that we have a future when he says things like this. "I'm sorry this visit has to be so short."

"Perfect doesn't have a timeframe," I whisper, dropping the voile curtain and turning in his arms. It doesn't have to last a lifetime. "No need to ask what our plans are for this evening." I keep my lashes lowered, not wanting to reveal my pained thoughts as I slowly walk my fingers up his right bicep.

"I wouldn't say that."

"Good. I wouldn't like to lose my air of mystery."

My chuckle sounds kind of dirty because there really is no mystery about the thing growing hard against my stomach. But before I can make a smart reply, a rap of knuckles sounds against the door.

"Best answer that."

"Or we could just ignore it."

"But it's for you."

"How can you tell?" I ask, pulling slightly away.

"I can't."

"Can't or won't?"

"Go open the door," he whispers, pressing his lips to my head. And then a smack to my butt as I slide around him.

"Hey, watch the merchandise."

"Don't worry, darling." His words stroke like a caress. "I've paid Madame extra for my unnatural tastes."

"Unnatural?" I reply, matching his tone.

"She said you were the best. I can't wait to discover that for myself."

My sultry laughter sounds all the way to the door.

"Mademoiselle Valente?" a chicly dressed woman of indeterminable age asks from the hallway. Her stature is small, her features bird-like, but there's an underlying sense of strength about her.

"Yes," I answer hesitantly.

"*Bon.*" One word and her attention swings away, her hands a flutter of movement.

"Can I help you?" She shakes her head, and I find myself stepping back from the door as she ushers a pair of girls about my age ahead, girls laden with all manner of garment bags and each pulling a suitcase behind them. "What is this all about?" I'm unsure if my question is meant for her or Whit, who, when I turn, is lowering himself into a chair. I also notice he is doing a pretty good impersonation of the Cheshire cat. Not so much in the grinning sense but the knowing.

"We have come to dress you," the tiny woman states imperiously, shooing me farther into the room. "Vite!"

. . .

It turns out Whit has no plans to give up his air of mystery this evening as he lounges in the armchair with a crystal flute of champagne dangling from between his fingers. I have a glass, too, but I've barely managed a mouthful of it thanks to *Madame*—no other name given—having the command of a drill sergeant.

"I like this one," Whit says as Madame instructs her assistant to straighten the hem on the third dress I've tried on this evening. It cuts across my arms and chest, Bardot style, the fabric pink and diaphanous. *And the label Chanel.* There's no price tag, and for that I'm grateful because I also love this dress, and I really don't want to take it off.

I also really don't want to try another on.

"You have a good eye, Monsieur." Madame's tone is approving. "This dress complements Mademoiselle's skin tone perfectly."

"It's so pretty," I say, glancing at myself in the full-length rococo-style mirror, swishing it this way and that.

"Made all the more pretty by you."

Madame beams at Whit's approval, and the two younger women with her cluck like little hens.

"Yes, this one," he affirms, rising gracefully from the armchair. He's so good at appearing impassive, I realize. It's a wonder no one else in the room seems to notice the heat in those tiger eyes of his.

"And the shoes?" she asks, her eyes appreciative as he draws closer.

"I'll leave that to you, darling," he says, pressing a kiss to my temple. "I'm going to hop in the shower." Madame's assistants giggle, but he pays them no heed as he saunters off in the direction of the bathroom.

I choose a pair of Valentino heels before it becomes apparent that the assistants aren't here to stroke Madame's ego when one of them produces a long roll of makeup brushes like a magician and the other, whose arms are covered in a sleeve of tattoos, begins to lift curling wands and straightening irons out of a Mary Poppins-style bag. I'm hurried to take a seat at the dressing table where the duo proceeds to primp, paint, poke, and preen me, all three women conversing in a flurry of French. They spare the occasional word for me but mostly communicate with each other. While I love this dress, this experience isn't exactly relaxing and not nearly as much fun, I contemplate, as being Whit's Sunday afternoon boutique Barbie Doll...

I jolt back to myself as the door to the bathroom opens, and in the mirror, Whit steps out. *Dressed only in a towel.* The girl with the tattoos blushes and ducks her head, intent on tidying a loose strand of my hair. The other woman is much bolder in her appraisal, not that it matters as he has eyes only for me as the fall of light plays across the muscles of his shoulders and chest, the crest of his hip bones rendered a smudge of shadow. He strolls to the ornate armoire and pulls out a leather washbag I've seen in his bathroom at home. *Home.* The word causes me a tiny pang of longing, though I'm distracted by the sound of the armoire closing. Whit turns and shoots me a wink before he saunters back the way he came, though I'm surprised he can move through the thick estrogen cloud. The bathroom door closes once again.

"Beau cul." In the mirror, I note how the makeup artist purses her lips appreciatively.

I feel myself frowning. *Beaucoup? Like merci beaucoup?* Is she thanking him for the show?

"She says you are a very lucky woman." The old woman catches my eye, her words diplomatic.

"Yeah," I reply doubtfully.

"He has, how do you say?" She frowns a little as though grasping for the words. "A backside like two boiled eggs in a handkerchief."

Words from the same school of thought as Aunt Doreen, apparently.

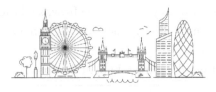

38

WHIT

THE STYLIST and her team leave, the door to the suite closing with a solid *thunk.*

"Got any more surprises up your sleeve, master of mystery?" Mimi takes a step closer, a vision of loveliness. She's always so beautiful, but there's something about this Paris version of her. *It must be the air,* I think to myself.

"I might have." My reply sounds husky as she comes to a stop in front of me and runs her hand up the satin lapel of my evening suit.

"So what are we all dressed up for?" Her hand lifts to cup my smoothly shaven cheek, purring appreciatively.

"I've decided that's up to you." *It's all up to you, darling.*

"Oh?" Her response sounds like the lift of a brow.

"But first, I have something for you."

Her peal of laughter is low and suggestive. "I can't wait."

I make a sound with my teeth and tongue—a *tsk* of disappointment, which she doesn't fall for. Not one bit.

"I bet you feel like you've created a monster, don't you?"

"No. We've created something quite beautiful." Something I'm loath to let fall through my fingers. Her head dips bashfully at my words, allowing me the opportunity to grab the velvet box from the armoire. Inspired by the look on her face while she watched TV from the sofa a little while ago, I hold the paperback-sized box out in my hand before opening it.

Her gaze dips, and her smile spreads slow and sweet, just like spilled honey. "Do you have something to say to me?"

"Do I?"

Both of us glance down at the box, though this time, Mimi's fingers are drawn to the tactile velvet interior. Of course, I play my part, snapping the lid on her fingers and making her bark out a surprised laugh.

"I totally knew you were going to do that," she says, her gray eyes shining with a mixture of mirth and pleasure.

"Then why did you put your finger in?"

"You sound like you've said that before," she answers just a touch smuttily. "You're supposed to tell me not to get too excited, that it's only on loan."

I shake my head. "Richard Gere must be a cheapskate."

"Edward Lewis," she says softly. "That was his character's name."

"Well, Amelia Valente," I murmur, bringing my gaze level with hers. "This is for you even though it feels a little like trying to gild a lily."

"Edward Lewis has nothing on you," she says as her lips brush mine, the pass as soft as silk.

"Turn around, darling." As she does, I take out the necklace and drop the box to the chair, sliding the delicate gold chain around her neck. Mimi touches the single diamond nestled in her cleavage in the milky mirror on the wall in front.

"It's so beautiful."

"Just like you." I press my mouth to her shoulder, and she shivers, her eyes rolling closed as my lips chart the skin of her neck. She turns in my arms, stretching toward me like a flower seeking the sun. My hand slides from her hip to her ribs, cupping her breast and thumbing her nipple, her soft moan an approval. "One of us needs to stop this," I rasp as her nipple pebbles beneath the silk.

"You'll have to do it." Her eyes flutter closed as she presses herself more fully into my hand. "I can't think straight when you're touching me."

And I can't think of anything but sucking her hardened nipple into my mouth. I tip forward, skating my tongue over the soft swell. "I had plans. Dinner. Tickets to the opera."

"Just like *Pretty Woman*," she breathes, willing me on with her body.

"You're not pretty, my darling. You're fucking stunning." With that, I slide my tongue under her neckline, and in turn, she pushes her hands into my hair.

"I need you, Whit. Please."

With a groan, I suck harder, swirling the hardened nub with my tongue. In my hands, she feels so good. All soft skin and womanly curves, but it's more than that. I want her with a strength that frightens me. I want to keep her, bind her to me. I want to make her happy. Be her mornings and her evenings. Her friend and her lover, her shield and her confidant. I love her so much I want to keep her forever.

"Fuck, darling. I've longed to hear you say that." My raspy voice brims with all the things that I can't yet say. How I want her to be by my side always, how my hands can't touch enough, how my heart can't love enough as I clasp and knead her body, pulling her closer. I slide my hand to her thigh and lift it to my hip, my cock aching and as hard as a pole between us.

Her frantic hand slides inside my jacket, over the plains of my back, desperately pulling at the cotton of my shirt. "I want to touch you. Need to feel your skin."

"Yes." I grunt as she buries her nails into my skin. Something inside me snaps, releasing a surge of need and possession. Everything becomes frantic for a moment, hands grasping, teeth biting as I pull her impossibly close, desperate to feel the soft press of her belly and the dig of her hips. The sound of her breath, her sharp gasp as I press my cock to her and the feel of her soft exhale as I push inside her. I imagine it all, I want it all, my fingers and my mind skipping ahead as I clasp her body to mine and carry her backward toward the bed.

"There will be other operas," I rasp, not sure which of us I'm trying to reassure. "Other days in Paris. Other nights in Rome."

"I just need you. Only you." Her words are achingly sweet and desperate as I lay her down on the bed. "Please, please hurry." Her fingers shake as she reaches for the end of my bow tie, the thing unraveling as I pull away. Her eyes are avid as I slide off my jacket, abandoning it to the floor. "In case I forget to tell you," she whispers as I loosen my cuff links and pull my shirt over my head. "You look so handsome tonight."

"Says the angel in the pink dress." I drop over her, my fingers frantic on the zipper at the side of her dress, but before I can complete my task, our mouths are fused again.

"Stop distracting me," I demand, pulling at the tiny hindrance. "I need to get you naked." I yank again. "Fuck it. I'll just tear the seam."

"Don't you dare," she says, rolling onto her side. "This is couture."

"And this is mine," I growl, pressing my hand to her hip

and sliding her back again. "This is mine," I assert, gripping her bared thigh. "And this is mine." I palm her pussy through her underwear, loving how her eyes darken and her body instinctively deepens the contact. "Isn't that right?" I demand.

"Yes. Yours. I'm all yours." Her exhalation is shaky.

"Because you were made for me, weren't you? You've always known it. I was just a little slower on the uptake."

"Oh God, Whit," she moans, throwing out her hands as she arches into me.

This time, I'm gentler with the zip, and it opens easily. I slip her dress down her arms. She's not wearing a bra, and as the fabric slips over her hard nipples, she shivers and releases a soft moan. I drop her dress to the floor, turning back to slide her knickers down her legs. My hands tremble as I undo my belt and make quick work of the rest of my clothes, coming back to the bed.

"This is mine," I whisper as I hook my hand under her knee, baring her to me. And because I can't resist such a delectable sight, I swipe my tongue through her wetness with a lengthy groan.

"Oh God. What are you doing to me?"

"Owning you, my darling." I begin to crawl my way up her body, tracing soft, open-mouthed kisses as I go. "Mine." The jut of her hip bones. "Mine." The soft flare of her hips. "Fucking mine." The underside of her breast and the point of her nipple. "Only for me."

"Whit, please."

I press the length of my body against hers, my lips hot at her ear. "You are so wet for me, my darling. I want to drown myself in you." She whimpers, her hand slipping between us in demand, but there's a method in this torturous kind of madness as I take her hand and press it above her head.

"This," I say, laying my palm over her heart. "Your heart is mine, Amelia. I know you don't want to admit it, but I see it in your eyes every time you look at me."

She shakes her head staccato and breathes my name as her eyes turn the color of rain.

"I have your heart," I whisper, pouring it into my words. "I have your heart, and you have mine." Lifting her thigh, I drive my cock inside her. Her body bows beneath me, shuddering as I withdraw. Crying out as, with my next thrust, I grind against her.

"Please, please," she begins to beg, her walls throbbing around me and dragging me closer to the edge.

"Yes, darling." I work myself deep inside her as I whisper soft incantations and prayers. "Go ahead, beg me. Let me hear how much you want this. Let the walls shake with your cries. Tell me how you love me." I know it's unfair, and I didn't plan for the evening to go this way, but it doesn't stop me from wanting to fuck the truth out of her.

"No, please." Her free hand slides to my shoulder, pulling me down as her thighs yield to the press of mine. "I didn't want to." Her words are a hot sob in my ear. "It wasn't supposed to be this way."

I turn my head, my mouth sliding over hers. "That's why it's called falling." I gently bite her bottom lip. "There's no stopping it. Only forward momentum."

"Like slipping down a cliff," she rasps with an unhappy laugh. "You're not selling it to me."

Her words sound wet, and though I hate this turmoil for her, I'm here for her admission as I push up onto my palms and solidly drive myself between her legs. "Give me this chance, darling. I will love you fiercely. Constantly. Inventively." She laughs again, her walls gripping me like a glove. "I will give you more love than you'll ever need. I will worship you eternally." I begin to thrust into her again and again when she chokes back a strangled cry, her body bowing from the bed. As her orgasm hits, she takes my arse in her hands, pressing me to her as she cries out her love. Cries out my name.

I don't last long, every one of my muscles tightening in the face of such abject pleasure as my orgasm hits. I shatter into a million pieces, showering my love over her.

39

MIMI

"I never liked the opera anyway," Whit murmurs as he traces a lock of hair across my back.

"Was it supposed to be part of the Julia Roberts's experience?" I say, not quite able to lift my head. Orgasm number three has taken the strength from my limbs as I lie on my front, one arm under my pillow, the other dangling from the edge of the bed.

"I suppose so, though the opera was Beckett's suggestion. He got me the tickets to *Madame Butterfly* in the opera house that inspired *Phantom of the Opera*, apparently."

"Nice."

"I'm just not that cultured," he says with a chuckle.

"You're more a couple of pints down the boozer with your brothers?"

"I'd say I'm more the type who'd prefer to spend his time adoring his beautiful girlfriend."

My heart does a little leap, pleasure spreading through me at hearing such a little thing. But I worry about the things I haven't told him. Secrets I'll have to share now. And that's when my worries will become his. Like he doesn't have enough on his plate right now. Like his heart isn't already stretched to capacity.

"We can term it some other way if you don't like the sound of being my girlfriend."

I huff a small laugh. There was no insecurity in his offer.

"A girlfriend by any other name is just as sweet?"

"There is no one sweeter than you." The bed dips with his weight as he drops closer and slides his mouth over the back of my neck. As though that's not close enough for his satisfaction, he hooks his arms around my waist, pulling me against him, the big spoon to my smaller one. We lie quiet for a beat, just satisfied to be near, but when he begins to speak again, my eyes make puddles on the pillow.

"I know you probably have things you need to tell me, and that's okay. I'm here when you're ready, okay?" His lips brush my shoulder as light as a butterfly's wing. "Whatever it is, we'll face it together. I'm in your corner now, darling."

How will I ever survive this? Wanting Whit. Will it ever go away? I don't think so because haven't I always loved him? Loved him without realizing, without him knowing what it really meant. It's like he knows me better than I know myself. My love for him feels clean and untouched by worry and fear. By anxiety. It feels like that stuff is all separate, like it can't touch me. I don't know how he does it. I don't know how he makes me feel so free because most of the time, I'm just pretending. Faking it until I make it. Going through the motions until I have to face the inevitable.

Make it. The thought is a scathing voice in my head. A mutter from my subconscious. I have to make it because the alternative is just like the saying goes: *a fate worse than death.*

If there is a fate worse than death, I think as I reach for the diamond pendant around my neck, it would be missing this. Missing my chance to love Whit.

"Maybe we should go to the Amalfi coast next," Whit suggests, taking the bag from my hand. That's the bag he packed for me without telling me. "I'll take a few days' vacation, and we won't be so rushed."

"We don't need to go anywhere. I still have so much of London to discover, not to mention the rest of England, Wales, and Bonny Scotland. And I still need to go back to Florida." His brow draws down, his expression darkening. "We'll talk about it later," I say, reaching for the bag, though his hand just tightens around it. "I have a thing I need to be back for." I release a worried breath, my words spilling like fast-flowing tears. "Can we talk about it when we get back?"

He waves off Jacques's tentative offer of help as he throws both bags into the trunk of the Mercedes. He pivots to face me, taking my shoulders in his hands. "Of course," he murmurs, pressing his lips to my head. "Whenever you're ready."

It's not like I want to confess to this ridiculousness. It's not like I want to admit that the Mimi he knows and loves is not who she seems to be. But the truth should come out sooner rather than later. It looks like today I'll be ripping off this emotional Band-Aid today.

The roads in Paris are quieter on Sunday mornings, and it isn't too long before we're back at the private airport terminal.

"Should we have bought a gift for your mom?" I ask as the thought suddenly occurs to me. It's a little too late, considering we're already making our way across the tarmac.

Whit just chuckles and tightens his grip on my hand. "She doesn't even know we're here."

"Really?"

He slides me a look. "We are adults, you know."

I make an uncomfortable gesture. "Old habits die hard."

"Well, it's time to make new ones," he returns, kissing the back of my hand. "Anyway, it serves Polly right for pushing me in the bloody Serpentine."

"She was just trying to help," I say doubtfully. If she'd pushed me in, we wouldn't be having this conversation because I'd be dead. The water was so cold.

"She's going to gloat, you know. Say this is all her doing, you and me, I mean. She'll say that she pushed me in the boating lake, that you appreciated my entry in the wet T-shirt contest, and fell for me on the spot."

"As explanations go, I think we could do worse."

Whit angles a puzzled look my way.

"You want to tell people how we really got together?"

"Yeah. I'll tell them you were relentless in your pursuit of me."

"Would that be before you fingered me?"

His feet halt, and he sucks in a sharp breath. "Mimi Valente, you little hussy!

"I was about to say you've rubbed off on me, but I guess I already did."

His delighted chuckle follows me all the way up the steps.

"I have news," he announces happily a few minutes later as he slides into the cream leather seat opposite mine. "Jody just had the babies. Polly sent me a text."

"Oh." My heart melts a little at the news. Babies are such a blessing, as my mother always says. "And everything went okay?"

"I think so. Polly sounded pretty ecstatic, so I imagine

they have ten fingers and ten toes apiece. I'm just waiting to see where her mind goes from here."

"Gosh, Whit. She's only just had her babies. She won't be thinking about coming back to work."

"I wasn't talking about Jody," he scoffs. "I was talking about Polly and her granny lust. Jody's husband is from up north somewhere," he adds contemplatively as he fastens his seat belt. "I'm banking on his parents not being around so much. Which, in turn, will give Polly a foot in the door. Everyone loves pseudo granny. She'll be another willing pair of hands. Because the alternative," he says, fixing me with a look, "isn't pretty. Especially when we tell her we're together.

"Polly is a granny without grandchildren. I am her eldest son, and you are my girlfriend, and she loves you. I don't think it'll be just me she makes puppy dog eyes at."

"But you don't want children."

"I never said that." His reply bypasses my brain and drops to my stomach like a lead weight.

"But you never wanted a girlfriend."

"I never said that I wasn't interested in settling down, just that I wasn't making much effort to." His mouth twists humorously. "There you go sprinkling glitter on red flags again."

"I don't know what you're talking about?"

"What kind of thirty-six-year-old man says he has no interest in settling down? Not everyone wants kids, but everyone wants to be loved, don't they?"

I didn't set out to be loved by Whit. I shouldn't have allowed it. Just a few moments ago, I was basking in his attention, feeling happy and lucky and all kinds of blessed. Terrified too, because of the things I have to confess. But I told myself it was worth it. More than that, I told myself to be worthy of him. There was no other way. And now I'm looking at him and wondering if my chance is about to slip away. Wondering if I'm brave enough to ask him.

"I know it's early in our relationship, but do you want kids?"

I'm not the girl for him. It was good to fool myself for a little while.

My heart suddenly breaks. It's not a misfiring of electrical signals like I'd been led to expect, but a snap, clean and loud like the break of a stem.

"I've never really given it any thought." My answer is automatic. On consideration, I wouldn't be surprised if the jet now drops to the ground.

Karma.

There was a short period just recently when I thought of little else, a time I'd investigated all that science had to offer, including gene therapy. Ultimately, if I struggled to accept my fate, then...

No. I can't go through this again.

"You seem deep in thought."

At Whit's concerned words, I lift my head and pray my smile is more bright than brittle. "I guess this weekend was a lot to take in."

"Is this where I'm supposed to say *that's what she said*?"

Is it wrong to be hurt that he doesn't see through me? I guess I'm being unfair because I've never been the real me with him.

40

WHIT

WE GET BACK to City Airport, where George waits to take us home. Though it's been barely twenty-four hours since we left, it feels like a lifetime has passed. But in a really good way.

We stop for sushi before dropping Mimi back at the apartment. I have to meet Beckett for an hour at Motcombs because he's off to New York next week.

"I won't be long," I tell her, pulling her body flush with mine outside my building. "Don't eat it all." I tap the lid of the sushi box.

"I won't."

Pressing my forefinger under her chin, I lift her gaze to mine. "You okay?"

"Just tired." She gives a tiny shrug. "All that walking yesterday, I guess."

I also kept her up last night, not that either of us would complain about that.

I watch her walk into the building and don't get back into the Bentley until she crosses the foyer, disappearing around a corner. As I pull the door closed, I suffer what I can only describe as a contraction deep in my chest. It's a physical sensation with an emotional cause: the sense that something isn't right.

"Belgravia, wasn't it, guvnor?" My eyes meet George's in the rear view mirror, and I nod.

"Yeah, Motcombs. I'll only be an hour."

"Right you are," he says, pulling out into the traffic.

I find myself rubbing my chest with my knuckles. She's just tired, I repeat to myself.

"Honey, I'm home!" I drop my jacket to the console table, stepping into a quiet apartment, which is odd. When Mimi's home, there's usually an audible trail. Music playing, a TV left on playing mindless soaps with a variety of British accents. The whirr of a dishwasher that previously went unused; this place hasn't been silent since Mimi arrived. The sound of her humming, the shuffle of her bare feet. The drip of a shower she's forgotten to turn off properly.

"Mimi?" I call, making my way to the kitchen. It's usually a good bet. Not because she's a fan of cooking but she is a fan of eating. I try the bedroom next. She's not there either, though from farther along the hallway I hear a thump and a muffled curse.

She's in one of the spare bedrooms.

"What are you doing in here?" I ask, pushing the door wide. The bed is covered with hangers and the walk-in closet is full. "Why are all your clothes in here?" My words sound dumb, my mind on delay. Two questions and she hasn't even looked at me yet. By this point of our greeting, usually we haven't come up for breath.

"I'm just making sure everything is organised," she says,

stepping back as she slides her hand down an evening dress I know she hasn't yet worn. "You can give these to Primrose maybe? They're brand new, and she'd look so pretty in them. Or maybe she'd like to sell them."

Before I can ask her what the fuck she's talking about, she turns and my stomach drops. At least one part of me instinctively understands.

"Sweetheart, you've been crying."

She nods and gives a brave yet wobbly-looking smile. "I can't help but feel sad. I guess it's inevitable when things come to an end."

"What are you talking about? What things?"

"Whit, I know you know this isn't real. I can't pretend anymore."

"You can't... what?" I shake my head as though I'm hearing things—as though my ears are waterlogged and need a good clean. "What are you talking about?"

"I made a mistake." Her eyes are suddenly rain-filled clouds. "I can't do this. I shouldn't have gotten caught up in the moment. I shouldn't have stayed here with you because I've ruined everything."

She begins to cry, and my instinct is to go to her, but she holds out her hand and rushes past me into the hallway.

It takes me a beat to process, but I'm quick on her heels.

"What the fuck, Mimi," I call after her. She doesn't turn back as she ducks right into the bedroom. *Our bedroom.* "What the hell is going on? I've only been gone an hour."

"I told you. I can't do this, not with you. It's not right," she says adamantly, pulling on a drawer and scooping out an armful of her underwear. She turns to the bed, and I notice her open suitcase, clothes hanging half in and half out, not sure if they're coming or going.

My fingers fasten around her arm as she moves to the chest again. "You can't love me, or you don't?"

"What difference does it make?" she says, wrestling her arm away. Her eyes are red and angry, her face the color of spoiled milk.

"It makes all the difference," I retort, getting between her and the drawers. "You can't say one thing and mean another. Something has happened, and I want to know what it is."

"I can't stay here," she says, her voice low and adamant. "I can't be with you, not without being someone else."

"What the fuck are you talking about?"

"This has all been an act," she shouts, throwing up her arms. "I'm not the woman you think I am. I'm not happy and carefree. It's all been a fucking lie."

"No." I stop and blow out the breath crowding my chest. "You can't fake it that well, darling."

She slides me a look full of spite and malice. "What would you know? How would you even tell?"

I bark out a laugh, but I'm not feeling very amused. "That's fucking classic," I grate out, catching her arm again. "You think my ego is that fragile? That you'll insult my prowess and I'll tuck tail and run? I've been making women come since you were wearing pigtails."

"I'm sure you're very proud," she retorts haughtily. "Release my arm. I'm going to leave, and nothing you can say will stop me."

Her expression. The malice in her voice. I want to throw her on the bed and kiss some sense into her—kiss her to compliance. But I'm not that man. I'm not a bully. So I release my fingers before I do something we might both regret.

I stalk from the bedroom, but I don't leave. Instead, I

pull a bottle of whisky from the cabinet and treat myself to a generous pour.

What's going through her head?

What happened in the past hour that made her so vehement?

She loves me. I know she does. I've seen it on her face, and I've felt it in her fingertips.

Bringing my glass to my mouth, I throw half of the contents back, relishing the burn. *This is ridiculous.* I'm not going to allow her to fuck things up for such flimsy reasoning—for a non-reasoning. She can barely look me in the face.

Maybe it was the diamond. She wasn't even wearing it. She must've taken it off. Maybe I should tell her I didn't mean anything by it. It's not a sneaky attempt at an engagement. What does she take me for?

The thoughts begin to churn and turn in my head.

Everything was okay until I mentioned children. I want kids, but it's a distant, vague sort of thing. I might change my mind—better the right person than the wrong one with ovaries.

Maybe that's what this is. Maybe she can't have kids, and it hurts too much to tell me.

Fuck it. I throw the rest of my whisky down my throat before the glass connects with the tabletop. If it's kids, we can talk about it. It's not a dealbreaker.

I take a step away from the table only to double back again. How do you ask that? How do I tell her it doesn't matter when it obviously does to her?

I know she can love me. I know it.

Something's going on. Maybe it's the same thing that brought her here—something other than her frank demands and her clumsy seduction. What was the root cause of this? I know what the outcome is. The tattered remains beating in my chest cavity.

I slosh more whisky into the glass, willing her to appear from the room. She's got to come out sometime, right? I dump the whisky down the back of my throat, hoping to wash away this disdain I have for myself.

She doesn't fucking love you.

She doesn't have to.

And you can't make her.

The fuck I can't.

My footsteps sound loud and purposeful as I stalk down the hallway, ignoring the canvas that cost me a quarter of a million from Sotheby's. Money fixes so many things, I consider, but it can't fix a broken heart. Not that I see any need to suffer one of those.

My feelings are hurt, that's all. My fucking pride. All that shit is fixable. I know there's more to this than meets the eye.

"You're not going anywhere," I grate out, pushing on the door. "Not until you give me a fucking reason. Half a reason —a drop. Don't think you can feed me bullshit."

The room seems empty, the afternoon outside blue and green and yellow, a day full of life. But inside this room, everything feels wrong. A minute ago, it was filled with angry energy. Right now, it lacks energy entirely. Her energy. Her perpetual sunshine and flowers. Her fucking... something is missing, and it's freaking me out.

"Amelia?" Her name comes out rough. *She can't have gone far,* I think as something swells inside me. Dis*quiet* is such a strange word because this sudden worried buzz in my head is anything but.

She isn't in the closet, the hangers half empty. The clothes we'd shopped together for, the Paris dress, they're all in the other room and her own clothes are in her case on the bed.

"For fuck's sake, Mimi." I push on the open bathroom door, but she's not there, either. Cosmetics litter the countertop and damp towels are scattered across the floor. How can one person make so much mess?

I storm from the bathroom as the fist squeezes tighter and tighter when something I can't define compels me to the other side of the bed.

"Jesus Christ!" I drop to my knees next to the sprawled form of the woman I love. She's on her front, her position awkward, her hair like a veil across her face. Has she passed out? I roll her over, and my heart rolls up my throat. "Mimi!" If I thought she was pale before, now she looks like—

I can't say it. I can't think it as I begin to shake her by the shoulders.

There's no reaction at all.

"Fuck, oh fuck." I press my finger to the pulse in her neck, then her wrist because my shaking fingers can't find one. My phone—where the fuck is my phone? I pat my pockets frantically at the same time as I arrange her flat on her back. *It's in my jacket pocket.* I almost go and get it as my hands hover over her chest, thoughts shooting lightning quick through my head.

Wasn't there something about apartment's smart system being able to dial for the emergency services? Voice activated?

I don't remember—I can't fucking concentrate as I reach over her prone figure and knock the landline phone from the nightstand and input the digits. On my knees still, I press my left hand to the center of her chest, interlocking my right fingers over it.

"Nine, nine, nine," says a voice from the phone. "Which service do you require?"

"Paramedics. Quickly. My girlfriend isn't breathing." With straight arms, I use the heel of my palm to push on her breastbone as I play that stupid Bee Gee's song over and over again in my head.

Staying-alive-staying-alive-ah-ha... again and again.

Tension spears between my shoulder blades, sweat standing on my brow, running down my face and mingling with my tears. Abject fear fills my heart, the motions of my chest compressions happening without real cognizance. As the eldest of seven children, I relish peace. I enjoy periods of solitude. But I never want to feel this alone ever again.

I hear voices in the apartment. The concierge from downstairs and a woman's voice. "In here," I shout. "Fucking hurry!"

A woman in a noisy green-and-yellow jacket appears by my side.

"Mush up, my love. I'll take it from here."

"She's not breathing." I move to the floor by her head. I'm not going far. "Please, for the love of God, just fucking do something."

"What's her name, my love?" The woman, the paramedic, is about my age. *Jesus, shouldn't she have a doctor?*

"I'm here first, so I'll have to do," she says without rancor as a companion arrives to continue the same pattern of compressions, and she gets fuck knows what out of her huge bag. "Name?" she repeats.

"Mimi. Amelia. Amelia Valente."

"Mimi, my darling, can you hear me?"

I drop my head to my hands because I don't think she can.

I hate hospitals, but who doesn't? Maybe people who love their jobs, I think, watching women in scrubs and porters in navy uniforms pass along the corridors. Some smile, some laughing. They're entitled to what fun they can glean because I wouldn't do their jobs for all the money in the world. Deal with death and heartache on a daily basis? I find myself shaking my head in denial, catching my reflection in the window. I look like a case of care in the community. My hair is a mess, and I'm muttering to myself.

Please, God, let her be okay. Casting my eyes to the ceiling, I bargain with the big fella, not for the first time today.

It felt like we'd been alone on that floor for hours, when it could only have been minutes before the critical care paramedics turned up with their portable defibrillator. They shocked Mimi—twice—before she regained a pulse.

She was dead. She was the lack of energy I felt, and I never want to experience that again.

Dead and they brought her back. How fucking amazing is that? And now she's in a coma; an induced coma is still a coma, whichever way you look at it. She's lying in a hospital bed, just feet from me, on a ventilator.

A door opens, and my head jerks up. I wish it hadn't when I spot a distraught family being led out. A husband and a wife, maybe, clinging to each other. Other people follow, grief etched into their faces.

How can anyone do this job? Numbers makes sense. Death does not. Not for someone as vibrant as Mimi. Elbows on my knees, I drop my head between my shoulder blades because I feel so fucking helpless.

No. I'm not doing this, I think, sitting upright again.

She's not dying. I won't let her. Except...

If they lead me to that room, I'm not going in, I decide. Fuck that and fuck this, she is *not* dying.

The plastic chair squeaks a protest as I control the things I can, pulling my jacket from where it's draped over the back of it. I fish Mimi's phone out from the pocket. I can't believe I had the foresight to grab it from the bed next to her case as she was carried out to the waiting ambulance. I input her code, also not sure how I know it.

Let's face it, I'm not fucking sure of much right now.

It's not the first time I've called Mimi's mother since we arrived at St. Barts, but she's yet to pick up. But this time, I won't use Mimi's phone, just the number from her address book.

The call buzzes, then clicks. Then it rings. And it rings. And then my heart stops at the sounds of a woman's voice.

"Hello?"

Keep it together. Come on. You've done this before, broken bad news. You did this when Dad passed because Mum wasn't in any fit state to. "Is this Mrs. Valente?"

"This is she," a wary voice replies. I suppose my accent is a dead giveaway for something out of the ordinary.

"This is Whit, Mrs. Valente. Connor's friend?" Not so good friend, as it turns out. Jesus Christ, how am I going to tell her this?

"Oh, yes, Whit," she says with a burst of audible relief. "How are you?"

"Mrs. Valente, I don't know if Mimi told you, but she's been working for my company."

"No, she never mentioned it. She called earlier, but I missed her call. I was at the dentist." I close my eyes. She didn't call. She can't because she's in a coma. I should've used my phone the first time. "Mimi told me she was working at a bank in the city."

"Yes." I close my eyes and pinch the bridge of my noise. "The bank." VirTu, my bank, I suppose. Springing up from the chair, I walk to the darkened window and press my forehead against the cool glass. *Get. The. Fucking. Words. Out.* "I don't know how to tell you this, except to say first and foremost that she's stable. She's okay." Sort of. "But she's in the hospital."

I hear the terrified intake of her breath, her words then falling in a rush, tumbling over each other like water over rocks. "Oh my God. It's happened, hasn't it? Her heart?"

"Yeah. Yes, they said it's her heart." There go the hairs on the back of my neck again. "A cardiac arrest, they're saying."

"But she's okay?" she demands frantically.

"She stable," I answer gravely. Stable is better than the alternative, right? Which would be unstable. Or worse still, completely fucking rigid, stretched out on a slab.

Stop. The glass rattles as I whack my head against it as though I can afford to waste brain cells. How on earth does a twenty-four-year-old suffer from cardiac arrest?

"I need to go—I need to book flights. No," she adds under her breath. "Tell me where, Whit? Which hospital?"

"Saint Barts—Saint Bartholomew's. It has a..." Does she need to hear this? Yes, I decide, there might be comfort in the knowledge. "It has a heart center. It's a teaching hospital, too. One of the best in London."

"Thank you, Whit," she breathes out. "But do they know?"

"Know what?"

"About her condition? About Brugada?"

"I don't know what that is," I answer confused and sorry and so fucking scared.

"Oh, Whit. Please go and find a doctor. Tell them, please. Let them know she has Brugada Syndrome. It's what killed Connor." Her mother bursts into sobs.

"I'll go and find someone," I promise. "Let me..."

"Yes, yes, you do that. Call me right back?"

I promise I will.

And I do, several more times between finding a doctor and explaining what her mother told me. Between googling what the hell Brugada Syndrome is and finally cursing Mimi Valente for her recklessness.

41

MIMI

"Oh, honey."

I wake to my mother, brushing my hair from my face.

"Mom?" My voice sounds croaky, and my throat is really sore. "What are you doing here?" But then a sinking sensation fills all the spaces in my brain and my aching body, where I feel hollow. I try to move, pushing up on one elbow only to lower myself back again. I feel like I've been hit by a truck. I hope that's not the case.

Wasn't it morning? Afternoon, maybe, last time my eyes were open? How is it dark?

"Hush now." My mother fusses with the blanket. Why is she here? She lives in Florida, and I live ...

"Mom, where *is* here?" I swallow audibly, and Mom brings a tumbler of water to my lips. Her expression. I know before she says it. I'm in the hospital. My brain supplies the rest. I'm in a hospital in London. And it happened.

"You gave us all such a fright, but you're okay now."

"Oh." She means okay for now. This much I know. Hey, but at least I'm not dead. I want to laugh before a black thought ripples through my head. Maybe I was dead, but

I'm still here. Everything seems to fade into the distance. It happened. The thing I've been trying to ignore while living my life happened—and I came out on the other side.

"Mom, where is—"

"Dad?"

No. The other one. Daddy. Whit. The man I love. The man I tried to make believe otherwise. But I nod because that's what she expects. "He's gone with Whit to get some of your things. Why didn't you tell us you were staying with him?"

"I didn't want to worry you," I say, pressing my head into the pillows. I don't want to talk about it, but I feel like there's a lot to be said. A lot of questions to answer as I lift my hand and press it to my chest.

"When he told me about the unexploded bomb. How crazy, sweetheart. You might've been hurt."

I ball my hand into a fist. Which ticking time bomb are we talking about? I survived the first and the second. The third, I guess we'll see.

"Well," she whispers, covering her hand with mine. "It's safe to say we haven't stopped worrying about you since you left."

"I know." Old habits are hard to lay down.

"The doctor will be coming around in a little while. They want to fit the ICD before you leave." Though her voice is strong, her eyes plead.

An ICD. An implantable cardioverter defibrillator. A machine that could shock my heart into a rhythm should I suffer... well, what just happened, I guess. But it could also shock the hell out of me whether I need it or not. In other words, my heart is the first ticking time bomb, an ICD the second.

But getting away was never just about that.

I sigh as, under my fingers, my heart beats like it should. For now. How long did it not beat for, I wonder. And who found me?

"Will you? Now?" My mother reaches for my hands. "Please, Mimi."

"I didn't say I wouldn't have it fitted. I just said I needed time."

"We nearly lost you," she whispers, turning her face from mine. She shouldn't spare me her tears. I know she should make me watch as I turn my hand under hers and offer her what little reassurance I have.

I'm here. It happened before I was ready for it. "I'll do it." Because really, what other choice do I have?

Doctors come and go, nurses, too. You're not allowed to sleep in a hospital, it seems. I'm told that, while in a coma, my parents and Whit were told it wasn't certain whether I'd survive the experience. I'm also informed I'm very fortunate because not only did I live but it seems I don't bear the scars. Neurologically, at least.

Almost two days in a coma. Where did I go because I have no memory of it?

How my parents and Whit must've suffered. How they must've worried.

It's safe to say I feel that guilt.

Given the choice, I'd still do it again. I'd still leave.

Sometime later, hours, I think—it's hard to judge when you're in the hospital—I open my eyes. It's still dark, but Whit is seated in a faux leather chair at the left of my bed. His sweater looks wrinkled, and his jeans look less than pristine. His jaw is covered in a thick rasp of stubble, and his hair is a mess.

"Hey," I whisper, reaching to rub the sleep from my eyes.

"How are you feeling?" His ankle slides from its place of rest on the opposite knee when he sits forward.

"Like I died, and someone shocked me back to living, I guess." I try to laugh, but it comes out more like a hacking cough. *My throat*, I think, pressing my hand to it. "I hope I look better than you do."

Something that looks like dark amusement skitters across his face as one of his beautiful hands slides across the bristles. "I haven't seen a mirror for a while, so I can't comment."

"Jeez. Kick a girl when she's down, why don't you?"

"Sorry." As his gaze dips, I experience a pang of regret. Why did I have to hurt him? And then I remember. He wants children. He wants children, and I have a genetic condition that killed my brother and my grandfather, and Lord only knows how many people before him. I have a genetic condition that could kill a child of mine with no advent of science to prevent it. That's ultimately why I had to let him go.

"No, I'm sorry," I whisper. "About everything." Because he knows my secret now. He knows about this thing I'm carrying. The rest he won't understand. No one ever does. "I'm sorry I didn't tell you."

He doesn't lift his head, and he doesn't immediately answer. But when he does, I feel incredibly small. "Your parents filled in the blanks when I called to tell them you were in a coma."

"Oh."

"When you were on a ventilator. A machine that breathed for you."

"I know what a ventilator is." My answer sounds harsher than it should. Harsher than I'd like it to.

"Then I told the doctors, which seemed to help them. Brugada Syndrome is genetic, right?

"Yes. It's what killed Connor, though we didn't know at the time."

"You've known for a couple of years. Had regular testing and watched for the symptoms."

"I see my parents have been very chatty."

He stands abruptly, and my unreliable little heart does a jig, settling again when he lowers himself on the bed, taking my hand between his. "What on earth were you thinking?"

"I was thinking I didn't want to live my life with a sword hanging over my head."

"So you thought you'd just take your chances. Dice with death?"

"It's not so cut-and-dried when you're looking at it from this side."

"If you'd had the surgery—"

"I see you've read the literature," I mutter, pulling my hand away. "But just the parts that spoke to you. The same parts my parents liked. How it'd save my life. Shock my heart when it stopped. But do you know how?" Before he can answer, I rush on. "By sending eight hundred volts of power into me. Worse than being kicked by a horse, apparently."

"A horse kick that would make sure you lived."

"That's why I came to London. To live. Before I gave in to fear because that's what having an ICD represents to me. Living in fear that I might die."

"News flash, sweetheart. You already did."

"I know—it wasn't supposed to happen. I've lived with this for years, and the symptoms only started to appear a few months ago. I figured I'd have time, and I was going to use that time to experience freedom for the first time in my life.

"I didn't mean for it to touch you. I didn't come here with the idea of seducing you. I thought you'd be way beyond the touch of a girl like me—and you were. You asked me if I believed in magic that afternoon at your mom's house." I feel the tears begin to fall, batting them away with my hands. "I didn't. Not anymore."

I don't know how it happened, but I was already falling for you when I left your apartment with my scrunched résumé in my hand, my insides still pulsing in time with your words.

"Stop. Calm down." I can see he wants to press me back against the pillows but restrains himself from doing so.

"Why? It's not like I'm going to die now." I'm behaving like a child, I know. I have to. I can't let this go on.

"Isn't it?" His voice is so arch as he watches me tap my fingers over my chest.

"No, because I'm in the hospital. I won't be leaving until I've had the device fitted." My fingers close over my chest and swallow over the ache of loss. I won't regret having the operation. I've found I have too much to live for. *Even if I can't have him.*

"I'll never understand it," he says, dropping his head.

"I wouldn't expect you to."

"I'll never understand how you could make that choice," he says, his head coming up, his gaze sharp and unforgiving. "You of all people. You lost your brother to this illness, and you decided to play fucking Russian roulette?"

"It wasn't like—"

"I'm not finished!" he bellows. My gaze slides to the door, expecting a nurse to come running. Maybe he already warned them. "All that bullshit about going back to Florida.

Were you really going to go back to live? Or were you set to die? To rob those who love you of your life."

"I've been living my life for other people since Connor died," I retort, my tone low and obstinate. "And you want the truth? I wasn't sure when I left home." God forgive me for my lie. The worst I'm guilty of is recklessness. "I wasn't sure what I wanted. I was just frightened for the longest time. We're all dying, Whit, from the moment we take our first breath."

"A nihilist to boot," he says with an unhappy laugh.

"I could've died without ever knowing I had Brugada, just like Connor. A death not chosen. The result out of my hands."

"Here one minute and gone the next?" he demands with a snap of his fingers. "Well, that nearly fucking happened." I hate that his hands are shaking. I hate that I've put him in this position and made him this angry. But I don't hate that he was there to save me. To give me another chance. Just because I can't have him doesn't mean I don't want to live.

"I know it might seem strange to you—"

"Doesn't seem strange at all," he retorts. "You weren't thinking of anyone but yourself."

His words land like a knife to the stomach. They are no more than I deserve.

"So what if I was?" My fear turns physical, a cold lump now in my stomach, my tears running freely now. "Dying or living with the threat of death? Living with the danger of eight hundred indiscriminate volts through my chest? Do you know how anxious I've been? No, you wouldn't know. How could you?"

"Exactly my point. I couldn't know because you never told me."

"I just wanted to be an ordinary person," I almost whisper.

"I won't pretend I can even imagine I have one iota of that understanding," he says, his voice softer. Even if he can barely stand to look at me.

"ICDs fail. They save lives, yeah. But they're not without their own problems." Not that I'll go into it with him. They can shock you into cardiac arrest for no reason. Parts of the device can be recalled; other parts just outright fail. Batteries need replacing and don't let your iPhone get anywhere near it! I shake my head. Like my phone was even a consideration given the severity of the circumstances. Getting an ICD is signing up for a lifetime of surgeries, possible infections, and complications. Those kill, too.

"It sounds like you were already weighing up your options for the best way to die when you arrived."

And now I lie.

"Maybe I was. Maybe you're right about playing Russian roulette. I considered that I might live a normal life without an ICD, bow out when it's time."

"You mean like last week?" he asks. "At the age of twenty-four? Did that time seem right to you?" Anger chases through his second question.

"I thought, hoped when I'd considered that an option, that I would be older. Or else I thought I might have the device fitted and have it kill me early anyway. I don't know how to explain it."

I won't say I never thought about these things, but the thoughts were only fleeting and now seem like distant memories. I guess I was afraid to examine them properly, but that's no longer relevant in the current scheme of things. I was working from a place of extreme fear. My fear, my parents' fear. Fear of what happened to Connor.

"And you thought running away might help?"

I shake my head. "It felt like buying time. One last hurrah before I gave in." I wasn't giving in to death. I was giving in to fear of what life with an ICD would mean.

"Gave in to what?" he asks angrily. "A life where you wouldn't drop dead without a second's notice?"

"To terror!" Weakness trembles through my body, but anger overtakes it. "I bore the burden of my family's fear for years. Can't you see that? That's why I lived at home. Why I didn't visit the gym, drink, or party with my friends. As long as I wasn't suffering symptoms, it was fine. I wasn't frightened. Everything was okay. But then at my last cardiology appointment, they repeated the stress test and laid out the news. I was at risk now. It was real—it was happening."

"That still doesn't explain why you'd put your family through the worry of a six-month wait."

"I wasn't sure I wanted the ICD." This is so true, but *want* didn't come into it. "Aren't you listening? It was like being placed between the devil and the deep blue sea. I couldn't think of their fears anymore because I had too many of my own. That's why I left. I wanted time to myself. Time to live, to experience life like other girls do. But then there was you."

"Me," he repeats gravely. "Another person you couldn't tell."

"I didn't want your pity." My gaze ducks to the hospital bedding. The crisp, white sheet and the blue-green blanket I run my fingertips over.

"Not even when I said I loved you?"

"Especially not then," I whisper, watching a fat teardrop soak into the cotton. "You deserve someone better than me."

"Someone who isn't selfish, you mean."

His words cut like a knife. I begin to understand that there's no coming back from this for him. Panic begins to swell inside me. I thought I could explain—I thought I could make him understand. To live or not to live doesn't seem too difficult now that I've had that choice taken away from me. And him along with it because he deserves better than me. Someone who can give him children. Someone far braver than me.

"I was trying not to be selfish." The words are choked and halting, but I don't want his sympathy.

It's just my heart, that troublesome, hurtful muscle. Well *now* it feels like it's breaking. I've lived for months terrified about what might happen, and now that it's breaking in two, it doesn't even have the decency of skipping a solitary beat. I hiccup a sob as a black thought hits: better to worry about what being shocked back to life feels like than actually experience it.

That's why I lied. Why I said I wasn't in love with you. Because I am. I really do love you. I love you so much, but I still need to let you go.

One hiccuping sob becomes two, and I give into my tears. It comforts me that his instinct is to come to me, to hold me. I see it in his aborted movement and how he balls his hands into fists as though to stop himself. I force myself to be strong, to choke back the tears and not fall apart. I can't quite manage it but try, swiping the meat of my palms under my eyes.

"People who love don't treat someone like you have treated me." He looks up, his golden eyes dim. "You were unresponsive, Mimi. Dead in my arms. I will never not see that image or feel that pain. And I will never understand how you could put another human in that position, let alone someone you profess to love."

"I'm sorry. So, so sorry." I run the back of my hand under my running nose. I must look such a mess. Dirty, straggled hair and a blotchy red face.

"I thought I knew you, but you only let me see what you wanted me to. You're not all sunshine. That was an act. You have depths you refused to show me, and the thing is, I would've still loved you if you had. But you couldn't see that because you're no more mature than Lavender or Primrose." The knife, it twists. "I have enough on my hands looking after them. I have no desire to add another to the burden."

"I'm sorry," I say again. Maybe if I say it enough, he'll believe me. He'll see through my tears and my hurtful words to an understanding. Doesn't he know he's become my whole world?

I don't fool myself for very long as he stands, his next words cutting to the brutal truth of it.

"I'm sorry too, but I'm not looking for someone else to look after." Through the haze of my tears, I see him by the side of the bed, and watch in slow motion as he lowers his head. "Goodbye, Mimi." He presses a kiss to my head. "I truly hope you find what you're looking for."

I already have, I want to say as I watch him walk away with my love.

42

WHIT

I LEAVE. I leave her room, the hospital. I leave my apartment, my family, and I leave the country. I get as far away from Mimi Valente as I can for the sake of my own sanity.

I can't watch her self-destruct. I can't be there and hold her hand for that. Yet I can't stay away, and I hate myself for it. Two weeks after moving to Zurich, after going to great lengths and great expense to move my office and support staff, I move back to London again.

Because I'm my own worst enemy.

I can't seem to stay away though I tell myself things will return to normal when Mimi moves back to Florida. As I understand it, this won't be too much longer. And where do I get my intel? Where else but Polly. She keeps in contact with Mimi's parents. She lets me know how her procedure went. How her subsequent checkups went. What her cardiologist says. And how quiet Mimi is when she visits.

While Mimi was in St. Barts, I gave up my place to her parents. When she was discharged, I arranged a small flat for them near the hospital. It didn't seem fair for her to return to a place with so many memories.

I can't stay there myself. All I can see is her lying prone on the floor, and when I do, I feel like I'm having my own fucking cardiac arrest.

But I'm there today because Polly wants to "pop around for a chat." I hadn't the heart to tell her I'm not staying there. I don't feel like answering the million questions she'll no doubt have, and I don't want her worried looks or her sympathy.

I just want to drink whisky and eat carbs from the room service menu and fucking well wallow until my arteries clog, which I manage that quite well in a suite in a nearby hotel.

"Hello, darling." Poll knows the code to the door, of course, and comes bustling in, dumping her Birkin on the floor. In her arm, she has chocolates and flowers, which she sets down on the island bench.

"Have you bought me flowers?" Jesus, I must look like a sad sack.

"No, silly. Those are for Mimi's mother. I'm popping over to their flat after our visit."

I bite the inside of my lip against the notion of asking for news.

"The chocolates are for Mimi, of course. I also bought a bottle of wine for her dad, but I dropped my bag on the way over, so now it stinks like a wine barrel."

I try not to grimace, thinking of the price of the bag.

"They think Mimi will get the all clear to go back home next week."

"Oh." Oh fuck. "I'm sure they'll all be very happy to see the back of London."

"Well, two of them will. One is a little sad that she's having to leave prematurely."

"It's for the best," I say gruffly. "Want a coffee?" Before

she answers, I'm already making my way over to the machine.

"Go on then," she says, "you've twisted my arm."

I make a couple of flat whites, thankful for the shopping service or else I'd be making coffee with cottage cheese, and hand one to Mum, mainly to stop her going around with a feather duster she's pulled from the cleaning closet.

"Mum, sit down. I pay someone to do this."

"I'm just making sure you're getting your money's worth," she mutters, bending down to swipe something up from under a sideboard. "See. Looks like they missed this," she says, handing me a notebook I've never seen before. "They can't be that good. They're clearly not vacuuming properly."

Black and unassuming, I twist the notebook around. It doesn't exactly scream *owned by Mimi,* but somehow, I know it's hers. *I shouldn't read it,* I think as I flip through the pages. And then I do as Mum rounds the island to wash her hands babbling on about making Lavender come and dust once a week in exchange for her keep. Frankly, I'd rather become a hoarder and live in squalor than have to listen to her complaining every week.

The notebook is blank but for one page where a feminine hand has penned a list

1. Stop caring so much about what other people think. You only have one life to live and what you do with it is no business of anyone else.

Well, she should put a line through that one because she fucking achieved it.

2. See some of the world. Pick a project. Do something just for you.

Check again. She saw London and Paris. Her project was

me. And what she did? That would also be me. She did me and she did me over.

3. Be fearless. Because what is fear but a monster of your own making? What's scarier than fear? Only the inevitable.

I sit with that one for a minute, not sure what to make of it. She was obviously scared of Brugada, but not enough to take care of herself. Maybe she's one of those people who can just bury their head in the sand. What was the inevitable? Surgery? Death?

4. Don't live in the cages other people build for you. Fly. Run, and not just because you feel like you're being chased for a change. Frolic. Have fun. Fuck—yes, fuck. The thing you were taught not to want, the expression of life itself. Do it. Enjoy it.

Number four makes my heart ache, even though she managed to use the *f* word.

5. Tell everyone you love how much you love them. Not only that but love them gently in actions and deeds. Love them hard, if they can take it. Love them however you want, but just make sure they know how much you love them.

Scrawled in the margins is a note that reads: *Love Whit but don't tell him. Maybe I've always loved him, and have just managed not to admit it. Don't spoil it, Mimi. He deserves someone better.*

Number five leaves a ball of emotion in my throat. Someone better or someone who won't lie to me?

6. Give up guilt. Live the best way you know how. The rest? Forgive. Forgive yourself and forgive others. None of us are perfect.

True. So true.

7. Stop being hard on yourself. Life can be hard enough without all that mind chatter.

I skim seven in favor of eight.

8. *Breathe while you can. A good life and a good death are the best a person can hope for.*

Something wanders over my grave and, for a second, I'm back in my bedroom, crying and kneeling on the floor next to her.

"What's that you're reading?"

I flip the notebook closed as Polly hops up onto the stool next to me. "Nothing much." Nothing I can make much sense of.

"Have you seen Mimi since she was discharged?" she asks so airily that I know this isn't a throwaway line.

I make a vague gesture meant to convey *no* as I lift my coffee cup to my mouth.

"It's such a shame what happened to her."

"Yep. A shame she didn't look after herself."

Polly tilts her head to one side. "That's a little unfair, and not at all like you."

"She went into cardiac arrest in my bedroom." I can't even sleep in there anymore.

"I'm so pleased you were there."

"What if I hadn't? What if she'd really died? Gone? I would've carried that guilt around with me for my whole bloody life."

"Well, that's what you do, Leif."

"What's that supposed to mean?"

"That you feel things deeply. That you take on responsibilities that aren't yours."

My expression twists in warning. *Dangerous territory, Poll.*

"I know you had to when your father died," she says, stretching out her arm, her hand covering mine. "I don't know what I would've done without you. But I'm here now.

I'm okay. When those little toe rags cause you any pain, just flick them back my way."

"It's become habit now," I say, staring down into the foam in my cup.

"And they know it. Honestly, I'm sure half the time they're just trying to make your life difficult. Taking the piss. Especially Lavender." My head jerks up at Polly's language. She rarely swears. "She just feels like she needs to be seen. If you take a step back, perhaps," she suggests softly. "I might be able to make some headway with her. And if you did that, you might have more time for Mimi."

"Stop," I say softly. "We tried, and it didn't work out."

"It's just so not like you," she says, frowning. "You never give up."

"I didn't give up. I got involved with a woman who wouldn't let me in."

"At first, maybe."

"You don't know what you're talking about, Mum. She's not the person you think she is."

"She's not the person you think she is, either," she retorts sharply. "Take off your blinders. See this for what it really is."

"And what's that?" I say, pressing my fist into my hip.

"She didn't have a death wish, Leif. When the tests came back, the advice from the cardiologist was that she should consider having an ICD fitted. Not that she had to that minute. That death was imminent."

"If that had happened to me, you would've sat on me—kept me in one place until I gave in and said yes to the thing."

"But that's what her parents have done her whole life. She's lived in fear—their fear. And then just think, she couldn't put their fear down because of the weight heaped on top of it. Not only was she facing her own mortality, but this device, this ICD, would keep her alive, but not without complications, physical and otherwise. Why, the emotional consequences alone—"

"The emotional consequences of staying alive, you mean."

"To have the operation, to have an ICD fitted, meant giving in. Admitting she was at risk. The risk of dying, not just physically but mentally, too. Imagine the stress, Whit. Just like the bomb found near her aunt's house, Mimi lived with the threat of Brugada ticking away inside her. And the device is no magic solution, either. It can become faulty and shock her into cardiac arrest for no reason. You're not even supposed to place an iPhone near it for fear of setting it off."

Fuck. Are they really that unstable?

"Getting an ICD is signing up for a lifetime of worry and potential complications. But more than that, according to Mimi's mother, she'd found it so difficult to come to terms with never being a mother herself."

"I don't—I don't understand."

"The Brugada gene is hereditary, Whit. I can't imagine the way she must be feel about that. Would I risk bringing a child into this world with those kinds of odds—without really knowing if I'd be passing on this burden? I really don't know."

And just like that, everything fits into place.

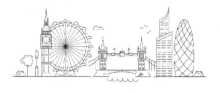

43

___

MIMI

"No. No, I don't want to be here," I say as the black cab pulls up at Marble Arch. "You didn't say we were coming here." My words hold a world of panic, and I find myself pressing my hand over the slight bump of my ICD where it lies under my skin. I've begun to touch it as a talisman of sorts. It's the weirdest thing to live with, to get used to, but I will.

"Polly chose the café," my mom cajoles, paying the cabbie as Dad climbs out.

"There are a dozen Pret sandwich shops in London." Why this one? Why the one next to Hyde Park? "And there are a hundred places much nicer to meet." I don't want to be here. It's hard enough trying to get over him.

"Mimi," my father says, holding open the cab door. "You've barely been out since you were discharged. A bit of fresh air will do you good."

"The air isn't—"

"It's a park," he deadpans. "Trees. Sunshine. Oxygen."

I feel tears gather because his words seem like an echo of Whit's statement that day. Swallowing over the lump in my throat, I catch the cabbie's eye, waiting for him to say

"What's it to be, love?" Then I'd ask him to take me back to the little flat we're staying in. I've had my final checkup and am free to fly home. Only Mom wants to stay for Doreen's wedding. She's marrying Frank next week at Haringey Civic Centre—the local council offices—before having a "good old-fashioned knees-up" in a local pub. Mom seems to be viewing it as an anthropological event.

"I'm clockin' off here, love," the taxi driver says instead.

"Out you go." My mother uses a tone she should reserve for toddlers.

"Just tell me," I say, swinging around to face her, my butt squeaking against the pleather seat. "Why here?"

"Gosh, Mimi. Such a fuss," she mutters. "I seem to recall something about Polly being here for a meeting. Something about a friend suffering from a raging menopause?"

Well, that odd story checks out, I guess. Which is how I find myself on the sidewalk, watching the cab pull away.

"Apparently, over there is the sight of the Tyburn hanging tree." My father stares at his phone, reading London tourist information.

"A tree hung with what?" Mom asks.

"People," I retort, turning toward one of London's many Pret a Manger sandwich shops.

"Gruesome. Oh wait, Mimi. Polly just sent me a text." She fumbles with her purse, pulling out her phone.

"How'd you know it was Polly?" I feel my gaze narrow suspiciously.

"Because she's the only person who calls me here," Mom retorts, not without frustration. "I got one of those travel SIM things, remember?"

"Yeah." I shake my head as though I could shake off this feeling. "Who wants coffee?"

"Oh, we've got to meet her over there."

"Oh, for fudge's sake," I mutter, swinging in the direction of the park, Whit's words echoing in my ear. Speakers' Corner. *It's where people go to get stuff off their chests.* Maybe I should've brought my own soap box.

We cross the busy road and head toward the small crowd of people milling where last time there was none. Sure enough, a woman in a sensible tweed skirt and cardigan stands on a little stepladder. She's so short it doesn't really give her much advantage. I spot Polly in the crowd, and she gives us a little wave before pointing at her wrist apologetically.

"Looks like things have overrun," Dad says. Thanks, Captain Obvious. "Let's grab a spot and hear what she has to say."

I slant my gaze his way. "Since when have you been a fan of listening to menopausal women?"

"I listened to your mother for years. Ow!" he moans following a well-deserved and well-aimed dig in the ribs.

"Watch it," she mutters, though she's smiling. "Look, there's a spot next to Polly."

"Hello, darling!" Polly's greeting is as enthusiastic as her hug. "Sorry about this." She points at the woman on the stepladder who seems to be reciting a poem. "She's a terrible poet," Polly adds with a laugh. "But it won't be much longer."

"She's attracted quite a crowd," Mom says with a weird gleam.

I half turn my head over my shoulder when Polly pipes up, "Oh, look! The man of the hour."

I press my hand over my heart, my fingers lying over the ICD. I want to turn, to walk away. To run, in fact, but I can't get my feet to coordinate. My heart and my head are at war at the sight of Leif Whittington. His lips quirk, the looks he sends his mother abashed. His gaze slides over my parents before reaching me. Through these treacherous tears, I still see his expression soften. He smiles; it's a small, tentative thing, but it still causes an ache to creep up the back of my throat. When he presses his index finger to the sharp divot above his top lip, my stomach tightens, becoming a mess of tangled nerves and knots.

Whit holds out his hand to help the woman in sensible tweed step down from the ladder, then he takes a step on it. And another. Then the third so he's towering above a not-so-insubstantial crowd. He throws his arms out and announces quite happily,

"I am an arsehole!"

"Nah!" comes a heckling retort from the back of the crowd. "An arsehole is useful at least once a day."

"Oh my Lord!" My mother chuckles, pressing her hand to her mouth.

"I am an arsehole," he repeats, "a poem by Leif Whittington." He takes a breath. "I am an arsehole because I couldn't see the love of a good woman, though it was parked on the end of my nose."

"Steady on, pervert!" yells someone else who sounds suspiciously like Primrose. Not that Whit is paying any attention because his eyes are only for me.

"There's this girl I knew, knock-kneed and pigtailed but so sweet. Her brother asked me to look after her, but I didn't do it well. So when she turned up on my doorstep, I thought I'd go to hell."

"Shakespeare's rolling in his grave!" yells a voice I don't recognize.

"Shut it. Let him speak." That one sounded like Brin.

"But I couldn't help myself," Whit adds with a theatrical shrug. "She was the most beautiful thing I'd ever seen.

Though her beauty was the least of her because her heart is generous and her laughter fair, and please don't get me started on her golden hair."

"Oh, honey." My mom's eyes are full as she turns to me.

"The worst of it is, she doesn't see herself as others do. But what good people in the world do?" He takes a deep breath as though about to shout, yet his next words leave his mouth so softly. "I really don't care about matters of maternity because, Amelia Valente, you are the torrid love affair I want to be part of for eternity."

"Shittiest poem ever!" shouts a warbly teenage voice, but I don't care because my love is in front of me. His hands are on my shoulders, and his smile is hesitant.

"I'm sorry," he says, his eyes bleeding love. "But if you give me a chance, I will love you as hard—"

"And as often!"

Whit frowns over my head, his gaze ultimately sliding back. "I will love you as hard as you can stand it for the rest of my life. What do you say, little fly?"

Tipping onto my toes, I press my hand to his cheek and my lips to his ear. "Don't give up your day job, Daddy," I whisper. And then I kiss him.

EPILOGUE
MIMI

"Happy birthday, dear Wh-it—"

"The poet wan-ker!" Brin and El sing.

I frown their way but don't lose my stride as chief birthday singer. "Happy birthday to you! Hip hip!"

"Hooray!"

"Hip hip!"

"Hooray!"

"Blow out your candles," I insist, clapping my hands like a seal.

"This is a fire hazard," Whit grumbles, but he does as I ask, blowing out the *at least* sixty candles on his birthday cake. This is what happens when you leave someone else to light them. Someone like Brin. "I'm cutting you all off," he adds as we all cheer. "Except you." His hand hooks around my waist, pulling me to him. "You're not going anywhere."

"I'm glad to hear it." Between my legs gives a little pulse at the way he looks at me the moment before he pulls me close.

"When can we send them all home?" His words are a hot whisper against my neck.

"Not for a while," I trill, pulling away.

"Oh, for fuck's sake," he grumbles as he catches El showing his date for the night his phone.

"You don't know that's what he's showing her," I say quickly, coming to his brother's defense.

"Of course it is. He delights in winding me up because I, the better man, won the girl."

"El was never interested in me." I scoff, but he's already stormed off.

"How many times do I have to pay to have this thing taken down?" he mutters. Whipping the phone out of his brother's hand, he begins poking at the screen.

"Oi!" El complains, taking it back. "Get your glasses on. You nearly poked my eye out!"

El doesn't confess that he's the one who loads the video to YouTube as soon as Whit has it taken down. That's the video taken at Speakers' Corner when he recited his sweet poem to win my heart. *Like he didn't own it already.* Some bystander (brother) loaded it to the platform, and it almost immediately went viral, and poor Whit was touted (taunted?) as the Poet Banker. British humor being what it is, this soon morphed into the Poet Wanker. Needless to say, he hates when anyone brings it up. But as he says, the embarrassment means nothing because he won the girl.

"I thought people were supposed to be nice to you on your birthday?" Whit complains, standing in the middle of our new home in Belgravia. Four bedrooms, a huge family kitchen, a beautiful garden with a tree house, and a playroom.

Crossing fingers and toes. I send my silly prayer into the ether.

"Everyone here is nice to you. Look at all the presents you've received."

"It would be nicer if they all buggered off home."

"Looks like someone has been hanging around Beckett too long." Olivia, Beckett's wife, laughs as she passes, champagne glass in hand.

"I'm nothing like Beckett," Whit complains, his brows lowering. Just like Beckett. But then Heather arrives by my side, shoving a sticky two-year-old girl into my arms. "Aunt Mimi loves a hug."

"Cookie," the kid demands, pointing at the cupboard they're kept in. Whit gets the jar out, takes little Dahlia, and thrusts her back into the arms of his sister. "Mimi is busy. She needs to help me with something in the cellar."

Whit's siblings are all doing well and mostly taking care of themselves. Primrose is studying to become a psychologist and has a long-term boyfriend. Lavender has become a bit of a renovation queen and is more likely to be seen wearing overalls and ripping down partition walls these days than smashing a love rival's window. Daniel married his Balinese backpacking girlfriend last year, and Heather and Archer have little Dahlia and another on the way. That just leaves El and Brin, who seem to enjoy sampling rather than settling down. I have noticed that Whit has been very firm since the next generation of Whittingtons is on the horizon. He doesn't exactly sound like a *funcle* when he categorically refuses to babysit. Despite my telling him it's okay and that I don't feel sad when I hold other people's babies, he's still very protective of me.

"The cellar?" I answer.

At the same time, Heather quips, "Because you need help lifting something heavy?" The insinuation is strong in this one. "Come on, little flower," she says, hugging her daughter. "Let's go find Gigi instead."

"Yes, do that. Your grandmother should be smothered in sticky fingertips at all times."

"Like Doreen, you mean?"

I groan aloud at Heather's words. "Please don't tell me she's been regaling you with smutty stories again."

"Okay, I won't say it. What I will say is that she's a hoot."

"Enough chatting." Whit grabs my hand and pulls me out of the kitchen behind him.

"Wave bye-bye to Aunt Mimi," Heather says. "It looks like Uncle Leif wants his birthday gift early."

"More like Uncle Leif wants his birthday gift to *come* early," he says, ushering me down the back stairs.

"We can't be away too long," I protest, turning back from closing the cellar door to find myself pulled against a wall of hard Whit. I shiver under his attention as he presses his mouth against my jaw. "You can't escape your own party."

"Sorry, what was that you said about long?" My hand in his, he presses it between us, and I giggle. "Long *and* hard," he asserts.

"Not quite," I purr. "But it has potential."

As though to reprimand me, his teeth press into my bottom lip, the sensation resonating everywhere. I open my mouth with a soft groan, and his tongue slips inside. He moves into this kiss as his body moves me against a wooden trestle table.

"Let's see what's going on under here," he whispers huskily as he lifts me onto the top of it.

"Really, Whit. We've got a houseful of guests, and you want to look at my underwear?"

He pauses in the action of lifting my dress over my knees. "Do you have a problem with that?"

"It would be a first, right?"

His lips tilt quite sinfully as he tips forward and presses

them to the inside of my left knee. "The benefits of having a nubile wife," he asserts smuttily.

"You're such a cliché, marrying your secretary."

He drops to his knees and slides his hands up my thighs. "I had to do something to stop her from being bent over other men's desks."

I laugh, but mainly because his hand has slipped around my inner thigh with a squeeze. Because he knows I'm ticklish. "Stop that!" I protest, pushing at his hand.

"Don't be mean. Let the birthday boy see his gift."

His gift.

Whit still sends me a gift card every Christmas and birthday. And I mean *every* birthday. Not just mine or his. It was Elvis the dog's twelfth birthday last week, and a gift card arrived in my inbox from Agent Provocateur. There was even a suggestion in the text that I might buy something themed. So I did. An underwear set that was little more than a crisscrossing of ribbons that came with a matching collar and leash.

It led to an interesting night and sore knees the following morning. *Totally worth it.*

"Oh, pretty." His words are a sultry purr as I lift my dress to my waist. "But let's get them off, shall we?" He hooks his fingers into the sides.

"Yes, let's lose the *knickers*," I intone, rolling the *r* dramatically. "God, I love saying that word."

"It rolls off your tongue as easily as they roll down your legs." And he does just that.

"It thought you wanted to look at them," I say as he shoves the scrap of black lace into his pocket.

"Later, darling. I'll take my time and make you work for it, but I just need a little taste for now."

Oh God. The things this man says.

His head bows, his elegant hands spreading my thighs wider, his tiger gaze burning bright as he slides his tongue along my pussy with a velvety groan.

"Oh yes." I fist my hand in his hair as he thrusts two fingers inside me, the invasion so slick as his tongue slips off the rise of my clit. "You're so giving on your birthday," I rasp, bucking up into him, "but Whit, please. I need you inside me."

"Ask properly," he demands as his tongue and fingers work me so well.

"Get up here, birthday boy." I pull on his thick dark hair. "Please, I need you to fuck me."

"There's my filthy-mouthed girl." The man delights in making me curse.

His jacket slipped off, his zipper undone, he lines himself up, and we both watch as my body accepts his thick crown.

"That never gets old," he grunts as his hips flex, filling me in one long drive.

I cry out and slide my hand to the back of his hair, bringing him closer. I can taste myself in his kisses as he begins to move. And move, my cries becoming louder and more desperate as he picks up the pace.

"I fucking love you, and I love fucking you," he grunts as he fills me again and again.

"Leif?" Our heads whip collectively to the door at the sound of his mother's voice. "Where've you gone? There's a delivery here for you, and it needs your signature."

"You locked the door, right?" he asks, his attention whipping my way.

"I think so. I'm not sure." *Did I?* "I really don't remember."

His eyes close as though in pain, but it's my walls

throbbing around him. "Better make this quick," he rasps, sliding his hands under my butt, changing the angle as he drags closer.

"Better get used to being interrupted," I whisper, pressing my palm behind me and letting my head fall back.

"Leif? Mimi!" his mother's voice trills.

"She's not moving in with us," he mutters as his whole body stills over me. He makes this noise, a masculine sort of *ungh*, as I laugh and react around his cock again.

"Not your mother." I take his face in my hands as though love bleeds from my fingertips.

"The adoption agency—" There's a lilt of a question in his words before he halts. We've both learned the hard way not to get our hopes up. But it's more than that, I want to tell him. This is fate's hand. And while I still have fears, I also have so much to give.

Love.

Love for Whit and for myself.

Love for a child somewhere in the world who needs it.

And love for another child unexpectedly created between my body and his.

My heart feels full as pleasure begins to pour through me, the rush of emotion and heat and love dragging Whit with me. I see stars burst, and I see universes created, each of them filled with love. I see our future. Our children, here in this house. I see us growing old together.

I see his mother... standing open-mouthed at the door?

Whit tips his head, oblivious, his body struck by the live line of his orgasm. "Best birthday ever," he rasps, collapsing against me.

As his forehead drops to my shoulder, I whisper, "Whit, your mom is at the door."

His shoulders move with a chuckle, but he doesn't move. "And that's what I call divine payback."

READ ON FOR MORE!

ACKNOWLEDGMENTS

My humongous thanks and eternal gratitude to Lisa, Elizabeth, Michelle, and Annette. I feel like we're a romance curling team. I'm throwing the stone and you lot are cleaning its path as it spins away from me. This might be a terrible analogy, but it works in my head.

Anyhoo, thank you for all that you do. Your kind words, encouragement, and time. You shore me up.

To the MoFo's because, great minds.

To The Lambs, thanks for being here.

To my family. You may commence talking to me again. Sorry for checking out.

To Sweep, I'm not sure how many books we have left together, but you're the best worst assistant EVER.

To Mike, thanks for everything.

ABOUT THE AUTHOR

USA Today bestseller Donna is a writer of love stories with heart, humour, and heat. When not bashing away at her keyboard, she can often be found hiding from her responsibilities with a book in her hand and a mop of a dog at her feet.

Get to hear all the news by joining her newsletter or come say hello in her private reader group, Donna's Lambs.

Keep in contact

Donna's Lambs
Donna's VIP Newsletter
mail@donnaalam.com
www.DonnaAlam.com